T0367530

THE DEJA VU CHRONICLES

BOOK 1: SINGING PUMPKINS

BILLY BRADLEY

authorHOUSE®

AuthorHouse™
1663 Liberty Drive
Bloomington, IN 47403
www.authorhouse.com
Phone: 1-800-839-8640

Published by AuthorHouse 9/18/2014

ISBN: 978-1-4969-3371-3 (sc)
ISBN: 978-1-4969-3370-6 (e)

Library of Congress Control Number: 2014914526

ACKNOWLEDGEMENTS

I would like to thank Russ Smith, Pete Kolodziejczyk, Greg Junod, Erin Genz, Christina Tarvin and Joe Ricotta for listening to me at work for over a year toying with the idea for this book on my lunch breaks – you're all the best! You'll never find a better staff to support military personnel.

I would also like to thank Marco Minoli and the rest of the staff at Matrix Games and 2X3 Games. If any reader would like to think that they could do better than the leaders of World War II, I invite them to purchase "War in the Pacific – Admiral's Edition". It is a very sobering experience and brought me the idea that I could do better, usually when I didn't.

I would be remiss to not acknowledge Linda Cirka and Kristie Wilson as my proofreaders. Thank you for reminding me how to actually speak my own language.

I would also like to thank all of the people I served with in the military; almost 9 years in the US Navy and 5 more in the Massachusetts Army National Guard. You all had a hand in making me the person I am today. In particular, all the members of the US Naval Academy's Class of 1998.

Finally, to the people at the Shovelhead Saloon, Sarges' Grill, Fountain Valley Bowl and VFW Post 3917 right here in southern Colorado Springs, where I hang out and drink with friends. I appreciate your support listening to me talk about my book and telling me where you all thought I might be wrong. You've made me better as a result.

Dedication:

This book is dedicated to my children.
I teach them every day that the mind
is the most powerful weapon.
They teach me every day that imagination
is the best ammunition.

NOVEMBER 30, 2014

These memoirs of my journal are the written record of my strange journey. Very strange indeed. I can scarcely even believe it myself; and I am still in the middle of the experience.

It was supposed to be a routine test. We were working on a simple power procedure on mini-super collider. The idea would be using the mini-super collider to push small portions of hydrogen into non-nuclear metals to see if it would fundamentally change. We had run these tests before. Today we determined that we'd up the power by 30% to see if the collided material would move to a more excited state. My task on the team as the software designer of the system was to observe and collect data to fine tune the equations. We, or more importantly I, didn't expect what would happen.

The command was entered and the system began to power up. Within seconds, there was a flash and an explosion. I was knocked against the wall and felt a strange static electricity run over my body as I fell unconscious...

NOVEMBER 30, 1941

When I came to, it was warm. Very warm and sunny; somehow I was outside. I could see palm trees and hear music in the distance. There were a couple of military personnel hovering over me; staring intently. When my eyes cleared, they pulled me up, put handcuffs on me and threw me in an old car, a very old car that was in good repair and well apportioned. When I asked what was going on, I was told to keep quiet and that I would be questioned by the military police. As I looked out the window of the car, I could see all the cars were old… almost like I was going to a classic car show.

I was very confused.

Though I majored in computer science at the Naval Academy (and was still a reservist), I did minor in history. Something was very very odd. I could see battleships… *battleships!* As I looked around as we drove I got the odd sense that I was in Pearl Harbor. The sea air scent, the palm trees and a lot of large ships; cruisers, battleships, destroyers, small craft of every type I could see from the car.

When we stopped I was ushered into a non-descript building. I was brought into a room and told to sit. When I asked for something to drink, they brought me a cup of coffee. I hate coffee. I sat there for about 30 minutes before a Navy Lieutenant (LT) came in and sat down in front of me. He questioned me about how I got onto the base and what I was doing there. To be honest, I didn't really know. I told him we were doing some particle experiments. He asked what that was. I told him about how the power output from the generator was supposed to move the uranium to a higher energy state. He stared at me with a look of incredulity. He asked me where I was from. I told him Massachusetts. He had my wallet and asked about the strange money and identification in it. I told him it was my military identification and my driver's license. He pulled out a dime and asked how the current president could be on coinage.

My heart almost stopped.

I asked him what the date was. He told me: November 30th, 1941. I stated that it was impossible as I was born in 1972. He got up and left the room.

About half an hour later, a Navy Lieutenant Commander (LCDR) came in. For some reason he seemed vaguely familiar, like I had seen his picture or something. He asked me about my birthdate and my statements of the technology I was working on. After a few minutes it hit me... he was Joseph Rochefort. I stated that I recognized him and told him his name. He stopped dead in his tracks from interrogating me (it seemed that he was probably the duty officer that day – he was a cryptanalyst).

He asked how I knew who he was. I told him about Station Hypo, JN25, the PURPLE decrypts, Japanese overtures to our Government and the coming attack. He ordered out all of the other personnel in the room and asked me how I knew all of that. I explained that I was a history minor at the Naval Academy, that my Master's degree was in Joint Warfare and that I wrote all my research papers on the War in the Pacific during World War II. When he stated that we were not currently at war I bluntly told him that in about a week that would change.

LCDR Rochefort had the security people come back in and remove my handcuffs. He had some food brought in so we could talk further. I asked him if his team knew where the main Japanese Carrier Force (the *Kido Butai*) was. He stated that he did not have that information. I told him that if he cross-checked his information he'd realize that there was no radio or other traffic from them starting from November 26th. He asked why. I stated that November 26th was when the carriers set sail from Japan. I went over strike numbers, the damage they would cause and how the diplomatic side would keep the situation muddled until after the attack had occurred. He stared hard at me. LCDR Rochefort left the room and had the Lieutenant from earlier in the day sit with me. The LT asked me how a grown man could make up that much bullshit. I asked him if he was stationed at Hypo or if he was somewhere else. He told me it was none of my business. I told him, fair enough; but if he believed in his duty, he'd have to believe in me.

LCDR Rochefort came back in about an hour later. He stated that I was to be kept on base, brought to quarters and to be kept on a 24 hour guard. He was going to see Admiral (ADM) Kimmel (current commander at Pearl Harbor). I got the impression that he had spoken with someone on Kimmel's staff. I was brought out of the room and driven to a fairly nice bungalow with some not-so-nice Military Police to guard me. I was told dinner would be brought to me and that I was more than welcome to listen to the radio. Radio… and to think that there was a good episode of the Jimmy Fallon show that was supposed to be on tonight.

The food was palatable. I sat down to start writing in my journal and then went to sleep.

DECEMBER 1, 1941

The "friendly" military police personnel woke me up at 0530 and brought me to what I recognized as the Old Administrative Building. We went in, went down some stairs and into a basement area. The Staff there was working feverishly on paperwork. After seeing LCDR Rochefort, I realized that I was inside Station HYPO.

The Lieutenant from the previous day introduced himself. His name was Joseph Finnegan, another protégé of LCDR Rochefort. I sat down to breakfast with the both of them and they explained to me what had happened over the last 9 hours.

LCDR Rochefort ordered one of his staff to find evidence of the *Kido Butai* having left home port to strike against Hawaii. He ordered LT Finnegan to find evidence that I was wrong. What they discovered was there were no radio reports or mentions of the ships at all… *at all*, since the 25th of November. Additionally, there was no radio traffic from Vice Admiral (VADM) Nagumo (the *Kido Butai* commander) since the 25th. Essentially, LT Finnegan had to admit that either a six carrier battlegroup had disappeared by accident or the Japanese Fleet was trying very very hard to hide them. It seemed the ships were not in port (they would not talk further on how they knew that), so very naturally, they were at sea. Since radio decrypts showed where many of the other major fleet units were, it only made sense that a heightened state of alert became necessary.

We then discussed what I remembered of the *Kido Butai* from my studies. They said that for a few hours we could put aside the flat impossibility that I was from the future, but for analysis sake, what could I tell them? I stated that I remembered the aircraft carriers Akagi, Kaga, Soryu, Hiryu,

Shokaku and Zuikaku. Additionally, there were supposed to be two battleships, the Hiei and Kirishima. I did admit that I could not remember all of the cruisers and destroyers.

LT Finnegan stared hard at LCDR Rochefort. I asked why he looked so worried? LT Finnegan said that those were the exact ships that they could find absolutely nothing about since the 25th of November. LCDR Rochefort told us to quickly finish breakfast; we had to see ADM Kimmel.

We quickly got into the car... I noticed that LCDR Rochefort waved away the Military Police. On the way over, LT Finnegan told me that he was stationed on the battleship USS Tennessee, but had shore patrol and met LCDR Rochefort that day. LCDR Rochefort asked for his transfer that evening. I guess I didn't need to be escorted anymore. It was a fairly quick drive over to ADM Kimmel's headquarters. When we were ushered in, he was sitting behind his desk looking at maps and the expected locations of enemy units. He told me flat out that he wasn't sure to believe my story, being from the future and all. But because I knew all these things made him believe that either I was a German agent, British agent or simply crazy enough to guess well. However, when LCDR Rochefort relayed the story from earlier this morning, his demeanor changed rather quickly.

Admiral Kimmel asked me how carriers could drop bombs that would pierce the armor on the battleships. I told him that they planned to use modified 800 kg armor piercing bombs. I pre-empted his next question by telling him the torpedo bombers would use modified Type 91 torpedoes designed for shallow water. When I was asked where they were I told him that I don't remember the exact location they would launch from but knew it was from north-west of Pearl. After more questions as to political overtures, other operations and just exactly how and why I was there we were dismissed so he could have a meeting with Lieutenant General (LTG) Short to determine what to do.

After we left his office, we went back to Station HYPO. LCDR Rochefort found an odd way to thank me. I asked him why. He said that he didn't really know that LT Finnegan was that good at cryptology. I told him that LT Finnegan was to survive the attack on the USS Tennessee and he would've been transferred to Station HYPO anyway. LCDR Rochefort stared at me again... I couldn't help but smile. The rest of the morning was spent reviewing data that was available. Shortly after lunch we were again ordered to report to ADM Kimmel.

Back at ADM Kimmel's office I was asked about what the Japanese Government was planning on doing from a diplomatic front. Admittedly, I could offer only some information on that front. LCDR Rochefort handed ADM Kimmel a message from PURPLE sources sent to the Japanese Embassy in Berlin that stated:

> "...extreme danger that war may suddenly break out... **undecrypted**... and Japan through some clash of arms and that the time of the breaking out of this war may come quicker than anyone dreams."

ADM Kimmel wondered aloud if that meant that they would attack the Soviet Union near Vladivostok and Siberia. I said that historically, the Soviets didn't go to war with Japan until after Germany was defeated and that the Soviets were aware that they would not be attacked. ADM Kimmel then asked how we could know for sure that Japan would strike against the United States instead of the Soviet Union. I explained that in the 'history', the Sorge Spy Information told Stalin that he would not be attacked by Japan. I then remembered what the attack order was. I told ADM Kimmel, his staff in the room, LCDR Rochefort and LT Finnegan that a coded message saying "Climb Mount Nitaka" would be the final order to execute the attack against Pearl Harbor. ADM Kimmel repeated the coded message and looked at his staff; he said we would discuss the spy information later. The room then got quiet. I could see the wheels turning in his head. He stood up and asked for his admin to send cables to ADM Stark; he felt he needed guidance from higher command. He did ask LCDR Rochefort to provide as much information as possible as to the location of the *Kido Butai*.

LTG Short looked very uneasy. He was taking notes and handed some of them to his aide who quickly retreated from the room. LCDR Rochefort didn't seem unduly concerned... it seemed as though the higher command was taking the threat seriously.

Before we were excused, ADM Kimmel reiterated his order to LCDR Rochefort to provide as much information as possible as to the location of the *Kido Butai*. We were then excused from the room to await further requests and orders from ADM Kimmel.

Back at Station HYPO I brought up another issue. I knew historically of all the problems related to the Mark 14 torpedo. LCDR Rochefort asked for specifics. I related my knowledge of the magnetic exploder, that it runs too deep and had a nasty tendency to circle back on the launching submarine. He asked for the local ordinance officer to pay a visit to the building to discuss the problems. I also related that the Bureau of Ordinance would deny all problems. After a short pause, LCDR Rochefort said that it would be best that we inform ADM Kimmel as well.

Dinner arrived shortly after 1700. The room was mostly quiet except for the new shift working on decrypts. I was tired, stressed and concerned. Being single, I technically didn't leave anyone behind, or ahead, depending on your point of view. I asked to take a walk, escorted if necessary. LCDR Rochefort agreed; to the walk… I would need to be escorted. After a pleasant meal I went for a walk. This time, the military police were much nicer. We discussed baseball and football while we walked. After a couple of miles, we got back to Station HYPO. LCDR Rochefort was retiring for the evening. I was escorted back to my bungalow, under guard, but at least now, a friendly guard. I turned on the radio and a show called "The Adventures of the Thin Man" was on as I fell asleep.

DECEMBER 2, 1941

The military police woke me up early. It was 0430; I was told to dress and that we were to be brought before ADM Kimmel as quickly as possible. When we arrived, LCDR Rochefort was already there. Everyone seemed tense. I asked what was happening.

LCDR Rochefort showed a decrypt that said "Climb Mount Nitaka". I felt unease in the room. ADM Kimmel asked if I was a Japanese spy. I denied it of course. He then asked LCDR Rochefort what he thought. LCDR Rochefort said there was no way I could know about the decrypt because the original message was sent four hours after our meeting with ADM Kimmel and at no time was I not either escorted by military police or in his actual presence. ADM Kimmel stared hard at me and then softened.

He asked his assembled staff what we should do. Messages were sent stateside asking advice and giving the information that was gained; nothing was mentioned about strange time travelers. Nothing as yet had been received back. ADM Kimmel thought that ADM Stark and VADM King were conferring and cross checking information. LTG Short indicated that he would keep units on a higher state of alert, but that there was only so much that could be done without violating orders.

We again went over what I knew of the attack, the weapons, the aircraft and the consequences. How do we defend without violating orders? How do we save the fleet? How do we take a war thrust upon us? Can we strike them pre-emptively? ADM Kimmel and LTG Short agreed that they would wait the day to see what other intelligence would come their way and to see if any guidance would come from the War Department.

Before being dismissed, ADM Kimmel asked LCDR Rochefort if there was any information regarding the *Kido Butai*. He indicated that no further information had come in to the best of his knowledge but would scour through the reports as soon as he got to Station HYPO. Before leaving, LCDR Rochefort indicated my knowledge about the Mark 14 torpedo and all of its problems. ADM Kimmel stated that he would call in the ordinance officers to discuss the problem and possibly do some tests. We were then dismissed.

I spent most of the day with LCDR Rochefort at Station HYPO. In addition to his regular duties he was getting paperwork ready to transfer LT Finnegan to his unit. There were many reports coming in, some about the combat in China, some about diplomatic requests; nothing that would be considered a smoking gun. There was a large backlog of messages that the crypto staff were working on in addition to the new ones that were coming in. As I was not a crypto guy myself, I didn't have much to offer.

Lunch was so-so. What I always referred to as "government nondescript". I read the newspapers, looked to see if there were any interesting trades in Major League Baseball (particularly my Red Sox) and waited quietly to see if I were needed in any way.

By dinner time, nothing was brought to my attention. For a while I thought they might have forgotten I was there. That all changed after dinner – a decent dinner; spaghetti with a not-too-bad sauce. We were ordered back to ADM Kimmel's office.

When we got to ADM Kimmel's office the entire staff was there, as well as LTG Short and his entire staff. LCDR Rochefort first reported that there were no indications as to the location of the *Kido Butai*. He could neither confirm nor deny that it was headed to Pearl Harbor. There were other reports about the combat in China, as well as fleet dispositions of the British, but no further information regarding Japanese intentions or the location of their major strike forces.

LTG Short reported that he had notified air group and squadron commanders of the possibility of an attack. However, the reliable reports from the mainland indicated that the main problem would be one of sabotage. Hence, the aircraft were still in neat rows so as to be more easily guarded.

ADM Kimmel then reported to the staff that he had been categorically forbidden to do any pre-emptive strikes on Japanese assets. This was ordered at the Presidential level. Apparently there was a meeting between the President, Secretary of State, Secretary of War, ADM Stark (Chief of Naval Operations), General (GEN) Marshall (Army Chief of Staff) and LTG Holcomb (Commandant of the Marine Corps). They decided that at the highest levels, no provocative action could be taken regarding the threat. ADM Kimmel spoke out loud that he thought he was being set up for failure.

A spirited discussion broke out about what to do. ADM Kimmel understood that the majority of the Fleet could sortie in less than 48 hours if ordered to do so and as such; decided that the best thing to do was to wait. He stated that if the Japanese do plan to attack on December 7th, then we had until the 5th to finalize plans.

ADM Kimmel wasn't happy, LTG Short wasn't happy. The staff wasn't happy. However, there was little we could do.

The staff was dismissed for the night. LCDR Rochefort stopped by Station HYPO to check on the evening staff before dropping me off at my bungalow. I was too tired to turn on the radio. I just listened to the wind on the trees as I fell asleep.

DECEMBER 3, 1941

I was brought to ADM Kimmel's staff meeting before breakfast. ADM Kimmel notified everyone that starting tomorrow a British Attaché would be available for relaying of orders between the British Command and the current staff. This was a good thing because once the shots were fired, coordination would be absolutely essential.

LCDR Rochefort read an interesting report from one of the previously intercepted messages that wasn't translated until last night. It sent a requirement to the Japanese consulate in Hawaii to make a report at least twice a week on the location of all major warships in Pearl Harbor. LCDR Rochefort thought it was almost a "smoking gun", but ADM Kimmel thought that it could simply be espionage and an attempt by the Japanese to update their intelligence.

ADM Kimmel ordered that I would be part of his staff from now on until the current crisis abated. I was given a desk in the Operations Section and would review data and coordinate what information I had. I spent the rest of the day helping gather information on ship readiness conditions, possible courses of action and had direct input to the two-a-day staff meetings with ADM Kimmel.

The evening meeting was pretty uneventful. No further information was found regarding the *Kido Butai* and no other interesting decrypts were reported. What was interesting is that some test firings were done from submarines with the Mark 14 torpedo just outside of Pearl. The torpedoes were running too deep and one circled around and almost hit the launching submarine. A series of messages were sent to Bureau of Ordinance. Because of the history of this problem, I plan to keep mentioning it.

Dinner was delivered to my bungalow. Not bad, but not great. I sat down to read the newspaper and turned on the radio. I laughed out loud when the radio show "Buck Rogers in the 25th Century" was being aired. I began to look for a book but eventually just went to sleep early.

DECEMBER 4, 1941

ADM Kimmel's morning briefing had some interesting tidbits today. The main report came from decrypts by LCDR Rochefort's crew at Station HYPO. The Japanese Ambassador in Washington and the Japanese Consulate in Hawaii were ordered to destroy all but one of their cypher machines, to destroy all secret documents and all secret codes. This was quite simply, a huge piece of information about impending war. Additionally, it seemed that all non-essential personnel have been leaving the Embassy and the Consulate to try to get back to Japan.

ADM Kimmel had this information sent back stateside and notified ADM Stark that he would take defensive measures if he was attacked. I was looking forward to the reply from the stateside headquarters. LTG Short sent the same information to GEN Marshall.

Right after lunch, the staff was assembled for a meeting with most of the commanders of the units at Pearl Harbor. VADM Pye was summoned (he was commander of the entire surface battle force) as well as Rear Admiral (RADM) Anderson (commander of all battleships), RADM Leary (commander of all cruisers) and RADM Draemel (commander of all destroyers). LTG Short summoned his equivalent flag officers to discuss defense measures; Brigadier General (BG) Wilson (24th Infantry Division), Major General (MG) Murray (25th Infantry Division), MG Bargin (Hawaiian Coast Artillery Command) and MG Marin (commander of all Air Forces in Hawaii).

Once assembled, they discussed the best way to do an emergency sortie of the fleet, where to send the ships and what actions could be taken at sea, on the ground and in the air.

Unfortunately, only the flag officers, their flag lieutenants and a single adjutant were allowed in the meeting. All of the rest of us were ushered out of the room. Every once in a while, a request would come out to the staff for action, but I was not included in any of them.

Dinner was served for the flag officers and we had a quick bite while going over fuel and ammunition requirements. When I left at 2200 to head back to my bungalow (I was no longer escorted) I had a quick beer and turned on the radio. It's interesting... I like listening to the radio shows. Tonight: "World News Roundup" followed by "The Jack Benny Program". Sleep came shortly thereafter.

DECEMBER 5, 1941

The entire battle staff was finally convinced that there was a real threat, though they didn't exactly do everything that I had hoped they would do. It was decided that a "quick drill" would be held beginning at 2200 December 6th at Pearl Harbor for a sortie. VADM Pye ordered the drill from ADM Kimmel telling RADM Anderson, RADM Leary and RADM Draemel from the previous day's meeting. The Flag Officers promptly got the orders down to the ship captains. Word on the waterfront was that the ship captains were pissed; the crews would not be happy. Ships began warming up the boilers as a "drill". The crews would be quietly told to return to their ships.

There would be a mass sortie of most of the fleet but not all capital ships because ADM Kimmel still thought that I was crazy; couldn't really blame him – what if I were in his shoes and some kid came in from the future? LTG Short agreed that some aircraft would fly patrols and that some anti-aircraft units would be supplied with ammunition.

In spite of my knowledge, it was decided that any ship that was in dry dock would not be put to sea and that the older battleships would stay in port. I warned them that it was sacrificial, but they scoffed. Most of the heavy cruisers, light cruisers and destroyers would sortie, as well as some other fleet assets.

The ships that put to sea would be sent to a location approximately 250 nautical miles southeast of Hawaii. I figured that it would be far enough away to keep them safe from Japanese patrols and air attack. Since the carriers were already out to sea, they were relatively safe. The operations section drew up orders to have them rendezvous southwest of Hawaii if the attack did materialize.

Of important note, my continual harping about the Mark 14 Torpedo has yielded results. More tests showed that the mass results of the actual warhead size caused the torpedo to run too deep. It looks like this is being fixed. Also, the magnetic exploder was ordered to be deactivated and some changes were going to be ordered for the contact exploder. Unfortunately, my training never taught me how to fix the circular running problem, and hence it was sent back to Bureau of Ordinance to be fixed. A message was received later in the day from the Bureau of Ordinance; they don't think there are any problems at all. This was to be expected.

ADM Kimmel voiced his opinion (to us on his staff and stateside) that he still wanted to sortie the fleet to the northwest to attack the incoming fleet. I was very worried about this. First, there were no carriers in place to support the battleships; second, I couldn't exactly remember where the enemy fleet would launch from. If the ships were damaged or sunk in the harbor, they could be raised, repaired and be able to fight again. If they were sunk out of the harbor, they were gone for good. It took a cable from ADM Stark to forbid him from trying to attack the enemy fleet with the battleships (along with a "friendly reminder" that pre-emptive strikes were against Presidential orders).

One thing I have to consider: I am changing the timeline. Does this mean that the Japanese High Command will change its attack plans? Of this I am fairly certain. They may change strategic issues and shipbuilding plans. I believe that I can be of help, but am I causing more damage by helping? These thoughts caused me to lose most of my appetite.

DECEMBER 6, 1941

Ship Captains were summoned again by ADM Kimmel's chain of command and given a surprise set of orders. The Captains didn't complain, but there was a look of concern on their faces with the "drill" that they were given. They were told to not discuss what was going on with anyone.

Orders were quietly given to the battleships USS Maryland, USS West Virginia, USS California, USS Tennessee and USS Pennsylvania to form Task Force 18. They were to top off their tanks and head immediately southeast of Hawaii a minimum of 240 nautical miles. Also in attendance would be the heavy cruisers USS New Orleans and USS San Francisco, 4 light cruisers and 18 destroyers. Captain (CAPT) Borowski was given command of the Task Force. It is important to note that an Army or Marine Corps Captain is abbreviated as CPT – CAPT Borowski is a Navy Captain, equivalent to an Army or Marine Corps Colonel.

Figure 1 - USS Maryland (BB-46)

Another Task Force was created (Task Force 42) of 12 destroyers, 4 destroyer minesweepers and 8 destroyer mine layers was created to follow Task Force 18. LCDR Beck in command.

Finally, a small anti-submarine force of 4 destroyers (USS Litchfield, USS Chew, USS Schley and USS Ward) would head roughly 40 nautical miles south of Pearl Harbor to look for enemy submarines. This was dangerous because there exists the possibility that they would come under enemy air attack. This was Task Force 43; Commander (CDR) Ahearn in command.

All that would remain in port would be the battleships USS Utah, USS Nevada, USS Oklahoma, USS Arizona, 2 light cruisers, 1 destroyer and support craft. I could not convince Admiral Kimmel to sortie any of the tenders, support craft or replenishment craft. This may be a problem in the long run if they are severely damaged or destroyed.

From the Army Air Corps orders were sent to all bomber squadrons to begin search sorties and keep 80% of the remaining bombers ready to attack enemy forces. The squadron commanders were not happy to have to do this on a weekend and I have doubts that it will amount to much. Fighter squadrons were to ready aircraft and prepare to have about a third of their aircraft ready for patrol and combat operations.

The commander of the Marine fighter squadron told Admiral Kimmel that they would be in the air if anything happened.

Navy Carrier groups were instructed by radio to rendezvous just south of Johnston Island. The group flagship carriers USS Lexington and USS Enterprise both acknowledged the orders and began moving their task forces.

Task Force 407 was near Canton Island with transports, cargo ships and a single heavy cruiser (USS Pensacola). They were instructed to offload their troops at Port Moresby (147th Field Artillery Regiment, 131st Field Artillery Battalion and two Army Air Corps support battalions).

No special orders were transmitted for units on the US West Coast.

No cable or radio traffic had yet been received from GEN MacArthur. We had no idea what was happening in the Philippines. Orders were sent via radio to have all at sea elements fall back to Soerabaja on the Island of Java to await further orders. These forces included some destroyers at Balikpapan, the light cruiser USS Boise, the light cruiser USS Marblehead (with 5 attending destroyers) and the heavy cruiser USS Houston. The four destroyers in Manila (Cavite Base) would have to wait out the attack.

The agreed upon plan would be to send some submarines out to interdict Japanese forces. These would fall mostly on the "S" class submarines for local attacks with the fleet boats ordered to other locations. Orders were transmitted but not acknowledged.

Then, right before midnight, a message was received from Asiatic Fleet Headquarters in Manila that lookouts had seen "objects floating in the straights that were not in the defensive minefield". Message followed that two minesweepers were sent to check things out and that four submarines had been sortied (USS S-37, USS S-38, USS S-40 and USS S-41) to wartime patrol locations. The submarine USS S-36 was already at sea in the vicinity and acknowledged a message to remain at sea. Asiatic Fleet Headquarters also acknowledged the emergency orders regarding the Mark 14 torpedo issues saying that all fleet boats using them had received copies.

The British Attaché had convinced his command that Singapore would be the prime focus of the Japanese attack on them, as well as an assault on Hong Kong. Not much could be done for Hong Kong. However, British fleet assets could be spared from destruction. The joint meeting involved a decision to have all assets fall back on Java. This would include en-route reinforcements of British and Australian units as well as air squadrons and ships.

Thus, orders were given to the three destroyers in Hong Kong to move to Soerabaja; also the motor torpedo boats were instructed to make as best they could to Manila for further moves south. The battleship HMS Prince of Wales and the battle cruiser HMS Repulse were to stay in Singapore for now and to not sortie; our staff convinced them that the risk of air attack was too great. This also left two light cruisers and nine destroyers in Singapore for future operations. British air units at Singapore were alerted and reported ready.

Task Force 422 was a transport force that was carrying the 53rd and 54th British Brigades as well as the 251st Recce Battalion (plus several thousand tons of supplies). They were instructed to offload their troops at Batavia or Tjilatjap on Java and then remain available to evacuate Singapore if necessary.

Task Force 427 was carrying the 46th Indian Brigade to Rangoon. Their orders were changed to Batavia on Java as well. They were instructed to sail to the south of Sumatra to avoid attacks.

All British Army units were instructed to build fortifications to slow the possible Japanese advance across Malaya. Particular attention would be paid to Malacca, Mersing, Johore Bahru and Singapore proper.

The Australians were persuaded to move troops to their northeast bases and to gather some forces for an immediate reinforcement of Port Moresby on New Guinea. There simply were not enough forces to go around for anything more than harassment strikes against the Japanese forces. Cruiser forces would meet at Port Moresby and ready themselves for quick strikes against invasion forces. New Zealand fleet assets would also be committed at Port Moresby.

The 7th Australian Brigade would move to Normanton, the 11th Australian Brigade to Cairns, the 2nd Australian Brigade to Townsville and the 14th Australian Brigade would move to Cooktown after getting off the trains in Cairns. It should take 2 to 3 days for the units to assemble and get on the trains; this should be enough time. Some units would be called back from fighting in North Africa, but it is currently unknown when they will be ready.

British Commonwealth troops would seek to reinforce Kohima, Chittagong and Akyab near India. They would dig in and dig in deep. The 19th Indian Infantry Division would begin to pack up and move to Chittagong and the 63rd Indian Infantry Brigade would pack up and move to Kohima. There aren't really enough troops to currently move anything to Akyab yet. However, there is considerable talk about moving the forces currently in Burma to Akyab, but the British High Command has not yet made a decision on those troops yet.

At approximately midnight, LCDR Rochefort ran into the staff area to immediately discuss with ADM Kimmel a series of decrypts. I asked him why… he said it was some very important decrypts from PURPLE sources. I bet him a beer that the message was to inform the Japanese Embassy in Washington to inform the State Department at 1 pm that negotiations were at an end. LCDR Rochefort stared at me in horror that I knew what the message said. I reminded him that I wrote a paper on it for my Master's degree. ADM Kimmel was informed and alerts went out to all commands in Hawaii. A message was being sent to the Philippines but no one was sure if it could be acted upon in time.

The respective staffs now promulgated orders. All we could do now was wait.

DECEMBER 7, 1941   DAY 1 OF THE WAR

<u>Hawaii</u>

The attack at Pearl Harbor came earlier than expected. They arrived at 0630... an hour and a half early. This may be proof that I have altered history; and not necessarily in a good way.

At 0500, reports came in from watchstanders that there were "objects" in the channel going into Pearl. The destroyers USS Aylwin and USS Phelps went to investigate and engaged a small submarine to no avail. At this point, the PBY patrol aircraft squadrons immediately began prep work to take off and search for enemy shipping. The alarm went out to the various commands. However, as previously indicated, the main attack came earlier than expected.

The main attack came in a single large wave of planes, 304 aircraft in all with Val dive bombers, Kate torpedo bombers and Zero fighters for escort. The only friendly aircraft that got off the ground were 2 P-40B's and 4 P-36A's. In the ensuing air battle 1 P-40 and 2 P-36's were shot down, the rest damaged.

The airfields were hit pretty hard. 48 aircraft were completely destroyed on the ground (hardest hit were the PBY Catalinas; 15 were completely destroyed); 210 more were damaged to the point of almost not being airworthy. The runways were trashed and the hangars and support buildings were also heavily damaged. I watched a Zero fighter come in and strafe our building... very very scary. Casualty reports were still coming in to the headquarters.

In the port itself, the battleships left in port were hit hard. The USS Utah was completely destroyed; she was hit with 11 bombs and 6 torpedoes; one of the bombs hit a forward magazine and the ship completely exploded. The USS Nevada was hit with 9 bombs and 4 torpedoes, the USS Arizona with 5 bombs and 7 torpedoes and the Oklahoma with 10 bombs and 3 torpedoes. Aside from the USS Utah, damage assessment was ongoing for the USS Nevada, USS Arizona and USS Oklahoma but it was obvious based on the heavy fires and visible damage that those ships would not be putting to sea anytime soon.

The USS Wright, USS Tangier and USS Curtiss (all AV type ships) were damaged and some other support ships were damaged, but all in all, it wasn't as bad as it could have been. The tank farm where all the fuel was stored did take a bomb hit but the fires were under control pretty quickly (assessments were being made as to how much fuel was actually lost). The main supply dump also took a bomb hit. A bigger problem was the damage to the port itself; a lot of the cranes, transfer boxes and docking equipment were damaged. This would take several days if not weeks to completely repair. The dry docks were also damaged by a few bombs.

The only losses to the Japanese attack force were a single Val and a single Kate. A few others were damaged and trailed smoke, but the only confirmed kills were shot down by flak, not by the fighters that managed to get airborne. Not a very good showing.

BROADER PACIFIC OPERATIONS

Guam was hit by a coordinated airstrike from Tinian and Truk by roughly 20 medium bombers escorted by 6 fighters; probably Betty bombers and Zeros for escorts. They hit a supply depot and damaged the airbase, but there were no casualties.

Midway Island was shelled by a couple of Japanese destroyers that were heading west. The 6th Marine Defense Battalion was dug in deep. No casualties were reported by the Battalion.

PHILIPPINE ISLANDS OPERATIONS

Clark Field in the Philippines was visited twice by enemy aircraft. The first raid came in at first light. This raid had a little over 50 bombers, half of them Betty medium bombers and the other half Nell medium bombers escorted by roughly 25 fighters. The 20th and 34th Pursuit Squadrons managed to get a total of 27 aircraft in the air. 2 of their fighters were shot down and another damaged without making any kills themselves, but they did damage 9 of the bombers. The airbase itself was hit hard with the runway cratered in several locations and the support facilities were damaged. Casualties on the ground were light.

The second attack was smaller with only 9 Nell bombers but with 20 escort fighters. The squadrons at Clark Field got 17 fighters into the air; 2 were shot down and the only damage to the enemy was the light damage done to a single Nell bomber.

Davao Port was attacked by 12 Kate torpedo bombers (armed with regular bombs instead of torpedoes). Some support equipment was damaged and the USS William B. Preston (AVD type ship) was hit with a bomb that started a fire on the ship. Damage and casualty reports should be available soon.

Iba was hit hard with a large air strike that consisted of a little over 50 Betty bombers escorted by roughly 35 Zero fighters (reports varied slightly). The 6th Pursuit Squadron (a Philippine squadron) got 4 P-26 fighters in the air, 2 were shot down and a P-40 was destroyed on the ground during the raid. No damage was scored against the enemy.

Tuguegarao Airfield was hit by 25 bombers escorted by 25 fighters. The airfield was hit hard with multiple small craters on the runway and damage to the airfield support facilities. The Japanese used smaller bombs in this raid; the commander on the scene thought they were only 100 kg bombs. The airfield should be up and operating again in less than 24 hours. No reports as to casualties.

Batan Island (north of Luzon) was invaded by a scratch Japanese force. They quickly took control of the island since we really did not have troops there.

CHINESE THEATER OF OPERATIONS

Hong Kong was hit by an air raid that had more than 50 bombers escorted by a few fighters. The reports coming in led the staff to believe that they were older lighter bombers. No major damage was reported and the troops in Hong Kong Fortress were busy preparing for the inevitable assault.

There were some air attacks on Chinese units, but the information was slow in coming into our headquarters. No reports were available as to casualties, raid sizes or objectives outside of what we could figure out via our own signals intelligence. I fear that there will be little precious information with regards to the Chinese theater of operations.

BRITISH AND ALLIED OPERATIONS

Rangoon was attacked several times. The first raid was a fighter sweep by about a dozen Zero fighters. 5 Buffalo fighters took off to challenge them with 3 Buffalos being shot down with no damage to the Japanese force.

The second raid was roughly 35 bombers escorted by 25 fighters. The types were not immediately apparent, but British Intelligence thought they were Sally medium bombers. 4 British aircraft were damaged on the ground and there was damage to the runway. No British aircraft took off in time to intercept the raid.

The second attack was by about 20 Betty bombers that attacked the port. 3 cargo ships were damaged and a single bomb hit one of the smaller supply dumps. There was negligible damage to the port facilities.

Major operations against British and Allied forces occurred on the Malayan Peninsula. Alor Star, Georgetown and Kota Bharu were hit hard by air raids. Also, an amphibious landing operation was begun at Kota Bharu. British Intelligence thought that the air raids against Kota Bharu were from aircraft based at Phnom Penh.

Alor Star was hit by two air raids. The first was a large raid of 50 bombers that caught the airfield by surprise. The runway was severely damaged along with support facilities and the supply dump. 2 light bombers were destroyed on the ground and a further 18 were damaged. 10 men were killed and another 4 were wounded. 2 enemy bombers were damaged by flak batteries at the base.

Later in the day, 25 medium bombers hit Alor Star again though they were escorted by 6 fighters. 5 men were injured on the ground, 2 more light bombers were damaged on the ground and the support facilities were heavily damaged.

Georgetown Airfield (at Penang Island) was first attacked by about 20 Oscar fighters coming in low and quick with light bombs at low altitude. One Buffalo fighter was destroyed on the ground with little damage to the airfield. One Oscar was shot down by anti-aircraft fire.

The second attack at Georgetown was by 25 Sally medium bombers. They were unescorted for some reason. 5 Buffalo fighters managed to get to altitude to intercept after the bombers had dropped their loads. 4 of the enemy bombers were shot down and a further 5 were damaged. One Buffalo was damaged on landing on the damaged runway.

Kota Bharu was attacked by 20 medium bombers with 4 fighter escorts early in the morning. They damaged the runway and did a little damage to the facilities. No aircraft were damaged on the ground or in the air.

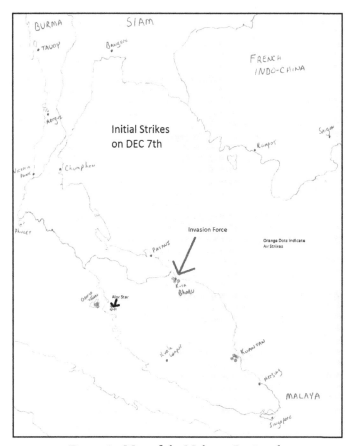

Figure 2 - Map of the Malayan Peninsula

Later in the morning, an invasion force appeared on the horizon. Some aircraft were launched to attack the force, losing a Hudson bomber shot down by flak and a further 4 damaged with no damage to the invasion force. By noon, a bombardment began to soften up defenses for an assault; there appeared to be a light cruiser with some destroyers doing the firing. The defending forces fired back on the invading ships and landing craft. During the exchange of fire, friendly forces reported 26 casualties (wounded) and reported no hits on the bombarding enemy ships. However, some of the landing craft were damaged. The commander on the scene thought that he had caused roughly 50 casualties on the enemy (some dead, most wounded with one landing boat destroyed). He asked for reinforcements and would send an estimate of how many enemy troops had landed. Requests were sent to see what information was available with regards to enemy units and movements.

INTELLIGENCE

OP-20 signals intelligence arrived around 1600 local to give a report on the information that they had managed to decode. The majority of the traffic dealt with enemy army units and where they were moving to.

Lingayen in the Philippines was indicated as a major target with the Japanese 7th Tank Regiment and the 9th Infantry Regiment being ordered to plan an attack. This meant that somewhere loaded on a transport were those units and they were either to land further north at Vigan or San Fernando and push south or they were to make a direct amphibious assault. Since no units were seen directly in the area, it is still a matter of conjecture where these units will land. The planning staff didn't seem too happy about this because there were not many units available to disrupt the landing (only 4 destroyers were available at Manila (Cavite Base).

Also of note for the Philippines was a series of messages that were decoded about elements of the 20th Infantry Regiment that is currently loaded on a transport moving towards Legaspi on southern Luzon. This means that there would be one major landing in southern Luzon and another somewhere in the North (Vigan, San Fernando or Lingayen). Philippine Army reserves were being called up, but the quality of the troops may be in doubt and it will be difficult at best to keep them adequately supplied.

Exact Japanese Fleet elements that are assigned to support these efforts are currently unknown.

The island of Borneo was mentioned by the decoders as well. Signals intelligence pointed to information that the 124th Infantry Battalion and the 90th Infantry Battalion are on transports moving to Miri on the north coast of the island. It is concluded that the destination is at Miri, but no other information is available as to the size of the naval force or if any other units are assigned to that operation.

SIGINT also determined that the 113th Infantry Regiment was ordered to prepare to attack Kota Bharu. It is unknown where this unit is, but it is known that the destination is now Kota Bharu. Reinforcements would be landed at Patani 80 miles north of Kota Bharu; the current reinforcements for the Japanese include the 148th Infantry Regiment. It was unknown how long it would take for these reinforcements to arrive. Radio transmissions were detected from Singora a little further up the coast, but the messages were not decoded.

There were a few other messages decoded, but these involved units that were identified on the Japanese Home Islands and a couple of units in the Chinese Theater of Operations. Of note, only one unit was identified that was ordered to plan an attack against Hong Kong; the 19th Independent Engineering

Regiment. The garrison at Hong Kong was told to prepare for a major assault.

Theories and Intentions

After the end of the first day of combat much was learned. First, the majority of the fleet was saved and could continue to hide until the Japanese Fleet left the area. I am concerned with the possibility of them launching another strike before retiring to Japan. Admiral Kimmel's staff believed that they would retire under cover of darkness. Time will tell who is correct.

Second, it was obvious by the number of strikes that both northern and southern Luzon would be invaded. It is currently unknown if the troops on the ground there will be able to resist the invasion. If an opportunity presents itself to hit an invasion force with the destroyers still at Cavite, then it will be taken. There was little information coming from the headquarters in Manila, so all discussion on the defense of Luzon was academic.

Third, the border between Malaya and Thailand was being attacked by Japanese forces located in Thailand. They will probably push down the peninsula until reaching the bottle neck at Singapore. The question is whether or not the British forces can hold or not. The staff was beginning to look at ways to hit the invasion and support forces with fast moving surface forces. The British battle cruiser HMS Repulse and the battleship HMS Prince of Wales were simply too slow to be used in this manner. Cruisers and destroyers will have to perform these quick strikes to be able to retire to friendly air cover before Japanese bombers can reach them. Sumatra will probably be next.

Figure 3 - Java Sea Area

Lastly, the island of Java will be the key to the defense of the entire region. Combat and support reinforcements will be brought to the island. The four initial critical areas to be fortified will be Batavia, Merak, Kalidjati and Semarang. If the island can be sufficiently fortified with troops and quick striking surface units kept on standby, then the island can be firmly kept in friendly hands. This is where the HMS Repulse and HMS Prince of Wales should be ready for strikes.

Strangely, Wake Island remained untouched. This is unnerving.

Late Day Reports

Information coming in from various sources indicated that there were many Japanese submarines operating within 50 NM of Oahu. There were 5 confirmed sightings of submarines by air patrol assets, 3 to the southwest and 2 to the northeast of Pearl Harbor. Staff discussions revolved around how to deal with the threat. Given the ability of the Japanese Fleet to continue to conduct strikes for at least the next couple of days, the best option available is air patrols to counter the enemy submarines. After it is confirmed that the Japanese Fleet has retired, some additional destroyer and patrol boat forces can be detailed to cover the threat. The submarines could not operate for long this far away from their bases; some recon assets will be detailed to see if there are any support ships in the area that are helping the submarines.

A heavily shot up PBY Catalina float plane arrived shortly after sunset with information that there was a "large concentration of ships" approximately 140 NM west-northwest of Pearl Harbor. When asked why they didn't radio in the information it was explained that the radio was shot out. ADM Kimmel wanted to attack, but with the extensive damage to air assets in Hawaii, there was little that could be done. Ground crews were working feverishly to repair aircraft, runways and hangars. Priority was being given to fighters, followed by recon aircraft and finally bombers. It would be several days before enough attack aircraft were repaired and available for sorties.

At approximately 2200, a radio report came in from the commanding officer at Kota Bharu via the British attaché. He stated that he had approximately 1800 infantry, 2300 support personnel, 7 artillery pieces and 8 mortars available for the coming battle; 2 of his artillery pieces and 4 mortars had already been destroyed by the shore fire support from the Japanese ships. The mortars and artillery were firing on the landing Japanese troops. He estimated that around 3100 enemy troops had already landed. He estimated that at Singora to the northeast, they had approximately 3900 troops. He also noted that his troops had spotted 12 ships off the coast that were landing the troops (including what his troops described as a light cruiser and a "few" destroyers). The troops were digging in and preparing a counter-attack. Few on the staff believed that a counter-attack would have its intended outcome.

At 2300, a report was received from the headquarters in Manila. Late day recon assets found a large task force of "cruisers and transports" 80 NM east of Samar. Another plane noted that Batan Island had roughly 14 ships and saw enough troops to convince the observer that an entire regiment had landed. One final plane noted that there were "over 40 medium and large ships" at Takao on Formosa. Further notes indicated that they thought that this is where the invasion forces are coming from. Shortly thereafter, I went to sleep.

<u>MORNING BRIEF</u>

During the night, orders were promulgated on the West Coast. Task Force 84 was formed consisting of the carrier USS Saratoga, the light cruiser USS Concord and 6 destroyers. Their orders were to sail for Pearl Harbor from San Diego and run anti-submarine air patrols while crossing the Pacific.

A supply force was dispatched from San Francisco to Victoria, British Columbia to bring badly needed supplies and ammunition to forces there. It was surmised that the request came at the behest of the Canadian Government and that they would soon make available some anti-submarine assets to protect the west coast.

A surface anti-submarine patrol consisting of 3 destroyers (USS Humphreys, USS Sands and USS King) was put together to patrol the west coast from 150 miles north and south of San Francisco to around 100 miles out to sea. This force is Task Force 84. They have support from land based aircraft.

The battleship USS Colorado is in dry dock in Seattle. She should be ready to put to sea in a little less than a month. Overnight, the submarine USS Thresher arrived at Pearl Harbor.

The 35th Infantry Division reported ready for deployment at Ford Ord in the early morning hours.

In the Philippines, the submarine USS Porpoise was sortied to patrol the areas in the northern South China Sea in particular between Batan Island and Formosa. There were concerns about the lack of troops in Vigan, Aparri and Laong. These will be the most likely landing sites. In the south of Luzon, there were only light troops at Legaspi. However, reservists attached to the 1st Philippine Army Division began assembling in Manila.

In the continuing stream of bad news, the ship USS William B. Preston that was damaged at Davao by a bomb had a catastrophic explosion when the fire spread to an ammunition magazine. The ship is a total loss.

On the Malay Peninsula there were some force changes. First, the battleship HMS Prince of Wales and the battlecruiser HMS Repulse put to sea from Singapore to go to Soerabaja. No. 36 Sqn consisting of Vildebeest torpedo bombers transferred from Kota Bharu to Singapore. No. 21 Sqn consisting of Buffalo fighters transferred from Georgetown to Singapore.

Enemy troops continued to land during the night at Kota Bharu. The commander at Kota Bharu radioed that he did not feel confident about holding the line before the airfield. Time would tell.

The garrisons at Addu and Diego Garcia were in need of supplies. Single transport ships would be sent from Africa (Cape Town) with the required sundries.

Damage assessments for USS Nevada, USS Oklahoma and USS Arizona were ongoing. Fires were slowly being brought under control and the Staff expected a report as to the material condition of the ships in the next 24 hours.

The Staff and I were expecting more intense attacks on the Malay Peninsula. There was a possibility of another strike against Pearl Harbor and I personally was expecting strikes against Wake Island. I wasn't sure if the landings would begin on the north coast of Luzon or not; but I was sure that it would be another long day.

HAWAII

There was another mid-afternoon attack at Hickham Field; this did not happen historically, I now know for sure that I have changed the timeline. 30 Kates were escorted by 10 Zeros. 14 fighters intercepted the force, shooting down 3 Kates, damaging another while losing 2 P-36s and 1 P-40 to air combat. 3 more aircraft were destroyed on the ground with a further 6 damaged. The runway at Hickham was cratered yet again (2 specific places). It was assumed that the strike force came from enemy carriers west-southwest of Pearl Harbor. Patrol elements were already airborne and it was hoped that the enemy task force would be found in time for a strike to be sent out.

Lihue on Kauai Island was attacked by a large enemy force. At least 60 dive bombers (probably Vals) and 20 level aircraft (probably Kates) escorted by about 15 Zero fighters hit the port and airfield hard. The supply dumps, fuel stores and runway were hit very hard (the runway had 28 separate craters that needed to be leveled). 28 fighters from various air units engaged the enemy; they were vectored in from combat air patrol from Pearl Harbor. 4 friendly fighters were shot down and 1 Zero was confirmed shot down. Not a very good showing from our fighter force. The port should be up and operating at full capacity in a couple of days, but the airfield will be out of action for about a week (at least).

The ASW force (TF 42) near Pearl Harbor actively engaged an enemy submarine in the late morning hours. The destroyer USS Chew located the submarine and commenced a depth charge attack. No word on damage to the enemy submarine. The task force was under attack at the time by enemy carrier aircraft. 2 fighters from Pearl came out to help, with 1 P-40 being shot down. No damage was scored against the task force, but also, no enemy aircraft were confirmed shot down. Four hours later, another attack group came at the Task Force, the destroyer USS Schley was hit by a couple of 250kg bombs (presumably from Kate bombers) hitting just forward of the superstructure. Large fires broke out and there was damage to the hull from the explosions. She sank later that afternoon; most of the crew was rescued.

BROADER PACIFIC OPERATIONS

Guam was attacked by a small force of medium bombers overnight. There was some scratch damage to the airfield but no casualties. The base commander radioed that the enemy force was around 8 bombers. That the enemy is conducting night bombing attacks is somewhat unsettling.

Guam was again visited by enemy bombers in the early afternoon being attacked by about a dozen Betty medium bombers escorted by a few fighters. The runway was hit hard and the airfield support facilities were partially destroyed.

Wake Island was attacked at roughly 0900 local time by a mixed force of Nell and Betty medium bombers. The commander at the scene noted that there were about 14 bombers in the force. He authorized one flight of F4F-3 Wildcat fighters to intercept them. For some reason, the bombers were NOT escorted. A single Nell was confirmed shot down and a Betty was seen leaving the area trailing smoke. The base suffered 8 direct hits by bombs. Crews were already working to repair the damage. No damage was suffered by the attacking Wildcat fighters.

Rabaul was attacked by a small force of bombers overnight; a few Bettys attacked the airfield. There was no damage.

A small Japanese force arrived at Makin Island and began unloading troops. The small radio team that was located there was quickly captured. Makin Island now belongs to the Japanese.

PHILIPPINE ISLAND OPERATIONS

The 2 minesweepers that were sent into the straights near Baatan did encounter a hastily laid minefield; probably by enemy submarine. They spent the day clearing the mines and had confirmed by sunset that they had located and destroyed 40 mines.

There were no confirmed landings of enemy troops.

CHINESE THEATER

There was word that a battle was developing at Pengpu in east central China. The 89th Chinese Infantry Corps was engaged with an unknown number of Japanese units. Reports were sketchy, but it seemed like that 89th Chinese Corps was being forced to retreat with heavy losses. Enemy casualties were unknown but it did look like the Japanese did take losses in their assault vanguards. Reports also came in that the Chinese forces were under attack at various locations by enemy airstrikes. Confirmed units and locations under attack were the 88th Corps near Hangchow under multiple airstrikes and the 74th Corps at Changsha.

BRITISH AND ALLIED OPERATIONS

There was much action at Kota Bharu. 3 separate smaller forces were landing troops. Reports coming in indicated that the forces that had landed included the 56th Infantry Regiment, the 12th Engineer Regiment and a company of Japanese Air Force Engineers; ostensibly to repair the airfield and get it up and operating a quickly as possible. There was a light cruiser, "several" destroyers and some smaller fleet assets firing on the friendly troops at Kota Bharu. The remaining troops were firing back with what artillery remained but not scoring many hits. In the ensuing ground battle, the base commander reported that he had sustained a little over 600 casualties and that his main defensive belt was penetrated. He held little confidence that he would be able to hold the base.

There were many air attacks on both the airfield and the troops defending the airfield. The airfield itself was heavily damaged. There were enemy fighter sweeps and bombing runs. Some Blenhiem bombers and Hudson bombers attacked the invasion forces and caused little damage to the enemy. In between attacks, enemy forces bombed the airfield and destroyed several aircraft on the ground. A report came in stating that there were two enemy battleships off the coast protecting the invasion force.

There were four separate air attacks against the base at Kuantan; this must be their next target. One overnight strike was made by several medium bombers (type unknown) and hit the runway. The runway was repaired by sunrise.

Later in the morning, there were separate attacks. The first attack was the worst. It was estimated that 80 medium bombers attacked around 0800. The runway was trashed and heavily cratered, the hangars were blown apart and the supply dumps were set afire. 3 aircraft were destroyed on the ground with another 17 damaged.

At 0900 another attack wave came in that contained almost 20 medium bombers. One of the observers thought that they were Nell bombers. They added to the general destruction at the base.

At 1100 the final wave came in that consisted of 27 Lily medium bombers. They added to the damage at the base. Shortly thereafter, a lone recon plane came overhead at the base; more than likely to take post-strike photos for the Japanese command.

At Hong Kong there was one large attack in the late morning. A mix of fighters, medium bombers and dive bombers attacked the Hong Kong Fortress and the port. One dive bomber (a Sonia) was shot down by anti-aircraft defenses. There was damage to two of the cargo ships in the port, one of which was burning brightly. The commander on the scene thought the ship that was on fire was the SS Hinsang, a 4100 ton cargo ship.

At Rangoon there was a single air attack in the early afternoon. At around 1300 local time, a force of 30 medium bombers escorted by 11 Zero fighters attack the airfield at Rangoon. No. 67 Sqn of the Royal Air Force managed to vector 4 Buffalo fighters to intercept. They confirmed shooting down 3 aircraft (1 Zero and 2 Sallys) and damaging a further 3 Sally medium bombers. A single Buffalo was shot down by enemy aircraft and only one bomb found its mark on the runway.

The HMS Prince of Wales and HMS Repulse were attacked by a Japanese submarine just east of Bangka Island. The Prince of Wales took a torpedo hit. The Captain reported that the ship could make 23 knots but had some flooding aft. He would have to retire to a drydock for repairs. The force would split. The Repulse would continue on to Soerabaja and the Prince of Wales would go to Columbo on the Island of Ceylon to the large base there to be repaired.

Figure 4 - British Battle Cruiser HMS Repulse

INTELLIGENCE

The 1600 intelligence report had begun. The main element from the intelligence report was information that was decoded regarding the Maizuru 2nd Special Naval Landing Force that was onboard a Kongo Maru AMC class ship moving to disembark their troops at Wake Island. The intelligence elements could not tell us how long it would be before they landed.

In the Philippines, it was confirmed via decrypts that Vigan would be one of the first targets with the 47th Infantry Regiment, 7th Tank Regiment and a unit only known as the "Kanno Detachment". Aparri was identified as a target for the 28th Japanese Air Force Battalion and an unidentified Infantry Regiment. Intelligence estimated that they would be able to land in less than 48 hours.

The British Liaison officer was notified that Miri on the northwest side of Borneo was a target for the 124th Infantry Battalion.

Aside from the ground units identified, no other specific fleet assets were identified. The intelligence directorate did indicate that they thought the Japanese carrier force near Hawaii would begin a slow withdrawal, possibly to assist an invasion of Wake Island. They also indicated based on the level of radio transmissions that there existed the real possibility that enemy submarines would be operating on the Pacific Coast of the continental United States.

THEORIES AND INTENTIONS

It seems obvious now that Kota Bharu and Kuantan are the first targets to be seized in Malaya. It doesn't seem possible for the troops in place to be able to effectively defend the peninsula. Singapore may be able to hold out, but since the reinforcement troops are going to Java, it seems unlikely that they will hold very long. The question is: Do you sacrifice Singapore to hold Java?

Northern Luzon will be invaded for sure in the next 48 hours at the latest. Philippine reservists are being called up, but I do not believe that they will be able to stop the Japanese Army. Delaying actions may be useful for falling back to Bataan which could be resupplied by submarine (if the orders are sent TODAY to have supplies brought in from Java).

The strike force that attacked Hawaii should now be falling back. They seem to be positioning their forces to support an assault on Wake Island. They have more combat power and the two carriers that we have would not be able to effectively attack them if they were in position. I think it may become important to begin planning an operation to take back Wake Island if it falls.

In the Australian Theater, forces are marshaling as quickly as possible. No enemy forces have been seen there, but it does not mean that it would not quickly become a hot spot.

LATE DAY REPORTS

There were still confirmed and unconfirmed reports of many Japanese submarines operating in the vicinity of Oahu. The staff would work through the night to try to scrape up assets for anti-submarine patrols to augment the air patrols. Late afternoon recon assets showed that the main Japanese Carrier Group was definitely moving west at an estimated speed of 20 knots. This would bring them into the vicinity of Wake in approximately 2-3 days assuming they do not head north.

The two main task forces north of Luzon were still headed southwest at approximately 15 knots. They would reach their landing objectives in the next 24 hours. Unfortunately there were no real troops to be sent to the previously mentioned landing sites to counter the invasion. American and Philippine forces would have to fight them inland, not at the water's edge.

The commander at Kota Bharu sent a radio message that he had approximately 1300 infantry and 2100 support troops available based on best information that he had (that is down from 3900 total the day before; the fighting must have been savage). He indicated that he will probably be pushed out of his position in the next 24 hours due to being outnumbered and based on the quality of the training that his scratch force of troops has.

A radio report came in from Kuantan at about 2300. The commander there stated he had 1100 infantry and 2300 support troops available. He had everyone digging prepared fighting positions and pre-registering available avenues of approach with the available number of mortars that he has. He also indicated in the report that the largest artillery pieces available were a number of BOFORS 40mm guns. He has no howitzers or field guns.

The British Liaison officer noted that there were no combat troops at Kuala Lumpur. However, there was a battalion of infantry and a field artillery regiment at Temuloh Base, a small base about 30 miles northeast of Kuala Lumpur. Temuloh would have to fall before the Japanese could move onto Kuala Lumpur.

A report came in from the commercial radio sources indicating that the Congress and the Senate had officially declared war against the Japanese Empire. President Roosevelt presented his historical "Infamy" speech. It was now officially a no holds barred war.

Reports came in from Port Moresby that there were no Japanese Task Forces found by patrol assets.

I went to the bungalow and fell asleep… in my clothes.

DECEMBER 9, 1941   DAY 3 OF THE WAR

<u>MORNING BRIEF</u>

Many reports came in overnight. First, VADM Brown took command of a combined US Carrier group (Task Force 405) that was made by absorbing Task Force 406. The carriers USS Lexington and USS Enterprise with supporting cruisers and destroyers were making their way to a location about 700 miles south-southwest of Pearl Harbor to avoid the Japanese Carrier group. Once it was safe for Task Force 405 to head back to Pearl Harbor, they would begin transit back to the base.

Task Force 18 (battleships, cruisers and destroyers that left Pearl the night before the attack) and Task Force 42 (a screening force of destroyers, destroyer minesweepers and destroyer minelayers) were maintaining their position southeast of Oahu. No enemy patrol assets were seen by the forces indicating that, at least for the moment, they were relatively safe.

Damage reports also were waiting for the staff meeting. The battleship USS Arizona was still burning fiercely and had extremely severe hull damage and many casualties. Because the ship was still on fire, it is still impossible to ascertain the full damage to the ship. The crew was working feverishly to get the fires under control with help from shore parties. It was obvious, however, from looking at the burning ship that the aft main gun turret was completely gutted and would need to be repaired (if not replaced). Smoke was pouring out of the #2 main turret forward; not a good sign.

The USS Nevada was moving under tow to the dry dock to begin repairs. The commanding officer CAPT Headrich reported that one starboard side 5" gun turret was destroyed and that two of the boilers in the engine rooms were destroyed. Deck and hull damage from the bomb and torpedo hits will require extensive repairs to the material condition of the ship as well as equipment that was destroyed. After consulting with the harbor master and the repair crews at the dry dock, it was estimated that it will take 13 months to completely repair the ship barring any unforeseen circumstances.

The USS Oklahoma faired only slightly better. USS Oklahoma's commanding officer CAPT Withers reported that he had a port side 5" gun turret destroyed, a boiler completely destroyed and several locations where deck damage due to bombs and particularly hull damage due to torpedoes were extreme. It would take a minimum of 9 months to fully repair the ship. USS Oklahoma would be towed to the dry dock after the USS Nevada was hard down. The harbor master reported that he thought it could be done for both ships before sunset.

Several other ships had to be brought to dry dock to be repaired. There was some damage to the dry dock itself, so not all of the ships could be brought in. There was a priority system set up by the staff with the dry dock crews. The battleships would be first, followed by support assets and then other combat ships. So, the USS Tangier and USS Curtiss were sent to the dry dock (roughly 3 weeks to repair the Tangier and a month for the Curtiss) followed by the repair ship USS Vestal (2 weeks to repair; but when she moves out of dry dock, she will be able to help repair other ships). For combat ships, the USS Taney (a small Coast Guard vessel that can help with anti-submarine patrols taken in by the US Navy, 10 days to fully repair) and the submarine USS Narwhal (6 weeks to repair; a torpedo from a Kate bomber went under the submarine at the pier, hit the pier, exploded and damaged the submarine).

Engineering crews were working constantly to repair the port, airfields and dry dock. The squadron commander's reports were rolled up and reported that there were 118 fighters, 18 dive bombers, 51 medium and heavy level bombers, 42 patrol planes, 2 cargo planes and 5 reconnaissance planes that were mission capable. It was decided that fighters would fly combat air patrol with a minimum of 40 aircraft in the air at any one time and that half the patrol planes would fly to search the areas around Oahu. The reconnaissance planes would take off if the patrol planes found something of interest.

The commander at Lihue radioed that he needed food and medical supplies to tend to the aftermath of the large raid at his base. The initial reports indicated that some of the supply dumps were damaged. In truth, the supply dumps were all but destroyed and burned through the day and night. It was too dangerous to dispatch a supply ship, so the 19th Transport Squadron with their single working C-33 cargo plane would begin making sorties to bring the barest of supplies to the base until it was safe enough to send a ship. It was calculated that the plane could carry between 1 to 1 ½ tons of needed supplies per sortie. It would provide the bare minimum for a couple of days (assuming the aircraft was not damaged).

A report came in from Wake Island from Major (MAJ) Devereux stating that his base was good with supplies with the exception of barbed wire and extra fighters and that his troops were digging in, manning all weapons and waiting to repulse the anticipated Japanese assault.

In the Philippines, Colonel (COL) Howard of the 4th Marine Regiment radioed via Manila Headquarters that his Regiment was leading the charge in preparing Bataan for an assault. They were preparing positions and stockpiling what supplies they could. The report requested supplies be dispatched, particularly machine gun ammunition, artillery shells, mortar shells and rifle ammunition. Curiously, he did not ask for food or medical supplies. Chilling.

US Army Forces in the Philippines indicated that they were short on troops and would not be able to oppose landings on the north shore of Luzon. They did note that the available fighter squadrons were running combat air patrols and that the small force of B-17 bombers available would be held in reserve to attack beach heads at enemy landing sites. Ground forces were to make prepared defensive positions near Clark Airfield, Manila and Bataan.

Asiatic Fleet Headquarters reported that 6 submarines had sortied during the night to attack enemy merchant and combat fleet shipping:

- USS Seal will patrol near the port of Cam Ranh Bay
- USS Salmon will patrol off the north coast of Borneo
- USS Tarpon will patrol west-northwest of the island of Groot Natoena (itself, around 300 miles east-northeast of Singapore)
- USS Skipjack will patrol the Sulu Sea
- USS Perch will patrol the Celebes Sea
- USS Sturgeon will patrol south of Davao off Mindanao Island in the southern Philippines

Figure 5 - USS Seal (SS-183)

This would leave 16 submarines awaiting orders at Cavite Base.

At Soerabaja, the submarine HNLMS O16 was sortied to patrol just east of Singapore. More destroyers and a couple of cruisers arrived and docked in the early morning hours; now assembled is a force of 3 light cruisers and 11 destroyers. Debates abound as to the mission of this force. The Staff believed it best to save them for quick runs to break up invasion forces. I expect the debate to continue until the first force able to be hit presents itself. This force should be augmented by the battlecruiser HMS Repulse when she arrives.

Reports from the British Liaison Officer stated that forces at Malaya are flying patrols, strike aircraft are preparing to break up invasion forces and ground forces are digging in. It would appear from his report that the forces at Kota Bharu are on their own.

He also reported that the Australian Forces are putting together a full division from assets already in place. They will take the 18th, 41st and 45th Infantry Battalions and mate them with the 1st and 9th Infantry Brigades in Sydney to form the 1st Australian Division. This force will then board transports for Port Moresby. It will take at least a week to have the forces assembled. It was also hinted that some additional forces may travel with the division (possibly anti-aircraft or base support forces such as aircraft maintenance and the like).

At the end of the brief, ADM Kimmel notified the staff that he was being transferred stateside on ADM King's staff to head the Operations Directorate. ADM Chester Nimitz was selected to replace him (he was promoted above several other Admirals; I remember that historically it happened closer to the end of the month). LTG Short also notified the Staff that he was going stateside to support the Army Chief of Staff. His replacement was named as LTG Richardson.

Stateside, the 8th Marine Regiment was ordered to pack up and move by rail to San Francisco. COL Jeschke was ordered to begin planning for a counter-invasion of Wake Island. The 57th Coastal Artillery Regiment with Lieutenant Colonel (LTC) Brors commanding, in San Francisco was ordered to start packing up equipment to move to Hawaii and then to Wake Island.

At Hawaii, a group of troops consisting of maintenance, operations and mission support personnel (LTC Lindsay commanding) was told to begin planning to go to Wake Island. Also, the 4th Marine Defense Battalion (COL Fassett commanding) was also told to prepare his Marines for Wake Island.

These movement notices told me that either they will be a reinforcement, or to be ready to retake the island after the Japanese assault.

Hawaii

During the day, the USS McFarland (an AVD type ship) arrived in port safely from a cross ocean transit from San Francisco. This was uneventful considering all of the carnage of late.

At 0900, Johnston Island was attacked by carrier based aircraft. Best radio reports indicated 40 Vals and 40 Kates escorted by at least 24 Zero fighters. They did scratch damage to the port and some damage to the airfield. Casualties on the ground were at a minimum. This indicated that the carriers had headed slightly south on their way west. This means that they are going to pass close by Wake Island.

BROADER PACIFIC OCEAN

At sunrise on Wake Island, an invasion force was seen on the horizon. The Wildcat fighters based there took off with 8 aircraft loaded up with 100 lb. bombs to strafe and bomb the enemy force. They managed to shoot up a destroyer with their machine guns but did no damage to the enemy transports. Half of the attacking fighters were damaged to some extent.

By 0800 local, shore bombardment began from the enemy fleet. At least three light cruisers, four destroyers and some smaller ships began firing on the island. The 5" gun batteries on the island fired back. Some scratch hits were noted on one of the light cruisers and a patrol boat was hit setting it on fire. The machine guns opened up on the landing craft when in range. MAJ Devereux reported that his forces had 13 wounded before the enemy troops landed. They started landing by 0900 local.

Fighting broke out as soon as the Japanese troops landed. By the end of the day, MAJ Devereux reported that he had 20 killed in action and 34 more wounded. He estimated 10 enemy dead and 290 wounded. He indicated that he could hold, at least for now. The Japanese were landing mostly around Wilkes Island.

At Tarawa, a radio operator on the island reported that he saw "many troops" landing. Shortly thereafter, he went off the air. It is safe to assume that Tarawa now belongs to the Japanese.

Guam was hit by a small but highly effective bombing raid at noon local time. 20 Betty bombers attacked the base and heavily damaged the runway, supply dump and support structures. Casualties were light, but for all purposes, the airbase is out of action.

PHILIPPINE ISLAND OPERATIONS

During the early morning hours all the way into the evening, the submarines operating near the Philippines were busy. Reports from the USS S-38 (LCDR Chapple in command) showed that they attacked an enemy force near Laoag. They fired two torpedoes at a destroyer that missed. They were then attacked by other ships with depth charges but managed to sneak away to make the report.

A couple of hours later, the USS Porpoise (CDR Brewster in command) was sighted by an escort when maneuvering in to position to attack. They were unable to make the attack but managed to slip away after being attacked by depth charges. They later caught up to the task force in the afternoon, launched two torpedoes for no hits and then they were attacked again. They managed to slip away by around 1400 and broke away to the east near the north coast of Luzon.

A few hours later, USS S-38 (LCDR Chapple) found another escorted freighter and attacked it with two torpedoes in the South China Sea, hitting with one. The torpedo struck forward of the beam on the starboard side and heavily damaged the freighter (Intel later reported that this ship is possibly the Hakodate Maru). No report yet as to whether or not the ship was sunk.

Late in the afternoon, USS S-39 (LCDR Coe in command) noted a small formation of three ships. She fired four torpedoes at a ship, registering no hits. Later, a patrol boat attacked them with depth charges with no damage to the submarine. USS S-39 reported that they would shadow the ships to try to make another attack.

At sunrise in Aparri and Vigan, enemy troops began to land from a fleet off the coast. There were no immediate reports as to the number and type of troops. The Intelligence team is gathering data to make an assessment.

CHINESE THEATER

Hong Kong was subjected to a minor attack of 3 dive bombers. The airbase took a couple of hits and 2 of the dive bombers were damaged by anti-aircraft fire. Type of bomber was unknown but would normally be either a Mabel or a Sonia.

No other reports came in from the Chinese Theater of Operations today.

BRITISH AND ALLIED OPERATIONS

There were two separate night air attacks at Georgetown. The base suffered light damage and there were no casualties to the attackers.

At first light, a huge force of 57 Nell medium bombers appeared. A single Blenhiem fighter version got airborne and managed to shoot down 1 Nell and damage 2 others. The airbase was almost completely destroyed. There were almost 100 craters on the runway, the supply dump was on fire and the supporting buildings, machine shops and repair assets were heavily damaged. The remainder of the aircraft of No. 27 Squadron were destroyed on the ground. Approximately 3 hours later, another raid of 24 bombers added to the general destruction.

Not to be completely out of the fight, 6 Bleinheims from Georgetown were away on a strike when the large force came in. They attacked enemy shipping at Patani. They came in level at 6000 feet and bombed a transport ship. They scored no hits.

4 of the Bleinheims were damaged by enemy fire but made it back to base just in time to be destroyed by the second raid of enemy bombers (those that weren't severely damaged on landing from the damaged runway).

There were two separate air attacks at Kota Bharu before noon. In total, 56 bombers attacked in a 60 minute period. The raids were not that effective probably because they were concerned about hitting friendly troops assaulting the base.

The assault against the base continued throughout the day. By the time the last assault started at 1600, most of the base was in enemy hands. By sunset, friendly forces had been pushed back and were retreating towards Temuloh Base to the southwest. Initial reports stated that friendly forces suffered 2100 casualties (1700 dead, a couple hundred wounded and some MIA and presumed dead or captured). There were no reports as to enemy losses.

Alor Star was hit by two separate attacks totaling roughly 40 medium bombers escorted by a few fighters. The runway was hit hard, but there was little damage to the support areas or the supply dump. Only one enemy bomber was damaged by anti-aircraft fire.

Further to the north, Rangoon was attacked by roughly 30 medium bombers escorted by 40 fighters (Zero and Oscar types). Some Buffalo fighters (a total of 9 in all) rose to attack the enemy force. Of the medium bombers, 6 were damaged (confirmed to be Sally bombers) and 1 Buffalo was shot down by enemy fighters. There was light damage to the base.

In the Australian area, there was a small raid on Rabaul that damaged two aircraft on the ground and destroyed one other. They were Hudson medium bombers. There were no fighters based at Rabaul to repulse the attack.

Intelligence

The 1600 intel brief indicated first and foremost that the troops that had landed on Wake were probably from the Maizuru 2nd Special Naval Landing Force. Reports also indicated that there were 2300 enemy troops landing on Wake or disembarking at Wake. MAJ Devereux reported that he had 208 infantry, 606 support troops, 13 machine guns left and five of six of his 5" coastal guns were still active (the gun battery on Wilkes Island was captured by the Japanese). The intel boys didn't think that the island would hold out long.

There was a report that the 124th Infantry Battalion was planning to attack Miri on the north side of Borneo. This was also corroborated with a late patrol report showing six ships heading towards Miri. The British Liaison officer sent the information to his command.

The rest of the report dealt with radio decrypts concerning the Philippines. The 65th Brigade was heading towards Vigan along with the 47th Infantry Regiment.

They also reported that they were having a hard time decrypting many of the messages. It was not reported if the Japanese changed their codes or if they were understaffed. In any case LCDR Rochefort was adamant that he was working his crews as hard as he could.

Theories and Intentions

It seems that the main objectives are Wake, the Malayan Peninsula and single islands in the Pacific to get a sensor net available. The intentions remain to be known about Rangoon, Java and Australia. Since attacks are beginning at Rabaul, it is possible that they will head south to secure their flank. An invasion of Australia would not be out of the question.

Since combat was continuing in China, the objective must be to gain resources. Oil is more important and oil is at Java, Sumatra and Borneo. Forces must be able to hold on to Java. That would allow our allies to have an area to springboard from to retake bases from the enemy and damage their supply lines.

LATE DAY REPORTS

Japanese troops and US Marines were still engaged in combat towards the end of the day. Luckily, the machine gun crews were keeping the enemy at bay, but sooner or later they'd start to run out of ammunition. The Marine on staff thought that MAJ Devereux would order a counter-attack to regain the initiative, but that seemed unlikely to me given the fact that they're outnumbered almost 10 to 1.

There were many ships in the Luzon area landing troops. There were at least 30 ships at Aparri, 30 at Vigan and there was a large force 80 nautical miles west of Laong heading east (presumably to land troops).

The large enemy carrier force in the Hawaiian area was moving west at approximately 20 knots. A PBY Catalina got close enough to take pictures. There were 6 confirmed carriers, at least 10 destroyers and a handful of cruisers and battleships. There was no way that TF 405 would be able to attack them successfully.

The night staff began to get reports ready for the morning brief. At that point, I left go to sleep.

DECEMBER 10, 1941   DAY 4 OF THE WAR

ADM Nimitz came in to introduce himself to his new staff. He did bring a couple of his people along and they made introductions. I had a separate introduction because of the... nature of my being on the staff. In college I read all about ADM Nimitz; he was my hero growing up. Now I'm standing in front of him. What do you say?

He gathered everyone and told them that whenever any operation is proposed, discussed or changed, all staff members must keep the following in mind:

1. Is the proposed operation likely to succeed?
2. What might be the consequences of failure?
3. Is it in the realm of practicability in terms of matériel and supplies?

ADM Nimitz stated that he wanted "decisions with reasons". If there were not decisions with reasons then the situation would be hard pressed for him to support it. He asked for everyone to nod in acknowledgement and agreement. He then sat back and asked his operations officer to begin the morning briefing from the night staff reports.

The Operations Officer began with the *Kido Butai*. They were last estimated as being 550 nautical miles west-southwest of Pearl. They were heading west at an estimated 20 knots. Their current course would take them near Wake Island, probably to assist with the invasion there.

The supply situation at Lihue was being worked on. There were a couple of flights late yesterday and this morning. Right now, there have been about two tons of supplies provided, mostly food and medical supplies. The current risk assessment precluded a supply ship being dispatched for at least another 24 hours.

Task Force 405 was maintaining the distance so as not to be ambushed by the *Kido Butai*. They are heading to their rendezvous location before heading back to Pearl. They have an aggressive combat air patrol up and are purely defensive. VADM Brown radioed that he would not engage the enemy unless he felt the risk met the reward. Current Task Force speed is 20 knots.

Task Force 407 is still proceeding to Port Moresby to unload the troops and supplies. They are currently just south of the Gilbert Island making roughly 15 knots.

Task Force 408 consisting of the heavy cruiser USS Louisville with 2 empty troop transports were making their way to Pearl Harbor from the vicinity of Baker Island. They were making 15 knots.

Figure 6 - USS Louisville (CA-28)

Wake Island was still being assaulted by Japanese landing forces. The enemy has complete control of the seas in the area and there is little that our forces were going to be able to do about it now that the *Kido Butai* is heading in that direction. The troops on the ground were still fighting, but they would probably not last longer than a few days. More troops landed during the night. There was not a night assault done by either the Marines or by the Japanese.

Pago Pago made a report that they were starting to run low on supplies. Somehow a supply ship would need to bring them more food and some ammunition. Plans were going into motion over the next 48 hours to have a ship dispatched from Australia or San Diego to resupply them. Reports were pending.

In the Philippines, large fleets were seen at Vigan (at least 30 ships) and Aparri (at least 40 ships). Enemy troops were landing and there were very few troops to stop them. There were reservists being called up in Manila and US Forces were digging in near Clark Field. The fallback positions would be on the Bataan Peninsula. Overnight, 7 submarines received orders and left port, there are 9 submarines still in port:

- USS Pike to patrol north of Brunei
- USS Shark to patrol east of Samar
- USS Pickerel to patrol south of Mindanao
- USS Stingray to patrol near Singapore
- USS Seawolf to patrol west of Batan Island
- USS Spearfish to patrol west of Mindanao
- USS Swordfish to patrol the straights between Celebes and Borneo

Kota Bharu was completely off the air. It was safely assumed that the Japanese have seized the base and are consolidating before moving on. There was no word on further casualties but the remaining forces were retreating to Temuloh. The British

Liaison officer was also told of a small force heading to Miri (6 ships were sighted).

US Forces arrived at Soerabaja overnight. The light cruiser USS Marblehead along with 9 older destroyers docked and began to refuel awaiting orders. Supply ships were going to be dispatched from the east coast to head to Cape Town with ammunition and torpedo reloads for the ships. There was a small supply of ammunition at Soerabaja but they would need more delivered to maintain viability. It would take at least 21 days for the supplies to arrive. The battlecruiser HMS Repulse arrived with 5 other destroyers and began to refuel. The battleship HMS Prince of Wales was passing Merak on her way to Columbo to repair torpedo damage.

The Operations Officer then concluded the morning report. No questions were asked. ADM Nimitz indicated that he would be having planning sessions after objectives are determined. In the meantime, everyone was to be calm and professional.

Hawaii

Aside from a confirmed sighting of an enemy submarine northeast of Pearl Harbor, there was little action in this area.

Broader Pacific Ocean

Wake Island was under attack the entire day. The remaining 5" gun batteries managed to damage a smaller patrol boat and registered hits on a larger freighter/troop transport. There was no major assault by the Japanese and aside from some probing attacks, the Marine Defense Battalion held ground and kept the enemy troops pinned down.

Guam was attacked by almost 30 medium bombers with escorting fighters. The airbase and port were hit. The minesweeper USS Penguin was hit by a small bomb, damaged and set on fire.

PHILIPPINE ISLAND OPERATIONS

More troops landed at Vigan and Aparri. Local civilians saw thousands of troops and called Manila to report it. No further communications were noted by 1200 local. Aircraft were sent to see how many troops. The pilots reported 8000 troops at Aparri and roughly 10000 at Vigan.

A report came in late morning that the minesweepers that had left Manila to work near Bataan had been attacked by Betty medium bombers. Fighters from combat air patrol at Manila and Clark Field were vectored in on the unescorted bombers. There were a total of 9 bombers spotted, 5 were shot down with no losses to the attacking fighters. The minesweepers were not damaged.

At 1400, a report came in from the submarine USS S-38 (LCDR Chapple) near Laoag that they were sighted and attacked by a Japanese patrol boat. They were under attack for about an hour before breaking away to make the report.

At nearly the same time, a report came in from the submarine USS Shark (LCDR Shane in command) that they had seen and attacked an enemy troop transport during transit to the submarines operating area. They fired 4 torpedoes at the transport, hitting it with 2. The enemy ship was heavily damaged and was on fire. A patrol boat then attacked the submarine for roughly 2 hours. The submarine was then able to make an escape and make the report. It is currently unknown if the troop transport sank.

Late in the afternoon, a report came in from Legaspi noting that enemy troops were landing. No information as to number of troops or number of ships. Hopefully, some late day information will let us see how large the force is. No further reports were received from Legaspi.

CHINESE THEATER

There were no reports to confirm combat operations in China, though it was probable that at a minimum there was low level combat across the theater.

BRITISH AND ALLIED OPERATIONS

There was a single night raid at Alor Star by roughly a dozen medium bombers. There was scratch damage to the airfield and no losses were suffered by the attacking force.

There were several attacks against Kuantan during the day. By sunset, the base had been visited by over 150 medium bombers. The airfield was cratered, 20 aircraft had been lost on the ground and 65 troops were injured during the raids.

Enemy troops began landing at Miri. It is unknown how many troops were landing, but there was a confirmed report of six ships doing the landings. The Liaison Officer thought that there would be an attempt to break up any landing that would be attempted at Kuching using fast moving destroyers from Singapore.

Rangoon was attacked by roughly 30 medium bombers (initial reports were Sally medium bombers) heavily escorted by 50 fighters. No. 67 Squadron managed to get 8 Buffalo fighters in the air and attack the force. A Sally was shot down and 1 Buffalo was shot down by the escorting fighters. The escorting fighters were kept very busy by the interceptors. The base was lightly damaged and crews immediately went to work repairing the damage.

Hong Kong was attacked by a mix of medium level bombers and dive bombers. The raid was ineffective, but did manage to keep friendly troops tied down while the Japanese moved troops into assault positions. The Japanese forces attacked the fortress area at noon. The commander of the ground troops radioed that he had 20 dead and a little over 200 wounded. He did not know how many casualties he had caused, but he thought they had to be pretty severe because the first assault was stopped cold.

Dutch aircraft from Singkawang on Borneo found and attacked a concentration of ships heading to Kuching. They bombed the force with 4 medium bombers scoring no hits.

Rabaul was attacked again today by a small force of Betty medium bombers. The base was heavily damaged; the bombers came in low (estimate was 5000') and the accuracy was uncanny. Facilities were heavily damaged and 5 casualties were reported.

INTELLIGENCE

The 1600 intelligence report began. LCDR Rochefort first reported that a message had been intercepted from the Japanese ship Terukuni Maru (12000 ton passenger ship now used as a troop transport). The ship reported that she had been torpedoed and asked for assistance. This report corroborates the combat report from the USS Shark. There was no information on the ship that was torpedoed yesterday by the USS S-36.

The next report dealt with Hong Kong. Intercepts indicated that the Japanese suffered 102 dead and 1300 wounded in the first assault on Hong Kong Fortress. The 66th Japanese Infantry Regiment was leading the attack.

The only other interesting piece of intelligence was that the 144th Infantry Regiment was ordered to Guam. This will be the major unit participating in the attack on Guam. It was not known when the attack will take place.

THEORIES AND INTENTIONS

Right now it looks like the next target will be Kuching. The British Liaison Officer thought that there would be a surface force sent from Singapore to break up any attempted invasion of Kuching. The attacking Dutch aircraft did not notice any escorting destroyers or cruisers indicated that there exists the possibility to strike a good shot at the enemy forces. Miri was already under attack and other attacks occurred on the Malayan Peninsula. The Japanese will probably push their troops down the peninsula with supporting amphibious invasions (though it is highly unlikely, given the strong sea defenses of Singapore that they would commit to an amphibious attack directly at Singapore).

With the supporting invasion of Legaspi in the Philippines it seems that Luzon is a higher priority at this point. We're hoping (the staff that is) that the rest of the submarines are sortied from Cavite Base and that something is done with the rest of the shipping. The only way supplies can be brought in right now is by submarine and that won't last long.

The operations area around Hawaii seems to be relatively secure except for the submarine threat. Hopefully a supply ship can be dispatched to Lihue tomorrow. Otherwise, marshaling of forces will be occurring until such time as friendly forces can strike back. Submarines seem the only way right now.

With daily attacks at Rabaul, we expect that invasion forces can't be far behind. There are a handful of cruisers assembling at Port Moresby, but to fully resupply, they'll have to retreat to Brisbane or Sydney. Some forces may be dispatched to Australia to help.

LATE DAY REPORTS

As the night operations team was coming in, there were some late day reports that the staff was beginning to work on.

First, reports came in via the British that there were an estimated 20000 troops attacking Hong Kong. The garrison in place might hold out for a few days but they will eventually be overrun without reinforcements or additional supplies.

Second, the commander at Miri estimated that 1400 enemy troops had landed with more on the way. The enemy was being engaged at the water's edge but would eventually push inland.

Third, the British indicated that they would send a surface force to Kuching to try to break up the invasion force that was heading there. They would use whatever they could scrape together from the forces at Singapore. By morning, they would have the operations orders in place to sortie the ships.

On the US side, reports also came in from Soerabaja late that indicated that the USS Houston (a heavy cruiser) and the USS Boise (a light cruiser) arrived near sunset. This would augment a complete US Force. The night staff would promulgate orders if a target presented itself that would be worthwhile to attack. Once it was determined who the senior officer is, they would liaise with the Dutch to maintain an active defense.

In the Philippines a report came in that was sketchy, but indicated that roughly 4500 troops were at Legaspi.

There was no further word on the *Kido Butai*.

I didn't turn on the radio when I got to my bungalow. I had a quick sandwich and fell asleep to the wind in the trees.

DECEMBER 11, 1941   DAY 5 OF THE WAR

Apparently, Hitler was just as stupid in this world as the last. He dutifully declared war against the United States making it easier on US/UK issues; it's a damn shame that he still believes that Japan won't lose a war just because they never lost one in the past. Sadly, my knowledge of the European Theater was not as well developed in college as my knowledge of the Pacific Theater. I am respectfully staying out of that area, unless specifically asked. This news was all I could hear on the radio this morning as I was getting ready.

MORNING BRIEF

After ADM Nimitz noted that we were now at war with Germany as well as Japan, he ordered that all reports on leftover German forces in the Pacific must be acted upon. He also ordered that there would be a brainstorming session to determine how to best use the limited attack forces that the Pacific Fleet has (vis-à-vis the current concentration of force). He then turned the floor over to his Operations Officer.

The Operations Officer began his report focusing on the *Kido Butai*. As it turned out, the *Kido Butai* was well west of Johnston Island and moving west-southwest at 20 knots. He noted that they could be heading to Truk or Kwajalein to refuel. There were no indications as to the next mission of the *Kido Butai* and the intelligence staff was tasked with providing as much information as possible to track it.

There were no new reports from Wake Island. Apparently the Japanese forces were confined to a small portion of the Island and were being kept at bay with machine guns and mortars. However, unless some kind of relief force is sent, the

Island will most certainly fall. Right now, it was too dangerous to push the issue because of the *Kido Butai*, but eventually some supplies and reinforcements must be sent. Barring that, the operations staff may receive orders for a counter-invasion. The 8th Marine Regiment immediately came to mind for this mission.

The task forces that had evaded attack were given orders during the night to begin heading back to Pearl. This included all battleships and the large surface force sent in support (the destroyers, destroyer minesweepers and support ships). Task Force 405 (the carrier task force) was heading back to Pearl as well. VADM Brown's report also stated that he had 160 aircraft ready for operations in his Task Force. Task Force 407 was still proceeding to Port Moresby at a steady advance of 15 knots.

A light cargo ship was leaving port this morning to head to Lihue with a total of 1700 tons of food, medicine, equipment and other supplies. They should reach Lihue in about 24 hours. It was noted that the ship was unescorted.

During the night, two submarines left Pearl Harbor for offensive patrols:

- USS Tautog would patrol just west of Wake Island
- USS Thresher would patrol the northern Marshall Islands

Also, from Manila the following submarine operations had occurred:

- USS S-39 arrived in port for refueling and rearming and was heading to patrol off of Saigon
- USS Permit would patrol near Formosa
- USS Snapper would patrol south of Hong Kong

- USS Seadragon would patrol in the southern Makassar Straights

This left 6 submarines waiting for orders in Cavite Base. These submarines would soon be sortied for offensive patrols. A couple of tankers and oilers were formed into a quick Task Force and were ordered to head to Soerabaja (Task Force 246).

On the West Coast, the submarines USS Gar and USS Grayling were ordered to transit to Pearl Harbor from San Diego to receive orders for offensive patrols. From San Francisco, the submarines USS Nautilus, USS Cuttlefish and USS Tuna received the same orders. Additionally, troop transports (the ships specifically designed to be troop transports known as "AP" types, not passenger liners converted over) were ordered to Pearl Harbor from San Diego, Los Angeles and San Francisco; a total of 9 APs would begin the transit. The converted liners that are being brought into Government service (known as xAP types) would be responsible for bringing troops and supplies to Pearl, but unless specifically noted, only "fleet" transports would perform actual assaults.

At Soerabaja, it was determined that CAPT Rooks, in command of the USS Houston was the senior officer. Radio reports indicated that he could sail on a 12 hour notice to perform missions as assigned. It was clear that he would use his forces to break up invasion forces near Java and southern Borneo. CAPT Farrell in command of the USS Boise would be force executive officer. CAPT Rooks also indicated that the Dutch forces in Java had moved 13 of their PT Boats to Batavia from Soerabaja.

From the British, reports came in that they had assembled two surface forces to attack landings at Kuching and Miri. For Kuching, Task Force 97 was composed of 6 destroyers under the command of CDR Swinley. For Miri, Task Force 116 was composed of 4 destroyers under the command of LCDR Thew. They were to make a quick run in, attack any ships present and fall back to Singapore. Apparently, both forces put to sea just after midnight last night. It was dangerous but could upset Japanese timetables.

They also reported that the battleship HMS Prince of Wales was making 23 knots and was 250 nautical miles west-northwest of Merak heading towards Columbo to utilize the dry dock there.

The Operations Officer concluded his report and opened the floor to questions. There were none. ADM Nimitz reminded us to be calm, professional and realize that victory will come with hard work. We were then sent to our respective stations.

HAWAII

Bad news came in before lunch. The small freighter (ship's name was Hirondelle) that was dispatched to bring cargo to Lihue was attacked around lunch time local. She had left port around 0600 and around 60 nautical miles away, a Japanese submarine surfaced; _SURFACED_ to attack the ship with guns. It took the Japanese submarine less than 15 minutes to hit the ship with the deck gun (at least 30 times according to the survivors) and sink the ship just as a PBY Catalina came in to support. No attack was possible against the submarine and the Catalina landed to pick up survivors. Another ship will need to be dispatched, this time, with escorts.

BROADER PACIFIC OCEAN

A report came in from Guam informing us that they had been under attack during the night by several bombers. They did not know the type, but there was a little bit of damage to the runway that was repaired by noon. Roughly two hours later, another raid of roughly a dozen bombers (probably Betty types) escorted by 8 or 10 Zero fighters attacked the base significantly damaging the supply dump and destroying one if the hangars.

At Wake Island, more troops landed during the night and early morning hours. A large transport came close in to the island escorted by some small patrol boats to land troops. The transport was hit by a couple of 5" shells from the shore battery and was set on fire. No major assaults were made during the day by either side. It seems like the Japanese are trying to get enough troops landed to make a major assault. The staff wasn't quite sure what to do given the number of enemy ships.

PHILIPPINE ISLAND OPERATIONS

On the ground force side, no Japanese troop movements were noted. It seemed as though they were consolidating the areas of Vigan, Aparri and Legaspi. There were plenty of enemy ships landing troops and supplies, but there were few friendly forces available to attack them. There were two separate attacks against the minesweepers in the Bataan Straights. In both instances, the Betty bombers were unescorted. A total of 12 bombers attacked over 2 hours. Friendly fighters shot down 2 of the enemy bombers; however, 1 of the P-40s was damaged on landing at Manila.

The submarines were very busy during the early morning hours straight through to the night.

A consolidated report from the USS S-38 (LCDR Chappel) showed them shadowing an enemy task force all day west of Luzon and attempting to make an attack. At 0900, they were sighted and attacked by an enemy patrol boat with no damage to the submarine. They broke contact at roughly 1030. They approached again at 1300 and were then attacked again by another patrol boat with no damage to the submarine. There were no further attacks by or against this submarine for the rest of the day.

A report from the USS S-40 (LCDR Lucker) indicated that they had found an enemy group north of Luzon at around noon and launched an attack. The report stated that they had fired 4 torpedoes at a destroyer scoring no hits. They were then attacked by a patrol boat with no damage to the submarine. They then broke contact surfaced and continued their patrol.

The report from the USS S-36 (LCDR McKnight) had information that showed an attack against an enemy patrol boat near Takao at 1400 local time. They fired two torpedoes at the ship, hitting with one of them. No indication as to whether or not the ship was sunk.

Near Laong, the USS Seawolf (LCDR Warder) had a very busy day. They reported attacking an enemy cargo ship, hitting it with one torpedo at 0900. No word as to whether or not the ship was sunk because the submarine had to dive deep and break contact because of the escorts. At 1100, they found another small force and fired two torpedoes at a patrol boat scoring no hits; they then dove deep to break contact. At around 1400, the submarine attacked another small freighter with two torpedoes, scoring no hits. A few hours after that, the submarine surfaced to attack a small cargo ship with their deck gun. They scored a few hits but were also hit by deck guns and machine guns from the freighter. The USS Seawolf will be ordered to Soerabaja in order to replenish and repair damage.

Just around 150 nautical miles southeast of Cam Ranh Bay, the USS Seal (LCDR Hurd) found and attacked a large convoy of freighters under escort. They fired two torpedoes at a freighter watched one of the torpedoes hit amidships. They reported that the ship literally exploded. They then dove deep and tried to break contact. They were attacked by several escorts over the next few hours but eventually escaped to the southwest to surface and radio in the report.

The USS Porpoise (CDR Brewster) attacked a small surface force at 1500, 150 nautical miles from Takao, firing four torpedoes at a destroyer. The torpedoes missed and the submarine was attacked for several hours. They managed to break contact to reload and recharge their batteries.

CHINESE THEATER

Reports came in about a large developing battle at Chengchow that indicated that the Chinese forces were being pushed back by the Imperial Japanese Army. It appeared that the entire area was in Japanese control by the end of the day.

Near Kaifeng, another battle was developing. There was a lot of low level combat but the Japanese were bringing up reinforcements. No indications as to casualties on either side.

BRITISH AND ALLIED OPERATIONS

There were several air attacks during constant ground combat at Hong Kong. There were four separate attacks during the morning. In entirety, 70 medium bombers attacked friendly forces at Hong Kong escorted by a total of 40 or so fighters. They heavily damaged the airfield and attacked friendly troops in the fortress area. This was happening during varying levels of high intensity and low intensity ground combat. No enemy aircraft were shot down during the morning. As the day wore on, another smaller attack came in by mid-afternoon. A few dive bombers attacked the port, damaging a couple of freighters but one of the dive bombers was shot down by ground fire. By the end of the day, ground combat had claimed the lives of 230 friendly ground troops with another 300 wounded in one way or another. The Japanese forces have brought up a lot of artillery to support their attacks. The fortress might hold out another day or two.

Figure 7 - Japanese Betty Medium Bomber

On the Malayan Peninsula there were renewed air attacks with severe consequences. Georgetown was absolutely pummeled by air attacks. There were three night attacks that caused scratch damage. At first light however, there was a large raid by 30 Betty bombers that came in at only 6000'. They hit the port and hit it hard. Many small craft were completely destroyed at the docks, the docks themselves took major damage and the fuel and supply dumps were set on fire. Luckily, this attack only caused a few casualties. In the early afternoon another attack by almost 60 medium bombers all but destroyed what was left in the port. The bombers were a mix of Nell and Betty medium bomber types. The freighters in port were sunk or heavily damaged, the fuel depot was in flames and the port structure itself was heavily damaged. It would take weeks to repair.

Alor Star was hit by a night raid and a small morning raid. There was little damage to facilities, but the crews still had to man equipment and this tired them out even more.

On Borneo, Miri was under attack by first light. Troops continued to land through the night and early in the morning. Japanese ships shelled the facility all day waiting for a mid-afternoon assault. There was a friendly Royal Navy gun battery engaged the enemy ships. It was unknown if enemy ships were hit or not. By 1600, the assault had pushed the Royal Navy forces out and they were in full retreat to Brunei. Miri now belonged to the Japanese. It was still up to Task Force 116 to attack the ships. It should take several days to complete the unloading, so the enemy force should be attacked sometime in the next 48 hours.

At Kuching friendly forces tried to bomb the invading ships. No hits were scored by a total of 8 Blenheim bombers on the invading ships. Troops began landing in the morning. One landing ship was hit by a friendly gun battery. By the end of the day, there were about 1000 enemy troops landed. The only defending unit was a small infantry force and some Royal Navy gun batteries.

Of note in the Australian Theater there was a single raid at Rabaul. A few bombers damaged the runway but caused no casualties. It was becoming obvious that this may become a target for invasion.

Intelligence

The intelligence shop came in for the daily briefing. LCDR
Rochefort again helped by revealing a Japanese report that the
freighter Saiko Maru was sunk today by an enemy submarine
(the registered tonnage was 2050 tons). LCDR Hurd thus
gains the first confirmed ship kill of the war. Another report
showed that the freighter Aki Maru was torpedoed as well
(which corroborates the USS Seawolf report). No information
was reported about the attack by the USS S-36.

There were few reports about enemy intentions or locations.
The only ones they knew for sure was that the 15th Naval
Guard Unit and a company of the 1st Sasebo Special Naval
Landing Force were going to Kuching. LCDR Rochefort was
thinking that the Japanese were changing their codes and his
crews might have to start from scratch.

Theories and Intentions

It's obvious that Miri, Kuching and Georgetown are the
next targets. This may be a bit of a misnomer because Miri was
already in Japanese hands. Since light attacks were occurring
at Rabaul it may be a future target, probably in a couple of
weeks. It is unknown where the *Kido Butai* is heading, but
that is the best indication for where the next enemy attack
would take place.

Troops hadn't started moving down the Malayan Peninsula
yet, but that couldn't stay the case for long. It should take the
Japanese one day, maybe two before they are consolidated
enough to begin the march. The heavy attacks at Georgetown
point to the ground forces heading there first. It should be
interesting to see what happens to the two Task Forces that

the British put together to break up the invasion forces at Miri and Kuching.

LATE DAY REPORTS

Most of the combat surface forces arrived in the early evening and worked their way into the appropriate areas. The battleships, cruisers and destroyers immediately began refueling. The late night staff was ordered to set up operations orders for another supply ship (this time under escort) to go to Lihue.

CAPT Rooks reported that four more Dutch submarines arrived at Soerabaja.

In the Philippines, a late report came in that indicated that there were at least 18 Japanese ships using the port of Vigan. It is possible that they may attempt to bomb the port with the limited number of bombers that they have available.

I decided to stop by the chow hall before going back to my bungalow, pasta yet again. Nothing interesting was on the radio as I went to sleep.

MORNING BRIEF

After an unimpressive breakfast, we all came in for the morning brief before dealing with the reports and problems of the day. ADM Nimitz seemed very tired today. Maybe he didn't sleep well.

First up this morning was an update from our allies. The British Liaison reported that their two destroyer task forces should achieve their objectives sometime in the next 24 hours. They would listen in for updates if the destroyers find enemy shipping.

Second, the 48th Light Anti-Aircraft Regiment was told to begin packing up to be shipped to Merak on Java. They have many 40mm BOFORS guns that would be very useful in defending the likely landing site by the Japanese.

Third, the HMS Prince of Wales was still making 23 knots and heading towards Columbo for repairs. Additionally, the troop transports are still heading towards Java with troops and supplies.

Fourth, the Australians are loading up a cargo ship with food, medical supplies and a few machine guns for Pago Pago. They also reported that the HMAS Canberra (a heavy cruiser) and the HMAS Perth (a light cruiser) arrived at Port Moresby. They will await reinforcements from New Zealand (they are sending a couple of light cruisers).

The British Liaison completed his report and the Operations Officer began his report. On the mainland, VP-91 a squadron of Catalina flying boats will begin transiting from the east coast to San Francisco. The 8th Marine Regiment should be in San Francisco by tomorrow ready to load onto troop transports to continue transit to Pearl Harbor.

Task Force 405 should arrive in Pearl Harbor late today or early tomorrow. VADM Brown reports no major problems on the carriers. Task Force 84 (carrier USS Saratoga with escorts) should arrive at the same time. Two separate task forces are currently being loaded up. The cargo ship USS Castor with 3 attending destroyers will resupply Lihue. The cargo ship USS Alchiba with 3 attending destroyers will resupply Johnston Island. This should alleviate supply problems on both islands for at least a couple of months.

In the Philippines, reports came in that had B-17 bombers based at Clark Field preparing a low level run on the ships at the port in Vigan. Additionally, the following submarines were sortied:

- USS Sargo will patrol the vicinity of Peleliu
- USS Saury will patrol east of Legaspi

This leaves 4 submarines waiting for orders. This concluded the morning brief. ADM Nimitz reminded us to be aware and beware. He told the staff that he felt something bad was going to happen at Wake Island.

SUBMARINE OPERATIONS

Since submarines will be operating across the entire Pacific, it makes sense for me to have my reports on those in their own section.

The USS Seawolf found and attacked an enemy patrol boat near Laoag. They fired two torpedoes for no hits and got away unscathed after 4 hours underwater sneaking away slowly. The patrol boat never found them.

I find it humorous that I picked today to have a separate section for friendly submarine operations and for today, the USS Seawolf report was the only one that came in.

HAWAII

There were no major reports near Hawaii today. The cargo ships under heavy escort are proceeding to their destinations and no confirmed sightings of enemy submarines were reported.

BROADER PACIFIC OCEAN

Near the US West Coast, the cargo ship SS Julia Luckenbach (8150 tons) was attacked by a Japanese submarine at 1500 local. The ship was torpedoed and then attacked on the surface by the submarine with the deck gun. The ship sank roughly 200 nautical miles west of Eureka, California. Catalina flying boats are looking for survivors. It is currently unknown how many Japanese submarines are heading to the West Coast.

At Wake Island, enemy forces continued shore bombardment to try to help their troops that were pinned down by the Marines. An interesting report came in about one of the shore 5" guns hitting a "large enemy transport" with several shells and setting the ship afire. The information was given to LCDR Rochefort and his intelligence team to see if some further information could be deduced from this report. The ground situation seems like a stalemate at this point. It seems like the Japanese are trying to wear down the defenders from a supply and support standpoint before making a major assault. MAJ Deveraux indicated by a radio report that he was concerned about ammunition levels.

There was a light air raid at Guam at roughly noon local time. There was some damage to the air base facilities but luckily, no casualties were reported.

PHILIPPINE ISLAND OPERATIONS

The Japanese yet again today sent Betty bombers to attack the minesweepers near Bataan. They sent 9 Betty bombers with no escort. P-40 Warhawk fighters from Clark Field intercepted them and 4 of the bombers were shot down with no loss to the attacking fighters. There were no reports of damage to the minesweepers. Some good news for a change.

The news then changed rapidly. A friendly force of 11 B-17 bombers from Clark Field escorted by 6 P-40 Warhawk fighters attempted a raid at Vigan Port where it was reported that almost 20 enemy cargo ships were unloading equipment, troops and supplies. The force was attacked by 28 Zero fighters. A single P-40 was shot down, but 5 B-17s were shot down and the rest damaged. There was only one good hit on the port facilities. This raid is to be considered a failure.

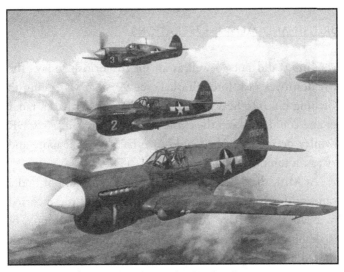

Figure 8 - P-40 Warhawk

At San Fernando, a Japanese tank regiment attacked friendly forces trying to push through them. The 11th Philippine Army Division put up a spirited resistance, destroying 3 enemy tanks and disabling 18 more. This is a considerable achievement considering the division is currently still receiving called up reservists (last reports from Manila indicated that the division only has 3200 troops currently in uniform). 88 Philippine Army troops were wounded.

CHINESE THEATER

There were reports of fighting near Kaifeng, Kweisui, Pengpu, Hangchow, Lang Son, Hwainan, Hwaiyin, Chengting and Canton. It seemed like there was a general offensive in the entire theater. There is currently no word as to how successful these Japanese attacks have been.

BRITISH AND ALLIED OPERATIONS

Things did not go well at all for the British today. The first destroyer task force (Task Force 97) that was going to Kuching ran into heavy fog. Only one destroyer had a radar set and could not keep the entire force coordinated. So, CDR Swinley decided that he would turn back for Singapore and try again tomorrow.

At Miri, the 3 destroyers (Task Force 116) did not find a transport force. Well, technically they did, but it was escorted by a Japanese Surface Action Group that had a couple of battleships, cruisers and destroyers. The reports that came in showed a running gun battle over 7 hours as the destroyers tried to break contact. When it was all over, the destroyers HMAS Vampire and HMS Jupiter were sunk with only one confirmed hit on an enemy destroyer (hit with a 4.5" shell from the HMAS Vampire). The destroyer HMAS Vendetta was heavily damaged, but managed to break contact. There was a heated discussion as to whether the destroyer should make for Singapore or Soerabaja to be repaired. Singapore had a larger dock but was more exposed. Soerabaja was smaller but farther away (and also not under immediate attack). The British Liaison said that the final decision would be made later in the evening.

Japanese troops continued to land at Kuching during the entire day. It was determined that the assaulting force was from the Japanese 124th Infantry Battalion (a couple of prisoners were taken during the day and were interrogated; this is where the information came from). It was estimated that roughly 1000 troops had landed and were being reinforced. During the day, friendly forces suffered 24 killed and 58 wounded. The radio report stated that 15 prisoners were taken and that roughly 150 enemy troops were wounded or killed. There was an attack by British Blenheim bombers at noon from Singapore coming in at 6000' to bomb the transports. No hits were reported on the enemy transports. Shore batteries were firing on the transports and it was reported that a small transport ship was hit and was on fire.

At Hong Kong, there were several air attacks during the day. At 1400 local, the main attack came in by 40 medium bombers that did extensive damage to ships in the harbor. 4 cargo ships were hit and set afire. At 1430 several dive bombers hit the fortified area causing a few casualties before the enemy assault began at 1445. The attack was made by nearly 30000 enemy troops. Friendly forces suffered 693 dead (best reports available) and the enemy suffered nearly 1000 casualties (unknown what the number of dead or wounded are). Friendly troops are in some truly savage fighting.

At Rangoon, there was a single large enemy raid that arrived at 1600 local time. The raid was by 20 medium bombers (reported as Sally types) very heavily escorted by almost 50 fighters (a mix of Zero and Oscar types according to the pilot debrief). Friendly Buffalo fighters attempted to attack them but were completely overwhelmed by the escorts. No. 67 Sqn lost 3 Buffalo fighters and only managed to damage 2 of the enemy bombers (no word on pilot losses). There was some damage to the airfield that was quickly repaired.

On the Malayan Peninsula combat continued at a high intensity pace as well. Overnight at Alor Star, there were 3 separate air attacks (more than likely, a single raid that got a little lost and then came in piecemeal). There was no damage to friendly facilities by these raids. At 0800 local, another raid by 25 medium bombers (reports indicated that they were Sally types) hit the airbase. The only real damage was from a single 250 kg bomb that landed near the hangars. Several Blenheim bombers were damaged by the explosion and one was completely destroyed. Ground based heavy machine guns managed to damage one of the attacking bombers (seen heading to the east trailing smoke).

Kuantan was hit with several air raids by medium bombers. By the end of the day, a total of 90 medium bombers from 4 separate raids had completely trashed the port facilities and set fire to the supply dumps there. There were scarce anti-aircraft guns and no enemy planes were reported as shot down. The Japanese seem intent on destroying this facility; it remains to be seen if they will have engineer units come in to repair the facilities or if it is to be completely bypassed.

In the Australian area, there was a single large raid against Rabaul consisting of 30 medium bombers. They did appreciable damage to the airfield (though there are no friendly aircraft at that base). It was reported that there were 8 wounded during the raid.

INTELLIGENCE

LCDR Rochefort did his daily report. Of interest, elements of the Japanese 53rd Division were headed for Kota Bharu. Also, elements of the 4th Infantry Battalion are heading towards Kuching on an unidentified ship. When asked about the Wake Island area, he stated that a partial decrypt from the Kinryu Maru stated that they were damaged by enemy shore fire during the day. This is a large ship (9300 tons) that can carry a lot of troops and cargo. The Imperial Japanese Navy saw fit to convert that particular ship into an Armed Merchant Cruiser (AMC). It is unknown how damaged the ship is.

He also stated that an older report that was decrypted indicated that the cargo ship Nako Maru was torpedoed on the 11th of December. The location and date corroborate the report from the submarine USS S-36.

There was no information on the *Kido Butai*.

There were no further reports from the intelligence unit.

THEORIES AND INTENTIONS

Since the Japanese are not being content with just damaging Kuantan but completely destroying it indicates that they are probably going to bypass the location until they have liquidated Singapore.

The appearance of Japanese submarines on the West Coast is disturbing. There simply are not enough escorts to go around. However, it will be difficult for the Japanese to maintain those submarines. They must have logistical support in the form of oilers/tankers and ammunition support. It may become necessary to scour some areas of the North Pacific to see if these support ships are out there.

The British suffered a setback at Miri… it remains to be seen what will happen at Kuching.

LATE DAY REPORTS

Task Force 405 arrived at Pearl Harbor. The carriers immediately began taking on supplies and shore based maintenance personnel to make the ships ready to depart when ordered. VADM Brown reported directly to ADM Nimitz for a closed door session.

The submarine USS Trout also arrived at Pearl Harbor.

USS Castor arrived at Lihue at 2000 and began offloading supplies, medical equipment, food and replacements. It will take a couple of days to offload everything, but the immediate crisis has been abated. The attending destroyers will work local patrols until it is time for the cargo ship to head back to Pearl Harbor.

On Java, CAPT Rooks reported that 3 more Dutch submarines arrived and were re-provisioning and waiting for orders. He also reported that the 3 destroyers from Hong Kong arrived (HMS Thracian, HMS Scout and HMS Thanat). He also relayed a report from the Dutch command that the PT Boats sent to Batavia arrived safely and were waiting for orders.

The British Liaison reported that Task Force 97 (the 6 destroyers) would be leaving Singapore again (and had probably already left after refueling) to attack Kuching again. Hopefully the weather would cooperate this time. He also reported that the damaged surviving destroyer from Task Force 116 (HMAS Vendetta) would be heading to Soerabaja for repairs. Also reported via the New Zealand officer was information that the light cruisers HMNZS Leander and HMNZS Achilles arrived at Port Moresby.

I left the headquarters building at 2030, grabbed a sandwich and went to my bungalow. I took a long shower and went immediately to sleep. As I drifted off, I thought about how good a Sam Adams beer would taste right now and then went sullen when I realized that I wouldn't be able to have one for about 50 years.

Morning Brief

First thing ADM Nimitz asked for was a list, by type, of all available US ships in the Pacific. This was to include ships in dry dock. He then began a conversation about how we were pretty much stuck with what we had because of personnel issues. From this conversation we discussed the hard core logistics of running a major war. As an example, to bring a civilian up to the basic standards (not even a specialist) for a ship would take a minimum of 3 months. This meant that we would not see a major expansion until at least late February at the earliest.

Additionally, stocks of ammunition were considered "adequate" but he cautioned that extravagant expenditures may hurt the overall war effort until all of the factories are churning out the equipment that we will need. As an example, he cited the destroyer USS Benson. She was laid down on 16 MAY 1938, launched 15 NOV 1939 and wasn't commissioned until 25 JUL 1940. He reasoned that even if production efficiencies could reduce the amount of time to build a ship, this efficiency wouldn't happen quickly. To point out another example, ADM Nimitz pointed to the ship lost on the 2nd day of the war, the USS Schley. She was an older "four piper" from World War I. Even so, it took 11 months from construction starting until she was commissioned. We need to strike at the enemy but must not waste resources to do so.

He brought up our ability to strike at the enemy. From a pure "Mahanian" viewpoint, we were going to pursue a *Guerre-de-Course* method. We would not intentionally engage enemy fleet forces without local superiority (or at least parity).

We would strike at logistical elements, freighters, cargo ships, oilers and tankers which presented themselves until such time as we had a major force advantage. If the opportunity arose to strike fleet combat assets, it would happen, but only if some advantage could be gained weighed against the risk of loss. We were not seeking a "Battle of Jutland" at this point. We were to minimize losses until we had clear superiority. "Submarines" he stated "will bear the brunt of our offensives during these next few months."

With that, he asked the Operations Officer to begin the morning briefing.

He did so. First on the agenda was an update on Task Force 84 (USS Saratoga Carrier Group); they were two days from reaching Pearl Harbor. Next was Task Force 407 (USS Pensacola with troop transports); they were near the Duff Islands and about a week from reaching Port Moresby with a speed of advance of 12 knots. Next on the list was Task Force 408 (USS Louisville with two troop transports heading to Pearl Harbor); they were at least a week out of Pearl Harbor located roughly 500 nautical miles west-northwest of Palmyra Island with a speed of advance of 16 knots.

Overnight on the West Coast, the 8th Marine Regiment began loading onto converted liners for a transit to Pearl Harbor. Their speed of advance will be 19 knots (fast for troop carriers) and should help mitigate the submarine threat.

In the Philippines, the remaining 4 submarines were ordered to Soerabaja to pick up supplies for troops in the Philippines (USS Sculpin, USS Sailfish, USS Searaven and USS Sealion). It will supply only a trickle, but it will help slow the advance of Japanese troops. More ships were sortied from Cavite Base; 2 of the 3 submarine tenders were to put to sea and are heading towards Soerabaja (USS Holland and USS Otus). Additionally, the 4 destroyers in Cavite Base will make a high speed run to attack any shipping near Vigan Port (Task Force 88 under command of CDR Musak). This will be dangerous but there were no confirmed indications of enemy ships larger than a destroyer (there were some cruisers at Aparri). This was deemed acceptable risk by the commander in Manila. ADM Nimitz winced when he heard this part of the report.

The British Liaison Officer reported that Task Force 97 (6 destroyers) headed out to attack shipping at Kuching. They were standing by to receive reports. Also, the HMS Prince of Wales could now make 23 knots on her way to Columbo for repairs. The HMAS Vendetta was still on fire but was making 17 knots heading towards Soerabaja. It would take roughly 5 days to get there.

The staff was then dismissed to begin the day's work.

SUBMARINE OPERATIONS

The submarine USS Seal (LCDR Hurd) was sighted by an enemy destroyer near Cam Ranh Bay and attacked with depth charges. They managed to sneak away and resume their patrol.

Near Laoag, the USS S-37 (CDR Easton) found a Japanese light cruiser and attacked. They fired 4 torpedoes for no hits. A subchaser was detached from the group to attack the submarine. After a 2 hour cat and mouse battle, the submarine managed to slip away and resume its patrol.

Near Hengchun the USS Seawolf (LCDR Warder) found and attacked a large cargo ship. The torpedoes were heard to hit the hull but not explode. This may be a continuing Mark 14 torpedo problem. In any case, the submarine was chased by an enemy destroyer and was depth charged. They managed to escape and continue their patrol.

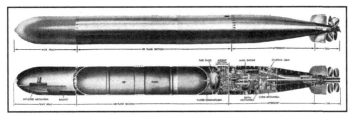

Figure 9 - Mark 14 Torpedo

HAWAII

Part of the staff reported back to ADM Nimitz after lunch. The available fleet forces as of 0800 local were as follows:

- Carriers (CV) – 3
- Battleships (BB) – 5 ready, with 4 repairing (USS Arizona, USS West Virginia and USS Oklahoma in Pearl Harbor with the USS Colorado in Seattle)
- Heavy Cruisers (CA) – 13
- Light Cruisers (CL) – 10
- Destroyers (DD) – 77
- Destroyer Transports (APD) – 1
- Fleet Troop Transports (AP) – 15
- Fleet Cargo Ships (AK) – 5
- Fleet Oilers (AO) – 12
- Submarines (SS) – 40 fleet, 12 'S' Class

It was not known how many British, Dutch, Australian or New Zealand ships were available. Current Japanese Fleet assets were also not available. There were a large number of merchant cargo ships available and a large number of converted liners available as well. The list provided showed only what were true "Fleet" assets. It was obvious by looking at this list that only operations with really good risk management were to be attempted.

BROADER PACIFIC OCEAN

At Wake Island, enemy ships continued to trade shots with the remaining shore based 5" batteries. MAJ Deveraux reported that his guns damaged another large enemy transport and a smaller patrol boat. He did report that he was concerned that he would run low on 5" ammunition. It is unknown why the Japanese are just sitting there and not attacking with the ground troops. MAJ Deveraux indicated that he may have his Marines counter attack if it looked favorable. Low level conflict continued, with snipers and machine guns dominating the small deadly space.

There was a small attack at Guam. A few dive bombers made an attack against the airfield. There was little damage to the airfield and no enemy planes were shot down.

PHILIPPINE ISLAND OPERATIONS

As it turned out, while we were having our morning briefing Task Force 88 reached their objective at Vigan and attacked enemy shipping. They ran into no enemy combat units save for a couple of small patrol boats that were escorting a large number of freighters, cargo ships and converted troop transports. CDR Musak immediately ordered an attack. By their count, there were 14 large ships and 10 smaller ships. They opened fire at 12000 yards and did a high speed run in for a torpedo attack. All of the destroyers scored hits on various transports. However, the USS Pope claimed a transport sunk and the USS Peary claimed 2 enemy ships sunk (mostly due to torpedo hits). 5 other freighters were seen to be on fire or damaged during the attack. They attacked for roughly one hour before retiring to head back to port before sunrise. A success!

This attack must have pissed off the Japanese something awful because the destroyers were attacked by a coordinated strike by 4 separate forces as they approached the harbor at Subic Bay. In all, 40 medium bombers, 4 dive bombers escorted by a total of 60 enemy fighters attacked over a 2 hour period in the late morning. The friendly squadrons in Manila and Clark Field managed to get 47 fighters in the air during the attacks. Losses by the end of the attacks included 5 medium bombers shot down, 2 enemy escorting fighters shot down for 9 friendly interceptors. No hits were scored against the destroyers returning to base.

There was only one further report from the Philippines. The 11th Philippine Army Division was attacked yet again at San Fernando. They were attacked by the 4th Tank Regiment and the 65th Infantry Brigade. They were pushed back towards Clark Field with heavy losses. Preliminary reports indicate that they suffered 1200 killed, wounded and missing. The 11th Division will try to re-provision and accept reinforcements at Clark Field.

Chinese Theater

There were no major reports. We're not entirely sure if it is because the Chinese Command doesn't want us to know the true state of affairs or if it is because they simply don't have the information either. They did admit that one of their infantry corps had been forced out of a defensive position near

Chenting. Outside of that, there was little reported from this operational theater.

BRITISH AND ALLIED OPERATIONS

During the night, Task Force 116 approached Kuching to attack enemy shipping. They found 20 freighters of various sizes along with a single patrol boat. As the fog was beginning to come in, they attacked before the weather got too bad. They managed to damage the patrol boat and put rounds into a couple of the smaller transports before the fog got bad enough that they needed to withdraw. They got within 11000 yards of the force before the fog got too thick. While not a complete success, they did manage to damage a few ships which in some way will still help the war effort.

The ground force situation was one of stalemate at Kuching, probably because the resupply operations were foiled by the destroyer attack (the freighters had to stop operations to try to defend themselves).

Rangoon was attacked by 30 Sally medium bombers escorted by 60 fighters. 3 aircraft were destroyed on the ground and a few enemy bombers were damaged (at least 4 were seen trailing smoke). The runway was heavily damaged and the supply dump was set on fire. It will take several hours for repairs to the runway to be completed.

Hong Kong was assaulted at first light after a short but intense artillery bombardment with supporting air attacks that threw off the defending troops. By 1400 local, the remaining troops had surrendered. 5200 friendly troops were either killed or captured. Hong Kong now belongs to Japan.

There was a small counter strike by Blenheims from Singapore against ships at Kota Bharu. There was no damage scored against the enemy (they attacked a solitary cargo ship). All aircraft returned safely to Singapore.

At Kuantan, there was a large raid that arrived at around 1030 local. Around 30 medium bombers escorted by 50 fighters attacked the airfield. There were some hits on the runway and one of the hangars was damaged.

In the Australian area, Rabaul was attacked by a single large force of Betty bombers. They caused a lot of damage to the runway and blew open the remaining hangars. There were 17 wounded on the ground and there were no enemy bombers shot down by friendly forces (light anti-aircraft on the ground).

Japanese forces landed at Medang on northeast New Guinea. Troop numbers are unknown and landing force size in terms of ships are unknown. The forces in Port Moresby may be sortied to attack this enemy incursion, but it is unlikely.

INTELLIGENCE

LCDR Rochefort reported that there was no new information regarding the *Kido Butai*. No radio traffic, nothing from coastwatchers or from patrol assets. Signals intelligence noted that units were planning for an attack against Guam; a mixed engineering and support unit known as the 15th Force was ordered to plan for an invasion.

The following intel was gained as well:

-   Elements of the 21st Division were loaded onto a troop transport and heading for Samah.
-   Troops from the 56th Recon Regiment were moving to Patani
-   A reinforcement company of infantry was heading to Kuching to support the 4th Infantry Battalion

- The Army General Headquarters was identified at Tokyo. Certain messages may now be decrypted.
- One of the damaged ships at Wake Island was confirmed as a destroyer (strafed by one of the fighters early in the invasion)

Ships damaged at Vigan were identified to a point. The ships sunk were identified by a merchant message. They were identified as:

- Toyokawa Maru, a 4875 ton Aden Class cargo ship
- Sugiyama Maru, a 3425 ton Ehime Class cargo ship
- Yasuteru Maru, also a 3425 ton Ehime Class cargo ship

There were a further four ships that reported damage from the raid, confirming the report from CDR Musak. It remains to be seen which friendly ships conclusively sank which enemy ships, but that information should be available after debriefs and analysis. LCDR Rochefort indicated that this success should shake up the Japanese command a little bit and make them a bit more timid. I personally didn't agree or disagree. When LCDR Rochefort was briefed on the Japanese response, he wasn't particularly surprised.

He ended the report by stating that they were still looking for more information.

THEORIES AND INTENTIONS

It is now obvious that the Japanese fleet can't adequately defend all of their transport forces. This explains the use of smaller "patrol boats" that are based on small freighter hulls. It is risky, but continued attacks by fast surface forces may be able to hit some of the supply convoys and troop transport forces. This will keep with ADM Nimitz's *Guerre de Course* strategy.

The intelligence reports show that more troops will be headed to the Malayan Peninsula. This is corroborated by a continuing set of operations heading down the Peninsula towards Singapore. It remains to be seen how the British will be able to defend against this incursion. The landings on the north coast of Borneo show that they are trying to secure the oil resources there.

LATE DAY REPORTS

At 1900, the HMAS Vendetta reported that they were sinking. The ship had severe fires that got out of control and caused a conflagration. The ship launched all lifeboats and they were heading towards the Borneo coast. Radio contact was then lost. Singapore will try to send some flying boats to their last known reported location.

Task Force 97 (destroyers) was refueling and re-provisioning at Singapore and would make another attempt at attacking the enemy shipping at Kuching. Late day patrols reported that another task force of transports was making its way to Kuching and would be carrying more troops and supplies. It was a ripe target because no escorts were evident. Tempting and dangerous all in one measure.

A Japanese submarine was sighted roughly 90 nautical miles east-northeast of Pearl Harbor. The staff was considering sending out some destroyers.

The supply situation at Lihue has been abated. A little over 600 tons of food and medical supplies have been offloaded so far. The fleet cargo ship USS Alchiba with attending destroyers was still 36 hours from reaching Johnston Island.

MAJ Deveraux at Wake Island reported that he was planning a counter attack against the Japanese forces. He stated that he had almost a full company of infantry and 13 supporting machine guns to mount the attack. This was risky, but I'm not the commander on the ground. It is natural to seek a counter attack.

CDR Musak sent a report via Manila HQ that he was re-provisioning his force but that Manila Depot was out of Mk 15 torpedoes. He had roughly half of a full battle load on his destroyers and that he would mount another attack in the next 24 hours.

It was a long day. I stopped by the Officer's Club, had a beer, a ham sandwich and went to my bungalow. Sleep came fitfully; there was a thunderstorm.

DECEMBER 14, 1941   DAY 8 OF THE WAR

The Operations Officer started quickly. ADM Nimitz looked like he needed to be somewhere. Maps were brought out with updates and the report began.

On the West Coast, patrol assets were being called and assembled in San Francisco to begin anti-submarine patrols off the coast. This would fall mainly on smaller ships as the fleet destroyers were needed elsewhere. VP-91, stationed at Mare Island would begin anti-submarine patrols.

The carrier USS Saratoga should be in port over the next 24 hours with her attending escorts. Orders were to have them immediately re-provision and stand by for an immediate sortie. That sounded to me like there was an operation that was ready to go down.

The Coast Guard Cutters Tiger and Reliance were ready to be absorbed into the US Navy and were assigned to a task force along with the destroyers USS Worden and USS Dale to perform anti-submarine patrols to the east-northeast of Pearl Harbor. They would begin their patrol near the location where the Japanese submarine was seen yesterday. They were assigned as Task Force 282 under the command of LCDR Rorschbach.

In the Philippines, Task Force 88 would plan another sortie to Vigan port to attack Japanese shipping. CDR Musak was still in command and wanted more kills. ADM Nimitz indicated that he should be awarded at Bronze Star Medal at the minimum. The Administrative Officer took note.

All other task forces were proceeding as planned, with no indicated threats or concerns.

The British Liaison Officer reported that Prince of Wales was well out to sea in the Indian Ocean and would provide no further reports on the ship until she entered port in Columbo.

He also indicated that the 48th Light Anti-Aircraft Regiment was boarding ships for transport to Java, with an eventual final location of Merak for local air defense.

CDR Swinley with Task Force 97 would again attack Kuching in the next 24 hours to try to sink transports and slow the invasion forces landing in Borneo. There was little more to be done near Borneo for the immediate future.

With that, we were dismissed with no additional notifications from ADM Nimitz. He quickly left with his aides and the Operations Officer was in command during his absence.

SUBMARINE OPERATIONS

At 0500 West Coast time, an enemy submarine attacked and sank the 4620 ton freighter SS Steel Voyager only 90 nautical miles west-southwest of Eureka, California. The ship reported they were under attack, took several torpedo hits and that they were sinking. A PBY Catalina was sent to the area to look for survivors; hence, no idea on friendly casualties. The ship, however, was destroyed.

At 1700 local time, a report was received from the submarine USS Sargo (LCDR Jacobs) that stated they had found an enemy surface action group and fired a spread of torpedoes at an enemy battleship (identified as a Nagato class battleship). They scored one hit on the battleship that struck midships on the port side. They were then swarmed by at least 4 destroyers. It took them three hours to sneak away. It is unlikely that a battleship would be sunk by a single torpedo, but it would indicate that the ship would need to return to drydock for repairs.

Figure 10 - Nagato Class Battleship

HAWAII

At 0930 local time, a report came in from Task Force 282 just northeast of Pearl Harbor. They reported that an enemy submarine had attacked them with torpedoes (no hits were scored). The destroyers and cutters then began a sub hunt. Several depth charges were used, but there is no indication that the enemy submarine was sunk.

BROADER PACIFIC OCEAN

MAJ Devereaux had his infantry attack Japanese forces at dawn Wake Island time. They used the machine guns to cover the assault. It was moderately successful; by the end of the day, MAJ Deveraux reported that his troops suffered 22 wounded, but killed at least 70 of the Japanese troops on the island while wounding scores more. He used the 5" gun batteries to support the machine gunners. The staff began to work on ways to get some supplies to the base. It looks like submarines are the only way to go, unless the carriers sortie to break the invasion force.

At Guam, a large raid came in at 1300 local that did severe damage to the port, the fuelling facilities and the piers. There was little the forces on the ground could do because all they had were machine guns and the bombers came in over the max altitude of the anti-aircraft machine guns.

PHILIPPINE ISLAND OPERATIONS

Right after CDR Musak and his destroyers left port, an overnight raid came in over Manila that attacked the airfield. The number of enemy bombers was not known, but a couple of PBY Catalina patrol aircraft were damaged on the ground. This was the beginning of several incursions by aircraft in the general Manila area during the day.

At 0900 local an attack by 9 Betty bombers escorted by 22 Zero fighters again attacked the minesweepers working near the Bataan Peninsula. One Betty was shot down for the loss of 3 friendly fighters.

Roughly 2 hours later, a flight of Nell bombers came in to attack the airfield at Manila. They were bounced by almost 20 friendly Warhawk fighters; 4 enemy bombers were shot down with no losses to the fighters.

At the same time, a small raid hit Clark Field damaging some of the B-17 bombers on the ground. Anti-aircraft fire claimed one enemy bomber damaged (however, this was not confirmed). A couple of hours later, another major air raid took place. A force of 20 Sally bombers came in escorted by 26

Zero fighters. Almost every available Warhawk scrambled. In the ensuing furball, 4 enemy fighters and 1 bomber were shot down for the loss of 6 friendly fighters. It was a very grueling battle.

The fighters barely had time to rearm and refuel before the next raid came at Manila. A force of 12 dive bombers (probably Sonia types) escorted by 12 Nate fighters came in to bomb the airfield. Friendly forces managed to get 11 fighters in the air. A total of 3 enemy aircraft were shot down and a single P-40 Warhawk was damaged on landing.

CDR Musak's destroyers caught up with some of the enemy ships at Vigan, but a heavy fog was developing. The destroyers made a quick run in heavily damaging a freighter and putting some shells in a couple of others. There were no confirmed sinkings of ships and the destroyers turned back for Cavite Base to resupply.

CHINESE THEATER

There were more reports on ground combat in China. It appeared that Japanese troops were on the move near Chuhsien, Kaifeng, Kweisui, Canton and Lang Son. No indications as to friendly or enemy casualties.

BRITISH AND ALLIED OPERATIONS

Madang, at Papua on northeast New Guinea fell to a Japanese landing force. The British Liaison officer believed that the Australians would sortie their cruiser force to break up the invasion force before having them fall back to refuel and re-provision.

There was also an air raid at Kavieng Island. The radio operator could not identify types, but the port was struck near the northwest area of the island. This could only mean that there would probably be an invasion. Since the types were not identified, there is no consensus as to whether they are carrier based or land based aircraft. This is dangerous.

At Kuching, Task Force 97 (CDR Swinley) caught up with transports offloading more troops and supplies. They attacked immediately. During a 3 hour running battle that started just before first light, the destroyers managed to sink what they reported as 2 destroyers, 2 freighters and damaged several more (4 enemy freighters were reported as "burning heavily"). There was no damage to any of the attacking destroyers and they quickly left the area to head back to Singapore. While this was occurring, the troops that had already landed managed to take the main part of the base and push the British and Indian troops towards Sambas. Kuching was in Japanese hands.

On the Malayan Peninsula, Kuantan was struck by a very large raid of over 100 medium bombers with escorts. The port was on fire as well as the fuel and supply depots. There was very little left undamaged at the port.

There were two separate raids at Alor Star, one at 1100 local and another at 1140 local. In all, 50 medium bombers escorted by 20 fighters bombed the airfield. There was extensive damage to the runway (that could be repaired) and a couple of aircraft were damaged on the ground. There were no losses to the enemy force and it would take at least 7 or 8 hours for the crews on the ground to repair the runway.

Further to the north, Rangoon was attacked at 1000 local by a force of 30 Sally medium bombers escorted by mix of Zero and Oscar fighters. The raid damaged the runway but did not hit the support structures or the supply dump. A single Buffalo fighter was shot down by the enemy fighters and 3 of the Sally bombers had damage of some kind.

Figure 11 - Japanese Zero Fighter

INTELLIGENCE

OP-20 Intelligence began their normal 1600 report. ADM Nimitz was back in the headquarters building after having a consultation with some of the force commanders on their flagships.

First on the intelligence update was concerning a Japanese Guards Mixed Brigade. A decrypted message indicated that elements of this unit were on a troop transport named the Keihuku Maru and were moving towards Wake Island. This would be a reinforcement unit to help take the island. After MAJ Devereaux's successful counter attack, they are probably trying to finish the job quickly.

There was a heavy volume of transmissions from the ocean areas north of Rabaul and Kavieng Island. This may indicate the next large scale assault.

There was no decrypted traffic to suggest the names or material status of damaged ships from CDR Musak's strike at Vigan, but they were maintaining vigilance to see if any information could be gained. There was also no traffic about the battleship that was attacked.

There was traffic that was decrypted concerning Kuching. As it turns out, the Japanese reported that two APD (destroyer transport) type ships were sunk, the Tsuta and Yomogi. They were small ships (roughly 935 tons each) and were carrying some infantry troops to Kuching. Also decrypted was information on the following ships:

- Freighter Thames Maru was sunk (4875 tons)
- Freighter Yubari Maru was sunk (2375 tons)
- 7 other freighters were damaged, 3 severely, no names

There was no information regarding the Japanese carriers, which was disconcerting. With that, the intelligence report ended.

THEORIES AND INTENTIONS

News of Japanese submarines attacking shipping on the West Coast is very troubling. The submarines could not reach the West Coast without some type of logistical support. There must be some location where they are refueling and re-provisioning. This was brought to the attention of ADM Nimitz. He surmised that it is *possible* that there could be ships set up "somewhere" in the North Pacific. Problem is the North

Pacific is vast. He would take it under advisement to see if any patrol assets could begin looking for these logistical tails.

That the Japanese are forced to send reinforcements to Wake shows that the Marines are fighting hard. I started a conversation about the possibility of sending our carriers to break up the invasion that sounded bold and dangerous. ADM Nimitz loved the idea *if* we could figure out where the Japanese carriers are. He did say that a quick in and out strike would not be out of the question and asked what we could gain from such a strike. I figured that we could completely off-balance the enemy attack and throw off their timetables. ADM Nimitz smiled and asked to see the operations officer.

Late Day Reports

USS Saratoga arrived at Pearl Harbor and immediately began refueling and re-provisioning. They were told to keep their boilers hot. The submarine USS Triton also arrived at Pearl Harbor late in the day.

USS Alchiba and her escort destroyers arrived at Johnston Island and began offloading needed supplies. A report came in from Hilo saying that they were running low on supplies (mostly food and fuel).

CDR Musak in the Philippines reported that his destroyers were almost out of torpedoes, but they had plenty of gun ammunition (4" and 3" guns) that could damage the enemy, but without torpedoes he won't be able to sink many ships. The stores available ashore held plenty of gun ammunition, so this would not be a problem.

An enemy submarine was spotted 125 nautical miles south of Pearl Harbor. Air patrol assets were shadowing the submarine.

In Australia at Sydney, the 1st Australian Division was beginning to form up. All of the subordinate units had arrived and they were shaking down and getting ready to board transports. It should take a couple of days to fully load the division to send it to Port Moresby.

A patrol plane noted that even more ships were at Kuching offloading troops and supplies. ADM Nimitz had a closed door session with the British Liaison Officer and then had notes for the night staff. I then left for some sleep.

DECEMBER 15, 1941   DAY 9 OF THE WAR

<u>MORNING BRIEF</u>

Military Police came and woke me up early this morning. It was 0415 when they came. I was told I was needed at the headquarters immediately. When I arrived, it looked like ADM Nimitz was up all night. He told me that the carriers USS Lexington, USS Saratoga and USS Enterprise would sortie with 4 attending heavy cruisers and 13 destroyers. They were to make a quick run to Wake Island, support the troops there and get out. They were to stay in the area for no longer than 36 hours. They would be called Task Force Rogers, and the operation was called Operation Buck. I was to go over the operations plan and make sure that the combat staff knew the contents. He ordered some of the other staff to work on some orders for our ships at Soerabaja.

By 0730, the task was completed and a light breakfast of toast, jam and some coffee was brought in. I asked for tea. At this point, the Operations Officer began the morning briefing.

He started with a quick brief of Task Force Rogers which was currently leaving port. They were to scour for enemy shipping and if none were found, to assist the troops on Wake Island by bombing the hell out of the enemy forces. CAPT Ramsay was in command of the Task Force and reported before leaving that 247 aircraft on the carriers were ready for battle.

He then briefed the orders given to CAPT Rooks at Java. He was to send a light cruiser and 5 destroyers to Kuching to help the British there. A quick run, damage or destroy as many enemy ships as possible and then fall back to Soerabaja. That force was called Task Force Alpha, under the command of CAPT Newman aboard the light cruiser USS Marblehead. It would take two days for the force to reach Kuching.

Also leaving port were the submarines USS Triton and USS Trout. They were loaded with food and ammunition to deliver to Wake Island.

A request for supplies from Palmyra Island led to the merchant freighter SS Florence D. to load up and take a destroyer escort to bring the supplies. They should put to sea in the next 24 hours.

On the West Coast, the 8th Marine Regiment was fully loaded on the transports and was waiting for the last of the supplies to be loaded. They should put to sea sometime today.

The Canadians started an anti-submarine patrol with some of their smaller ships near the border with the US off of Vancouver Island. They will also fly some patrol aircraft to help with the threat.

The patrol squadron VP-51 was released from the East Coast and should be at San Francisco in the next day or so for further tasking.

In the Philippines, CDR Musak's destroyers would attempt another attack at Vigan.

Task Force 407 was six days from Port Moresby. When they offload, they will make for Sydney, Australia for further orders.

Task Force 408 was only three days away from Pearl Harbor. The heavy cruiser USS Louisville with the two troop transports will be most welcome.

The British Liaison Officer reported that a strike force was being sent from Port Moresby to Madang to attack enemy shipping. That force will then fall back on Sydney to refuel and re-provision. Also, the light cruiser HMS Mauritius will sortie from Singapore to attack shipping at Kuching. The destroyers from Task Force 97 need time to repair wear and tear damage from all the high speed runs.

With the end of the report, ADM Nimitz told us he was taking a nap in his office and to wake him in case of major developments. We ate some food and went to work.

Submarine Operations

The first report from submarines arrived at roughly 1100 as an early lunch was being brought in. USS S-41 (LCDR Holley in command) had sighted and attacked a smaller Japanese freighter. They fired two torpedoes and hit with one, the ship was seen to have broken in half and sank quickly; the submarine was then attacked by enemy patrol aircraft with no damage. We will wait to see if corroborating information is available from intelligence. A few hours later they sighted another enemy freighter and attacked. They again fired two torpedoes hitting with one just aft of the beam on the starboard side. Again, enemy patrol planes attacked and forced them deep. The first activity was closer to Hengchun, while the second attack was closer to Laoag.

Later around noon, a report from the USS S-40 (LCDR Lucker) indicated that they had seen a lone freighter and attacked. They hit the ship with a single torpedo and broke contact due to enemy air activity. This was near Takao.

Both the USS Permit and USS Seawolf sent reports that they were attacked by enemy surface forces. USS Permit near Calayan and USS Seawolf near Batan Island. No damage was scored against either submarine.

Around 1400, USS S-37 reported attacking an enemy patrol boat near Hengchun, missing with the torpedoes and then having to escape from the ship they attacked. No casualties to either side.

Hawaii

There were no major events in the area today.

Broader Pacific Ocean

MAJ Deveraux had his Marines keep pressure on the Japanese forces. They managed to get a few Wildcat fighters off the ground to intercept other land based medium bombers. 40 Nell medium bombers came in from the south at noon to attack the base. They scored several hits and caused some casualties on the ground (22 wounded). The fighters managed to shoot down one bomber and damage two more.

Another wave came in at 1500 local time and consisted of 14 medium bombers. Again, a few fighters got in the air, shooting down one bomber. The fighters landed safely, though the Japanese were shooting at them with their rifles as they came in. But, for now, the Marines were hanging on.

Guam was hit by a mixed group of carrier aircraft. Val dive bombers and Kate torpedo bombers on level runs. The airfield was hit hard with some casualties, but all that could be gained was that the aircraft came in from the north. The carriers must be there as well. This is a hard piece of information.

Philippine Island Operations

CDR Musak and his destroyer squadron were very busy. They ran into three separate groups of enemy ships and attacked each on the way into the objective point and on the way out. The initial reports stated that he was concerned that the 4" guns didn't have a lot of stopping power so they would have to close with the enemy ships to make the guns more effective. Between all groups of ships, two enemy ships were sunk and a further 11 were damaged.

CDR Musak ordered the destroyers to within 2000 yards of the last group of ships; a troop transport was hit by all guns (including .50 caliber machine guns) and was one of the ships sunk. After four hours of combat, only one friendly ship was damaged; USS Pillsbury was hit by either a 4" or 5" enemy shell which exploded on the bulkhead in the engine room. There was a little flooding but the ship's captain (CDR Enderson) indicated that they could make 25 knots. The ship needs repairs and a dry dock. The force may be ordered to Soerabaja. It would be interesting to see what intelligence reports will come out of this battle. USS Pope was credited with sinking one of the enemy freighters.

Figure 12 - USS Pope (DD-225)

As the destroyers were pulling back in at sunrise, a mixed force of medium bombers, dive bombers and some fighters appeared over Manila to attack the airfield. At final count, 6 dive bombers and 4 fighters were shot down by friendly fighters. No friendly fighters were damaged. There was some damage to the runway, but for the most part, the 17th and 21st Pursuit Squadrons put up a very effective defense.

CHINESE THEATER

No further information was gained in this theater, combat was occurring in the same locations as yesterday.

BRITISH AND ALLIED OPERATIONS

Near Australia, Rabaul was hit with a total of 40 bombers over a 30 minute raid. They hit the port hard since there were no anti-aircraft defenses or fighters at the base. They came in low and slow at 5000' to make sure they hit the targets hard. The damage was beyond the capacity of the troops in place to repair.

Some of the ships fleeing from Hong Kong were massacred near Iba. A series of Betty bombers came in on torpedo runs. All three of the small cargo ships were sunk (SS Joan Moller, SS Halldor and SS Soochow). They were too far away to send flying boats to check for survivors.

Kuantan was hit hard by a large raid late morning. There were over 100 medium bombers with a mix of Betty and Sally bombers. The port was hit very hard and there was a large fire. The crews on the ground were going to have a very hard time trying to put out the fires and repair the damage. The port would not be useful for a very long time.

Alor Star was hit by two large raids in the morning. Each raid had roughly 25 medium bombers (ground forces said they were Sally types). The aircraft on the ground could not take off because the damage to runway was not fully fixed. The rest of the facilities were heavily damaged and the remaining aircraft on the ground were either destroyed or heavily damaged. This did little to help the Japanese ground assault however. The Indian troops managed to hold against an armored regiment that was attacking the base (not without casualties, the base commander reported that his troops suffered 140 wounded). 22 enemy tanks were disabled and 1 was completely destroyed.

Rangoon was hit at sunrise by a large force of bombers. Reports indicated that there were 30 medium bombers escorted by 45 fighters. The base was hit pretty hard, with the runway being heavily damaged and the supply dump taking a hit that set a large fire. No friendly fighters managed to get off the ground. It was reported that two of the enemy bombers were hit by anti-aircraft fire and were damaged. The base was taken by surprise by this raid because the bombs started falling literally as the sun came up.

To complete the bad news on Malaya, Victoria Point was attacked from out of the jungle by Japanese infantry. They swiftly overran the base and pushed the small scratch force of engineers and support troops north into the jungle. There were no reports of casualties or intentions of the commander. The radio station was offline and it was obvious that Japanese forces controlled the area.

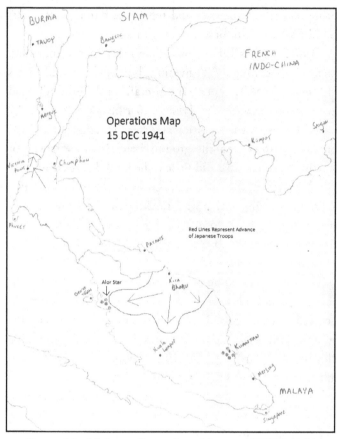

Figure 13 - Malayan Operations Map on 15 DEC 1941

INTELLIGENCE

LCDR Rochefort had little information today. His crew was having trouble decrypting most of the traffic. They were still understaffed. The only piece of information that was gained was that an Engineering regiment was heading towards Davao, or at least told to prepare to go to Davao. We gave him the information about the enemy carrier strikes at Guam. He took notes and thanked us for the data.

We also let him know about the action at Vigan and from the submarine attacks during the day. He now had some information to bring back to his crews to start looking at focused decrypts.

THEORIES AND INTENTIONS

Another day of combat. Between the submarines and CDR Musak's destroyers, we hurt the enemy. Since the start of hostilities, our forces have confirmed sinking 7 enemy freighters. The British have destroyed 2 enemy freighters and 2 destroyer transports. All told, 34000 tons of enemy shipping has been destroyed.

I'm sure that ADM Nimitz will ask for a rollup of destroyed shipping vs. what we have lost. We should begin to round up the data.

LATE DAY REPORTS

There were no reports about the Japanese carriers. It is possible that they were near Pagan Island. If it is the *Kido Butai*, then they have bypassed Wake Island. This may allow Task Force Roger the needed 36 hours to pound the enemy at Wake Island and allow the resupply submarines to bring needed food and ammunition (probably 80 tons of supplies at best, but it will feed them for quite a while until a full relief force can be sent).

There seemed to be a lack of information. We weren't sure if it was a problem with the radio section or if there was simply not much new information.

There was also a report that showed a force of 6 ships heading towards Tarakan on Borneo on the Celebes Sea side. There aren't any forces available to attack them if there is an invasion.

We were all tired. I had some chicken (or a chicken like substance), took a shower and went directly to sleep.

DECEMBER 16, 1941   DAY 10 OF THE WAR

<u>MORNING BRIEF</u>

After a light breakfast I went straight to the headquarters building. ADM Nimitz seemed better rested but still a bit tired. The Operations Officer began his morning report.

Early this morning the submarine USS Tambor arrived at Pearl Harbor and began a quick maintenance cycle before being readied to patrol somewhere in the Pacific.

The cargo ship USS Alchiba was now unloading supplies at Johnston Island under the watchful eye of the escorting destroyers. It should take a few days to completely unload the ship; the pier equipment was sparse and most of the supplies have to be unloaded by hand.

Task Force 408 (USS Louisville with a couple of empty troop transports) is now only one day out from Pearl Harbor.

The merchant freighter SS Florence D. left port this morning with some destroyers to bring supplies to Palmyra. They are Task Force 303.

Task Force 89, the converted liners carrying the 8th Marine Regiment left San Francisco last night. They are running at 19 knots in order to make it difficult for enemy submarines to attack them. It is risky without escorts, but they should be relatively safe.

In the Philippines, reports came in about enemy troops being seen at Lingayen on the west side of Luzon. Friendly forces there amount to about 6000 troops. They were expecting an attack.

Task Force 88 under CDR Musak will head to Soerabaja to repair and resupply on torpedoes. CDR Musak reported that he will take his ships by Legaspi to try to hit enemy ships before leaving the area. It is unlikely that they will return to the Philippines.

Three gunboats under the command of LT Jordan are leaving Subic Bay to try to attack enemy shipping near Vigan.

The British Liaison Officer reported that enemy troops at Alor Star were likely to push friendly troops out. This was not good news, but also not unexpected.

Task Force 97 (CDR Swinley) would spend a couple of days in Singapore repairing damage to the destroyers. They would be ready to sortie if absolutely necessary. The large number of quick run ins to attack shipping at Kuching caused a lot of wear and tear to the ships. None of the damage was major, but still needed to be repaired in order to maximize ship efficiency.

The light cruiser HMS Mauritius should reach Kuching sometime in the next 24 hours. Force Alpha sent from Soerabaja was notified of this and they were to quickly coordinate their strikes. CAPT Newman (in command of the force) acknowledged the message.

There were no new developments near Java.

The Australians sent the freighter SS Steel Worker loaded with food and medical supplies to Pago Pago. The ship should take at least a week to get to Pago Pago; she left Sydney late last night.

The Australians also reported that their cruiser force had been sent back to Port Moresby because of the threat of air attack. It remains to be seen what ships will be in that area in the next few days. The Operations Officer thought it was prudent but unsubstantiated.

Also, Task Force 407 was roughly four days from reaching Port Moresby with troops and supplies.

With that, the briefing ended and we started what was one of the busiest days since the war began.

Operation Buck

Task Force Rogers is under radio silence unless a major event occurs. No radio information was received today. They should be on course and on time to arrive at Wake Island.

Submarine Operations

USS S-37 found an enemy small cargo ship and fired two torpedoes at it for no hits. Enemy aircraft were in the area so the submarine had to remain submerged and could not catch up to the ship for another attack. Later that afternoon, she came across a larger enemy ship and attacked on the surface. The report indicated that the enemy ship was hit by at least eight 4" gun shells and a torpedo (the enemy ship was reported as "on fire and heavily damaged"). The submarine was also hit by some enemy fire (probably a smaller deck gun and machine guns). The submarine will leave the area and head for Soerabaja to repair. No word on friendly casualties on the submarine. Just a little too aggressive by that skipper.

Near Cam Ranh Bay, USS Seal spotted a convoy and was positioning to attack when she was sighted by an enemy escort. She dove deep to avoid attacks and broke away.

Roughly 50 nautical miles to the west, USS S-39 sighted a small enemy cargo ship and fired two torpedoes. One torpedo hit the enemy ship and according to the radio report "the ship blew apart". Intel information will be sought out about this report to confirm the kill.

HAWAII

There were no confirmed enemy submarine sightings and other than cargo forces unloading at Lihue and Johnston Island, there are no major events to report here today.

BROADER PACIFIC OCEAN

There was a Japanese raid on Wake Island that hit just as the sun was rising. The fighters on the ground had no warning and the runway was hit in a couple of places. MAJ Deveraux kept pressure on the enemy troops left on the island (for some reason, the Japanese ships left; not sure if they're waiting on more ships to come in or if the troops were simply left there). In any case, the Marines were still fighting and hanging on. However, they were running short on supplies. No mention was made to them about Operation Buck.

Guam was hit by carrier aircraft in two separate raids. The Ops Boss thought that it meant that the Japanese carriers were somewhere near Saipan. That puts them at just a two day steaming time from Wake Island if that's the case. Regardless, there was some damage to facilities at Guam with a few casualties on the ground.

PHILIPPINE ISLAND OPERATIONS

The Japanese were very busy in the Philippines. The ground battles had died down a bit as the weather was not very cooperative in northern Luzon. In the air, however, there was a lot of action.

The day started with a naval strike against a couple more of the small freighters that had escaped Hong Kong. The freighters SS Yat Shing and SS Chengtu reported that they were under air attack and then went off the air. It is surmised that both ships were sunk by torpedo bombers.

CDR Musak's destroyers came under air attack near the island of Busuanga. The enemy aircraft came near Clark Field on the way down Luzon and were intercepted. The fighters gave chase. They were dealing with enemy escort fighters almost the entire time. Luckily, no hits were scored on the destroyers, but 5 friendly fighters were lost and there was only one confirmed damaged enemy bomber.

Around the same time, another strike hit Clark Field. Friendly fighters got into the air in time. The strike was 20 medium bombers (Lily types) escorted by 10 Zero fighters. A wild furball of air combat broke out. When the raid was done, one Zero and four Lilys were shot down. Friendly forces lost four fighters (2 P-40 and 2 P-35 types).

Late in the afternoon, another strike was seen heading in the area of Bataan. A small force (3 Nell bombers escorted by 6 Zero fighters). A mixed bag from the fighter squadrons put up 12 fighters to intercept them. The bombers were going for the minesweepers still working in the straights. One Zero and one Nell were shot down for no losses to the friendly fighters. Of note, 1st LT Brownewell (1LT) of the Army Air Corps 17th Pursuit Squadron achieved ace status during that fight with his 5th confirmed kill. The minesweepers suffered no damage.

CHINESE THEATER

There were a couple of real reports today from China. One was a confirmed report that Chinese ground forces had suffered a defeat at Kweiteh. Chinese infantry forces were pushed out of the area by the Japanese 36th Division.

The other is that Chinese forces successfully defended against a Japanese attack near Loyang. They pushed back the enemy assault with heavy losses.

KUCHING, BORNEO

This particular location deserves its own section for today. A lot had happened at this location. We found out late in the day that it was agreed upon that the British light cruiser HMS Mauritius would head in, break up the formation of enemy ships and get out. This would be easier due to the fog situation in that particular area and allow the US Force (Force Alpha) to attack enemy shipping with concentrated fire.

HMS Mauritius dutifully went in alone and attacked enemy shipping. At roughly 2200 local time, she made the run in. First thing she came across was a large freighter escorted by a single small escort. Her 6" guns made short work of the escort and then the enemy cargo ship was hit again and again by all the batteries of the ship. In the report, the crew counted at least 36 hits on the enemy freighter which sank in the presence of the bridge crew.

This must have caused panic because ships came running out helter skelter. At 0100 local, almost 30 freighters of all sizes went running. HMS Mauritius engaged a couple of enemy freighters and began moving out of the area to make sure that she would not accidentally be mistaken as an enemy ship by US Forces. Two enemy ships were reported as being hit, one of them being "severely damaged". At this point, HMS Mauritius broke out to the northwest to allow US Forces to come in.

Figure 14 - HMS Mauritius (C80)

According to the plan, US Forces would head in at the 50 nautical mile mark beginning at 0230. HMS Mauritius was well out of the area by the time Force Alpha began the run in. At 0315, the first ships encountered were a single freighter escorted by a small ship at the edge of a rain squall. Some lightning in the background had given them away to the lookouts. CAPT Newman ordered the ships in at a moderate pace and withheld fire until only 2000 yards away from their targets. USS John D. Edwards (a destroyer) fired a full tight spread of 3 torpedoes at the freighter; 60 seconds later, USS Marblehead (light cruiser and flagship of the force) fired at the escort with her 6" guns. The freighter was hit by all 3 of the torpedoes and simply came apart; she sank in less than 2 minutes. The escort blew up when hit by a 6" shell; the escort must have been small or an ammunition magazine was hit. Either way, these two ships were the first kills of the night for the US Force.

Figure 15 - USS Marblehead (CL-12)

Fog had reduced visibility to around 5000 yards; CAPT Newman had the destroyers come to within 4000 yards of his ship at the center to maximize searching capability. For the next two hours, the force was slowly making way into the area where the enemy freighters should be. By 0530, it was beginning to get light, so CAPT Newman ordered a general retirement.

When the force turned around to break out of the area, sunlight was making it very dangerous for the force if enemy aircraft were sent to the area. The fog was lifting and the force was working up speed to get out of the area. Around 0700 local a lookout noticed smoke on the horizon. CAPT Newman made the decision to head in that general area to check it out. They ran into a gaggle of 30 freighters re-assembling. He ordered an attack.

They were initially spotted at 20000 yards… he did not allow any friendly ships to open fire until at a range of 5000 yards. For the next two hours, a shooting gallery of torpedoes, main guns, machine guns and cannons rocked the area. At one point, two of the freighters collided trying to break from the area and scatter. Friendly ships also took some damage.

The destroyer USS Barker was hit by a large shell on her aft main 4" gun turret from a deck gun from one of the freighters. The turret is out of action and will need to be repaired when the force gets back to Soerabaja; 7 sailors were injured on the destroyer. The destroyers USS Alden and USS John D. Edwards also took some light fire from the enemy ships. When it was all over, 6 enemy freighters were confirmed sunk and 8 others damaged to some extent (3 severely damaged and burning brightly). CAPT Newman then ordered a high speed exit from the area to minimize the possibility of enemy air attack, put the ships back in formation and began the transit back to Soerabaja to repair and re-supply.

Thus, the operation netted two small escort ships, 8 freighters sunk and at least 8 others damaged. That is how a well-executed operation is defined. The reports were sent over to LCDR Rochefort to see if any signals information could be gained concerning the ships damaged and sunk.

BRITISH AND ALLIED OPERATIONS

First reports from Singapore indicated that a strike of 10 Blenheim bombers headed to Kuching to try to hit more ships. They arrived unscathed but failed to hit any of the ships.

Kuantan was hit again, but by a much smaller force (only 13 bombers in total). Luckily, there was little on the ground for the bombers to hit, so casualties were at a minimum.

Rangoon was hit around noon time local with a large raid. Roughly 30 medium bombers escorted by almost 30 fighters. The airbase was damaged and the fighters would not come down to strafe ground targets (machine guns were apparently noted on the ground and avoided).

At about the same time, a sustained attack began at Alor Star; tanks with some supporting infantry but no heavy artillery. By sunset, troops from the 6th and 15th Indian Brigades had stopped the assault cold. Some enemy tanks were destroyed as well as some confirmed ground kills. Friendly forces suffered 11 dead and around 80 wounded.

There was a single large enemy air raid at Rabaul. A total of 40 medium bombers came in and bombed the port. The remaining equipment there was more or less destroyed. Local forces are going to be hard pressed to defend against an amphibious assault. The British Liaison thinks that Rabaul will be a major target for the Japanese. Sadly, there are no forces that could be delivered to the location prior to an enemy assault.

INTELLIGENCE

When LCDR Rochefort came in, he was smiling. He said he had a lot of information that had been decoded. First, he noted that his team broke the call sign for the Japanese fleet oiler Toei Maru. They would now be able to follow the ship around whenever it made a call.

He confirmed that call signs from the carrier Zuikaku were noted in the area of Saipan. This confirmed earlier reports from the strike force that hit Guam. He also reported that his team broke messages that showed the 77th Infantry Regiment loaded on ships heading towards Kota Bharu; more than likely a reinforcement unit for pushing down the Malayan Peninsula.

Next he got to the shipping issues. First was a report on the freighter Kumakawa Maru. This ship was confirmed to be sunk near Hengchun by a submarine. This corroborates the radio report from USS S-41 yesterday. Also, the freighter Kosei

Maru and liner Naminoue Maru were confirmed to be sunk via radio message at Vigan. This corroborates the report from CDR Musak's force when they had attacked there yesterday.

With regards to Kuching, he stated that heavy radio transmissions started at about the time indicated by the attack messages from Force Alpha and HMS Mauritius. Apparently the HMS Mauritius had really taken them by surprise, because a message in the clear was intercepted from the submarine chaser Ch-19 (438 tons) which was attacked. That ship was escorting a large freighter, the Kogyo Maru (6400 tons). When they were sinking they sent out distress calls. As it turns out, the Kogyo Maru was carrying quite a few troops and a lot of equipment.

When this was going on, Japanese headquarters ordered all the freighters to scatter and get out of the area. When Force Alpha arrived, they found another submarine chaser, Cha-2 and the freighter Ada Maru. Both were confirmed as destroyed.

As the information coming in was being decoded and the situation developed, it turned out the Force Alpha was lucky. When no contact was seen over the next three hours, headquarters ordered the freighters to meet at the location where they were spotted by Force Alpha on the egress. The confirmed ships destroyed by Force Alpha are as follows:

-   Submarine chaser Cha-2 (100 tons)
-   Freighter Ada Maru (4875 tons)
-   Freighter Argun Maru (4875 tons)
-   Freighter Ryuun Maru (4875 tons)
-   Freighter Sugiyama Maru (4875 tons)
-   Freighter Chojun Maru (2375 tons)
-   Freighter Yamura Maru (2375 tons)
-   Freighter Yamakuni Maru (2375 tons)

Reports from the commander of the Japanese force indicated that from the troops that were onboard along with the equipment, a total of roughly 1150 troops were unaccounted for and a little over 700 troops had been rescued from the water. This amounts to almost two battalions of infantry that could have been destroyed while still on their transports.

This well planned attack had destroyed a combined total of 33500 tons of enemy shipping. It was a piece of good news during a dark period.

He had no information from his team about the attack by USS S-37 or by USS S-39 with confirmed kills as of yet but would keep his team working on it.

ADM Nimitz had a smile on his face after hearing this report.

THEORIES AND INTENTIONS

Nothing like this so early in the war historically. We know that the Japanese have vulnerable points that can be exploited. I guess we will see what happens next with Operation Buck.

It seems evident that Rabaul is definitely a target for the Japanese. There's simply nothing we can do about it.

LATE DAY REPORTS

By the end of the day, Task Force 408 had arrived at Pearl Harbor. The ships were refueling and performing maintenance and should be ready to accept orders in the next 24 hours.

If my calculations are correct, Task Force Rogers should be somewhere between French Frigate Shoal and Laysan Island. They should be about 3 days from Wake Island.

Patrol aircraft noted that there were "a lot" of enemy ships trying to unload at Kuching. Best estimates put it at 40 to 50 ships. CAPT Rooks in Java sent a message that he was readying more US Forces to attack. He put together his own ship the heavy cruiser USS Houston, the light cruiser USS Boise and four destroyers to make a run in to Kuching to attack shipping. He acknowledged that there were enemy surface forces at Miri (what looked like a light cruiser and a few destroyers). Force Alpha should be back at Soerabaja sometime in the next 24 hours.

One more late day report showed a "few" enemy ships, probably cruisers at the entrance to Davao on Mindanao.

With that, the night shift was coming in. ADM Nimitz left about an hour ago. I really needed a beer.

DECEMBER 17, 1941   DAY 11 OF THE WAR

I was told this morning that there were still going to be a few debriefs for me as to how I arrived. As it turns out, the FBI sent people to my home town to check on my grandparents. They were told nothing about me, but I had given them the names of my mother and my uncle who are children back in Adams, MA. My father's family is still in Spartanburg, SC.

The Operations Officer began the morning brief. Task Force 303 that consists of the freighter SS Florence D. escorted by four destroyers were proceeding to Palmyra Island at 12 knots.

We were to expect reports from CDR Musak and his destroyers (Task Force 88) as they approach Legaspi prior to heading to Soerabaja. It is unknown whether or not they will find enemy ships or if the force will be too large to attack. Time will tell.

The trio of gunboats from Subic Bay should reach the enemy forces at Vigan and we were to expect some type of report. That looked more like a suicide mission to me.

Near Australia, a heavy cruiser (HMAS Australia) escorted by three light cruisers left Port Moresby to attack enemy shipping at Madang. It should take them two or three days to get there. They are Task Force 170.

Task Force 407 is now three days from Port Moresby and should begin offloading the troops as soon as they arrive.

In Sydney, the 1st Australian Division fell under the command of MG Cyril Cloves. He was readying the division for transport to Port Moresby. It will take them a few more days to pack up all of their equipment.

At Java, CAPT Rooks put to sea to head to Kuching to attack enemy shipping. They are known as Force Gable.

In Rangoon, the All-Volunteer Air Group sent their 1st Squadron of fighters to Rangoon to assist the British forces there. They should be able to fly sorties immediately.

Closer to home, the fires on the USS Arizona were finally out. The Harbor Master reported that the ship will take a *minimum* of 18 months to repair. The ship was towed to docks to begin repairs. It may be prudent to take the ship back to the west coast when the ship has enough power and stability to make the trip.

Johnston Island and Lihue were still having the supplies offloaded and this should take a few more days for the task to be completed.

With that, the report ended and we were dismissed to our tasks for the day.

OPERATION BUCK

Just like yesterday, no reports came from Force Rogers. This is to be expected. The operational plan will continue to be followed unless something happens that will cause the force to break radio silence.

SUBMARINE OPERATIONS

A report came in from USS Salmon that they had found and attacked an enemy ship escorted by a single patrol boat near Balabac. The freighter was hit by at least one torpedo and was heavily damaged. The submarine then had to dive to avoid the patrol boat and break contact from the area.

USS Seal attacked an enemy freighter near Saigon, firing torpedoes at a single freighter. No hits were recorded and the submarine needed to dive to get away from enemy air assets.

HAWAII

There were no major incidents and all cargo ships and escorts were proceeding according to plans.

BROADER PACIFIC OCEAN

There were a couple of air raids at Guam. One that came in just prior to sunrise that struck the runway. The number of bombers was not immediately known. They were probably medium bombers. Then as the crews were working another strike came in that was made up of carrier based aircraft. They did a lot of damage to the barracks and the supply dump. There were no losses to the enemy.

PHILIPPINE ISLAND OPERATIONS

Sad news: The gunboats sent to Vigan were intercepted by an enemy cruiser force. All of the gunboats were sunk. Survivors were not thought to be likely after the engagement. The gunboats USS Isabel, USS Asheville and USS Tulsa were written off of the Vessel Register.

Figure 16 - Gunboat USS Tulsa (PG-22)

On the ground at Lingayen, the 11th Philippine Army Division used their artillery and smaller direct fire guns to lay an ambush against a probing attack by the Japanese 7th Tank Regiment. One enemy tank was destroyed and a further five were disabled and abandoned by their crews.

More bad news came in later in the morning. More of the freighters that had escaped Hong Kong were attacked by enemy aircraft just off the coast of Luzon near Batangas. In all, six freighters were in the force and sunk;

- SS Hanyang
- SS Bennevis
- SS Munlock
- SS Fatshan
- SS Hai Lee
- SS Haraldsvang

Flying boats were sent out (PBY Catalinas from Manila) and managed to pick up a few survivors, but the freighters were all sunk with a heavy loss of life. Additionally, one of the minesweepers in the straights near Bataan was sunk by an enemy bomber; USS Finch was sunk with only two survivors plucked from the water. No friendly fighters were available because they were fully defensive over Manila and Clark Field. During several hours of sorties, bombing raids and casualties, friendly fighters managed to shoot down two enemy fighters and two enemy bombers for the loss of five fighters. Not very good, but they were outnumbered the entire day.

To round out all the bad news, a couple of freighters were ambushed by an enemy force near Manado. The freighters SS Governor Wright and SS Ravnas were sunk by a force that was reported in the clear as being a couple of battleships with escorts. Not sure if more information could corroborate the report.

Task Force 88 under CDR Musak reported that there were too many enemy escort ships going into Legaspi and he declined to attack. He was now taking his force to Soerabaja for re-supply and repair.

CHINESE THEATER

A single report from China indicated that the 89th Corps had been defeated by Japanese units near Hwainan and was forced to retreat.

BRITISH AND ALLIED OPERATIONS

The day started off rough for friendly troops at Kuantan. A total of three separate air raids took place in a 7 hour period. In total, almost 150 medium bombers attacked during the morning. The port suffered more damage and there were almost 90 wounded on the ground there. Makes one think that the Japanese are using this location as a "live fire" training exercise for their bomber crews.

Alor Star was hit by two fairly large raids, each containing roughly 24 bombers and a few fighter escorts. The airbase was hit pretty hard and there were a few casualties on the ground. There was no assault by enemy troops; they are regrouping for a major attack.

In the Bismarck Islands, Kavieng was attacked by a small force of carrier aircraft. There was little damage on the ground and since there were no real forces at the base (except for some observers and a radio operator), there was no damage to the enemy.

Rabaul was hit by a mixed force of carrier aircraft and medium bombers. There was scratch damage to the facilities on the ground and no damage was scored against the enemy.

INTELLIGENCE

LCDR Rochefort didn't have much information today. He confirmed that the freighter Hakka Maru was indeed confirmed as sunk by Japanese intercepts. This corroborates the report from USS S-39 yesterday. It was a small freighter, only 830 tons, but it is a confirmed kill. The rest of the report was concerning breaking the codes and trying to figure out where enemy shipping was located. He looked very very tired.

THEORIES AND INTENTIONS

It seems that the enemy still has their sights on all mentioned targets, Malayan Peninsula, Wake Island, Borneo and Papua New Guinea. I am fairly confident that the Japanese will try to reinforce the troops they've already landed at Wake. If we catch the force, it could be a great victory. Prudence and caution must be taken as well, it seems the *Kido Butai* is in the area of Saipan; only two days away.

LATE DAY REPORTS

The Harbor Master reported at 1700 that repairs to the destroyer USS McCall have been completed and the ship and crew are ready for orders.

A report also came in from CDR Easton, the commanding officer of the submarine USS S-37. The damage to his submarine was slight, but it was still prudent, due to light hull damage, to move the submarine to Soerabaja for repairs and further patrols.

Force Alpha arrived at Soerabaja. Material conditions of the ships were fairly good, but the destroyers USS Barker and USS John D Edwards need to go pier side for repairs. USS Barker took the hit to her aft 4" gun turret, it will take two days to completely fix, and USS John D Edwards took machine gun and light cannon fire. She should take two days as well. The other ships have wear and tear repairs to make. USS Marblehead will need a full week to repair everything, but CAPT Newman's report stated that these were not mission critical and the ship could sail as is.

The British Liaison reported that HMS Mauritius arrived safely at Singapore and would be ready to sail after re-fueling and taking on more ammunition.

He also reported that Task Force 420 arrived at Batavia with the 44th and 45th Indian Infantry Brigades. They immediately began offloading. Task Force 428 is a couple of days behind with the 48th Gurkha Brigade onboard. More troop forces are following. British High Command will send a briefing to inform us where the reinforcements are going to dig in and await Japanese assaults.

With that, I left for the night. They served fish at the Officer's Club. I had a sandwich instead, went to my bungalow and went to sleep. I was really thinking that I wanted to read a book. Have to pick one up tomorrow.

MORNING BRIEF

ADM Nimitz was not there for the morning brief. We were told that he was conferring with the Harbor Master. We were now eating breakfast during the report; everyone was just too busy.

The Operations Officer began the briefing. First was Force Gable under CAPT Rooks near Java. They were expected to make contact with the enemy at any time during the next 24 hours. We were to stay alert to get the information up the chain of command. Force Alpha was now safe in Soerabaja and performing repairs to the ships (late report from yesterday).

Force Rogers was now two days from the strike location. No radio messages were received by the force indicating that they have not been spotted as of the time of the Operations Report.

Task Force 303 was now about three days from Palmyra. There are no confirmed reports of enemy ships in the Hawaii Operating Area. Lihue and Johnston Islands are still offloading the cargo ships under the eye of the destroyers escorting them. No additional information was available.

Task Force 407 was 36 hours from Port Moresby. The troops and supplies are badly needed. Enemy carriers are north of Rabaul which makes the unloading a priority.

The British Liaison Officer reported that Task Force 170 (Australian cruisers) should reach Madang in the next 24 hours or so… they will beat a quick retreat after attacking enemy shipping to ensure that they are not caught by the enemy carriers.

On the West Coast, six tankers and ten civilian freighters will be moving from Los Angeles to San Francisco. Additionally, two fleet oilers will depart Los Angeles to head to Pearl Harbor. Four additional smaller Coast Guard Cutters were taken into US Navy service at San Francisco and will be available to escort shipping on the West Coast.

OPERATION BUCK

Again, like yesterday, no reports came from Force Rogers. This is to be expected. The operational plan will continue to be followed unless something happens that will cause the force to break radio silence. They should reach their objective in roughly 24 hours. They will then commence strikes. It should be a surprise to the Japanese.

SUBMARINE OPERATIONS

USS Porpoise (CDR Brewster) attacked an enemy freighter on the surface in a rain squall near Takao. The enemy ship was hit by a torpedo and by at least 10 rounds from the submarine's 4" gun. Enemy aircraft came in against the submarine and she was forced to do a crash dive. It is unknown if the enemy freighter was sunk.

USS S-36 (LCDR McKnight) was sighted by an enemy destroyer and attacked about 30 nautical miles west of where USS Porpoise was. USS S-36 managed to get away without damage.

HAWAII

There were a few interesting developments in the Hawaii Area. First, a confirmed sighting of a Japanese submarine was reported roughly 120 nautical miles south-southeast of Pearl Harbor. The submarine was attacked by the PBY Catalina with no results.

At 1300 local, a report came in that showed a few "large tanker type" ships spotted almost 200 nautical miles north of French Frigate Shoals. This could indicate a refuel spot for Japanese submarines heading to the West Coast. The carriers are taking part in Operation Buck and were not to be taken off that mission. It is probable that further reports of this force may cause ADM Nimitz to send a surface force to attempt to intercept them. In any case, a few B-17 bombers took off and managed to find the ships at 1700 local, they initiated an attack from 6000' but scored no hits against the enemy force.

BROADER PACIFIC OCEAN

A report came in from the West Coast Command. The destroyer USS Sands was attacked by an enemy submarine while on patrol roughly 75 nautical miles south-southwest of Eureka, California. The enemy torpedoes missed and USS Sands was supported by the destroyer USS King to commence the sub hunt. It is unknown whether or not the enemy submarine was damaged.

Guam was hit by a smaller strike force of Japanese carrier based bombers at 0930 local. They caused 14 casualties (2 dead, 12 wounded) on the ground and suffered no losses themselves. Another strike group of dive bombers came in at 1100 escorted by some fighters. They bombed defensive positions near the naval base (probably to try to soften them up prior to an amphibious assault).

Wake Island was hit by two closely separated air raids. VMF-211 managed to get the three remaining Wildcat fighters in the air. They shot down two Nell medium bombers, damaged a few others with no losses suffered. The runways were hit hard (it was later estimated that 50 medium bombers attacked, mostly Nells, unescorted by Japanese fighters). Reports indicated that the Japanese hold all of Wilkes Island and the very western end of Peale Island near the reefs. It is difficult for the remaining fighters to take off because of the winds; this brings them directly over the Japanese held portion. It is to be assumed that friendly aircraft from Force Rogers will be attacking Wilkes Island.

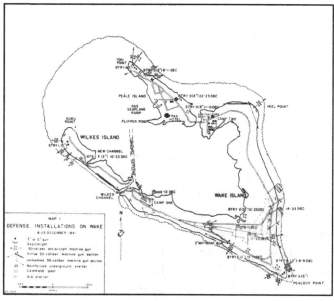

Figure 17 - Wake Island Atoll

Philippine Island Operations

There were two major air raids on Luzon. First was at 1000 local when a force of Betty medium bombers attacked the city of Manila. 11 Warhawk fighters rose to intercept them. Over the next 40 minutes, a fur ball of twisting aircraft machine gun fire was over the city. When it was all over, two Warhawks were lost and two Zero fighters were confirmed shot down. None of the bombers suffered any damage.

At 1130 local, Clark Field was under attack from 25 Sally medium bombers that for some reason were unescorted. Warhawks from the 20th Pursuit Squadron rose to attack them. A total of 7 Sally bombers were confirmed shot down and a further 6 were damaged. There were no losses to friendly fighters. This was a huge success.

There was some low level fighting at Lingayen, but no major assault took place on either side.

Chinese Theater

Sketchy reports had come in from China. What was confirmed was that the Chinese Forces had been pushed out of Chengting and Chuhsien. Casualties were unknown at this time. However, reports indicated that they were holding at Lang Son, Kweisui, Kaifeng and Canton against repeated Japanese assaults.

British and Allied Operations

CAPT Rooks was notified that there existed a high probability that the ships at Kuching had been reinforced with escorting destroyers and cruisers. The message to him also stated that it was his call whether or not to make the run in to engage the force. Force Gable hadn't reached Kuching yet; he will tomorrow if he does not turn around.

Ternate came under enemy amphibious assault at first light. Ternate is a small island off the larger island of Moluccas. The islands are owned by the Dutch and they have few forces available to hit the enemy. The commander at Soerabaja was notified of the assault and he consulted his higher command for instructions. It is possible that we will be asked to help break up the invasion. A battleship was seen with the invasion force.

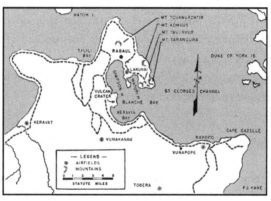

Figure 18 - Rabaul

Rabaul was also invaded at first light. A force of ships began unloading troops and some destroyers were providing shore fire support (reports indicate that they came ashore at Talili Bay). The total number of enemy ships and enemy troops are currently unknown. There were several air strikes to support the invasion forces. Carrier based aircraft and medium bombers all took part in the strikes. The port area seemed to take the biggest beating, in the vicinity of Lakunai since the troops were likely to get there after cutting off the peninsula.

There is only a scratch force of friendly troops there and it is unlikely that they will be able to hold the area. Rabaul has an excellent harbor area for a large anchorage. The commander of the Lark Battalion indicated he was moving his troops to prevent the Japanese from cutting off Rabaul from the rest of the island near Talili Bay. He also reported that it looked like the enemy had landed about 1200 troops so far.

On the Malayan Peninsula, Alor Star was hit by a sizeable attack force of enemy bombers escorted by some fighters. They hit the airbase hard and kept pressure on friendly forces trying to defend against a determined assault. This assault was continued in earnest at 0800 local after some probing attacks during the night. An artillery bombardment began that lasted almost an hour, followed by a coordinated attack by infantry supported by some light tanks. After fighting for nearly 7 hours, the Japanese had broken the lines and entered the airfield. The 6th and 15th Indian Brigades fell back with heavy losses (the 155th Field Regiment was also badly damaged). All told, friendly forces suffered nearly 2000 killed and missing, along with 350 walking wounded that managed to fall back with the combat forces able to do so. It should take the Japanese a good amount of time before they will be able to use the airfield, but the base no longer belongs to British Forces. Not a good sign.

At Kuantan, more large raids hit the port. There were three separate raids, the largest being the first, by almost 100 medium bombers coming in low, followed by a raid of 30 medium bombers and another raid of 30 medium bombers two hours later. Friendly forces have completely pulled out of the port area and are setting up defenses in other areas of Kuantan.

INTELLIGENCE

LCDR Rochefort reported that decrypts indicated that the 28th Engineering Regiment was bound for Kota Bharu. There was also a large amount of traffic from Samah.

He had no information regarding the tanker force north of French Frigate Shoals. They were either in complete radio silence or they simply had not received or decoded any information about them.

He also had no information about the freighter that USS Porpoise had attacked earlier today.

THEORIES AND INTENTIONS

Now that the Japanese have indeed invaded Rabaul, it is clear that they will follow (at least in that area) what they did historically. What is unknown is how unfolding operations will affect the timeline. Historically, the mission that Operation Buck is trying to pull off did happen; only that the carriers were pulled back before reaching Wake. It does not appear that ADM Nimitz will pull back. He really wants to strike back.

The invasion at Ternate is also somewhat disconcerting. They seem to be ahead of their timeline in this area; I sincerely hope that diverting reinforcements to Java will prevent the island from falling altogether.

We did find logistical elements in the North Pacific. Question is: Do we have enough forces to do anything about it? The only force that is large enough for sure would be the carriers. It is possible that a cruiser force could be sent (they carry floatplanes that would be able to recon the area and look for the enemy ships). They would also be fast enough to run down the tankers if they tried to run away. This should be an interesting topic at tomorrow's briefing.

LATE DAY REPORTS

The Harbor Master's Report indicated that enough space had opened up for the minelayer USS Oglala to move in to be repaired. This should take roughly a week to complete.

Also at Pearl Harbor, a force of six fleet troop transports arrived (full fleet AP type ships). They were refueling and re-provisioning.

Task Force 407 arrived at Port Moresby a little earlier than usual; the reports of enemy carrier aircraft at Rabaul caused the force commander to order a higher speed to get the troops and supplies offloaded as quickly as possible. They began unloading at sunset, local time.

At Soerabaja, the submarines USS Sculpin, USS Sailfish, USS Sealion and USS Searaven arrived to take on supplies (mostly food and engineering supplies like barbed wire and the like) for delivery to Bataan.

The British Liaison Officer reported that the battleship HMS Prince of Wales arrived today at Columbo and was immediately brought to the dry dock. Preliminary reports indicate a period of 10 weeks to fully repair the ship. Work began immediately.

He also reported that the 19th Indian Infantry Division arrived at Chittagong and were to immediately begin fortifying the area and using their engineers to build up the airfield. It seems that this area is to be a lynchpin to their defense of India.

In Australia, the 7th Australian Infantry Brigade arrived at Normanton on the north coast to provide local defense in case of a Japanese incursion. He indicated that he would have a report on the 1ˢᵗ Australian Infantry Division tomorrow.

I then left for the day. The FBI agents asked to have dinner with me. I of course obliged. They asked me about other family members and how this sort of thing could have happened. As for the science of time travel I told them they should talk to Albert Einstein; I was a computer scientist, not a theoretical physicist. They asked what a computer was… I told them it would take a while to explain. We talked for about an hour and they told me that they would probably have more questions for me in the near future. I told them that I'm still asking a lot of questions myself.

DECEMBER 19, 1941   DAY 13 OF THE WAR

<u>MORNING BRIEF</u>

First thing, as breakfast was being served, something happened that I remember from Nimitz's biography. He told us that he was going to the shooting range for a little while this morning to fire his practice pistol. This means that he is very stressed out and worried about an operation. I'd place money it's about the carriers. (If he were less worried, he'd be practicing putting in his office)

The Operations Officer began the morning report. First, Task Force 407 was unloading US Troops and supplies at Port Moresby. Additionally, it was reported that the 1st Australian Infantry Division was now loading onto troop transports for the transit to Port Moresby.

Next on the agenda was what to do about the enemy logistical elements north of French Frigate Shoals. During the night, orders were given to the light cruisers USS St. Louis and USS Helena along with six destroyers to head out to sea, head north and work with patrol assets to try to intercept the tankers. It was risky (from the standpoint of finding a small force 300 miles out to sea) but would be worth it if it could disrupt enemy submarine operations on the West Coast. They were to be Task Force Tambourine (CAPT Hoover in command). I wondered idly who thinks up these force names. In any case, they put to sea at 2200 last night and were moving at 25 knots. They were in radio communication with Pacific Fleet HQ waiting on reports from patrol planes.

Task Force 303 was a day out from Palmyra Island. They have encountered no issues.

Task Force Gable under CAPT Rooks should hit Kuching sometime today/tonight. We were to stand by for any reports. Additionally, the submarine tenders USS Holland and USS Otus arrived at Soerabaja from the Philippines and were to assist with friendly submarines that will eventually be headed there. The four friendly submarines that arrived there last night will be loading up on supplies to bring them to Bataan. It is thought that at least 175 tons might be brought in. It's dangerous but necessary work.

The Australian cruiser force should be in line to hit Madang today. We were ordered to stand by to act on those reports as well.

Task Force Rogers under Operation Buck should be making reports based on strikes. They should be hitting Japanese troops at Wake today (long range strikes). They were still at least a day from reaching their patrol point for 36 hours of operations.

It should be a busy day and we were told to be ready for it. With that we were dismissed for the day's work.

OPERATION BUCK

Operation Buck and operations at Wake Island are now combined. As such, all action at Wake will be reported here until Force Rogers leaves the area to head back to Pearl Harbor.

MAJ Devereaux reported that his lookouts had seen "many more" enemy ships on the horizon. They began to bombard the island and its defenses at first light. The shore batteries returned fire noting hits against enemy shipping. A couple of Wildcat fighters managed to get into the air and strafe enemy landing boats as they were attempting to land. It seemed like thousands were ready to land. Codewords were sent in the clear indicating that they were in danger of being overrun.

By noon, Wake Island time, fighting was savage at the water's edge. Just then, some SBD Dauntless dive bombers appeared from Force Rogers. There were only a dozen of them, but they immediately dove on the enemy ships. A freighter offloading supplies and a couple of troop transports were hit by bombs (explosions that caused large fires) that threw off the timetable of the invasion. The force must have thought that they were under a major attack because they withdrew some distance away from the Island in order to get maneuvering room. The dive bombers also strafed enemy landing boats as they approached the shore. When the larger ships pulled out to distance themselves, the landing boats did not have the range to get back to the troop transports (many enemy casualties resulted from this) and some of them swamped on the run into the invasion beaches.

As such, a report from Force Rogers came in that indicated that the small force launched was from volunteers from the airgroups. The strike would be near the maximum range of the aircraft (with carriers moving closer to the Wake Island that effectively extended their range). Force Rogers may now break radio silence as the airstrike indicated to the Japanese that they are in the area. The clock is now ticking but it is now possible to smash an entire invasion force with our carriers. It will still be difficult to resupply the island.

Enemy casualties are unknown but are thought to be heavy.

SUBMARINE OPERATIONS

The submarine USS S-36 reported that they had attacked an enemy freighter escorted by a small patrol boat near Takao.

No hits were scored against the enemy and they were forced deep for several hours due to enemy aircraft and the enemy patrol boat. They later broke contact and made their report. Later in the morning, USS S-41 reported attacking an enemy freighter near Laoag, hitting it with one torpedo. They then broke to the west due to enemy aircraft and surfaced a few hours later.

Another report came in from USS S-36 as dinner neared. They had found an enemy freighter while recharging their batteries on the surface. They fired several torpedoes and hit with two of them. They also reported hitting the enemy freighter with their 4" deck gun "quite a few times" before an enemy aircraft appeared that required them to dive. They broke away slowly to the southwest conserving battery power before surfacing again to make the report.

Hawaii

A PBY Catalina noticed the tanker type ships from yesterday at around 1100 local and radioed in their location. The Catalina then began to shadow the force for roughly an hour while their location was sent to Task Force Tambourine. As it turned out, Task Force Tambourine was only 110 nautical miles away. They radioed back to us that they were working up to full speed (30 knots) and were on a course to intercept the enemy ships.

The destroyer USS Craven was in the van of the force and spotted the enemy ships by smoke plumes on the horizon. CAPT Hoover ordered the ships into battle formation and moved to attack the enemy force. Two enemy destroyers were noted escorting seven large fleet tankers. One of the enemy destroyers laid a smoke screen and fired on USS Craven and

USS Gridley. The second enemy destroyer was alternating fire between the light cruiser USS Helena and the destroyer USS Henley. Firing began immediately between the forces.

Over the next two hours, the enemy tankers were hit repeatedly by 5" guns from the destroyers, 6" guns from the light cruisers and at least one of the enemy tankers was hit by a torpedo (lookouts from all of the ships reported that the tanker hit by the torpedo had sunk). The enemy destroyers were hit by 5" shells from the friendly destroyers.

When it was all over, the light cruiser USS Helena was hit by an enemy shell that caused problems with some internal systems. The destroyers USS Henley, USS Craven and USS Gridley were hit by enemy shells and were damaged pretty badly. All three friendly destroyers had fires on board and were making their way back to Pearl Harbor. The destroyer USS Patterson was also damaged by enemy fire and suffered a few casualties but the fires were quickly put under control.

Initial reports stated that one enemy tanker was sunk, both enemy destroyers were damaged and on fire and that the remaining tankers were all damaged heavily and were burning heavily. With friendly ships low on ammunition and several of them damaged and on fire, CAPT Hoover ordered a withdrawal to Pearl Harbor. The destroyers on fire could not make full speed and were making best speed back to Pearl Harbor. A full report will be submitted upon arrival (including damage to friendly forces).

As friendly ships were heading back to port, a few B-17s from Hickham Field went out to bomb what was left of the enemy forces. The bombers found an enemy destroyer but no tankers. The destroyer was on fire and heading west. No hits were scored by the bombers on the enemy destroyer.

BROADER PACIFIC OCEAN

The destroyer USS Humphreys was attacked by an enemy submarine west of Eureka, California. USS King (another destroyer) joined in the sub hunt. There was no damage scored against USS Humphreys and there is no data to suggest that the enemy submarine was destroyed. This seems to be a main operating area for enemy submarines.

Guam was hit by a combined force of land based medium bombers and at least 60 carrier based dive bombers and small level bombers (a mix of Val and Kate aircraft). There was a minimum of 16 casualties on the ground and there was no damage to enemy aircraft from the combined raid.

PHILIPPINE ISLAND OPERATIONS

The Philippines were relatively quiet. There was a sizeable raid against Clark Field that brought up whatever friendly fighters were still in a condition to fly. As such, a total of 13 P-40 Warhawks managed to get into the air. The raid was escorted by several enemy fighters. Over the next 30 minutes, a single friendly fighter was shot down and there were two confirmed kills of enemy bombers (the pilots reported them as Sally types). It seems like the Japanese are consolidating current gains and getting ready for their next push.

CHINESE THEATER

Chinese forces were pushed back at Chenting during the day. There were several other battles near Kaifeng, Kweisui, Lang Son, Hwainan, Hwaiyin and Canton.

BRITISH AND ALLIED OPERATIONS

Figure 19 - USS Houston (CA-30) - CAPT Rooks' Flagship

LCDR Rochefort arrived during the day and asked if there was something major going on near Kuching. We informed him that CAPT Rook's force should have been attacking. He said that was obvious based on the frantic Japanese radio traffic coming from that area. We, on the operations staff, had not received any reports yet but we were now looking forward to them.

When the reports began coming in, they were greeted with adulation. It seemed that CAPT Rooks had brought his force into the area on a fogless night (that it was also a new moon meant that visibility was still low). They found a large enemy force of freighters trying to unload their supplies and opened fire. The heavy cruiser USS Houston, light cruiser USS Boise and the destroyers USS Paul Jones, USS Parrott, USS Whipple and USS Stewart took individual targets and kept hitting enemy ships until they were sunk. The report from CAPT Rooks onboard the heavy cruiser USS Houston stated that "many enemy ships were sunk" and "more were damaged". LCDR Rochefort will indeed be busy trying to figure out the carnage that occurred.

A couple of hours later a simple report came in that stated that "11 large freighters and 4 small freighters were sunk with several others damaged" but neglected to provide information about damage to his force. He was retiring to Soerabaja at 25 knots. This particular operations report was forwarded to LCDR Rochefort.

Kuantan was hit by another large raid of enemy bombers (nearly, if not slightly over 100 enemy medium bombers). There was nothing on the ground for friendly forces to fight back with.

The scratch Dutch force at Ternate was more or less destroyed by Japanese troops and the base was taken.

The US tanker SS Manatawny radioed that they were torpedoed by an enemy submarine around 60 nautical miles from Balikpapan. The crew was abandoning ship and heading to the lifeboats.

The British Liaison Officer reported that a major invasion was occurring at Rabaul. Reports from the radio operators indicated that heavy cruisers along with at least one carrier are assisting the landing of enemy troops. He also noted that it appeared that the Japanese 90th Infantry Battalion along with some supporting units had landed on the Talili Bay side. The only major friendly unit present was a battalion of infantry without major artillery or armored support. Friendly troops were under attack by enemy aircraft all day along with large caliber sea based fire (mostly from heavy cruisers using plunging fire from the Talili Bay side).

It was estimated in the reports that a little over 1000 troops had landed during the first few hours. Sea based forces include at least three heavy cruisers, a half dozen destroyers and at least one enemy carrier. It is currently unknown if friendly forces are hunkering down or if they will move to meet the enemy in order to not be trapped on the peninsula.

However, some good news came from the Australian cruisers that had headed towards Madang. A late day report came in that indicated that they had run into an escorted enemy force of four ships (two escorts and two freighters). All four enemy ships were sunk by the cruiser force. When leaving the immediate area of Madang, they ran into another enemy freighter that they promptly shot up and sunk. They are now breaking free from the area and will return to Sydney for a full ammunition reload (large rounds and torpedo reloads are not available at Port Moresby).

Intelligence

There was a different officer presenting the intelligence report. As it turns out, LCDR Rochefort was incredibly busy still working decrypts. With that, the report began.

Intercepted traffic from radio intercepts indicated that indeed, a total of three freighters were sunk and a couple of patrol boats. Only one of the names was known at this point, the Hokkai Maru, but the intelligence crew was busy decrypting more messages.

It was apparent that at least one light carrier was supporting the invasion of Rabaul. It's possible that this carrier is the Shoho, but there is nothing confirmed at this point.

Intelligence believes that the main fleet carriers are near Guam supporting operations there which puts them two days away from Wake Island.

With regards to CAPT Rooks' foray into Kuching, there was much traffic, but only part of it was fully decrypted. Reports were sketchy but it was apparent that the Japanese had suffered fearful losses to our ships. The only names that were confirmed were the Keihuku Maru, Okuyo Maru and Seian Maru. The other traffic is still being decrypted. However, there were more confirmed losses of enemy ships; just the names were not yet known.

The engagement north of Lihue was confirmed as well by intelligence. They let us know that a total of seven tankers were present based on radio escorted by two destroyers. One of the destroyers was identified as the IJN Akebono and a tanker was confirmed as sunk (the Toei Maru, a 10000 ton tanker). The other ships were still transmitting but it seemed like they were in a dire situation with regards to damage. More information should be forthcoming.

Figure 20 - IJN Akebono (Destroyer)

Lastly, a freighter transmitted in the clear that they were under attack by a submarine. That ship was the Brisbane Maru and the information indicated that they were near Takao. They were sinking and the crew was taking to the lifeboats. This confirms a report from USS S-36.

Other information pointed to elements of the 3rd Infantry Regiment being aboard ships moving towards Kota Bharu. An additional message showed that the Japanese 52nd Infantry Division was heading towards Jolo and that the 40th Infantry Brigade was moving to Rabaul.

There was also an unusually high volume of radio traffic coming from Cam Ranh Bay. The intelligence crew wasn't sure why, but it was important enough to put into the daily report.

The Intelligence Officer then concluded the report by reminding us that more information will be available over the next 24 hours.

THEORIES AND INTENTIONS

The Japanese don't seem too worried about escorting ships near Kuching. This may indicate that they consider it to be a secondary target. If that is the case, we should hit all of their secondary targets like this.

Now that aircraft from Task Force Rogers have hit enemy shipping near Wake Island, it is possible that enemy carriers may move out to strike them. It will be a hard decision to make to support operations there. Additionally, there are problems with the number of replacement aircraft available. ADM Nimitz was concerned that any major losses may take up to a month or more to replace. He asked the supply officer for aircraft production figures and the number available in depots.

LATE DAY REPORTS

The only late day reports concerned Task Force Tambourine. It seems that a few of the destroyers were damaged pretty badly and the force was broken into two separate forces for the return to Pearl Harbor. The heavily damaged destroyers could only make 20 knots. This was an unusual decision but one that makes sense since they are so close to friendly air cover.

A late report also came in from CAPT Rooks that stated the destroyer USS John D. Edwards was fully repaired and ready for further orders.

Ham again for dinner. Sick of ham. Nothing good on the radio either.

DECEMBER 20, 1941   DAY 14 OF THE WAR

ADM Nimitz began the morning by formally ordering us to get information about how many replacement aircraft were currently available in depots; to include Hawaii and the West Coast. This was also concurrent with availability of ships coming to the Theater. We were ordered to continue to conserve resources for now (with the notable exception of Operation Buck). With that, the Operations Officer began his report.

Operation Buck should reach the culmination point today as they should reach their operational area today and launch multiple strikes (weather permitting). They were to stay no longer than 48 hours in this location (approximately 75 nautical miles northeast of Wake).

Canton Island reported that they were running low on supplies. A small force would need to be sent with food and building supplies soon.

Task Force 303 is offloading their cargo at Palmyra Island. This should take several days.

Several ships arrived this morning from the West Coast. The submarines USS Nautilus, USS Cuttlefish and USS Tuna are pierside replenishing right now. Also, the troop transport USS Barnett arrived. This was a fleet troop transport.

Task Force 407 was continuing to offload troops and supplies at Port Moresby. This should take another day or so, but the troops on the ground were already supporting building fortifications and finding firing locations for the artillery pieces. The artillery was to be split between defending against a seaborne invasion and against land forces that may come out of the mountains. Commanders on the scene were to use their own discretion.

The 1st Australian Infantry Division was still loading onto transports with their equipment. This should take another day or so, with a couple more small escorts meeting them at Sydney before leaving for the transit to Port Moresby.

Task Force Gable was passing Billiton Island on their way back to Soerabaja. No further orders were sent to CAPT Rooks.

For Java, the British Liaison Officer reported that the 44th Indian Infantry Brigade was fully offloaded at Batavia and had received orders to march to Kalidjati and begin fortifying the area against an enemy amphibious assault. The 45th Indian Infantry Brigade also had offloaded and received orders for Merak with the same mission to prepare the area against an enemy amphibious assault. The 48th Gurkha Brigade was to head to Buitenzorg and fortify that area. These developments greatly enhance the ability of friendly forces to hold the eastern end of the island. More forces were on their way to the island.

He also reported that the light cruiser HMS Mauritius with six attending destroyers were going to sortie and hit Kuching. CAPT Stevens is in command of this force which will be referred to as Task Force 131.

This concluded the morning report. We were dismissed to our duties for the day.

OPERATION BUCK

Task Force Rogers encountered bad weather for most of the day, but there was a clearing beginning around 1300 local that allowed them to launch a strike by 1500 today. They managed to get 30 Dauntless dive bombers, 15 Devastator torpedo bombers in the air escorted by 11 fighters to hit the enemy ships at Wake Island.

This was good timing, because the weather also halted landing of enemy troops for most of the morning. When the aircraft arrived on the scene, landing boats were loaded and heading towards Wake Island in the south. A confused series of attacks began that ended with bomb hits on what was reported as "a small destroyer, a large destroyer and several freighters/ troop transports". One of the freighters was hit by a torpedo from a Devastator that caused a massive explosion – the ship sank within minutes. The small destroyer was claimed as sunk as well as another freighter; the large destroyer was claimed as damaged. The aircraft then strafed landing boats until they had to return to their carriers. Only a single Devastator was damaged by enemy anti-aircraft fire.

The problem is that the strike force also reported that there were at least twenty other ships in the general vicinity. It is anticipated that they will launch another attack in the morning.

As such, MAJ Deveraux was now radioing that he was critically short of ammunition, particularly machine gun ammunition and 5" shells for his shore defense guns. His stocks of mortar rounds were also running low. The carriers may attempt to do a makeshift airdrop of machine gun ammunition from their stores tomorrow. ADM Nimitz notified us that he intends to order a general withdrawal for the force if they decide to stay longer than 48 hours. It was obvious, however, that the 1st Marine Defense Battalion needed all the help they could get. The supply submarines were at least another day away.

SUBMARINE OPERATIONS

No major reports came in from any at sea submarines today.

HAWAII

There were no major reports. Task Force Tambourine ships should begin arriving sometime today.

BROADER PACIFIC OCEAN

Guam was attacked by carrier based and land based bombers yet again today. The enemy was concentrating on the airfield today, cratering the runway and causing some damage to the airfield perimeter. There was nothing that the troops on the ground could do.

PHILIPPINE ISLAND OPERATIONS

Clark Field was subjected to several air raids during the day. In total, four separate raids kept the pilots, ground crews and anti-aircraft units busy. When the fighting was all done, four more friendly fighters were destroyed while shooting down one enemy fighter and one medium bomber. The airfield suffered significant damage that the engineers were having a hard time keeping up with.

There wasn't much good news on the ground front. Enemy troops coming up from Legaspi had captured Antimonan, cut off Boac and had their eyes probably set on Lucena. On the good side, there were roughly 3000 Philippine Army troops in the area of Lucena, but they were still assembling and having a hard time trying to set up a defense near the choke points between Atimonan and Lucena.

**Figure 21 - Luzon with original disposition
of air units at start of war**

At Lingayen, low level combat claimed some Japanese tanks destroyed, but the commanders there were asking for more ammunition; this was a problem for the entire area as stocks were still being distributed to the units shaking out into the field for battle. It also didn't help that the supplies located at Aparri were captured in the initial assault.

And, speaking of Aparri, enemy troops had moved out and assaulted the area of Tuguegarao in the Cagayan Valley.

The only friendly troops there were more or less destroyed (an assembling Philippine Army Infantry Battalion). The town shortly fell to the Japanese.

CHINESE THEATER

There were reports of heavy combat at Canton, Kaifeng, Kweisui and Lang Son. No other reports were received.

BRITISH AND ALLIED OPERATIONS

Combat operations at Rabaul continued. There was a lot of enemy shore fire support attacking the couple of harbor defense guns on the other side of Talili Bay. In some instances, even the freighters and troop transports were getting close enough to provide shore fire support. Reports came in indicating that some enemy freighters and troop transports were damaged by the guns, but nothing that would cause one to smile. No enemy transports were sunk. By the end of the day, nearly 4000 enemy troops were in combat with the single battalion present in the area. They were also under attack by land based medium bombers and carrier based planes. They did manage to slip away from the peninsula and are concentrating their efforts on preventing the two ground forces from linking up. Friendly forces have suffered 47 wounded. Enemy casualties are unknown.

Recon aircraft have reported that there are now destroyers in the vicinity of Kuching on escort duty. Task Force 131 was notified and acknowledged receipt of the message.

Rangoon was raided by a few enemy bombers. Apparently, the Japanese did not notice that the airfield was augmented by All-Volunteer Squadron fighters. A total of nine bombers attacked unescorted and five were shot down by friendly fighters (all confirmed).

Tavoy was also under enemy air attack most of the day. Tavoy is a small town down the Burmese side of the Malayan Peninsula. Reports were sketchy, but it seemed that at least 20 medium bombers had attacked the small airfield there during the early morning hours. The British Liaison Officer was trying to get more information.

INTELLIGENCE

The intelligence officer arrived to begin the daily report. More information had been broken regarding CAPT Rooks' attack at Kuching. More ship names were available. The following ships were confirmed as sunk and added to the list:

- Hukuzyu Maru
- Seikai Maru
- Tohuku Maru
- Hokutai Maru
- Yomei Maru

We were informed that they were still working on finding out more about that attack; they were also confirming the tonnages of each ship sunk. There was a lot of message traffic concerning these issues by the Japanese high command and the merchant ships in the area.

A report was intercepted concerning the Japanese 19th Infantry Division. It seems that they have been tasked with leading an attack against Lingayen on Luzon in the Philippines. That message was also sent to the headquarters in Manila.

Additionally, Balikpapan has been identified in several Japanese messages with forces being detailed for the assault. This information will be passed to forces at Java with planning instructions for CAPT Rooks to see if he might want to attack there pending further information.

The report ended there, though the intelligence officer reminded us that the cryptologic crew was still working on breaking more messages.

THEORIES AND INTENTIONS

Now that the Japanese are attacking in Burma, it seems that they are laying the groundwork for a run up the coast with their troops. While it is a big problem for the British, we need to stay on top of it for support purposes.

What remains to be seen is how long friendly forces will hold out at Rabaul. They can't hold for long, they're massively outgunned.

ADM Nimitz is very concerned about Task Force Rogers. He wants to hurt the Japanese fleet but he doesn't want the force to be ambushed by enemy carriers. He goes over all the reports from the Task Force with a fine toothed comb.

LATE DAY REPORTS

The reports were available as to the reserve of aircraft available for the Navy. It was not pretty:

- 10 Wildcat fighters
- 15 Buffalo fighters
- 4 Dauntless dive bombers
- 6 Devastator torpedo bombers

All of the PBY Catalinas were being put directly into squadrons. ADM Nimitz was not happy about any of this. The problem is that you just can't turn on an industry that quickly. Reports indicated that maybe 30 fighters a month could be turned out at the current rate, but that was simply not enough. There simply could not be any major loss of aircraft at this rate.

The situation wasn't much better for the Army Air Forces; in fact, it was worse. LTG Richardson reported that there were NO reserves of aircraft, not in fighters, patrol planes, bombers, nothing. They were all being held stateside for training and constituting new squadrons. There will be a trickle of aircraft coming over the next few months but major replacements won't be forthcoming until probably March or April.

Everyone winced.

With that cheerful news I left for the night. I'm sure there were a few other reports, but that was all I could concentrate on. To put it in perspective, if industry at home could put out 30 fighters a month, it would take four months to completely outfit Task Force Rogers from scratch. This makes any combat even more important when trying to figure out risk versus reward.

I really needed a beer. I picked up a few at the BX and drank a couple of them in my bungalow as I listened to some jazz music on the radio.

DECEMBER 21, 1941   DAY 15 OF THE WAR

<u>MORNING BRIEF</u>

ADM Nimitz was out of the office as the morning brief began.

The Operations officer told us that the troop transports USS Harris and USS William Ward Burrows arrived and were ready for operations. Also, the submarines USS Gar and USS Grayling arrived from the West Coast.

Task Force Rogers would be making major attacks today. The Operations Officer was sure that there would be a large argument over whether or not to withdraw the carriers pending intelligence assessment.

CAPT Hoover arrived late last night with the light cruisers USS St. Louis and USS Helena escorted by the destroyers USS Henley and USS Patterson. As it turns out, during the battle, USS Henley was hit by an enemy shell that had temporarily jammed their rudder and caused them to collide with USS Helena. That little piece of information was kept out of the radio reports. I think that's why ADM Nimitz wasn't in the office. The Harbor Master was onboard USS Helena at 0500 this morning and estimated that it would take almost a month to completely repair USS Helena; the damage was almost all due to the collision. USS Henley would take about a week pierside to fix the damage.

The remainder of the Task Force Tambourine should be arriving in port in the next 24 hours or so.

CAPT Rooks' force arrived at Soerabaja and stated that all ships would be ready to sortie in less than 24 hours. This was good news and implied that there were no major problems for the ships.

USS Porpoise arrived for a quick turnaround at Subic Bay overnight. They refueled and reloaded ammunition and went back out to sea. They were in port for only six hours.

A radio report was received from Christmas Island indicating that they were also running low on supplies. When one of the forces currently re-provisioning Lihue, Johnston Island or Palmyra finishes, they will be turned around for more missions.

The 57th Coastal Artillery Regiment was released for use in the Pacific. They will be loading up on transports and heading to Pearl Harbor in the next couple of days.

The British Liaison Officer reported that the freighter SS Steel Worker is about a week away from Pago Pago. After unloading, they will head back to Sydney.

The 1st Australian Infantry Division will be putting out to sea today to head to Port Moresby. They have several escorts and are also loaded up with building materials, engineering materials, food, medical supplies and extra ammunition. This convoy must reach Port Moresby.

Task Force 131 should reach Kuching sometime in the next 24 hours. We were all standing by for reports.

With that, the report ended, we grabbed some food and then went to our work stations and got ready for the day's work.

Operation Buck

Recon and estimates by MAJ Deveraux concluded that there are roughly 4000 Japanese troops on the Wake Atoll. As earlier indicated, they were concentrated on Wilkes Island. This should have been the main target for aircraft from Task Force Rogers.

However, the first strike of the day (at 0830, after patrol aircraft reports were back at the carriers) was concentrated on a light cruiser that was damaged and escorting a small freighter. The ships were attacked by 33 Dauntless dive bombers. The small freighter was hit by several bombs and sank while the air units were still in the area. The light cruiser was hit by at least 4 bombs and was burning heavily. The aircraft then turned to head back to the carriers.

Another strike took place at 1430 that was dedicated to supporting Wake Island. This gave enough time to turn around the dive bombers and make sure that the Devastator torpedo bombers were armed with bombs. The Devastators did a level run at 5000' and dropped their 500 lb. bombs. Next came the dive bombers. They began their dive at 10000' and released anywhere from 4000' to 2000'. In all, 44 Devastators and 82 Dauntless aircraft made strikes; they were escorted by 63 fighters, a mixed bag of Wildcats and Buffalos. The only friendly casualties were a single Dauntless that was damaged by some ground fire wounding the rear gunner. All of the aircraft returned to the carriers safely and the damaged Dauntless was being repaired.

According to MAJ Deveraux on the ground, the strikes were very effective but there were no indications of the count on enemy casualties. Problem is that MAJ Deveraux did not have the forces necessary to attack an estimated 4000 enemy soldiers on Wilkes Island. Another method would have to be found to permanently eject the enemy from the Atoll.

Another report from Wake indicated that all stores were exhausted and the supplies that troops currently have is all that is available. Luckily, the submarines with food and ammunition should be there in the next 24 hours or so.

Submarine Operations

A report came in after lunch from USS S-38 (LCDR Chapple) that they had found and attacked a freighter near Laoag. They fired two torpedoes and hit with one midships on the port side. Enemy patrol aircraft were there in a matter of minutes requiring the submarine to stay submerged and break from the area.

USS Seal (LCDR Hurd) came under attack by an enemy escort that caused no damage.

Hawaii

There were no major reports near Hawaii today.

Broader Pacific Ocean

Guam was hit by enemy carrier aircraft again today. Mostly Val dive bombers attacking facilities and troops on the ground. It won't be long before an invasion occurs.

Philippine Island Operations

Manila was under constant air attack during the day. There were only a few Warhawks remaining and they sortied to meet the attackers. By the end of the day, the remaining fighters were either shot down or received so much damage that they were barely airworthy. The city was damaged and the small airfield there was cratered and no enemy aircraft were shot down. The air force there is now effectively destroyed.

There were probing attacks by both sides at Lingayen. A few Japanese tanks were damaged and there were no casualties to friendly forces.

Philippine Army units were still marshaling in Manila and near Clark Field. Weapons and supplies were trying to be located for them.

CHINESE THEATER

There was ground combat at Wenchow, Canton, Kaifeng, Kweisui, Lang Son and Chuhsien. At Kweiteh, Japanese forces pushed back the 89th Chinese Corps and resumed a significant advance.

BRITISH AND ALLIED OPERATIONS

There was more combat at Rabaul today. More enemy troops were landed during the day and the troops on the ground were severely outnumbered and outgunned. Fire was coming in from the Talili Bay side as well as from ships near the lagoon. The accurate shore fire support helped the Japanese troops on the ground as well as accurate strikes by carrier based aircraft. By the end of the day, all friendly forces had been pushed out of Rabaul. By radio report, 900 troops were killed, wounded or captured. The British Liaison was trying to get information about what troops were left. This is not going to help the strategic situation in the Australian Theater.

Kuantan was attacked again today by enemy bombers. Not as severe as in the past, but a total of 40 medium bombers had visited the area during the day. There was also a troubling report that enemy troops were seen massing to the north.

Tavoy came under air attack again today as well. A total of 50 medium bombers escorted by some fighters made a concentrated strike against installations there. There were 14 casualties on the ground and no damage was scored against the enemy. There were no notifications of enemy troop movements, but the enemy will probably begin to move troops up the coast. They need to attack and capture Rangoon in order to get the oil supplies there.

Some good news came from Task Force 131. They made their run into the Kuching area and found many enemy ships at roughly 0200 local time. CAPT Stevens had assigned exclusive sectors for each of his ships as they made their way in. There was calm weather and a sliver moon that provided a little light. They overtook a small force on the way in that was a single large freighter escorted by a small patrol boat and a small destroyer. All three ships were quickly dispatched.

This did alert the other ships in the area (they could hear the gunfire). At this point, radio transmissions were made; apparently calling for help. Another force coming in from the northeast (CAPT Stevens was coming in from the west-northwest hugging the coast) had a larger destroyer. This enemy destroyer ran headlong into the British force and managed to put some hits in on the light cruiser HMS Mauritius (the flagship) and the destroyer HMS Electra. HMS Mauritius was hit by a 5" shell on her port side that penetrated the superstructure and exploded causing some casualties and destroying a 20mm anti-aircraft gun emplacement. A wild melee ensued over the next 30 minutes that ended when the destroyer HMS Stronghold hit the enemy destroyer with a torpedo at a range of only 1000 yards. The torpedo struck forward of the beam against the destroyer and must have lit off an ammunition magazine because HMS Stronghold was peppered with debris from the enemy destroyer. During this part of the engagement, another patrol boat and freighter were shot up and sunk.

Figure 22 - HMS Electra (H27)

CAPT Stevens was concerned about a fire onboard his ship and the exploding enemy destroyer. He signaled to his force to do a slow withdrawal to the north at 15 knots. They encountered another patrol boat escorting a single freighter which was summarily attacked. The patrol boat was claimed sunk and the freighter was heavily damaged. More ships were seen in an unorganized fashion and at 0445 a small escort (possibly a submarine chaser) escorting a freighter were attacked and both sunk. At 0540, a single freighter was seen and attacked with main guns and torpedoes. The ship was sunk quickly.

At 0650, when the sun was coming up, CAPT Stevens was just about ready to order a withdrawal when a large gaggle of ships was seen by lookouts at approximately 8 nautical miles to the east. The ships worked up speed and ran straight into a large convoy of freighters escorted by a single patrol boat. For the next two hours, gunfire and torpedoes tore into the enemy convoy. More freighters and the patrol boat were sunk (CAPT Stevens claims that 6 more freighters were sunk).

At 0925, lookouts noticed more ships coming in at long range. They appeared to be a single heavy cruiser with some escorting destroyers. CAPT Stevens immediately ordered a withdrawal at full speed to the west-northwest to head back to Singapore and radioed in the enemy combat force to headquarters units.

If the reports were to be believed, 12 enemy freighters, 2 patrol boats, a large destroyer and a small destroyer were all sunk during this engagement. The intelligence cell would be very busy trying to collate all of this information. Still, by any measure, it was a resounding success.

Intelligence

The 1600 report started a little late. There were a few last minute reports that had been decrypted that the intelligence crew wanted in the report.

A report came in from the freighter SS Nanning indicating that they were attacked by an enemy submarine near Tawi Tawi. I don't even know where Tawi Tawi is... I'll have to find that on a map. In any case, the ship was severely damaged and would try to make for a friendly port.

More information was available from CAPT Rooks' attack at Kuching on the 19th. The names of more ships were available:

- Hokumai Maru
- Hokutatsu Maru
- Buyo Maru

Also, from the Australian attack at Madang the following sunk ships were identified by radio intercepts:

- Kosin Maru #3 (a patrol boat)

179

- Sydney Maru
- Kunitu Maru

From carrier based air attacks near Wake Island yesterday, the following sunk ships were identified by radio intercepts:

- Kowa Maru (troop transport)
- Amagisan Maru (freighter)
- Hashidate (small destroyer, 1010 tons)

There was extensive traffic from the British engagement at Kuching, but the intelligence and decryption teams were still hard at work sorting through all of the information. The only major piece of information was that the Japanese area commander had stated that "many of our ships were sunk".

There was a little more information. It appeared that elements of the Japanese 30th Infantry Regiment were moving to Kota Bharu. They were probably going to be used for pushing down the peninsula towards Singapore. The British Liaison Officer took note of that information.

Theories and Intentions

More attacks at Tavoy show that the Japanese will push down the Malayan Peninsula as well as pushing up towards Rangoon. It remains to be seen where the 30th Infantry Regiment will be heading once they land at Kota Bharu.

The continued successes at Kuching can't last. They now seem to have some quick reaction forces in the area. Their timing was off, but that won't last for long either. They will learn as we learn.

LATE DAY REPORTS

The transports carrying the 8th Marine Regiment arrived this afternoon from San Francisco. The troops, equipment and supplies were now unloading. Rumors abounded about the commanding officer of the Regiment being ordered to see ADM Nimitz in the morning.

The 57th Coastal Artillery Regiment was now out to sea from San Francisco on the transports of Task Force 17. It will be several days before they get here.

Task Force 407 has completed the unloading of US Forces at Port Moresby. An artillery regiment, two separate artillery battalions and a lot of ground support and aircraft maintenance troops were unloaded. They are now going about their mission of securing Port Moresby along with our Australian allies.

At Soerabaja, CDR Musak's Task Force 88 arrived. They are going pierside for repairs and re-provisioning. Full report as to the material condition of the ships should be available in the next 24 hours.

I had a quick bite, grabbed a couple of beers and sat on the porch of my bungalow listening to a show called "The Great Gildersleeve". It was kind of funny. This installment was called "Christmas Gift for McGee". After the show ended, I went to sleep.

DECEMBER 22, 1941   DAY 16 OF THE WAR

<u>MORNING BRIEF</u>

Some toast and butter for breakfast. I was quickly losing weight and needed to reconsider my diet and some exercise. ADM Nimitz seemed very tired and when we came in we heard him talking about the collision between friendly ships and how angry he was. He was not angry at the crew, but at the situation. Preliminary investigation showed that the jammed rudder from enemy fire caused the collision; but to lose trained crew to something like that… he must have found it infuriating.

The Operations Officer started by explaining that we were still waiting on information regarding CDR Musak's destroyers that just entered port at Soerabaja. It is thought that the majority of the ships should be just fine from a material standpoint but that USS Pillsbury might need some major repairs; this ship was damaged in the Philippines.

The carriers of Task Force Rogers were to remain on station for one more day to provide support and then return to Pearl Harbor. So far, the operation has been considered a success with enemy ships sunk and damaged and ground support to the 1st Marine Defense Battalion at Wake Island. It was hoped that the carriers would find a major enemy invasion force, but this was not to be. In any case, force preservation was still the order of the day.

A group of three freighters were detailed to make shuttle runs from San Francisco and Pearl Harbor to bring supplies, food and ammunition. The first run should be putting to sea today. The Operations Staff was ordered to liaise with the

Supply Staff to make sure high priority items are being brought from the mainland.

A request came in to detail some destroyers to head to San Diego. As it turns out, the carrier USS Yorktown was due to be out of drydock in a week or so and would immediately be available for operations. They would complete engineering trials and shakedown on the way to Pearl Harbor.

Task Force 407 was still heading towards Sydney to await further orders. We were to monitor progress.

The submarine USS Tuna was leaving port this morning to patrol in the area around Eniwetok to attack enemy shipping.

The remaining four destroyers from Task Force Tambourine should be getting to Pearl Harbor later this morning. Any reports from the Harbor Master should be brought to ADM Nimitz's attention immediately. We all nodded in confirmation of the order.

The British Liaison Officer notified us that the 46th Indian Infantry Brigade was still unloading at Batavia and should be ready for orders in the next day or so. A report also came in that indicated that there seemed to be a major concentration of enemy fleet assets near Ternate on Moluccas Island. This may indicate future intentions of the enemy.

There were no major changes to other Task Force orders or dispositions. As such, we were dismissed for the day's work.

OPERATION BUCK

The unthinkable and unhistorical happened. Task Force Rogers landed a few aircraft with extra machine gun ammunition and a little bit of food and brought information that a large strike would hit the Japanese controlled areas around 1300 local time. This makeshift airlift (done by

Dauntless dive bombers without their rear gunners) brought in just enough machine gun ammunition (a few dozen units of fire) to allow the 1st Marine Defense Battalion to aggressively defend against a single enemy attack. The food was parceled out to the defenders and a few of the badly wounded were set in the rear gunner seats for transport to the carriers. One pilot had orders to request an up to date operations map to brief the pilots. MAJ Deveraux drew out where his and the enemy forces were and that last pilot took off to head back to the carriers.

At 1100 local, a radio message was received by our headquarters from MAJ Deveraux that indicated that the Japanese were seemingly assembling for an attack. The report also indicated that the time of the Japanese attack was unknown.

By 1230 local, the Japanese troops were ready for their attack because the Marines near the western end of Wake Island proper were beginning to receive mortar rounds from Japanese forces that were mostly confined to Wilkes Island. It seems that their attack was meant to be timed with low tide so that the small strip of land between Wilkes and Wake would be larger to allow for more troops to move.

At 1250 local, friendly strike aircraft were in the air from Task Force Rogers. Dauntless dive bombers hit the areas closest to friendly forces near the eastern end of Wilkes Island with the Devastator bombers doing a level bombing run along the long axis of Wilkes Island at 5000' with drop zones near the western side of the island. Each Dauntless was armed with a single 1000 lb. bomb and the each Devastator was armed with a pair of 500 lb. bombs.

Over the next hour, 44 Devastator torpedo bombers, 114 Dauntless dive bombers escorted by 52 fighters (a mix of Buffalo and Wildcat types) attacked the Japanese on the Wilkes Island. A total of 202 bombs fell on the Japanese which sent their troops into a panic. When the bombers finished their work, the fighters came down on the deck to strafe the remaining enemy troops they could find.

This must have completely thrown off their attack because the Japanese troops did everything they could in order to get close to the Marine defenders (it is difficult to hit only the enemy when they are in close combat). In the panic, Japanese troops were mown down by the machine guns and rifle fire at the western end of Wake Island.

By 1345, a banzai charge of remaining enemy troops came at the Marines; one of the defending machine gun teams was killed to a man and many other Marines were wounded. However, by 1415, all organized resistance by the Japanese had ceased. There were reports by Marines indicating that individual Japanese soldiers were shooting themselves.

By 1500, all aircraft had left the area and there was no fire coming from Wilkes Island. MAJ Deveraux lead a heavily armed party to scout the edge of Wilkes Island looking for information. There were no Japanese to be seen. He then ordered a full platoon to reconnoiter Wilkes Island. A few Japanese prisoners were taken (9 prisoners in all, a few from the Maizuru 2nd Special Naval Landing Force and a few from the Guards Brigade), but for all intents and purposes, the Japanese forces were completely destroyed (over 1000 enemy dead were counted) and Wilkes Island was secured.

At 1800, MAJ Deveraux radioed that his battalion was in complete control of Wake Atoll. This was completely unprecedented.

Will the Japanese attack again? How will we get more forces to the island with Japanese land based bombers in striking range? We expected to be very busy with these questions. In the meantime, it was the first major victory that could be enjoyed by our forces. The submarines will hopefully be able to quickly drop off their supplies because Task Force Rogers was leaving the area to head back to Pearl Harbor.

SUBMARINE OPERATIONS

An enemy submarine attacked and sank the freighter SS Elcano trying to get into Soerabaja at 1330 local time today. They were attacked roughly 125 nautical miles east-northeast of Soerabaja. A floatplane will be heading to the area to look for survivors.

Nearly the same time, a report came in from the freighter SS Dos Hermanos near Pamekasan that they were under attack by an enemy submarine. The freighter was hit by several shells from the submarine's deck gun. We are standing by for further reports.

Another Japanese submarine attacked a destroyer group near Eureka, California. The destroyer USS King was heavily damaged and was trying to head back to San Francisco. USS Sands, another destroyer attempted to depth charge the submarine. No word on damage to the enemy.

USS Snapper (LCDR Stone) attacked an enemy freighter off the coast of China near Swatow. The freighter was hit with two torpedoes and was most likely sunk. Enemy patrol aircraft prevented the submarine from maintaining contact. Reports will be sought as to this attack.

HAWAII

The cargo ship USS Castor arrived from Lihue this morning with the three attending destroyers after completing unloading supplies. They are awaiting further orders and would probably be sent on another mission within a day or so. There are several other islands waiting for supplies.

The remaining destroyers from Task Force Tambourine arrived around lunchtime. The destroyer USS Craven was brought immediately to the dry dock. Initial reports indicate that it will take 11 days to fully repair the ship. USS Gridley would also take 11 days to repair. The wounded and dead were taken off the ships (a total of 28 wounded and 5 killed). The other two destroyers had minor damage and would be available for operations in a day or so. The ship's captains from all four destroyers were to debrief ADM Nimitz at dinner.

Figure 23 - USS Gridley (DD-380)

BROADER PACIFIC OCEAN

Guam was attacked by enemy carrier based planes. The raid was directed against the troops, not against the infrastructure. There was little that we could do about these attacks and there was no immediate information about casualties.

PHILIPPINE ISLAND OPERATIONS

There were several air attacks against Manila and Clark Field today. Unfortunately, the remaining fighters were pretty much unable to get into the air due to lack of spare parts and damage to the planes. The airbases had taken a lot of damage and there were no confirmed kills by anti-aircraft batteries during the day. One of the raids had attacked the port at Cavite Base and damaged a few ships there. Reports were sketchy but it was confirmed that one of the PT boats in the harbor was destroyed.

There was some low level combat at Lingayen as well. There were two Philippine Army infantry divisions in the area providing for the defense. The Japanese had sent a reconnaissance in force (a reinforced platoon of light tanks) to ascertain friendly locations. One of the battalion commanders had laid in an ambush and destroyed three enemy tanks (and damaged two others) with no losses to his troops.

There were no other reports from the Philippines.

CHINESE THEATER

There were confirmed reports of combat at Canton, Hwaiyin, Kweisui, Lang Son, Hwainan, Loyang and Kaifeng. No information was available as to losses on either side.

BRITISH AND ALLIED OPERATIONS

Kuantan was hit by several raids during the day, most of them with between 30 and 40 aircraft. It was unknown exactly how many enemy aircraft visited the area for strikes during the day, but the ground forces still present have retreated to the jungle edge to make sure they stay alive long enough to run back to the base for any kind of defense.

On the Indian Ocean side, there is apparently a small base south of Tavoy known as Mergui. They were under several air attacks during the day that caused quite a few casualties on the ground (the British Liaison officer had a report that showed 65 wounded). This will probably be a target for Japanese troops if they decide to push up into Rangoon.

At Sambas Base, just to the west of Kuching, some ships were providing support and landing a few troops to assist troops coming overland from Kuching. It is unknown how many enemy troops are in that area.

At Java, more troops were unloading. A disposition of defensive plans should be forthcoming, but we don't expect to see the entire plan (US Troops won't be involved, so this is purely informational for us).

INTELLIGENCE

LCDR Rochefort reported that the Japanese had changed some of their codes and his teams were working very hard at trying to crack the new codes. Not all of the codes have changed however, so some new information was available.

On the ground combat side, it appeared that elements of the 12th Infantry Division were going to be heading towards San Fernando in the Philippines. This is more than likely a reinforcement unit since some of the Japanese forces there have not been making progress towards the Imperial High Command time table.

A message in the clear from the freighter Tazima Maru (6475 tons) was received from a location near Swatow that they were torpedoed and sinking. This confirms the report from the submarine USS Snapper.

More confirmed kills were decrypted over the last 24 hours. The freighter Tyoko Maru (4875 tons) was confirmed sunk near Laoag from being torpedoed by an enemy submarine. This confirms the report from USS S-38.

Merchant ships confirmed sunk at Kuching were identified by radio decrypts (ships sunk by the British):

-	Hakkaisan Maru	2780 tons
-	London Maru	6475 tons
-	Kaiun Maru	2780 tons
-	Nissyu Maru	6400 tons
-	Showa Maru #3	215 tons

Also confirmed sunk was the destroyer Urukaze and the escort ship Uruyame.

Near Wake Island, the small freighter Tamaki Maru was confirmed sunk by decrypts. This ship was more than likely sunk by Dauntless dive bombers from the previous day. While there were no other radio reports about the light cruiser Kashii, there was no data to suggest that the ship was sunk. It was confirmed that the Kashii was in the area of Wake Island over the last few days.

More data was being analyzed from the merchant decrypts and fleet decrypts to see which other ships were sunk or damaged.

THEORIES AND INTENTIONS

There is absolutely no doubt that the timeline has changed. Carriers supporting Wake Island never happened and a complete destruction of enemy troops at Wake Island never happened. The problem now is a different one; how do we keep them supplied?

Unescorted freighters can't be sent to Wake because of enemy medium bombers located at Kwajalein Island. The freighters would be slaughtered. Destroyers alone may not have enough anti-aircraft defenses to allow the freighters free reign to unload which means an alternative method must be found. Submarines can help in the short term, but it is definitely not a long term solution.

This assumes, of course, that the Japanese will not attempt another invasion. Task Force Rogers is now returning to Pearl Harbor which again makes Wake Island very difficult to defend. Time will tell.

LATE DAY REPORTS

The destroyer USS King sank late this afternoon off the California coast. All but three of the crew were rescued. Enemy submarines will be a problem for the foreseeable future. However, the logistical elements that were damaged and destroyed should help ease the problem in the short term.

Three more small freighters arrived at Soerabaja from the Philippines and were ready to accept orders if needed.

CDR Musak reported that USS Pillsbury would need about a week to fully repair. The Dutch shore crews were working feverishly on the destroyer. CDR Musak indicated that this would be his last report as force commander and that he had already reported to CAPT Rooks that his ships were now under CAPT Rooks' command.

The British Liaison Officer reported that the 46th Indian Infantry Brigade was being detailed to Semarang to build up defenses and to make ready to repel a Japanese amphibious assault.

I left just in time to get dinner. I was too tired and too stressed by the day to do much of anything. I went for a quick walk after getting to my bungalow – it was raining and I love walking in the rain. I went to sleep shortly before midnight.

DECEMBER 23, 1941   DAY 17 OF THE WAR

MORNING BRIEF

The morning report began a little early. ADM Nimitz was not at the meeting this morning and would be back briefed by the Operations Officer.

Freighters from San Francisco were leaving port today to bring supplies to Christmas Island. As a result, Task Force 184 with the fleet cargo ship USS Castor would remain at Pearl Harbor until needed. Other freighter forces (Palmyra and Johnston Island) were still unloading their cargo and would remain in place.

The converted troop transports that had delivered the 8th Marine Regiment had left Pearl Harbor overnight and were headed back to San Francisco for more missions. It should be a few days before they get back to the West Coast.

There were no plans made as of yet on how to deal with the Japanese submarine threat on the West Coast. Destroyers were in short supply everywhere. It remains to be seen how much damage was caused to enemy operations by damaging and sinking the enemy fleet oilers north of Lihue.

More ships were being released from the East Coast. They are moving to the Panama Canal. Right now, there is a light cruiser, several destroyers, a fleet cargo ship and a couple of fleet aircraft cargo ships (AKV types). The cargo ship and aircraft cargo ships have already left the Panama Canal area to head to Pearl Harbor – the fleet cargo ship USS Procyon and the fleet aircraft cargo ships USS Hammondsport and USS Kittyhawk.

The British Liaison Officer reported that troops were still moving on Java to support the Dutch. It would be a few days

193

before they were at their appropriate duty stations. He also reported that a couple of British Army brigades should be arriving at Java in a little less than a week.

Task Force 131 had arrived at Singapore and the ships were repairing damage and performing maintenance pending further orders.

We had a sidebar conversation about ADM Nimitz's dinner last night with the ship captains. It appears that they were not going to be admonished in any way. This was actually good news because those skippers were part of the few that have actual combat experience right now. It was also determined that CAPT Rooks and CDR Musak were both written up for a Silver Star and that CAPT Newman was being written up for a Bronze Star. There were rumors of unit awards as well; nice to know that the administrative staff will be as busy as we are.

The final piece of information was that a large convoy of ships had left the East Coast to head to Cape Town in South Africa. The convoy was carrying main gun and secondary battery ammunition (everything from .50 caliber machine gun ammunition up to 8 inch rounds for USS Houston), replacement torpedoes for surface ships and submarines (Mark 10 and Mark 14 torpedoes for the submarines and Mark 15 torpedoes for the surface ships), spare parts, food, extra uniforms, everything. The report indicated that they had left port on December 10th and should be at Cape Town on December 30th or 31st. The supplies would then have to be shipped to Java from Cape Town. The British Liaison Officer was notified and plans were being drawn up to get the shipping to take care of the last leg (US freighters were ordered to return to Norfolk after unloading at Cape Town). There were enough stores brought from Manila to allow for roughly one full reload of ammunition for US surface ships (with some to spare). Submarines were to reload at Subic Bay or Cavite

Base if possible, otherwise, there were only a few reloads; however, Mark 10 torpedoes could be used in place of Mark 14 torpedoes (the Mark 10 was smaller and could be used in fleet boats if necessary). A few freighters that got out of Subic Bay had replacement torpedoes in their cargo holds along with a little bit of ammunition. The British and Dutch don't have this problem. There are large stocks at Soerabaja, Columbo, Singapore and Brisbane (Australia and India are capable of producing munitions).

Word also reached us that another supply convoy was going to leave for Cape Town sometime in the next week. Logistics was going to be a nightmare.

With that, I had a bowl of oatmeal and went to my desk to start the work day.

OPERATION BUCK

Task Force Rogers is transiting back to Pearl Harbor. It will be several days before they get back.

SUBMARINE OPERATIONS

Thankfully, there were no confirmed attacks by enemy submarines today.

USS Skipjack (LCDR Freeman) ran into many enemy ships today near Balabac Island (straights near Palawan). It appears that they found a Japanese convoy and had attacked them several times during the day. They had hunted ships and fought off escorts and patrol aircraft several times during the day. When it was over there were only 8 torpedoes left on the submarine (full load is 22 torpedoes – they were a very busy crew to reload the tubes for multiple attacks). The submarine had torpedoed three freighters during the day while under depth charge attack from escorts. This report was sent to the Intelligence crew.

USS Snapper (LCDR Stone) ran into a surface ship off the coast of China near Swatow. They attacked with torpedoes and the deck gun. They hit the cargo ship with a torpedo and with several shells before being hit by the deck gun from the freighter. The freighter called in patrol aircraft which arrived during the attack at which point they submerged and withdrew from the area. It is unknown whether or not the enemy ship was sunk.

USS Tarpon (LCDR Wallace) found a small convoy near Groot Natoena and managed to attack an enemy freighter. The freighter was hit with two torpedoes and was heavily damaged. An escort then looked for the submarine (they managed to break away to make the report).

USS Thresher (CDR Berg) attacked an escorted freighter near Roi-Namur. The torpedoes missed and the submarine was undetected but unable to reposition for another attack.

USS S-40 (LCDR Lucker) attacked an escorted convoy near Pescadores. The torpedoes missed and they were attacked by an enemy destroyer. They dove deep and slowly broke from the area to make the report. They also reported that they are heading to Subic Bay to refuel and rearm (they only have a "few" torpedoes left). They will run in during the night hours; the shore facilities at Subic Bay were hit hard (see the report below).

HAWAII

There were no major reports for the operational area around Hawaii today. No confirmed sightings of submarines or any enemy aircraft. This is a welcome report.

BROADER PACIFIC OCEAN

There was some bad news in this area.

Guam was hit by a couple of raids, one of them was a mixed medium bomber and carrier based aircraft attack that caused considerable damage to the facilities at the base. It is still unknown when the Japanese are planning to invade the island.

Ocean Island (also known as Banaba Island) was invaded by Japanese troops. I remembered that historically this didn't happen for a long time, like the summer of 1942; this is more proof that I have changed the timeline. At any rate, it is unknown how many enemy troops are on the island. It will surely fall.

PHILIPPINE ISLAND OPERATIONS

A large air strike hit the port facilities at Subic Bay. A total of 33 bombers (mix of Sally and Betty types) came in at only 6000' and hit the ships and port facilities located there. A full list of damaged ships is not available, but the report that came in used the word "catastrophic". Many of the smaller ships were destroyed outright (PT boats, patrol boats and the like). It was known that there was extensive damage to the port area. We were standing by for further reports.

Figure 24 - Japanese Sally Medium Bomber

Clark Field was hit by a fairly large raid. The 20th Pursuit Squadron managed to get a single P-40 Warhawk into the air. This fighter was bounced by "many" Zero fighters but still managed to put some machine gun rounds into a medium bomber (probably a Sally).

There was some small unit action at Lingayen on Luzon, but the Japanese did not seem to be putting forth any major probing actions at this time. The Philippine Army units were digging in and trying to get more information on enemy intentions.

CHINESE THEATER

There were reports of ground combat at Canton, Hwaiyin, Hwainan, Lang Son, Kweisui, Loyang and Kaifeng.

Loyang has a major concentration of troops for the Chinese. They are hoping to smash a Japanese drive in this area.

British and Allied Operations

Hudson and Blenheim medium bombers from Singapore executed a raid against enemy shipping at Kota Bharu. They came in at 6000' but did not hit any ships. Of note, it appeared that escort ships were scarce in the area. This may allow the British to do a quick run with fast ships in the manner of Kuching from last week. The British Liaison Officer smiled at this report.

There was a confirmed report of an enemy heavy cruiser at Kuching. It appears that the Japanese have finally provided serious escorts to the shipping in the area.

Not surprisingly, Kuantan was hit again by several raids. Total number of enemy bombers is unknown but the radio report said the raids were "substantial". The British Liaison Officer didn't seem happy about the reports from there.

Sambas was under attack yet again today. There were invasion ships unloading troops along with some fire support from destroyers and light cruisers. By the end of the day, nearly 700 enemy troops were estimated to be in the vicinity. No enemy ships were damaged but several of the landing boats were shot up by defenders on the beaches. Friendly bombers from Singapore attacked the enemy shipping but no hits were noticed and one of the Blenheim bombers was damaged (but managed to make it back to base). However, for now, the defenders were holding.

Georgetown was captured by enemy troops today in a determined assault. The majority of the friendly troops were support types for the airfield. Quite a few managed to escape off the island and head north. It is unknown how many survivors or casualties there were, but at last count, there were a total of 1500 friendly troops at that location.

The approaches to Temuloh Base was attacked as well. This base is located on the main road between Kuala Lumpur and Kota Bharu. All that was known was that several hundred dead and wounded were suffered and that the remaining troops were retreating towards the Base. This is not a good thing; there are few troops to defend Kuala Lumpur so Temuloh Base will have to be defended.

Mergui was attacked by a total of around 50 medium bombers with fighter escorts. They were specifically attacking the troop concentrations around the base while trying to leave the base unscathed. This indicates that they plan to use the facilities in the future if they manage to take the base. The base commander radioed that he had 12 dead and 54 wounded. He asked permission to retreat to the north if enemy forces attacked.

INTELLIGENCE

Radio signals were detected and some traffic decrypted concerning a mortar regiment that is being detailed to help out at Lingayen. This would indicate a general buildup of forces there meant to push out the Philippine units there.

The name of a patrol boat that was sunk near Madang on the 19th was decrypted. The ship was called the Chokai Maru (830 ton small patrol boat). This ship was confirmed sunk by Japanese radio traffic by Australian ships.

It was determined that a "large convoy" was attacked by submarines near Balabac. It seems that the Japanese thought that they were under attack by several submarines, not just USS Skipjack. Ships were confirmed sunk but the names were not yet available. LCDR Freeman must have given them hell.

The only other report was that there was an unusual amount of radio traffic coming from Truk. The messages have not yet been decoded.

THEORIES AND INTENTIONS

The taking of Ocean Island is purely strategic. If they choose to fortify the island, it will require supply convoys to head further south before heading to Australia from the West Coast. The Operations team was divided on whether or not we needed to take it back. It may be possible to detail the 8th Marine Regiment to this task, but we still weren't sure if the Japanese would re-invade Wake Island or not.

Now that Georgetown has fallen, the Malayan Peninsula has strategically been cut in half. Any British or Allied troops south of there can now only be supplied by ships coming into Singapore and that will be difficult at best.

LATE DAY REPORTS

Three light freighters arrived at Soerabaja from the Philippines. They were the SS Escalante, SS Sarangami and SS Taurus. They managed to bring along some ammunition and torpedoes from the stores at Manila. This will help alleviate some of the supply problems but the main shipment from the US will not be there for several weeks. In the meantime, they are being unloaded to the shore facilities and being readied for US ships at Soerabaja. CAPT Rooks was very pleased and sent a radio message that indicated they had roughly one and a half reloads available for all ships (critically short is 8" ammunition, but there was an abundance of 6" ammunition and 4" ammunition). USS Houston will have a partial reload if they go completely empty.

Reports from Manila indicate that the damage to the port facilities at Subic Bay was extensive. They can take small ships and submarines, but all of the large ships were burning and there were hundreds of casualties. A full accounting was not possible at this time due to continuing air attacks and the massive level of damage. Not good at all. However, they should be able to refuel and rearm the submarine USS S-40 when they get there in a couple of days.

With that, I left for the day, had some dinner and walked along the road for some exercise. I was mentally exhausted and sleep came quickly when I got to my bungalow.

DECEMBER 24, 1941   DAY 18 OF THE WAR

The morning brief began with ADM Nimitz in attendance; he told us that much had happened during the night and new orders were to be going out this morning. With that, the report began with the Operations Officer taking the floor.

First was a report from Asiatic Fleet Headquarters that they were going to close up shop and try to head to Soerabaja. They also reported that the submarine USS S-40 was going to Subic Bay to refuel, resupply and then head to Soerabaja. They would take some of the staff with them.

A further report indicated that enemy troops were massing at Lucena south of Manila and were planning to attack. The 51st Philippine Army Division was defending the area while waiting for reinforcements. The division itself was accepting reservists and was short of artillery but did have a battalion of 75mm pack guns available. It would be a near thing if an attack materialized.

Next was the report that 7 older destroyers were being sent from Pearl Harbor to San Francisco for further anti-submarine operations on the West Coast. The ships being dispatched were:

- USS Allen
- USS Talbot
- USS Dent
- USS Crosby
- USS Kennison
- USS Crane
- USS Kilty

Also being dispatched were 5 destroyers to San Diego for the purpose of joining the carrier USS Yorktown when she leaves dry dock. Those ships dispatched were:

- USS Ralph Talbot
- USS Patterson
- USS Jarvis
- USS McCall
- USS Maury

Word came from Wake Island that the submarines had dropped off their supplies and were now heading back to Pearl Harbor. In total, nearly 90 tons of food, medical supplies and ammunition were delivered. More was needed however, and the submarines USS Tambor, USS Gar and USS Grayling were loading up with supplies this morning to head out to Wake Island. They were also loaded with food, medical supplies and small caliber ammunition. It should take them several days to get there. In addition, MAJ Deveraux asked for even more supplies to be ready for another invasion. I personally doubted whether or not a ship would be sent until the danger level had dropped. The 1st Marine Defense Battalion had a full load of small caliber ammunition and there was food enough to build up a reserve.

ADM Nimitz then reported that a total of 10 civilian freighters were ordered to transit the Panama Canal for use in the Pacific Theater. They should be arriving in San Francisco from the Canal in the next couple of weeks. Reinforcements were finally coming. There was no word yet on additional combat ships or aircraft.

West Coast command notified us that 4 tankers were to begin shuttle runs to Pearl Harbor from San Francisco. They began loading today. Also, 4 tankers were to make the long haul from San Francisco to Sydney with a stop off at Pearl Harbor to refuel. They were also loading today.

Additionally, five more civilian freighters were detailed to begin shuttle runs to Pearl Harbor with general supplies, ammunition, food and sundries. They were also loading today.

The British Liaison Officer reported that the freighter SS Steel Worker should be arriving at Pago Pago in the next 24 hours to resupply our troops there. The trip for the freighter was blissfully uneventful.

The next report from the British concerned the 1st Australian Division. Their task force was now passing Rockhampton heading north to Port Moresby. They should reach Port Moresby in the next 5 days.

Next came reports about the cruiser force that had attacked Madang. The cruisers had arrived safely at Sydney and were refueling and rearming. They also needed a few repairs – these would take a couple of days.

Last on the list concerned Singapore. The commander there was sending the light cruisers HMS Danae and HMS Mauritius to Sambas to break up the invasion forces there; Task Force 170 under the command of CAPT Stevens. The destroyers HMS Stronghold, HMS Isis, HMS Express, HMS Encounter and HMS Tenedos were to head to Kota Bharu to break up shipping there; Task Force 260 under the command of CDR Swinley.

Figure 25 - HMS Danae (D44)

With the completion of the report, we were to work on further orders and to stand by for reports. I just had some toast with jam and a glass of orange juice and went to work. So much for a quiet Christmas Eve.

OPERATION BUCK

Task Force Rogers is continuing transit back to Pearl Harbor. Only normal reports were received. Nothing out of the ordinary.

SUBMARINE OPERATIONS

There were no enemy submarine attacks made today. This is always good news.

Northeast of Bikini Island USS Thresher attacked an escorted enemy freighter hitting it with three torpedoes and watching it sink through the periscope. The submarine then continued its patrol. This report was sent to the intelligence crew.

A report arrived from USS S-36 from their attack against an escorted freighter near Swatow. They hit the ship with a single torpedo and then broke from the area. The report stated that they were sure that the ship later sank (though there was not a visual of the sinking). This report was also sent to the intelligence crew.

HAWAII

With the destroyers leaving Pearl Harbor, they were all that was tracked leaving the area. No enemy ships, submarines or aircraft were seen.

BROADER PACIFIC OCEAN

Guam was attacked by a concentrated carrier air strike. Nearly 70 level and dive bombers attacked escorted by almost 30 fighters. They were attacking the base perimeter and defense emplacements. They were leaving the airfield itself alone.

Another attack occurred on a small island – Canton Island was attacked by a landing force that came out of nowhere. There is a small force of Navy support personnel at the base with a couple of gun emplacements. They fired on the landing troops but to little avail. It is unknown how many troops were landed and it was highly unlikely that we could get reinforcements to the island to help. It looks like another defeat.

PHILIPPINE ISLAND OPERATIONS

Manila has a couple of smaller airfields in the general area; Nichols and Nielson. Both were hit today along with a strike against the port (yet again) and a smaller strike against Clark Field. In total, over 100 fighters and medium bombers hit the targets. The air units left in the area were incapable of getting any fighters into the air.

The port was hit especially hard. There is scarcely a ship left that is not damaged and the piers suffered some damage as well. The piers and loading equipment are taking priority to prepare for the submarines that are going to come to the port to reload and take off senior staff members. A full accounting of the damage was not yet available, but GEN MacArthur was not one to state "catastrophic damage" very lightly.

There were no reports of ground combat, but the commander on the scene at Lingayen reported that additional

Japanese forces had arrived. He thought that they were cavalry/recon assets to begin patrols to see where his lines were.

CHINESE THEATER

There were reports of ground combat at Hwaiyin, Canton, Lang Son, Kweiseui, Loyang and Kaifeng. In all cases, reports indicated that the Chinese forces were holding the line. There were also reports of air strikes against Chinese forces on the ground. No specifics were available.

BRITISH AND ALLIED OPERATIONS

Singapore was attacked overnight by a small force of enemy medium bombers. They caused no damage but did wake everyone up.

Kuantan was attacked by several air raids during the day; this is not surprising. In all, almost 170 medium bombers attacked over 5 separate raids all of which were escorted. The airfield was hit yet again and heavily damaged though the ground crews were not working very hard at repairing the runway (there were no aircraft left stationed there).

A patrol plane noted the appearance of a Japanese battleship at Kuching (it was reported as the Haruna, but this has not been confirmed).

Mergui was attacked yet again by a fairly large raid of 30 medium bombers with fighter escort. They seem to be attacking the support section of the base targeting troops and equipment on the ground. The raid came in at an estimated 7000' and caused some casualties on the ground (the commander on the scene said he had 27 wounded).

Intelligence

LCDR Rochefort looked tired as usual… he had a large stack of papers with him as he came in.

The first report concerned the attack by our forces at Kuching back on the 19th. A couple more ships were identified that were sunk by our forces, the Gyokurei Maru a light freighter of 1650 tons displacement and the Asahisan Maru, a 3675 ton freighter.

They had information that had identified the *Kido Butai* in the vicinity of Saipan based on radio intercepts. He had no information regarding where they were going or what their mission was.

Theories and Intentions

There are no new intentions noticed as we do not know where the *Kido Butai* is heading. The only major change was that the Japanese are now specifically targeting the port facilities near Manila. The Operations Officer did not look happy about this.

Late Day Reports

As it turns out, the port facilities near Cavite Base were worse than we thought. The submarine tender USS Canopus was destroyed along with almost all the PT boats that were stationed there. The British motor gun boats that had escaped from Hong Kong were destroyed as well. All of the freighters had some damage and most of them were sunk. There were two troop transports stationed there that were destroyed. All told, nearly 30000 tons of our shipping was now sitting at the bottom of the harbor. There was little that could be done.

The submarine USS S-37 reached Soerabaja. CDR Easton estimated three days for repairs. A rollup of the submarine's patrol will be sent up the chain soon.

Submarines also reached Bataan Peninsula with much needed food and small arms ammunition. It should take them about a day to unload everything after which they will head back to Soerabaja for further orders.

I was tired. It was depressing because it's Christmas Eve. Real war. Nobody is happy.

DECEMBER 25, 1941   DAY 19 OF THE WAR

MORNING BRIEF

Merry Christmas. A happy one to be sure; sarcasm noted.

ADM Nimitz brought us all some wine to be shared at the end of our shift. A rumor abounded about a turkey dinner at the Officer's Club. Either way, it was still 12 hours off.

Here at Pearl Harbor, the 4th Marine Defense Battalion and the 2nd Marine Engineer Regiment were told to begin packing up for transport to Christmas Island (the irony was palatable). At the same time, the fleet cargo ship USS Castor with an escort of three destroyers USS Dunlap, USS Fanning and USS Mahan were to bring cargo, building supplies and other sundries for the Marines to begin fortifying the Island. ADM Nimitz broke in at this point to let us all know that this was under his direct orders because he thought that the Japanese would try to take the island to further isolate Australia.

A roll up report came from the submarine USS S-37. CDR Easton's report shows only one enemy freighter attacked; a kill could not be confirmed as of yet. They were going to repair and await further orders.

Reports from the Philippines indicated that the Japanese were consolidating their gains while preparing for the next push. Our troops were digging in and trying to prepare for an assault. The problem is one of air cover; most of the fighters stationed there have been destroyed or are out of commission for lack of parts. Aside from the small amounts of supplies that submarines could bring in, there was going to be great difficulty trying to get them resupplied. Some on the staff thought that the Philippines were being written off altogether.

A report came in early this morning from CAPT Rooks at Soerabaja on Java. It stated that the Dutch were sending a submarine to patrol east of Borneo in the Celebes Sea. The submarine was the HNLMS KXIV.

The British Liaison Officer reported that he thought that surface forces should be reaching Sambas and Kota Bharu today. They were to attack enemy shipping and then fall back to Singapore.

With the end of the report, ADM Nimitz wished us all a merry Christmas. At that point, LCDR Rochefort came in and said that there is a "lot of radio activity near Kota Bharu". The British must have arrived. We then went to work.

Operation Buck

Task Force Rogers is continuing transit back to Pearl Harbor. Only normal reports were received. They should be back at Pearl Harbor in the next 72 hours.

Submarine Operations

There were no reports of attacks by any submarines today, either ours or theirs. Just routine reports.

Hawaii

There were no reports around Hawaii.

BROADER PACIFIC OCEAN

Guam was hit by several raids during the day, a mix of medium bombers and carrier based aircraft. Over 130 aircraft were over Guam during the day. There were some casualties on the ground and there was little that could be done to alleviate the situation.

Canton Island and Ocean Island were still under attack and the Japanese were landing more forces to take the islands. Again, there was little that could be done. Personally, I thought that Canton Island should be retaken but few on the staff agreed with me.

PHILIPPINE ISLAND OPERATIONS

Clark Field came under a massive air raid. The runways were heavily cratered and the base facilities were more or less completely destroyed. The supply dump took a few hits that started another large fire; it's unknown how many supplies were lost. There are no fighter aircraft left to get into the air. There was nothing that could be done.

The small airfields outside of Manila were hit by smaller air raids that had little effect because there were no aircraft at the sites. It is unlikely that the damage will be repaired.

A new development concerned a large carrier based raid against facilities at Butuan on the Island of Mindanao. This could be the first part of an operation to begin the liquidation of Mindanao.

CHINESE THEATER

There was a report that a Japanese assault was stopped cold just west of Canton. A full report was not known but the Japanese forces in the area did not seem to be advancing. There were also reports of combat at Hwaiyin, Hwainan, Kweisui, Lang Son, Loyang and Kaifeng. There were additional reports of heavy Japanese air activity all along the Chinese Front.

BRITISH AND ALLIED OPERATIONS

As best we could tell, the British destroyers had arrived in the vicinity of Kota Bharu overnight. They formed up into a forward/aft line and followed the lead ship into the fray. They had found a fairly large group of ships at 2300 local time and attacked. The initial reports indicated that there were 5 freighters escorted by a couple of destroyers and a small escort.

The first two destroyers were tasked with attacking enemy escorts while the following three destroyers were ordered to hit the freighters. Reports indicated that the two destroyer type ships were sunk along with two of the freighters (combination of torpedo and shell hits). The remaining freighters were damaged and the small escort was hit by a single shell.

There were quite a few ships in the harbor area that were shot at in no particular manner, but a couple of other freighters were damaged by a few shells. However, there was a particularly large freighter that drew shots from all five destroyers (the ship was burning brightly, but did not sink). However, the destroyers did not want to get too close to the harbor if there were shore batteries ready to fire, so they headed north for about an hour and then turned around to head back to Singapore.

Figure 26 - HMS Tenedos (H04)

After turning around to head back the force ran into a small destroyer escorting a single freighter. Between small caliber shots (20mm anti-aircraft guns used to fire at the enemy ships) up to 4.7" quick firing main guns, the freighter and small destroyer were shot up and were sunk with visual confirmation.

The destroyers are at full speed and heading back to air cover provided by the fighters based at Singapore. The only damage to the destroyers reported was a single non-critical hit against the HMS Tenedos. A success! Sadly, that was the only good news for the British.

The light cruisers heading to Sambas to attack shipping saw a battleship at 26000 yards... they wisely declined to attack and turned back to Singapore at full speed.

Singkawang, which is a city on the far western end of the Island of Borneo came under intense air attack during the day. This city will probably be the next target if the Japanese manage to take Sambas to the northeast. Three separate raids hit the area during the day totaling around 100 medium bombers. The port area was hit as well as the small airstrip just outside the city. No enemy bombers were shot down or even damaged.

Ground combat continued at Sambas with the tactical situation approaching a stalemate. An attack by Japanese troops was stopped with losses by a battalion of infantry in the outskirts of Sambas.

Blenheim and Hudson bombers took off from Singapore to attack enemy shipping at Kuching. They came in at 6000' to attack some freighters. No hits were scored on the freighters and four of the Blenheim bombers were damaged to some extent.

Meanwhile, back on the Malayan Peninsula, Japanese troops had moved down the coast from Alor Star and attacked Taiping. In this case, the Japanese were stopped cold with casualties. It seemed like the Japanese had attacked with light screen infantry followed by light tanks. Machinegun fire had separated the infantry from the tanks and then both were defeated piecemeal. It is unlikely that the Japanese will make the same mistake twice. Unknown numbers of troops are coming down from Kota Bharu.

Further up the coast the areas of Tavoy and Mergui came under air attack. At Tavoy, the Japanese were attacking the town itself while at Mergui they were specifically targeting the small base there (just like yesterday). This is also probably part of their plan to move troops up towards India.

At Kuantan, a single raid of 26 bombers (as reported by the troops on the ground) unescorted by fighters had attacked the port yet again. This attack added to the general destruction of the port facilities. There were also reports of Japanese patrols coming out of the jungle from the northwest.

INTELLIGENCE

The only report concerned the action at Kota Bharu. There was a lot of radio traffic from the area from both Army and Navy commands. Apparently, there were thousands of casualties from reinforcements arriving on the freighters that were struck by the British destroyers. Best estimates from the Army intercepts showed 6300 casualties, the majority of them killed. It is unknown which enemy ground units were affected by the sea battle, but it should be considered a victory for the defense of Singapore.

LCDR Rochefort hoped to have more information for the staff meeting tomorrow.

THEORIES AND INTENTIONS

New attacks at Mindanao indicate a new objective for the Japanese High Command. No invasion forces were seen, but carrier strikes are a strong indicator.

More attacks up the Malayan Peninsula show that they plan to move both up and down the Peninsula. It is unknown how long Taiping can hold out, but they did manage to stop the Japanese advance for now.

LATE DAY REPORTS

There was a rollup of United States aircraft destroyed or written off since the beginning of the war and a list of what was available in reserve. Though the war had only been going on for 19 days, the losses were bad, a total of 237 aircraft:

-   P-40 Warhawk variants: 100

- Catalina variants: 42
- P-35 fighter: 22
- SBD Dauntless variants: 20
- B-17 bomber variants: 17
- P-36 Hawk fighter: 14
- B-18 Bolo bomber: 10
- F4F3 Wildcat fighter: 6
- A-20 Havoc bomber: 5
- F2A-3 Buffalo fighter: 1

From the rollup of reserves available the Navy and Marine Corps have the following in reserve:

- F2A-2 Buffalo fighter: 7
- F2A-3 Buffalo fighter: 13
- F3F-3 Wildcat fighter: 12
- Catalina variants: 2
- SBD-2 Dauntless: 3
- SBD-3 Dauntless: 4

The Army Air Forces have worked up a reserve… a grand total of a single P-39D Airacobra. Industry is slowly working up, but it's going to be a long time before we have a sizeable reserve.

Stateside, a report came in that the 140th Infantry Regiment reported they are ready for duty. They're a National Guard unit that is part of the 35th Infantry Division. They are training on the West Coast and providing local defense for now… if memory serves, that Infantry Division goes to Europe.

Other reports showed that there was an inordinate amount of enemy shipping located at Kuching. Also present seemed to be an enemy battleship.

The British Liaison Officer reported that the HMS Mauritius needs to go to the drydock for about four days to fix some unknown problems; at least the British Liaison Officer did not know what the problem was.

He also reported that the 46th Indian Brigade arrived on station at Semarang on the Island of Java and was preparing defensive positions.

A report came in from Asiatic Fleet HQ at Manila that the submarine USS S-41 completed replenishment and was heading to Soerabaja. They also took 20 staff personnel for the trip.

With that, a very busy Christmas ended. When I got to my bungalow, there was a bottle of beer with a ribbon on it from LCDR Rochefort. I laughed as I drank it and listened to Christmas music on the radio. I then went to sleep.

MORNING BRIEF

The Operations Officer looked very tired this morning. One of the other staffers told me that he was called in to help with the night shift because of all the traffic coming from Stateside. ADM Nimitz also looked tired this morning.

First up on the list was a local mission handed down to the civilian freighter SS Laida; they were to load up with supplies for Hilo so that the cargo planes could stand down for repair and for the pilots to get a little rest.

Continuing with local issues the Operations Officer notified us that USS Castor was well out to sea with attending destroyers to deliver building supplies, food, ammunition and other sundries to Christmas Island in anticipation of the Marines being stationed there. Along those lines, reports from the 4th Marine Defense Battalion and the 2nd Marine Engineering Regiment showed that they should be ready to pack up onto transports mid-day tomorrow. COL Fassett (commander of the 4th Marine Defense Battalion) was in attendance in this morning's meeting and was in a closed door session with ADM Nimitz after the briefing.

Task Force Rogers was still transiting back to Pearl Harbor and there were no known problems or concerns since change of shift yesterday.

A report from the Philippines indicated that the submarine USS S-40 also completed replenishment at Subic Bay and was heading down to Soerabaja to await further orders.

Next came all the reports and work concerning orders and requests from the War Department and the West Coast.

First on the list was a message that eight more freighters were being detailed to the Pacific Theater. They were crossing the Panama Canal and were to head to San Francisco to await further orders from West Coast Command. It's important to note that while West Coast Command was technically under ADM Nimitz's command, they still had to check with the War Department on certain issues. This made for some of the problems that we have been dealing with.

Second on the list, the fleet cargo ships USS Bellatrix, USS Betelgeuse and USS Arcturus were ordered to leave San Diego and head to Pearl Harbor to be under Pacific Ocean Area Command (ADM Nimitz's technical name for his command).

Third, four civilian freighters were tasked with providing all types of supplies for the Australians. They were to leave San Diego, refuel at Pearl Harbor, and then head to Sydney via the long route south to avoid any Japanese ships. When one of the staffers asked why, the next item came up.

Fourth: The 31st Pursuit Group (P-39 fighters) and the 22nd Bombardment Group (B-26 Marauder medium bombers) were to begin heading to San Francisco to be loaded up and sent to Australia. More than likely, when they get to Australia they would then head up to Port Moresby. When the US Forces got there from the transports last week, there were a lot of ground crews among the troops. Politically it was decided to help out there since Australia can't be allowed to come under invasion. It will still take a few weeks to get those forces there, but it is a good show of faith with our Allies. The British Liaison Officer nodded in agreement.

Fifth and finally: ADM Nimitz was "requested" to provide some ships to go along with the heavy cruiser USS Pensacola that was escorting the troops transports to Port Moresby. It was decided that Task Force 113 under the command of CAPT Dawley would be created consisting of the light cruisers

USS Raleigh and USS Detroit escorted by the destroyers USS Cummings, USS Drayton and USS Lamson. Task Force 113 would then meet with USS Pensacola and stand by for further orders. Supplies for those ships would also be in the freighters making runs to Sydney.

With that, the British Liaison Officer began his report. The 1st Australian Division was now passing Cairns on their way to Port Moresby. They should be at Port Moresby to begin unloading in the next 72 hours.

It was also reported that the Australian Command was moving the fully replenished cruiser force north to Townsville to be ready for quick strikes. The port facilities there are adequate but they will require some work at one of the piers in order to be able to transfer the larger main gun rounds to the heavy cruisers. This will take time but it still allows the cruisers to react quicker to enemy advances.

Lastly, there were reports that more merchant ships and a few armed merchant cruisers were assembling at Cape Town awaiting the US convoy with supplies for the forces at Soerabaja on Java. The US convoy will have about 100,000 tons of supplies for CAPT Rooks' ships. The British will 'combat load' the ships and may have to take a couple of trips to get all the supplies to Java (with space for British and Dutch sundries as well). It's going to be a big undertaking.

With that, breakfast was served. I quickly shook hands with COL Fassett and wished him luck. We had a toast to victory with orange juice and then I left the area to head to my desk for work.

OPERATION BUCK

No updates for Operation Buck. Task Force Rogers is proceeding as planned to Pearl Harbor.

SUBMARINE OPERATIONS

The destroyer USS Cushing was on patrol about 75 nautical miles from the border of Oregon and Washington State when she was attacked by an enemy submarine. The destroyer was hit aft of the beam on the starboard side. Several of the crew were killed (first count is 17 killed and 39 wounded) but most made it off the destroyer as she sank. Catalina flying boats are picking up survivors. The ship was torpedoed at 1600 local and sank at around 1730. The commanding officer was confirmed as the last soul off the ship.

Figure 27 - USS Cushing (DD-376)

The submarine USS Seal sent a report that they had gotten into a duel with a Japanese patrol boat. A couple of torpedoes were fired for no hits and the patrol boat had attacked them with depth charges. There was no damage to either side.

More bad news as the unescorted group of four freighters detailed to resupply Australia were attacked by an enemy submarine just south of San Clemente Island on the California coast. The freighter SS Steel Ranger took a hit from a torpedo at roughly 1300 local that caused the ship to slowly sink (the ship slipped under the waves at around 1530 local). All but three of the crew managed to abandon ship and the lifeboats were seen by a Catalina flying boat approaching San Clemente.

Not a good day for us on submarine operations.

HAWAII

There was nothing significant to report around Hawaii today.

BROADER PACIFIC OCEAN

Radio operators at Ocean Island sent a final message that the Japanese were just outside their building and then went off the air. The Japanese now control the island.

There was a night air raid against Wake Island. Best estimates put it at roughly a squadron of medium bombers. A couple of the bombs landed on the runways and will need to be repaired.

Guam was hit by four separate raids during the day, three in the morning and one in the afternoon. Three of the raids were from carrier based aircraft and the first of the day was from land based bombers. They were attacking the port facilities and the troop concentrations leaving the runway alone. There were a few wounded on the ground but there were scarce anti-aircraft guns so the attacks were relatively unscathed.

Philippine Island Operations

There were some night air attacks against the city of Manila. A few fires were started but they were put out relatively quickly. It is unknown if this was by accident or purposeful (the bombing target).

Shortly after sunrise a large raid hit Clark Field, roughly 40 medium bombers escorted by 30 or so fighters. They did extensive damage to the runway and damaged more of the support facilities. In an odd twist of fate, they are actually helping us by destroying these facilities because base personnel were ordered to destroy anything that couldn't be carried (hence, no further repairs will be done).

At about the same time, a strike by carrier based aircraft hit the small airfield near the city of Davao on Mindanao. The runway was hit a few times as well as the support facility. Casualties were unknown. The report stated that the enemy bombers came in level at high altitude (estimates were 18000' or so). This reduced accuracy of the bombers but put them at an altitude where ground fire could not hurt them.

Roughly at noon, a strike hit Nichols Field outside of Manila. The runway was heavily damaged but the facilities did not get damaged. There were around 30 medium bombers in that raid.

Starting around 0800 local, the areas around Cabanatuan came under assault by several thousand enemy troops with artillery. The 91st Philippine Army Division was completely overwhelmed and were forced to retreat towards Clark Field with heavy losses. As it turns out, the division was only 2300 strong and waiting for reservists when they were attacked. They suffered over 1100 casualties in the defense and the retreat; including an entire battalion of 2.95" pack guns. Not good at all.

South on Luzon, the Japanese troops attacked the area around Lucena trying to push up north. The 51ˢᵗ Philippine Army Division put up a well disciplined and tough defense that stopped the Japanese cold. It was more of a terrain issue for the defenders since the approach to Lucena was a narrow isthmus. This allowed them to concentrate artillery fire and machine gun fire. For now, the 51ˢᵗ can hold.

CHINESE THEATER

There were reports of combat at Wenchow, Kweiteh, Canton, Kaifeng, Loyang, Kweisui, Lang Son, Hwainan and Hwaiyin. Wenchow must have been pretty bad because information reached us that Japanese troops had pushed out the Chinese Army units there. No word on casualties as usual. ADM Nimitz was trying to get the State Department to get more information.

BRITISH AND ALLIED OPERATIONS

Singkawang came under attack again by Japanese bombers. This time a few fighters managed to get into the air and attack the unescorted bombers. A raid by 40 Betty bombers was attacked by three B-339D fighter aircraft (B-339D was a "de-navalized" version of the Buffalo fighter sold to the Dutch and British). They managed to shot down one of the Betty bombers and damage two more. Two other raids hit the airfield while the aircraft were being rearmed and refueled. No damage occurred to the fighters but the runway required four hours of work before aircraft could use it to take off.

Figure 28 - British B-339D Fighters

Kuantan was hit by three more raids today that were unopposed. The ground crews were no longer trying to repair the damage. Concerns were raised that Japanese troops were seen to the northwest. This could indicate an imminent ground attack.

INTELLIGENCE

LCDR Rochefort came in for the 1600 brief and told us that he had some more information.

First was that there was information concerning the Japanese 24th Infantry Regiment. They had received orders to prepare to attack against Davao. Their current location was unknown (whether or not the regiment was shipboard or currently on Luzon).

Also with regards to ground intelligence, elements of the Japanese 12th Division were onboard troop transports heading towards San Fernando on Mindanao.

He also had information regarding enemy shipping. There were no updates about the *Kido Butai*. They were looking for more information. However, there were updates as to Japanese ship losses on the 21st:

- Sub Chaser CHa-14 (99 tons) sunk at Kuching by the British
- Freighter Sinno Maru (4875 tons) sunk at Kuching by the British
- Freighter Saiho Maru (4875 tons) sunk at Kuching by the British
- Patrol Boat Kantori Maru (830 tons) sunk at Kuching by the British

From our submarines:

- Josho Maru (3675 tons) sunk by USS Tarpon near Groot Natoena
- Kiyozumi Maru (3425 tons) sunk by USS Skipjack near Balabac

The intelligence crew also noted that the USS Skipjack had sunk a couple of other ships and the crew was looking for information on them. There was no other major information that the intelligence crew could provide.

THEORIES AND INTENTIONS

It seems that strikes against Mindanao in the Philippines are intended to soften things up in preparation for an invasion. The intelligence report about the Japanese 12th Division corroborates the theory that Mindanao is the next target.

The staff is working hard to try to find weak spots against the enemy outside of submarine attacks against the supply lines. There are talks of a counter invasion at Canton Island; this may be rejected because Wake Island is still vulnerable. ADM Nimitz is still concerned about the material condition of the fleet overall and is looking for locations to attack the enemy where we have local superiority. I was thinking that even if we could find parity it would be worthwhile. At least supplies are now moving from the continental United States to the war zones. We have to make sure those supplies will be used wisely.

LATE DAY REPORTS

The Harbor Master reported that repairs to the USS Taney (formerly the USCGC Taney) were completed and the ship is ready for operations. The ship was formally taken in for service by the US Navy.

There were late patrol reports about a couple of separate Japanese surface groups halfway between Truk and Guam. Direction and speed were unknown.

There were at least 12 enemy ships in the vicinity of Rabaul. Apparently, a few of the troops stayed behind with a crank operated radio to report from time to time on Japanese force structures in the area. Very dangerous work, but may be the difference in giving us an edge.

A British patrol aircraft noted "many many" ships in the area of Kuching. This could indicate consolidation or as a jumping off point for new assaults. There is also a confirmed report of at least one battleship.

Task Force 260 (five destroyers) under CDR Swinley arrived safely at Singapore and are replenishing in anticipation of further orders.

A transport force arrived at Batavia on Java loaded with a couple of British Infantry Brigades and a recon battalion. It is unknown where the troops will be sent.

Lastly, at 1830 as I was leaving for the day, LCDR Rochefort came in to report that they had some "strong evidence" that the *Kido Butai* is more than likely in the Celebes Sea. This could indicate a foray into the Java Sea area. This may be a good reason to sortie additional submarines from Soerabaja.

I left with LCDR Rochefort and grabbed a quick dinner. LCDR Rochefort asked my opinion about the *Kido Butai*. I said that historically they do attack Java, but this is an opportunity to lay down a blanket of submarines to attack the carriers.

Sleep came quickly after a long hot shower.

MORNING BRIEF

This morning was cloudy and gloomy, depressing in all truth. Didn't seem like it was going to be a good day.

The Operations Officer began this morning's report with information about the Dutch on Java. CAPT Rooks sent a report about submarine movements. The Dutch were going to flush out five of their submarines to the Makassar Straights to try to attack the *Kido Butai* if it were possible. This is a good choke point that should increase the odds of finding the enemy ships. Other submarines were also patrolling the area. Their deployment dispositions are as follows:

- HNLMS K XI would patrol the southern approaches to the Makassar Straights
- HNLMS K XII would patrol the northern approaches to the Makassar Straights
- HNLMS O19 would patrol just east of Balikpapan
- HNLMS K XVIII would patrol west of Madjene
- HNLMS K XV would patrol the east central Java Sea

The British Liaison Officer reported that more tanker assets were moving to Columbo and that fuel would be delivered there as well. Some of the tankers would be detailed to take fuel to Australia. It was dangerous to try to get tankers out of Java and Sumatra.

The British Liaison Officer also reported that the troops being unloaded at Batavia comprised the 53rd, 54th and 55th British Brigades along with the 251st Recce Battalion. There was an argument at British High Command about how to best use the troops; it revolved around massing the entire division around a single location or if the Brigades should be sent to various locations to prepare for an attack. For now, it was not fully decided.

The Operations Officer then took the floor back. He stated that the destroyers dispatched yesterday were making good time and should be on the West Coast in a couple of days or so. He also reported that the gaggle of freighters moving from Panama to San Francisco were moving at a speed of advance of 12 knots.

The last report dealt with the fleet cargo ship USS Alchiba. She was still unloading supplies at Johnston Island. The port facilities there were very rudimentary and the cargo ship was unloading by small boat. They were roughly 35% unloaded but it was going to take a good long time to take the rest of the equipment, supplies and sundries off the ship. It might be a good idea to get an engineering unit there to improve the facilities.

With that report, the day's work began after a quick breakfast.

OPERATION BUCK

Task Force Rogers was only 24 hours away from being back in Pearl Harbor.

SUBMARINE OPERATIONS

A Japanese submarine attacked and sank the MV Macdhui which was a 4480 ton passenger and cargo ship that was heading back to Sydney from Port Moresby. The ship was sunk 90 nautical miles west-northwest of Sydney and was unescorted at the time. Flying boats were heading to the area to look for survivors. Some anti-submarine assets will have to be detailed to the east coast of Australia.

There were no attack reports from friendly submarines during the day. Merely routine reports.

Figure 29 - MV Macdhui

Hawaii

No major activity at Hawaii today.

Broader Pacific Ocean

Wake Island was hit by a small night raid that managed to put a single bomb on the runway to cause some damage. The majority of the bombs fell wide of targets and landed in the ocean and in the lagoon. Later on in the morning a couple dozen Betty medium bombers attacked the airfield. The

Marines managed to repair three Wildcat fighters and engage the bombers. One Betty was shot down and two more were damaged and trailing smoke. For some reason, the bombers were flying at only 6000' which was designed to concentrate their bomb loads. This ended up working. They flew down the long axis of the runway and dropped many bombs (it seemed that they were loaded with a couple of larger bombs and a "cluster" of smaller bombs. This brought them under ground fire from M1918 3" anti-aircraft guns. One of the Betty bombers took a hit on the wing and crashed a couple of miles offshore and exploded.

Damage to the runways was pretty extensive. The fighters were almost out of fuel when enough runway space was leveled to allow them to try to land. One of the Wildcat fighters was damaged on landing and would take several days to repair.

MAJ Devereux also reported that they were still very low on supplies. The submarines on their way to the island would not be there for several days.

PHILIPPINE ISLAND OPERATIONS

Each of the small fields outside of Manila was attacked today. However, an enemy medium bomber was shot down over Nielson Field. Aside from the anti-aircraft fire from the few guns, there was little that could be done to stop the raids.

At Clark Field, another large raid damaged the facilities on the ground. There were a few casualties and none of the enemy bombers were damaged (they flew above the max ceiling of the guns).

On the southern end of Luzon at Lucena, the 51st Philippine Army Division came under an intense assault by what appeared to be a reinforced Japanese infantry division.

THE DEJA VU CHRONICLES

The 51st only had 3200 troops assembled when the attack came. It seems that the attack against them yesterday was a probing attack. Reports indicated that at least three full enemy infantry regiments attacked and were supported by artillery, recon assets and combat engineers. The 51st fell back to the north with heavy losses. Initial reports show almost 2300 casualties (killed, wounded and missing). Though the remnants of the 51st Philippine Division are falling back to some other defensive locations, the road is almost completely open for Manila to fall from the south now.

The Island of Jolo which is part of the chain that separates the Sulu Sea from the Celebes Sea saw Japanese troops landing. There are only a few locals on the island with no friendly troops. They are still transmitting for now.

Luckily, there were no major Japanese offensives north of Manila today. It still seems that they are consolidating their gains and preparing for major assaults.

CHINESE THEATER

Some information came from Chinese Communist and Nationalist sources indicating ground combat at Sinyang, Kweiteh, Canton, Kaifeng, Loyang, Kweisui, Lang Son, Hwainan, and Hwaiyin. There were no major victories or defeats and the front line seems to have stabilized somewhat.

BRITISH AND ALLIED OPERATIONS

The ground situation at Taiping looked good at the beginning of the day, but the Japanese brought up reinforcements and attacked the city again this morning. After a full day of combat, Taiping had fallen and all Allied ground units were falling back towards Singapore. A radio message was received that reported a little over 2000 casualties for Allied forces. The defense was disintegrating.

Air strikes continued on the Malayan Peninsula with Kuantan being hit by three separate raids. In one raid, nearly 70 Betty bombers were flying in formation attacking the port facilities. Casualties on the ground were at a minimum because the troops had pulled back to the edge of the jungle to the southeast of Kuantan to get better defensive positions when the Japanese either land or attack from the northwest.

Further to the north, Tavoy in Burma was attacked by roughly two dozen medium bombers. There was scratch damage to facilities on the ground and no damage to enemy bombers that were flying over the max altitude of the anti-aircraft guns to engage.

On Balikpapan on Borneo, a Japanese Invasion force had landed intent on taking the facilities. There were some shore potteries present and they got into a duel with landing ships, escorting combat ships and troops that had made it to the beach. At least one enemy freighter was seen to have hit a mine (the ship was burning brightly but was still afloat). By the end of the day, several enemy ships were damaged but none were sunk. Roughly 600 Japanese troops had made it ashore and were engaged with a battalion of Dutch infantry.

The small area of Samarinda to the northeast was attacked by carrier based aircraft; a single friendly B-339D fighter managed to get into the air and dove on the enemy dive bombers before they reached the target area. The fighter managed to shoot down a Val and was then attacked by enemy Zero fighters. The pilot dove for the deck and circled the airfield low in the coverage of friendly light anti-aircraft guns (the Zero fighters refused to head down to the deck). Further to the north, the small island of Tarakan was also attacked by enemy carrier based planes. Overall, the situation looked dire on the east coast of the Island of Borneo.

On the other side of Borneo, low level ground combat continued at Sambas. There were no major gains by either side and a situation of stalemate seems to have developed.

On the Island of Celebes proper, the area of Makassar on the extreme southeast tip was attacked by enemy carrier based aircraft as well. The port facilities took some minor damage. The enemy bombers flew level at roughly 12000' and dropped their bombs. This reduced their accuracy. An amphibious invasion at that location cannot be ruled out.

INTELLIGENCE

LCDR Rochefort did not deliver the intelligence report today. However, the officer giving the report stated there was a "high probability" based purely on signals intercepts that there were enemy carriers in the Makassar Straights. When we informed him of the attacks against Balikpapan, he stated that enemy reinforcements were already heading to that location because of "intense enemy fire on the landing boats". We were also told that there existed a high probability that major carrier based strikes will hit that location in the next 24 hours.

There was scant information on other ship kills and/or troop movements. The crew was working diligently on trying to break more messages. With that, he concluded his report.

THEORIES AND INTENTIONS

With enemy carriers in the Makassar Straight, our ships could not even attempt a sortie from Soerabaja with any hope of success of breaking up the enemy invasion at Balikpapan.

They would be sunk on the run up the Straights by the aircraft. For now, they were safe at Soerabaja; this is where they would have to stay. However, if the carriers leave the area, this would allow for a robust counter-attack strategy with quick surface forces.

With Taiping captured by the Japanese, they were only about 350 miles from Singapore with a large concentration of troops. Kuanatan was only 200 miles from Singapore, but the lack of major roads would slow down the Japanese troops. The next targets would be Temuloh Base and then Kuala Lumpur.

LATE DAY REPORTS

The only late day report that came in concerned enemy carriers in the Makassar Straights. The Operations and Intelligence groups were both trying to figure out where they were going next.

I had a quick dinner of roast beef, mashed potatoes and peas at the dining facility and then went straight to my bungalow. I was very tired.

DECEMBER 28, 1941   DAY 22 OF THE WAR

<u>MORNING BRIEF</u>

ADM Nimitz received word that ADM Kimmel had reached the War Department in Washington DC. ADM Kimmel is now working for the War Department as the Chief Operations Officer. It is expected that sometime in the next couple of weeks there would be some kind of major strategy conference. Orders were being promulgated to get GEN MacArthur out of the Philippines; he would probably go by submarine. It was suggested that the strategy conference take place in Hawaii.

With that information the Operations Officer told us that we were to start thinking about how and where we should think about striking back. The morning briefing then began.

Overnight, a couple of fleet replenishment ships (AO type ships) had arrived from the West Coast. They came into the harbor and were standing by for further orders.

The submarine USS Nautilus was to take on supplies for delivery to Wake Island. It was thought that another 40 or so tons of food and supplies could be brought by the submarine. They would put to sea in the next 24 hours.

Task Force Present was formed with a couple of light cruisers, four destroyers and seven fleet troop transports under the command of CAPT Frederick to bring the 2nd Marine Engineering Regiment and the 4th Marine Defense Battalion to Christmas Island along with more supplies to build up port facilities and the airbase there.

There were no new reports from any other groups currently out to sea; unless the groups reach their destination or there are any problems, there will not be major reports.

With that, the British Liaison Officer started his briefing. All elements of the 18th British Division were now unloading at Batavia. The individual brigades will more than likely be parceled out to likely invasion sites. Unless more troops arrive the division will not be concentrated at any one location.

The 1st Australian Division was now unloading at Port Moresby. They were unpacking equipment and working with US Forces already there to provide for an all-around defense. The artillery will be used for counter invasion with secondary positions if enemy troops come out of the jungle.

Lastly, the Dutch were going to try to sneak in a group of four destroyers to Balikpapan to break up the invasion forces. The Dutch commander thought that the small size of the destroyers along with tactical maneuvering on the way in and out would provide acceptable risk for an attack. ADM Nimitz didn't seem to agree.

The morning briefing then ended. We had a quick breakfast… I don't know who thought these were pancakes, but well, whatever.

OPERATION BUCK

Task Force Rogers should be arriving sometime today. If there are no other reports, this section of my journal should end.

SUBMARINE OPERATIONS

USS Sturgeon (LCDR Wright) managed to attack a Japanese convoy roughly halfway between the southern end of Mindanao and Sangi Island in where the Celebes Sea meets the Philippine Sea. They managed to torpedo a patrol boat (the torpedo completely destroyed the patrol boat) and a small ship that is more than likely a transport. The submarine was then attacked by a couple of destroyers. They depth charged the submarine with little effect; however, it took almost 5 hours for the submarine to break from the area to surface and recharge the batteries.

The destroyer USS Humphreys was attacked by an enemy submarine about 125 nautical miles west of Eureka, California. The destroyer was not damaged and the enemy submarine was attacked with depth charges. There was no word on damage to the enemy submarine.

HAWAII

With the exception of Task Force Present heading south to Christmas Island, there is nothing to report today.

BROADER PACIFIC OCEAN

Guam came under assault today from the sea when a formation of at least ten ships was seen on the horizon at sunrise local time. Japanese troops began the assault at 0700 local and had landed at least 600 troops despite the fire from shore batteries. It is unknown how long our troops will be able to hold out. We were trying to find information on how many troops we had on the island. It didn't look very good.

A report came in indicating that Nauru Island was being overrun by Japanese troops. The island is only 8 square miles and was administered by Great Britain, Australia and New Zealand. The troops quickly took over the island and there were no further radio reports by 1100 local time.

PHILIPPINE ISLAND OPERATIONS

More Japanese troops were landing at Jolo and there was no way to get any help for the few people on that island. They were on their own. They were still transmitting for now, but they will fall in the next couple of days.

At Nichols Field, enough parts were cannibalized to allow a few P-40's to get off the ground. They managed to surprise a strike of 20 Sally bombers escorted by 30 Nate fighters. One of the Nate fighters was shot down and a couple of the Sally bombers were damaged. The port facilities at Subic Bay were damaged again by the bombers. The fighting was severe because there was only one airworthy P-40 left at the end of the day.

Another strike hit Clark Field that was unopposed. One of the Betty medium bombers was damaged by ground fire but the airfield was extensively damaged yet again.

It was currently unknown how many troops were moving north to follow the 51st Philippine Army Division from Lucena. We were still standing by for reports concerning this division.

CHINESE THEATER

The Chinese were asking for more supplies to arm more troops. Right now there were not enough weapons and supplies for our forces. However, supplies would be going to the Chinese as soon as some were available. This did not sit well with the State Department or the War Department but President Roosevelt thought that if we armed the Chinese they would tie down even more Japanese formations. Time would tell.

There were Japanese attacks at Canton, Kaifeng, Loyang, Kweisui, Lang Son, Hwainan and Hwaiyin. The Chinese had their biggest concentration of troops at Lang Son.

BRITISH AND ALLIED OPERATIONS

The Dutch destroyers left port overnight to try to find a position where they could use the weather to their advantage at a location where they'd be able to make a high speed run into the area of Balikpapan to attack enemy transports. The problem was that the destroyers (HNLMS Evertsen, HNLMS Kortenaer, HNLMS Piet Hein and HNLMS Van Ghent) literally ran into the enemy carrier force at around 0330 local.

To the credit of the Dutch commander (CDR Velthuizen) he managed to "cross the T" which is a maneuver where he put the enemy ships on his beam while they were sailing towards him. This allowed his ships to have all gun batteries to bear on the enemy while the enemy could only use their forward guns. One may ask where the problem was; it was that the enemy force consisted of three carriers, a battleship (identified as a "Kongo" class) and at least five escorting destroyers.

The escort destroyers opened fire on the Dutch destroyers at a range of 9000 yards at which point the Dutch destroyers returned fire. The battleship opened fire as well. A single large shell from the battleship hit the HNLMS Evertsen which blew up the ship instantly. The rest of the Dutch destroyers managed to damage a couple of the Japanese destroyers and put a round into one of the carriers (CDR Velthuizen thought it was the Akagi).

The HNLMS Kortenaer and HNLMS Van Ghent each took rounds from the main guns of the enemy destroyers. By 0445 CDR Velthuizen ordered a retreat to the east in order to get away from the enemy battlegroup. The destroyers then headed back to Soerabaja and got there by around noon. Overall, the operation was a failure; one destroyer sunk and two damaged for two damaged Japanese destroyers.

Because of the overnight surface battle, the Invasion of Balikpapan went on without disruption (though a couple of the troop transports were hit by shore fire). By the end of the day, 2500 Japanese troops had landed and were engaged with a Dutch infantry battalion and the shore batteries.

The enemy carriers were not slowed down though, because there were airstrikes against Pamekasan, Balikpapan and Soerabaja. The strike against Pamekasan did scant damage, but the strike against Soerabaja did damage a couple of ships in the harbor (the destroyer HNLMS Witte de With was hit with a 60 kg bomb that damaged the deck and started a fire; the remaining ships had superficial damage only from small bombs). Anti-aircraft fire was intense from the shore facilities and from the ships in the harbor. However, only one enemy aircraft was shot down.

Figure 30 - HNLMS Evertsen (EV)

On the Malayan Peninsula, the Japanese conducted air strikes against Kuantan (two large strikes), Mergui (one large strike) and Tavoy (medium sized strike with 20 medium bombers). Kuantan was still heavily damaged and facilities at

Mergui were lightly damaged. The strike against Tavoy was relatively ineffective (casualties were light).

At Temuloh Base, some Japanese light infantry came down the road with some light tanks and were ambushed by infantry from the 2nd Argylls Battalion. They estimate that they killed 20 and wounded about 200 other Japanese troops (they also report destroying an enemy tank). The Argylls suffered 13 wounded.

Low level combat was still occurring at Sambas. There was no major change to the front lines there; it is surmised that the Japanese were trying to move troops overland from Kuching.

Intelligence

There were no new names of enemy ships sunk. The intelligence crew did note that since the carrier group in the Makassar Straight had only three carriers that the other carriers must be somewhere else. In any case, the concentration of force is more than enough to be a problem to any battlegroup that we could put out there right now (with the exception of the ENTIRE carrier force in the Pacific right now) would not be powerful enough to survive. This gives the Japanese at least two separate carrier forces that really cannot be touched.

They were woefully short on information. The decrypt crews were working as hard as they could.

Theories and Intentions

Depending on what direction the enemy carriers take will show their intentions. If they stay in the Makassar Straights, then they are supporting all operations there. If they head to the west and pass Java heading towards Singapore, then it shows where they feel they need the additional firepower. If they head east to northern Australia, there would be a separate set of problems.

LATE DAY REPORTS

There were quite a few late day reports. First concerns Task Force Rogers; they arrived in Pearl Harbor late this morning. ADM Nimitz immediately left to confer with the carrier captains. They were to refuel, rest and be ready for further operations.

The submarines USS Plunger, USS Pollack and USS Pompano arrived at Pearl Harbor as well and are replenishing in anticipation of further orders. They were in good material condition.

From the West Coast a few reports came in. First, the converted liners that had brought the 8th Marine Regiment to Pearl Harbor arrived safely in San Francisco.

Second came reports concerning more troops massing back in the Continental United States. The 144th Infantry Regiment reported that they had all of their personnel reported in and that they were standing by for more equipment and they were ready for operations at Tacoma, Washington. Down in Los Angeles, the 125th Infantry Regiment reported the same.

Also released were regiments for the 40th Infantry Division (the 160th Infantry Regiment, 185th Infantry Regiment and the 108th Infantry Regiment) for transfer to ADM Nimitz' control. They were packing up to move to San Francisco. The docks at San Francisco were also filling up with all kinds of supplies to head out to the Pacific. It was to become a very busy port.

At Soerabaja, CAPT Rooks sent a report to ensure the command that his ships were still combat ready despite the Japanese attack. The Dutch were repairing the remaining ships from the ill-fated foray to attack shipping at Balikpapan.

They had arrived right after the air attacks and reported their material condition. The HNLMS Van Ghent needed to go to the dry dock and it would take roughly six days to repair. The HNLMS Kortenar would need six days pierside and the HNLMS Piet Hein only needed one day. The HNLMS Witte de With that was hit by a 60 kg bomb would need two days to repair the damage.

At that point I took my leave. I needed a walk and some food. Dinner was so-so… ham again. Tired of ham. I must have walked at least three miles; I needed the exercise. The night air felt good. I took a long shower and promptly went to sleep.

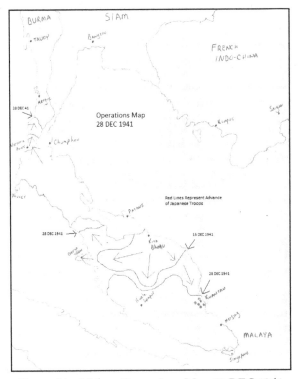

Figure 31 - Malaya Operations Map 28 DEC 1941

DECEMBER 29, 1941   DAY 23 OF THE WAR

I got up early and took another walk. It seemed to calm me down a bit. After a quick shower, I headed over to the headquarters building. ADM Nimitz was just coming in and asked how my walk was. I replied it was nice. He said he saw me as he was in his car coming back from seeing the Harbor Master. It was a nice quick chat.

The Operations Officer began the report with routine updates to forces already at sea. The groups heading to San Francisco, Christmas Island and the supplies continuing to be unloaded at Palmyra were covered, as well as some information about shipbuilding stateside.

He also reported that the material condition of the carriers was good and that the squadrons were having all of their aircraft undergoing maintenance. They should be ready to sortie again if necessary within 24 hours.

With the end of the American information, the British Liaison Officer began a lengthy report.

He began with a report from the Dutch High Command at Soerabaja. They were going to try to send another force of three destroyers to try to attack Japanese shipping at Balikpapan. ADM Nimitz looked visibly disturbed by this report. He point blank asked the British Liaison what the Dutch hoped to gain; to this ADM Nimitz received a shrug. He then motioned for the British Liaison to continue his briefing.

Next concerned the British 18th Division; they completed unloading at Batavia and the brigades received their orders. The 53rd Brigade would head to Tjepoe to dig in and prepare to repel an amphibious assault. The 54th Brigade would head to Merak to reinforce Dutch troops already there and the 55th Brigade would head east to Banjoewangi and build up defenses. The Division headquarters and the recon battalion would stay in Batavia for now.

On the Malayan Peninsula at Singapore, CDR Swinley was ordered to take four destroyers to attack enemy transports at Kota Bharu. They were taking advantage of some bad weather to hide on their way to the objective.

From the Australian Theater, the 1st Australian Division completed offloading all of their manpower at Port Moresby and the equipment was still coming off the ships. It should take a couple more days for all the equipment to be offloaded.

It was also reported that the Australian 4th Anti-Aircraft Regiment was released for transport to Port Moresby. This was welcome news because of the shortage of fighter aircraft in that area. The regiment was equipped with 36 40mm BOFORS anti-aircraft guns; a very good piece of artillery. When shipping is available, they will also move to Port Moresby.

Lastly, the Australian cruisers were going to sortie to Madang, yet again, to try to attack Japanese logistical shipping. It was dangerous but could yield excellent results.

With that, we were dismissed for the day's work.

Submarine Operations

Late this morning, USS Porpoise (CDR Brewster) came across a small convoy near Itbayat Island. They weren't in a great position (according to the report) but decided to launch an attack. They fired four torpedoes at a troop transport for no hits. The submarine was attacked by a pair of enemy destroyers; the submarine was depth charged several times for no damage and managed to break away.

USS S-39 (CDR Clark) was sighted on the surface by an enemy escort and they were forced to crash dive. They were damaged (though not severely) by a couple of close depth charges but eventually managed to slip away. CDR Clark stated that the damage was not bad enough to break away from the patrol but they would monitor the situation and provide regular reports.

There were no reported attacks against our shipping by enemy submarines.

HAWAII

There was nothing significant to report at Hawaii today.

BROADER PACIFIC OCEAN

Some enemy medium bombers visited Wake Island overnight that did not cause any damage to the base or personnel on the ground. It did, however, continue to tire the Marines on the ground due to the shaking out for battle stations overnight. No damage was scored against the enemy bombers. Shortly after sunrise, another strike hit the installations that caused quite a bit of damage to the runway and the small support facilities. There was no aviation gas to get any of the Wildcat fighters off the ground. Some needed to be delivered in order to get fighter cover up and operating again. There was also a request to provide some more anti-aircraft guns.

More enemy ships were unloading troops at Guam and the scratch troops at the various posts were beginning to take ground fire. By mid-morning, at least 6000 enemy troops were known to have landed and the radio reports were frantic. A report was received at around 1400 Guam time that indicated that they were being overrun and then the radio station went off the air. At this point it is safe to assume that Guam now belongs to the Japanese.

At Canton Island, more enemy troops were also unloading and it was unknown how long the small friendly force would last (there were only 400 lightly armed troops). When this report was given to ADM Nimitz he called for his Marine Liaison Officer to his office for a closed door session. We (Operations) then asked to see how long it would take to change the orders of the 8th Marine Regiment.

Philippine Island Operations

Clark Field fell under three separate raids that were closely spaced in the late morning. The first raid had 17 medium bombers with 10 fighters, the second had 16 medium bombers with 23 escorting fighters and the final raid had 24 medium bombers unescorted. The main damage was not to the runway but to the support facilities. There were "quite a few" casualties on the ground (reports did not indicate how many). There were no airworthy fighters at Clark Field that could get off the ground.

At around the same time that the last raid was hitting Clark Field, Subic Bay came under attack by dive bombers that caused some damage to the port facilities. One of the enemy dive bombers was damaged (the report indicated that it was a Sonia type) and there were roughly 20 wounded on the ground.

Right after noon, a strike hit Nichols Field just outside of Manila. There were enough cannibalized parts to allow a single P-40 Warhawk to get airborne. The pilot managed to do a quick diving attack against a single enemy fighter (a Nate) shooting it down. The pilot then dove for the deck to force enemy fighters to come into range of ground based machine guns if they wanted to attack. The bombers (reported as Sally types) damaged the runway and some of the support facilities. The P-40 managed to land when the fuel tanks were almost dry.

While all of these air attacks were occurring, a major assault came out of the jungle in the vicinity of Lingayen. The 11th and 21st Philippine Army Divisions initially put up a spirited defense before a massive barrage of enemy artillery shattered front line units. After the artillery barrage, almost 40 tanks came out and attacked separated platoons, companies and broke into battalion areas. The Divisions then began to fall back. It quickly turned into a rout with tanks firing on troops falling back. The survivors of the attack fell back towards Clark Field.

When reports came in, MGEN Brougher of the 11th Philippine Army Division reported that he only had 1200 men left and BGEN Capinpin reported that he only had 2600 men left. They also reported that they had lost most of their artillery and most of their supplies. If the reports were to be believed, it means that between the two divisions they lost 2100 men (the divisions were undermanned to begin with). Enemy casualties were not known but were believed to be light.

Another report came in from the troops that had retreated from Lucena yesterday. The 51st Philippine Army Division had completed their retreat to Batangas and reinforced the 41st Philippine Army Division in prepared defensive positions. MGEN Jones of the 51st Philippine Army Division reported that he had 1700 men ready for combat while MGEN Lim of the 41st Philippine Army Division reported that he had 3500 men under arms and that he was still waiting on reinforcements and additional supplies. Enemy troops were not far away preparing to attack; time was not on the side of friendly troops.

Chinese Theater

As usual there were reports of Japanese air strikes to support their ground troops; as usual we had little knowledge of their effectiveness. There were reports of combat at Kweiteh, Canton, Kaifeng, Loyang, Kweisui, Lang Son, Hwaiyin, Sinyang and Hwainan.

British and Allied Operations

Balikpapan on Borneo became the focus of much action today. The shore defenses were fairly robust with a mix of 75mm and 120mm guns in reinforced encasements. They were shelling the incoming ships when able. One of the Japanese ships was hit several times and was seen to be burning brightly; even then, the ships were still disgorging troops to assault the base forces in the area. Carrier based aircraft also attacked the facilities causing little damage during the day (the aircraft came from enemy carriers south in the Makassar Straights). The Japanese forces had landed around 1500 troops by the end of the day and there was a land battle going on between them and elements of the 6th KNIL Battalion (Dutch Infantry). It was hoped that the destroyers dispatched from Soerabaja would help break up the invasion. They should reach Balikpapan tomorrow.

On the other side of Borneo, Sambas saw more Japanese troops landed from ships offshore. It was estimated that roughly 200 more enemy troops had landed and were consolidating a beachhead so that they could push inland. The problem is that the roughly 400 friendly troops did not have the manpower or firepower to push them out. It was determined that defensive firepower would be more appropriate to keep the Japanese troops out.

The Japanese carriers in the southern Makassar Straights also completed strikes against the airfield at Makassar, port facilities at Soerabaja (no damage to friendly shipping) in addition to the aforementioned strike against Balikpapan.

On the Malayan Peninsula, there were several strikes against Kuantan. Estimates of enemy bombers during the day settled in on two large separate strikes with a combined total of 90 medium bombers and 50 escorting fighters. They simply added to the general carnage of damaged facilities on the ground. There was nothing that could be done.

Further up the peninsula, troops retreating from Victoria Point were attacked by enemy aircraft along with a small strike at Mergui. Troops were falling back on what would be a heavily defended Mergui and troops south were heading towards Singapore for a last stand. There were apparently plans being put into place to have some troops leave Singapore and have them go to Java.

INTELLIGENCE

The 1600 intelligence briefing began on time with another officer that not been seen before. His first report centered on the Japanese carriers. They were confirmed to be in the southern Makassar Straights (this we already knew). The end destination of the carriers was not yet known, but for now they were supporting ongoing operations on the east coast of Borneo. They also reported an unusually large amount of radio traffic at Truk and that the Japanese 40th Infantry Brigade was located at Truk.

There were no major reports made to confirmed sinkings of enemy ships. The crews were still working on those reports. It was thought by some on our staff that the intelligence crews were being presented with a new Japanese code; of course, we could not confirm it and the intelligence crew would not speak of it.

THEORIES AND INTENTIONS

The main thrust against the Philippines shows a pincer move coming in from the south and the north at the same time. The capture of Lingayen and the reports of enemy troops at Batangas indicate that the Japanese intend to attack Manila when both forces can attack at the same time.

The continued attacks at Canton Island (part of the Phoenix Island Chain) indicate that the Japanese are intending to cut off Australia from being supplied by the United States. It makes the round trip much longer. ADM Nimitz is concerned about this; these southern islands may become the focus of our attention.

LATE DAY REPORTS

At San Diego, the carrier USS Yorktown reported that they were out of dry dock and ready for orders. The destroyers dispatched to escort the carrier were still two days from reaching San Diego. After a quick replenishment, the destroyers will escort the carrier back to Pearl Harbor.

Right before dinner a report came in from a patrol aircraft that a Japanese submarine was sighted roughly 100 nautical miles northwest of Lihue. There were no immediate assets available to attack the submarine; the patrol aircraft did try to attack the submarine to no avail.

The Harbor Master reported that the destroyer USS Henley had complete repairs and was ready for service. The commanding officer was reporting the same up the chain of command.

A dinner of chicken and potatoes were served that was actually fairly decent. With that, I went to my bungalow for some rest. I listened to the radio; the Lux Radio Theatre presented "The Bride Came C.O.D.". It was fairly interesting. Sleep came fitfully.

Figure 32 - USS Yorktown (CV-5)

MORNING BRIEF

Some fresh fruit came in; mostly pineapple, but it was a welcome sight. The Operations Officer quickly began the morning briefing.

The first set of information regarded Christmas Island. It now seems that this is going to be the bastion for the springboard back into the island chains in that area. Supplies were currently being offloaded in anticipation of friendly troops landing as reinforcements. The troop ships should arrive in four days… in the meantime; the current troops would prepare for the reinforcements and dig defensive positions in case the Japanese do push that far. A couple of tankers were going to leave San Diego with fuel for ships and aircraft and would be there in about a week or so.

Canton Island will probably be counter-invaded if possible, thus, we were to prepare for the possibility that the 8th Marine Regiment may be sent to take the island back if necessary. Christmas Island would be the key to maintaining control of the area.

Next came information on the West Coast. USS Yorktown reported ready and was currently waiting for destroyers to escort her to Pearl Harbor. The carrier's stores were loaded and the aircraft were to maintain anti-submarine sweeps as she crossed the Pacific.

At San Francisco, troops and aircraft to reinforce Port Moresby were assembled but shipping was not yet available to take on all the aircraft, equipment, supplies and troops yet. Several ships were heading to San Francisco but were still a few days out. An entire Pursuit Wing (what I would call a Fighter

Wing) of P-39 Airacobras and an entire Bomber Wing of B-26 Marauder medium bombers were ready to load up. More support troops (mechanics, armorers, maintenance crews, etc.) were also assembling to go to Port Moresby. They would all probably go to Sydney first and then move up to Port Moresby.

As a tie-in, the British Liaison Officer began his briefing. He reported that the 1st Australian Division was still offloading supplies and equipment at Port Moresby and that they should be fully unloaded in a couple of days. However, most of the critical equipment was already offloaded.

The Australian Cruiser force was still heading to Madang to attack enemy shipping. It should take them a couple more days to get to the objective area.

The Dutch were hoping that their small force of three destroyers should be able to reach Balikpapan (if they weren't already there) to attack enemy invasion forces. If they could shoot up the transports they might be able to throw off the invasion. It is very risky and ADM Nimitz did not like their chances; he also had no choice. US Forces would stay in Soerabaja for now; he forbade them to sortie to Balikpapan with enemy carriers so close.

Lastly, destroyers from Singapore were still trying to make their way up the peninsula to attack enemy shipping at Kota Bharu. It should take them a day or two to get up there; they were using bad weather to hide from Japanese aircraft.

The briefing ended and we went to our desks for the day's work. There seemed to be many Marines in the area today; I assumed that this had something to do with a strategy shift regarding Canton Island.

Submarine Operations

There were no attacks against shipping by either our submarines or by the Japanese. The only reports that came in were routine; no combat summaries.

Hawaii

Nothing significant to report. The submarine seen yesterday has not been found. It is unknown if the submarine has left the area.

Broader Pacific Ocean

Wake Island was bombed yet again today. Roughly 40 Betty medium bombers came in and did a concentrated strike against the runway and nearby support buildings. Two more Wildcat fighters were destroyed on the ground (there is still no aviation gasoline to get the fighters into the air). There were a few men wounded on the ground. Submarines will help the supply situation, but a real cargo ship needs to get there at acceptable risk.

More Japanese troops had landed at Canton Island. The total number of troops was estimated at roughly 1000. The Japanese did not make a determined attack today; they only consolidated their beachhead (small as it was). We would not be able to get troops there in time even if we wanted to.

Philippine Island Operations

Considering the carnage of late, the Philippines were quiet today. There was only a single air raid against Clark Field and this didn't do much damage. After further review it was noted that the weather was pretty bad over much of the area and this may have curtailed combat operations. In any case, it was a breather for our troops on the ground (even if a wet one).

Chinese Theater

More of the same today, a mix of Japanese air strikes and continued ground combat at Canton, Hwaiyin, Hwainan, Lang Son, Kweisui, Loyang, Kaifeng and Kweiteh. There were no reports to suggest that the front line had changed any. However, reports indicate that the Chinese have major forces at Loyang; this must be strategically important.

British and Allied Operations

More bad news on the Malayan Peninsula: Mergui came under attack from troops that crossed the border from Thailand. They swiftly overran the base and there has been no word at all from the troops that were stationed there. It is assumed that they were all either captured, killed or that they lost their radio equipment. This cuts off the troops that were retreating from Victoria Point that were trying to retreat towards Rangoon.

The Burmese troops in garrison at Tavoy were attacked by two separate air raids. There was damage to the garrison area and the commander reported that he had 19 troops wounded. The Japanese are obviously making Tavoy the next target.

The Japanese also sent a couple of raids against the facilities at Rangoon. It was thought that around 20 medium bombers (types unknown) managed to attack the airfield. They landed a 250 kg bomb directly on a Blenheim bomber on the ground in an encasement. The aircraft was completely destroyed. No other damage was suffered at the base.

The approaches to Temuloh Base were attacked again today. The 2nd Argylls Battalion managed to ambush the lead elements of the attack but were eventually pushed back due to superior Japanese mortar and artillery strikes. They did manage to give the Japanese a bloody nose before pulling back a couple of kilometers to prepare for the next attack. The topography of this section of Malaya doesn't allow for major maneuver; there are only a couple of roads in the area that allow for movement and the 2nd Argylls is attempting to take this into account for their defense.

Kuantan was hit yet again today by roughly 70 medium bombers escorted by 40 fighters. The results were predictable with extensive damage to what was left of the facilities. No reports from the garrison regarding casualties on the ground.

There was a strange report that was received saying that troops were seen landing at Guadalcanal. Must have come from some Australian or Dominion personnel located there and there were no further reports. The British Liaison Officer was notified.

In the Borneo area a lot was happening. First, at Sambas, more Japanese troops were unloading. It was unknown how many troops were now engaged with British troops (estimates ran from 250 to 600 enemy troops). They were holding for now.

On the eastern side, the Dutch destroyers managed to pull off something pretty amazing. The three destroyers went into the vicinity of Balikpapan in a fog at 0445 local and managed to find a couple of transports which they attacked and damaged. This first part of the battle didn't last long because of the navigation issues related to the fog and the danger that ships moving that quickly could actually collide.

So, the Dutch commander (CDR Chompff) ordered a slow withdrawal to the east.

When the fog began to lift with sunrise, CDR Chompff ordered his ships back to the west and then to the south to begin to egress from the area. They found no enemy ships until they turned south – it appeared that the Japanese convoy commander had ordered his ships to head away from the destroyers (which headed east) by heading south. By 0920 local, CDR Chompff had seen a couple of "large freighters" at a range of 21000 yards. He then ordered the destroyers up to full speed and began an attack.

The destroyers (HNLMS Banckert, HNLMS Van Nes and HNLMS Piet Hein) engaged in a running gun battle with what was reported as six small freighters, five medium sized freighters and three "large" troop transports which may have been converted passenger liners. The destroyers laid fire into the enemy formation for around 90 minutes with accurate 120mm fire (but no reports of torpedo hits). CDR Chompff's verbal report (via radio) stated that he was "sure" that one of the ships was the Brazil Maru (8200 ton converted passenger liner taken in by the Imperial Fleet). Radio silence was disregarded because obviously the Japanese would radio that they were under attack.

HNLMS Banckert and HNLMS Piet Hein concentrated their fire on the Brazil Maru while HNLMS Van Nes attacked the smaller freighters. The Brazil Maru was burning heavily after around 30 minutes of being under fire and visual confirmation of the ship sinking was reported before the destroyers broke from the area.

Figure 33 - HNLMS Piet Hein (PH)

When it was determined that Brazil Maru was sinking, CDR Chompff ordered concentrated fire on the next largest ship seen which was already burning (possibly from shore batteries over the previous days or possibly from being hit in the fog during the first part of the battle). This ship suffered an explosion after only a few hits (perhaps a fuel explosion or some cargo exploding – we will never know). At that point, ammunition was running low and CDR Chompff ordered a high speed retreat to the south when a Japanese patrol plane was seen. HNLMS Van Nes reported sinking one of the small freighters with gunfire and all of the Japanese ships seen had suffered damage of some kind (verbal report: six of the enemy ships were "burning heavily").

By 1300 local, the ships had broken contact and were almost 60 nautical miles from the battle scene and had slowed to 20 knots. They were then attacked by some medium bombers (the sticks of bombs were easily avoided by the destroyers as they fell from an estimated 8000'). The destroyers then moved into a rain squall and continued south without incident. They should reach Soerabaja sometime tomorrow.

Elsewhere in the region, the Japanese carrier force was seen moving east near the southern end of Makassar Island. They conducted air strikes against Makassar, Kendari and Flores Island (a large island that was easternmost of the Java Island chain). These strikes caused damage to facilities on the ground. It is currently unknown if they plan to invade the region at this time. They did not attack Java proper and did not send assets to attack the retreating Dutch destroyers.

INTELLIGENCE

Signals intelligence cracked a message that Ternate was to prepare to have engineering units stationed there with the express purpose of building up defenses, repairing port facilities and lengthening the runway. This indicates that they plan to use this as a major facility in the future.

It was also determined from signals intelligence that the Japanese 25th Infantry Division was located at Kota Bharu. It is unknown if this applies only to the headquarters element or major portions of the division.

The Japanese carriers were confirmed to be in the area of Makassar based on radio intercepts. They indicated that they still did not know where the final destination for the carriers would be but were working on it.

Messages were also decrypted concerning Japanese ship losses. Kill confirmations were as follows:

- Hakubasan Maru – 6475 ton freighter sunk by the British near Kuching on December 21st
- Iwaki Maru – 3675 ton freighter sunk by the British near Kuching on December 21st

-   Chihaya Maru – 3475 ton freighter sunk near Balabac which corroborates to the submarine USS Skipjack from the action of December 23rd
-   Enju Maru – 3675 ton freighter sunk near Balabac which again corroborates to the submarine USS Skipjack from the action of December 23rd

The intelligence officer stated that they were still working hard on decrypting more messages and that they knew that there was a major action near Balikpapan because of the high volume of messages (friendly and enemy) that came from the area in the last 18 hours.

THEORIES AND INTENTIONS

It was strange that the Japanese carriers did not attack the retreating Dutch destroyers. Is this good or bad? Bad because they managed to coordinate with the land based bombers to conduct the actual attack against the destroyers or good because they didn't get any radio information that the destroyers were retreating? There is no data to suggest either with any firm probability.

LATE DAY REPORTS

On the West Coast the destroyers heading to San Diego picked up speed to get into port to support USS Yorktown (the carrier also took onboard a few spare Devastator torpedo bombers today). They required a day to replenish and then would be able to put to sea to escort the carrier to Pearl Harbor.

The Harbor Master in San Francisco reported that three small ships had been refitted for local anti-submarine patrols.

These are "yard patrol" craft (I'm thinking much like the small ships I trained on at the Naval Academy) with limited weapons but are better than nothing to work right off the coast.

Back here in Pearl Harbor, the submarines USS Triton and USS Trout came into port from the supply run to Wake Island. They reported that they will be ready for more missions in about a day.

The civilian freighter SS Laida was back at Pearl Harbor after dropping off supplies at Hilo. We were working on orders to have this freighter escorted by a minimum of four destroyers to head to Wake Island with aviation gasoline, ammunition and food, and to take civilian workers off the island and bring them back to Hawaii. Focus would be on destroyers with the best anti-aircraft armament.

My work for the day was done. I was told that I did not have to report until noon tomorrow because I haven't had a day off yet and it was New Years' Eve. I took advantage of the small gift of time by having several beers at the Officer's Club. I had a decent buzz on as I went to my bungalow.

DECEMBER 31, 1941   DAY 25 OF THE WAR

<u>MORNING BRIEF</u>

I spent my morning off by sleeping in and then having a friendly FBI agent take me into town for a drink and some decent food on Waikiki Beach. There was no questioning of me by the agent and it was actually a very nice morning. I was expected to report by noon; I got back to base around 1100 and was back at the headquarters building by 1130 ready for work.

I got a quick back brief from the Operations Officer. First, supplies for our forces on Java were unloading at Cape Town. They will then be loaded on British vessels for the next part of the run to Java. There would be more supplies sent to Cape Town. It was up to ADM Nimitz to determine if they go to Australia or to Java. Right now, Java has priority. Supplies for our forces going to Australia are coming from the West Coast.

Second, another fleet cargo ship was released – USS Almaack was transiting the Panama Canal and had orders to proceed to Pearl Harbor. Good to see that we were being reinforced, albeit slowly.

Third, the civilian freighter SS Laida was going to bring supplies to Wake Island with the destroyers USS Porter, USS Selfridge, USS Phelps and USS Balch. The force was under the overall command of LCDR Reynolds. Priority offload would be fuel for the fighters followed by all other cargo.

Lastly, the British had sent a force of two light cruisers and two destroyers to Sambas to attack shipping there (CAPT Stephens was again in command of the force); they put to sea late last night. There was no word from the destroyers under CDR Swinley as of yet.

I was then dismissed to go to work at my desk.

SUBMARINE OPERATIONS

USS S-41 under the command of LCDR Holley arrived at Soerabaja completing the submarine's first combat patrol. Rolling up the data shows that one enemy ship was sunk, a light freighter on 12/15/1941, with two other freighters damaged that might have sunk but were not confirmed. The submarine and her commander are officially credited with sinking 2050 tons of enemy shipping and for now, damaging two other freighters. If kills are later confirmed, they will be added to the confirmed kill list for this submarine. LCDR Holley is replenishing his submarine and repairing some light damage. They should be ready to sail again in a few days.

USS S-39 (LCDR Coe) was breaking patrol in the South China Sea to head to Soerabaja mostly because the submarine is running low on fuel. It should be several days before the submarine arrives.

USS Seal (LCDR Hurd) sent in a contact report that they had found a Japanese freighter while on the surface. The freighter was identified as a "Lima Maru" class freighter and was attacked. The freighter was hit by two torpedoes and a hit from the submarine's deck gun. The ship sank in the presence of the bridge crew. This report was sent to the intelligence section.

USS Porpoise (CDR Brewster) made visual contact with a Japanese freighter that was escorted by a small escort. They fired two torpedoes at the freighter with no hits and were summarily attacked by the enemy escort ship. CDR Brewster managed to slip away fairly quickly to surface and recharge the batteries. CDR Brewster also indicated that the submarine suffered no damage and will continue the patrol.

There were no reports of enemy submarine attacks today.

Hawaii

The outgoing force under LCDR Reynolds heading to Wake Island was the only major movement that was tracked today.

Broader Pacific Ocean

Yet more enemy troops were unloaded at Canton Island today. A sketchy radio report was received that had information on enemy troop levels. It seems that the Japanese have unloaded 2400 troops. If that is the case, then the island will fall. Our troops were still on their way to Christmas Island.

Philippine Island Operations

There was bad news from the Philippine Islands. There was an air strike against Nichols Field at noon local that caused a little damage on the ground. Three P-40 Warhawks managed to get airborne (the ground crews were becoming quite adept at cannibalizing parts) and attacked the incoming raid. A single Japanese fighter was shot down for no loss to the 17th Pursuit Squadron.

The problem concerned our troops in the vicinity of Batangas just south of Manila. Reports indicated that friendly troops were assaulted by a full strength Japanese Infantry Division (intelligence believes that it is the 16th Division). The defenders were completely overwhelmed and fell back with losses to the southern approaches to Manila. Initial reports indicated that over 2000 casualties were sustained in the battle and that almost a quarter of the friendly artillery was lost. It was not noted how many were killed, wounded or captured.

However, having lost over half the division in a single day means that there is a serious problem holding off Japanese attacks.

Manila is now at risk.

CHINESE THEATER

The front lines did not change today in China. There was low to mid-level combat at the usual locations, Canton, Hwainan, Lang Son, Kweisui, Loyang, Kaifeng, Kweiteh and Sinyang. There was a significant enemy air strike at Changsha. No indication to friendly or enemy casualties.

BRITISH AND ALLIED OPERATIONS

CDR Swinley's destroyers found a small force of enemy freighters near Kota Bharu at 0130 local. The moon was almost full and offered help seeing ships even though it was partly cloudy. A small formation of three ships was seen and attacked. The engagement started with a full torpedo spread from all four destroyers. Each of the freighters was hit (multiple times) by the torpedoes. Very little gun ammunition was used. The destroyers then turned to head back to Singapore having "bitten off the ships from the Imperial Fleet".

On the western side of Borneo, the British force of two light cruisers and two destroyers reached the area of Sambas in the early morning to find enemy troops still unloading. CAPT Stevens thought it would shake up the Japanese if he attacked at first light instead of a night attack. Around 0700 local time a pair of freighters was seen approaching the area of Sambas from the South China Sea. Both of them were quickly destroyed by 6" gunfire from HMS Danae and a torpedo attack by the HMS Tenedos.

By 0900 local, another pair of ships was seen; another freighter escorted by a small warship. As the force attacked the enemy ships, enemy bombers were seen by lookouts approaching the area. A little over 20 medium bombers were seen (identified as Betty types) coming in for torpedo runs on the British ships.

While the small escort (identified as a submarine chaser) was racked by 6" shells from the HMS Mauritius, all four British ships were fighting off the enemy bombers. At least three of the bombers were damaged (one severely, seen with an engine on fire as it fled to the north) as they made their runs. The last Betty bomber to make a run in hit the HMS Danae with a torpedo on the starboard side that caused much damage and flooding.

CAPT Stevens ordered the force split at this point. HMS Mauritius and HMS Stronghold would make for Singapore; HMS Danae would take HMS Tenedos as an escort and head to Soerabaja for repairs. Both forces then left the area around 1130 local to head in their separate directions.

While valiant and with some misfortune, the plan came to naught. The forces landed overnight added to the consolidated beachhead and launched an assault while the sea battle was occurring. Japanese troops had overrun the base and the remaining troops were falling back towards Singkawang.

On the eastern side of Borneo, a report came in from the garrison at Balikpapan that was quite interesting. It seems that some damaged ships were trying to head in to support the Japanese troops on the ground but had run into the defensive minefield. At least four separate explosions were seen during the day in the waters around Balikpapan. As a result, the low level combat seen on the ground did not change any of the positions by either the Japanese or by Dutch troops.

The Japanese carrier group moved what seemed to be slightly east just south of Kolaka on the southeastern peninsula of Celebes Island. They launched air strikes against Makassar and Koepang causing considerable damage.

On New Guinea, Japanese troops were seen to have landed at Finschhafen. These ships came in *after* the Australian cruiser force had passed the area heading to Madang. Orders were being sent to turn the cruisers around to attack the Japanese landing force before retiring to Sydney to rearm (the facilities at Townsville were not developed enough to move around crates of 8" rounds).

Back on the Malayan Peninsula, more appropriately on the strip of Burmese land that makes up the peninsula, a small strike of aircraft attacked the airfield at Tavoy. There was little damage done on the ground and no enemy planes were shot down. Tavoy is the last major obstacle for the Japanese army for almost 150 miles heading north until reaching an area known as Moulmein.

Further to the north at Rangoon, a sizeable strike of escorted medium bombers attacked the airfield. Elements of the American Volunteer Group flying H81-A3 fighters (a modified P-40 Warhawk for export) were in the air. Additional fighters got off the ground to attack the incoming bombers. In all, four Betty bombers were shot down as well as an escorting fighter (the after action report identified the fighters as Oscar types). One friendly fighter was shot down in the furball and another was destroyed by bombing on the ground.

Not surprisingly, Kuantan was hit yet again by a total of 50 medium bombers with 20 escorting fighters. Again, nothing could be done and none of the damage on the ground was being repaired.

Intelligence

Signals intelligence determined that elements of the Japanese 2nd Recon Regiment were tasked with transit to Balikpapan to assist with the assault. There was also a report that a new air defense battalion had been activated for service in Tokyo.

Sadly, the intelligence section did not have any new information on enemy ships sunk. They were provided with the operations reports that we had received during the day and were to try to find information regarding those attacks.

Theories and Intentions

The Japanese were firmly pushing up the Malayan Peninsula probably with the intention of taking Rangoon. There were plenty of oil fields there and this would feed their war machine. Sumatra and Java also have oil.

In the Philippines, Manila is now at risk and may find itself in a pincer movement from the north and south. This situation is bordering on untenable.

ADM Nimitz is concerned that the Japanese advances in the south central Pacific are intended to cut off Pearl Harbor from Australia. Nothing as of yet has come out of the closed door sessions with senior Marine commanders.

Late Day Reports

Last reports received before I left for the day were concerning Java. CAPT Rooks reported that the Dutch destroyers had returned to port and were replenishing fuel and ammunition.

Also of note the four submarines that had brought supplies to the Philippines had returned. The submarines are USS Sculpin, USS Sailfish, USS Sealion and USS Searaven. They are replenishing and awaiting further orders.

The British Liaison Officer reported that the 54th British Brigade had arrived at Merak and was taking up defensive positions. They are to hold the area at all costs.

As I left there was quite a party going on at the Officer's Club. I simply had dinner and an early New Year's toast to victory and then went to my bungalow. I was very tired.

MORNING BRIEF

There seemed to be many more people here on this New Year's Day. I was quietly told that ADM Nimitz had a few things to go over and that some of the new people were from the Administration Section and the Supply Section. They had some reports as well. There was also talk of a new operation that had been floating around.

ADM Nimitz started by wishing us a happy new year and reminding us that this year will be better than the last. He reminded us that we got punched in the face hard – but now we'll jab the enemy while we build up strength. He asked the Supply Officer to go over US ship losses and aircraft losses to date to begin the briefing.

The Supply Officer stood up and started by going over the ship losses. First was the battleship USS Utah which was completely destroyed in the initial attack. There were the destroyers USS King, USS Schley and USS Cushing that were lost in combat operations as well. As best as he could make out, six PT boats were lost in the Philippines as well as the three gunboats. Six minesweepers were also destroyed along with two aviation support destroyers (destroyers designed to support float planes in a pinch – like the Catalina). The USS Langley was confirmed destroyed at Cavite Base as well; this ship was the first carrier and was being used as an aircraft ferry where the planes could take off from the carrier and land at a base. A submarine tender was also lost at Cavite and a full size aviation support ship as well. On the civilian side, seven standard size cargo ships (larger than 2500 tons) and three light cargo ships were sunk by the enemy since the start of hostilities. A tanker was also sunk just off the California coast near San Diego as well. In all, 36 ships of all types were lost.

With regards to aircraft, he produced the following information:

Fighters Lost:

-	P-40 Warhawk variants	101
-	P-35A	22
-	P-26A Peashooter	16
-	P-36 Hawk	14
-	F4F Wildcat variants	9
-	F2 Buffalo variants	1

Dive Bombers Lost:

-	SBD Dauntless variants	21

Medium and Heavy Bombers Lost:

-	B-17 Flying Fortress variants	18
-	B-18 Bolo	10
-	A-20 Havoc	5
-	B-10	2

Observation, Cargo and Patrol Aircraft Lost:

-	PBY Catalina variants	48
-	SOC-1 Seagull	7
-	O-47A observation aircraft	6
-	OS2U Kingfisher	4
-	C-33 cargo plane	1

When the tallies are taken, aircraft losses through 25 days of combat and operational losses total 285 aircraft of all types. It was noted that aircraft production should be ramping up, but to put things in perspective, current production of the P-40E (the only P-40 model in production as the most up to date) is capping at 35 aircraft a month; in real terms just the Pacific Theater used up a little more than three months production of aircraft in just 25 days. This production number is total; that is, it's what is being produced and we in the Pacific Theater have to fight for resources as well as stateside training commands, Lend-Lease operations and any squadrons that would go to Europe. It did not look good.

Because of the buildup that is occurring stateside, US Army Air Corps has no workable reserves of aircraft right now. All production is being used for standing up squadrons, for training or being sent to Lend-Lease. The Navy and Marine Corps have the following reserves of aircraft:

-	SBD Dauntless variants	27
-	F2 Buffalo variants	25
-	SB2U Vindicator	18
-	F4F Wildcat variants	3
-	TBD Devastator	3
-	PBY Catalina variants	3

Not much of a reserve, but at least there are 79 aircraft available to be used in an emergency.

ADM Nimitz looked at all of us and saw the look of near horror in our faces. He paused to let the information sink in before reminding us that we need to make sure that we hit the enemy where our assets will not be wasted. He then asked the Operations Officer to proceed with the morning briefing.

The older destroyers dispatched from Pearl Harbor to San Francisco arrived early this morning without incident. They need a day or two to replenish and repair at which point they will be available for offensive anti-submarine patrols off the West Coast.

There will be a meeting with the Harbor Master concerning USS Nevada. The battleship may be repaired enough soon that she could make the run up to Seattle for longer term repairs; this would open up badly needed dry dock space here in Pearl Harbor. No firm orders have been issued yet. The Harbor Master also reported that the destroyer USS Craven had completed repairs and was now ready for orders.

The carrier USS Yorktown is leaving San Diego today to head out to Pearl Harbor with the destroyers that arrived yesterday. It should take a few days for them to get here and they were to have the fighter aircraft perform training while the dive bombers and torpedo bombers fly anti-submarine patrols to protect the carrier.

Submarines arrived safely at Wake Island and are dropping off the much needed food, ammunition and medical supplies. Another submarine is a few days behind them and the freighter SS Laida with escorting destroyers are now out to sea on their way to Wake Island with almost 3000 tons of aviation gas, food, medical supplies and building materials.

The latest report on the enemy carriers has them continuing to the southeast with a possible mission of striking northern Australia near Darwin. They could then pass south of New Guinea and head up to Truk, but this is speculation.

Supplies for CAPT Rooks' forces at Java should begin loading up at Cape Town in the next 24 hours for shipment. The British have provided four freighters for the job and intend to keep supplies moving to our forces there. More convoys from the East Coast will keep Cape Town supplied so our forces can draw from there. There are almost 100,000 tons of supplies offloading now and each run to Java will have between 20,000 and 30,000 tons.

Midway radioed that they were running low on supplies. Right now there are no transport assets to bring them supplies but there should be very soon.

The British Liaison Officer then took his queue and reiterated the report about shipping supplies to Java and stated that other consumables were available to US Forces already there (food and fuel). The real concern was ammunition for our forces that was not compatible with British or Dutch weapons.

He also reported that the Australian 19th Brigade was released from duty in the Middle East and should be available for transport back to Australia or wherever the High Command deems necessary. The unit should be available in a week or so.

It was also decided that the Australian cruiser force that was heading to Madang would turn around and attack the Japanese shipping near Lae and Finschhafen. They would then head back to Sydney.

ADM Nimitz then took the floor and told us to start operational planning for what was being called Operation Singing Pumpkin. This was going to be an operation to land the 8th Marine Regiment at Canton Island. Strategically, Japan is trying to cut off Australia. By taking back the islands in the south central Pacific, we can keep the supply lines open without having to constantly move around Japanese bases. It will also put the enemy on notice that we will fight them anywhere and let the people at home know that victory at Wake Island was not a "one off" thing.

With that, we were dismissed to our daily duties after a quick breakfast of substandard oatmeal.

SUBMARINE OPERATIONS

There were no Japanese submarine attacks today. We're lucky, we hit their logistics tail or they've returned to port for some reason.

Figure 34 - Heavy Cruiser IJN Myoko

A report came in via the British Liaison Officer from the Dutch submarine HNLMS K XI (CDR De Boer). They had spotted a group of Japanese ships and dove to attack. They fired two torpedoes at a small freighter and hit with one. The submarine then dove deep and broke _towards_ the escorts. While reloading their tubes (these submarines actually had two _different_ types of torpedo tubes) they came to periscope depth and found themselves only 2000 yards or so from a Japanese heavy cruiser (reported as a Myoko class). They quickly fired two torpedoes and hit with both. At this point, Japanese destroyers were all over them and they had to dive deep. They were depth charged for a little over two hours but managed to break away and make a report. There was no damage to the submarine and all of the Japanese ships had left the area; there was no way to know if the Japanese ships sank or limped off. They then resumed their patrol on the surface.

Another report came from the HNLMS K XII. They spotted an enemy patrol boat and launched an attack. The torpedoes missed but they were able to escape relatively easy after being depth charged a few times. They then surfaced and resumed their patrol.

HAWAII

Nothing significant to report here today.

BROADER PACIFIC OCEAN

Wake Island was attacked yet again by a little over 30 Betty bombers. They damaged some of the facilities and caused a few casualties on the ground. Yet again, the remaining Wildcat fighters could not get off the ground because there was no fuel. Anti-aircraft fire was also ineffective; no Japanese bombers were shot down.

Task Force Present reached Christmas Island and began offloading the 2nd Marine Engineering Regiment and the 4th Marine Defense Battalion. The engineers immediately went to work on facilities on the island starting with defensive positions for their fellow Marines. Next would be extending the airstrip and then building more port facilities. It should be a couple of days before the equipment and troops are fully unloaded.

At Canton Island, it was estimated that 1500 enemy troops had landed (reports were conflicting). They were exchanging gunfire with the US Navy personnel located there. There was not much that could be done to help them. In any case, planning for Operation Singing Pumpkin had begun.

PHILIPPINE ISLAND OPERATIONS

A coordinated strike against both Nielson Field and Nichols Field arrived at noon time local with the intention of hitting the runways. Again, due to cannibalizing parts and flying with some damage, a total of three P-40 Warhawks got off the ground to challenge the attack. They dove down from 18000' onto the fighters escorting the bombers at 12000'. One Nate fighter was shot down and then the P-40s dove for the deck to get into ground based friendly machine gun coverage. Nielson Field's runway was heavily damaged so the fighters landed at Nichols. No enemy bombers were shot down.

There was also a raid at Clark Field at 1400 local. Roughly a dozen Betty bombers made a run against the runway at an estimated 12000'. A few bombs hit the runway but did no further damage to the support facilities.

The raid occurred during a Japanese attack against Clark Field proper. It was estimated that 20,000 enemy troops were in the vicinity of Clark Field and an artillery duel began in the early morning hours. By noon, there were 22 dead and 30 wounded among US and Philippine Army forces. Right now, friendly forces were holding at Clark Field and there was talk of a couple of battalions of US light tanks making an attack against the Japanese.

Another battle was developing at Iba, slightly to the northwest. The 31st Philippine Army Division was defending the area along with some support troops. The battle began with a Japanese probe with infantry on the forward lines of the 31st Philippine Army Division; this probe was beaten back with machine gun and mortar fire. It was unknown if the infantry was line infantry or recon infantry/dismounted cavalry.

CHINESE THEATER

Not much change in the front lines. There was low to mid-level combat at the usual locations, Canton, Hwainan, Lang Son, Kweisui, Loyang, Kaifeng, Kweiteh and Sinyang. There was a significant enemy air strike at Lo Yang with a combined dive bomber and medium bomber attack. Of interesting note, it was revealed by Chinese Nationalists that the main Japanese assault unit is the 35th Division. No indication to friendly or enemy casualties.

BRITISH AND ALLIED OPERATIONS

The Australian cruiser force did in fact turn around and headed toward the area of Finschhafen. They entered the area near midnight local time and found a single Japanese freighter escorted by a small combat ship (reported as a submarine chaser). Both ships were quickly shot up and sunk. The cruisers then worked up to speed and began a withdrawal to Sydney to replenish the large caliber rounds.

The only other action during the day in the Australian area involved Japanese air strikes against Kavieng. There were significant casualties on the ground and the radio report did not even identify the type of bombers that attacked.

Near Sambas on the west side of Borneo, CAPT Stevens aboard HMS Mauritius decided to run interference for HMS Danae until that cruiser could break from the area. As such, the Japanese had sent a small surface action group to attack the retreating ships. This group had a battleship, a light cruiser and a couple of destroyers. CAPT Stevens actually attacked them and tried to draw them off to the north to allow HMS Danae to escape (she could only make 8 knots). Skillful maneuvering during the night battle allowed CAPT Stevens to make the battle last longer than he originally intended. Varying range between 9000 and 12000 yards he managed to make it difficult for the battleship to bring the main armament to bear; the range was too close for plunging fire and just far enough away to cause problems for flat trajectories.

After a 4 hour running battle, the only damage caused to HMS Mauritius was by a round from one of the Japanese destroyers that did not penetrate the armor of the cruiser. The enemy battleship was hit by a 6" shell (which would not penetrate that much armor) from HMS Mauritius and one of the enemy destroyers was hit by some small caliber rounds from the destroyer HMS Stronghold. A rain squall approached the battle area around 0400 local and was used to full effect by CAPT Stevens (after which he made his high speed withdrawal towards Singapore). Dangerous work skillfully done by CAPT Stevens.

On the eastern side of Borneo, there was more low level ground combat at Balikpapan. Total friendly troops numbered around 1400 and it was estimated that the Japanese had landed 1500 troops. Neither side had enough superiority to launch a major attack to push the other out.

Meanwhile, back on the Malayan Peninsula, Tavoy and Temuloh Base came under attack in weather that was rainy all day. The troops at Tavoy managed to defend themselves well enough (though with losses) and stop the Japanese attack, but at Temuloh Base it was another matter.

We found out later via the British Liaison Officer that photo reconnaissance showed a massive buildup of Japanese troops. However, the message did not get to the commander of the 2nd Argylls Battalion in time; they had no idea that they were outnumbered 10-1. The Japanese didn't even try to mask the assault; thousands of troops with tanks moved their way up the main road to the base using superior firepower to push out Allied troops. The battle lasted the entire day and shortly after nightfall Allied troops were in full retreat towards Kuala Lumpur. Initial reports were that over half the Allied force was killed, wounded or missing (only 70 walking wounded made it to Kuala Lumpur out of a force of a little over 700 prior to the battle).

Of note, heavy rain spared Kuantan from an air raid today and it is surmised that the rain might have helped put out some of the fires.

INTELLIGENCE

The intelligence report centered on information regarding the Japanese carrier group; no firm data on their location was known but it was surmised that they were heading towards the areas north of Australia. It is probable that Darwin will be struck.

Signals intelligence noted that there was an "infantry group" at Finschhafen; I wasn't quite sure what a group was over say, a regiment.

Last dealt with confirmed ship kills:

- Meisho Maru (3675 tons) was confirmed sunk on December 21st near Kuching (sunk by the British)
- Kaika Maru (830 tons – light freighter) was confirmed sunk on December 21st near Kuching (sunk by the British)
- Lima Maru (6475 tons) was confirmed sunk on December 24th near Bikini which corroborates the report of the submarine USS Thresher

There was also talk of a major Japanese operation going down sometime in the next 45 days. The intelligence cell did not have a target or more specific timeframe, but there is an unusual amount of radio traffic from the Japanese High Command to Truk Headquarters and Saigon Headquarters. The intelligence section was monitoring this development.

LCDR Rochefort hasn't been seen at our headquarters for several days. It is assumed that he is very busy with decrypting information.

OPERATION SINGING PUMPKIN PLANNING

In between operations reports and trying to follow ongoing combat operations, we were also tasked with setting up this operation. It was determined that the 8th Marine Regiment, 56th Coastal Artillery Regiment, the 3rd Marine Defense Battalion and some base support troops (aircraft mechanics, armorers, etc. to set up aviation operations) would be the ground troops for the operation.

The plan would be for the 8th Marine Regiment to perform the assault and consolidation of the island. The other troops would arrive a couple days later while the 8th Marine Regiment would egress from the island and return to Pearl Harbor. There also existed the possibility that this invasion could springboard from Christmas Island – this decision has not yet been made.

In any case, the first iteration of the plan that is being developed revolves around four major forces:

- Task Force Loadstone: The invasion force with the 8th Marine Regiment, 2 battleships, 2 heavy cruisers, 4 destroyers with 6 troop transports

- Task Force Recline: Supplementary force with the other troops for consolidation, 1 light cruiser, 3 destroyers, 4 troop transports and 4 cargo ships
- Task Force Decamp: Surface action group in case a major enemy surface group arrives, 2 battleships, 2 heavy cruisers, 2 light cruisers and 6 destroyers.
- Task Force Stampede: Carrier force for strike and air defense, 3 carriers, 2 heavy cruisers, 2 light cruisers and 7 destroyers.

It won't be necessary for tanker assets; if ships need fuel they can fall back to Christmas Island. There are also going to be separate supplies set up at Christmas Island as well.

The problem right now is that the only two battleships that will be ready in time for the beginning of the operation (set as January 25th) are USS Maryland and USS West Virginia. All of the battleships are undergoing a refit that was planned prior to the attack on December 7th; USS Pennsylvania, USS California, USS Tennessee are also undergoing major refit and repairs and won't be available until late February. USS New Mexico and USS Idaho are in dry dock in San Francisco and won't be available until close to the end of the month.

According to the first iteration of the plan, the only other element short is a single light cruiser (there will be four available instead of five). If the staff includes elements currently at sea that can be called in after their current operations are complete including assets being sent to Pearl Harbor from the East Coast, (listed as "incoming") the following can be used for the operation:

Ship Type Needed for Operation:		Available (incoming):
Carrier	3	3 (1)
Battleship	4	0 (2)

Heavy Cruiser	6	11 (0)
Light Cruiser	5	2 (2)
Destroyer	20	9 (20)
Troop Transport	10	3 (10)
Fleet Cargo Ship	4	0 (7)

Since the battleships won't be available there are a couple of courses of action. We could forgo Task Force Decamp altogether or use the available battleships for Task Force Decamp while increasing the number of heavy cruisers in Task Force Loadstone. I was in favor of the second option.

The first iteration of this plan will be presented to ADM Nimitz in the morning. This operation will take up the majority of the entire Pacific Fleet; risk and reward are both great.

THEORIES AND INTENTIONS

After spending the majority of my day running back and forth between Operation Singing Pumpkin and combat reports my ability to think clearly was seriously infringed upon. Operation Singing Pumpkin… seriously, who thinks up these names?

History has changed. I am no longer sure if I'm an asset or a detriment. However, I will always obey orders – no matter what time I live in, I swore an oath to the Constitution. None of my training ever prepared me for something like this.

In any case, the first iteration of the operation is complete. Not much else has changed; Luzon is still under attack, Malaya is being overrun a mile at a time and Borneo is still a hotbed of combat. It is surmised that the Japanese carriers are still heading towards the Banda Sea on their way to northern Australia.

LATE DAY REPORTS

There were only two late day reports. The first concerned the British as delivered by the Liaison Officer. CAPT Stevens arrived with HMS Mauritius and HMS Stronghold at Singapore. CDR Swinley arrived with his destroyers as well. They are replenishing and should be ready for more orders in a day or two.

The other report came from CAPT Rooks at Java. The submarine USS S-40 under the command of LCDR Lucker completed her combat patrol and was replenishing at Soerabaja. A rollup report of the patrol should be available in the morning.

I had a meal of ham with potatoes for dinner. I also had a bottle of Coke. I was laughing as I was drinking it – this is serious "Classic Coke". Sleep came quickly.

JANUARY 2, 1942   DAY 27 OF THE WAR

Morning Brief

ADM Nimitz had spent the evening reviewing our first iteration for Operation Singing Pumpkin. He liked the overall look of it, but would have a few changes and questions for us during the day.

The Operations Officer began with operations close to Pearl Harbor. First concerns the civilian freighter SS Laida. She was passing French Frigate Shoals along with the destroyer escorts.

The fleet cargo ship USS Alchiba was still offloading supplies at Palmyra Island. The lack of port facilities means that the supplies have had to be offloaded by small boat. So far, roughly 3000 tons of supplies have been offloaded; that is roughly half of the ship. It may take a week or two to complete the unloading at this rate. The ship may be pulled back early to support Operation Singing Pumpkin.

The converted liner SS President Coolidge (now USS President Coolidge, a fleet transport) was tasked with loading up supplies needed for Midway Island. This is advantageous because the ship can sail at 21 knots making it difficult for submarines to attack it. Because it is set up as a troop transport, it has several landing craft that can quickly offload the cargo. She should be putting out to sea today.

Four more civilian freighters are assembled and putting to sea to bring supplies to Pearl Harbor from San Diego. This group will be making shuttle runs to keep Pearl Harbor supplied. No further reports from this group will be made unless there is a delay, problem or attack.

More fast converted liners are assembling in San Francisco to bring troops and supplies across the Pacific. There are groups of ships that will be put in 19 knot convoys and 21 knot convoys. It is thought that the 31ˢᵗ Pursuit Group and the 22ⁿᵈ Bombardment Group will be loaded up on these ships for safe and quick transit across the Pacific to Sydney. Orders have not yet been given for this but it seems the most obvious conclusion.

A report was also received that that battleship USS Colorado had completed repairs and refit at the shipyards in Seattle. This could provide some relief to Operation Singing Pumpkin.

The final item from the Operations Officer concerned a report about the 47ᵗʰ Bombardment Group which was equipped with heavy bombers. They were being sent over to the East Coast for eventual deployment to Europe.

**Figure 35 - An Arcturus Class cargo
ship like USS Alchiba (AK-23)**

The British Liaison Officer then began his piece of the briefing. There were two elements to the briefing. First was a report on the freighters at Cape Town. As of now, five freighters were loading up with US supplies and munitions to head to Merak on Java. It was expected that the one way trip would take two weeks. Between the five freighters it was expected that roughly 27000 tons of supplies could be delivered (submarine and shipboard torpedoes, ammunition of all types, food, uniforms, everything). The freighters were loading a little bit of every type on each ship in case one of the ships is lost. It was hoped that none of the ships would be attacked.

The other dealt with the 1st Australian Division. The convoy that brought the troops and supplies to Port Moresby was almost finished with the unloading. They should finish today and then head back to Sydney for more orders.

With that, we had breakfast and went to work. Decent pancakes and for the first time in a long time, bacon...

SUBMARINE OPERATIONS

The small escort USS Vigilant (a patrol craft) found a Japanese submarine near Alliford Bay off of British Columbia north of Washington State at sunrise. They commenced an attack against the submarine but could not confirm any damage to the enemy submarine.

A report came in from USS Seadragon (LCDR Ferrall) right after lunch indicating that they attacked an enemy freighter on the surface after coming out of a rain squall near Madjene. In the report, the ship was identified as an MFM code class for a freighter of the Ada Maru class. The ship was fired on with a full spread of four torpedoes (three hits) and a few hits from the deck gun of the submarine. The freighter sank and the intelligence section was notified. I was curious about the codes; when I asked I was provided with a copy of ONI-208-J; this is the book that identifies the majority of the Japanese Merchant Fleet. Most submarines have a copy, but not all. Certainly no Allied submarines will have this document.

HAWAII

Nothing significant to report.

BROADER PACIFIC OCEAN

Wake Island was attacked by medium bombers at first light. They attacked the north side of the island where supplies would be brought in. It was estimated that 33 enemy bombers were involved in the attack and they were all Betty types. None of the bombers was hit by anti-aircraft fire and after the bombing run, the bombers all headed back to the south.

At Canton Island, Japanese troops continued to slowly land. It was estimated that just under 1500 enemy troops were on the island. The scratch Navy personnel located there were attempting to hold them away from the sensitive area of the island with rifle fire, but they lacked heavy weapons and there wouldn't be much they could do if the Japanese perform a determined assault.

PHILIPPINE ISLAND OPERATIONS

The good news was that Japanese troops have not yet tried to push their way into southern Manila. The bad news is Clark

Field was hit by a raid that caused several casualties and the really bad news concerned Iba to the northwest.

The Japanese 48th Division attacked the troops at the small airfield there and cut them off from heading south to try to link up with other friendly forces. They were steadily pushed back to the northwest all day and eventually surrendered. In total, the 31st Philippine Army Division and some support troops at the base were completely written off as captured or killed. There were a few friendly fighters at the base as well and these will also be written off.

Luzon is going from bad to worse.

CHINESE THEATER

We did not receive any messages today from the Chinese Theater. Disconcerting, but it does happen from time to time.

BRITISH AND ALLIED OPERATIONS

Transports arrived in the early morning at Batavia and immediately began unloading the 48th Light Anti-Aircraft Regiment. That unit is earmarked for Merak. The thirty-six 40mm Bofors anti-aircraft guns will be most welcome.

Overnight Tavoy was bombed by what was estimated as 20 medium bombers. Only one bomb fell in the base area. No damage was scored on the enemy bombers. Shortly after sunrise, Japanese troops came out of the jungle and attacked the Burmese Infantry and some Royal Air Force base troops. They were quickly pushed out of the airfield and out into the jungle to the north. Casualties are unknown.

Through a rainstorm in the area of Victoria Point, retreating British and Indian troops were bombed by several medium bombers (Sally types). It was unknown how many bombers were involved because the radio report was cut short.

Further to the north at Rangoon a heavily escorted strike of light bombers attempted to hit the airfield. Aircraft from the All-Volunteer Air Group rose to meet them. They managed to get 11 fighters in the air and attacked the Japanese formation. Unfortunately, the friendly fighters were outnumbered almost three-to-one. Four of the friendly fighters were confirmed lost and only one enemy aircraft was claimed shot down (a Kate torpedo bomber).

On the west side of Borneo, Singkawang was hit by a concentrated bomber strike. It was estimated that 50 bombers came over in the raid that was concentrated on the port facilities. There were hits on the port, but luckily, the bombs that did manage to hit the piers and storage areas were smaller bombs (it was thought they were 60kg bombs).

On the east side of Borneo, a few Japanese prisoners were taken by a Dutch infantry patrol. It was confirmed that the enemy troops are from the 8th Special Naval Landing Force. Just like yesterday, the ground combat at this location was at a stalemate.

There were several Japanese carrier aircraft strikes against Celebes Island in the vicinity of Manado on the north east extreme and at Kendari on the southeast side of the island. There were no reports of casualties. There was also a strike against Ambon Island further to the east on the approaches to New Guinea.

INTELLIGENCE

The only information from the Intelligence Section today concerned the enemy carriers. The intelligence officers were "sure" that the Japanese carriers were going to attack northern Australia. They were still working on other reports and trying to confirm enemy ship kills; but for now they had no new information on this front.

They also stated that there was no new information on enemy ground units or their locations. We did give them copies of our operations reports so they could cross-check information.

OPERATION SINGING PUMPKIN PLANNING

ADM Nimitz reviewed our first iteration shortly after the morning briefing and sent word that while the force structure of Task Forces are ok, the ships in them need to be changed. He agreed that the available battleships should be in the surface action group and taken out of the main invasion force (should the Japanese send major units to break up our invasion, our battleships should not be tied to the transports). So, by the end of the day we had our second iteration of the plan as follows:

- Task Force Loadstone: The invasion force with the 8th Marine Regiment will have 5 heavy cruisers, 5 destroyers and 6 troop transports. USS Salt Lake City will probably be the flagship (she has ten 8" guns instead of nine like the other heavy cruisers).
- Task Force Recline: Supplementary troops (56th Coastal Artillery Regiment, 3rd Marine Defense Battalion and base support troops) will have 1 light cruiser, 3 destroyers, 4 troop transports and 4 fleet cargo ships.
- Task Force Decamp: Surface battle group will have 2 battleships, 2 heavy cruisers, 2 light cruisers and 6 destroyers.

- Task Force Stampede: Carrier battle group will have 3 carriers, 2 heavy cruisers, 1 light cruiser and 7 destroyers.

The operation will begin on January 25th, 1942. Task Force Loadstone will leave port followed by Task Force Decamp and Task Force Stampede on January 27th. Task Force Recline will leave Pearl Harbor on January 30th.

This is the majority of the Pacific Fleet. Left in reserve will be 1 carrier, 1 battleship, 2 heavy cruisers, 8 destroyers, 3 troop transports and 3 fleet cargo ships. ADM Nimitz appreciated the risk level of the operation. This second iteration will be reviewed by the staff tomorrow morning.

We received word from COL Jeschke (commander of the 8th Marine Regiment) that we would receive a briefing from his staff on the invasion plans. In the meantime, he provided a table of organization and equipment. In typical Marine fashion, his report showed *exactly* 4778 Marines ready in his reinforced Regiment. He had 1571 infantry in three battalions each of three companies, his service troops along with a reserve infantry company with attached medium and heavy machine guns. He had requested some reinforcements for his Regiment, which is why the troop numbers are so high. He is being reinforced with an artillery battalion of five batteries (three 75mm pack howitzer batteries and two 105mm howitzer batteries; all of four guns each), an "ad-hoc" anti-aircraft battalion that has four batteries; three equipped with thirty-six .50 caliber machine guns each and a "heavy battery" with twelve .50 caliber machine guns, two 90mm heavy anti-aircraft guns and five 37mm anti-aircraft guns, a reinforced anti-tank company with 37mm anti-tank guns, a mortar company with twelve 81mm mortars and a combat engineering company.

The anti-aircraft battalion has dual use; that much heavy machinegun firepower can be used to support the infantry as well. I personally thought that the anti-tank guns would be overkill, but then again, I'm not a Marine Colonel.

The planned briefing would also include the dive bomber and torpedo bomber operations officers so that coordinated fire can help the Marines as they land. It would be expected that zones of fire will be set up on a timetable for shore bombardment as well.

THEORIES AND INTENTIONS

Nothing is really new today. We're still working on getting troops to Canton Island, the Philippines are still untenable, submarines are still attacking and we're trying to get supplies to our forces at Java.

I am concerned that we're betting the entire Pacific Fleet on Operation Singing Pumpkin; this is ahistorical.

LATE DAY REPORTS

CAPT Rooks reported that the Dutch had told him that the destroyer HNLMS Witte de With had completed repairs and was ready for sea. He also reported that all US Navy ships at Soerabaja were ok.

The only other report concerned the Japanese carriers. Apparently a patrol aircraft sighted them heading *north* on the east side of Celebes Island. They were parallel with Loewoek and were still heading to the northeast. This report was sent to the Intelligence Section; so much for "sure".

I had dinner and went for a walk. The breeze felt good. There wasn't anything interesting on the radio so I sat out on the veranda of the bungalow with a soda until I got tired and went in to sleep.

JANUARY 3, 1942   DAY 28 OF THE WAR

It was a fairly quick meeting this morning. The Operations Officer was needed in more planning conferences for Operation Singing Pumpkin. Colonel Jeschke would be arriving with two of the three rifle battalion commanders to brief the invasion plan sometime this afternoon. In the meantime, we were to continue planning.

Word came from Continental Army Forces that the 132nd Infantry Regiment was being released for duty in the Pacific and would be heading to San Francisco.

Overnight 11 civilian freighters arrived at San Francisco from the Panama Canal zone. It was unknown what their mission would be, but it would probably involve resupplying Pearl Harbor. Orders would be following shortly regarding these ships.

The 31st Pursuit Group was loading up on fast converted liners to head to Sydney (via Pearl Harbor to refuel and another stop at Christmas Island to refuel). These will be four fast liners travelling at 22 knots; they will only stop for refueling. In the meantime, two fleet oilers escorted by four destroyers will bring fuel to the tank farms being upgraded at Christmas Island by the 2nd Marine Engineering Regiment. The Marines are hard at work with all manner of construction (combat bunkers, additional port facilities and lengthening the runways).

All other US Forces were proceeding as originally planned.

The British Liaison Officer reported that the ships from the 1st Australian Division have completed offloading all of their supplies and are heading back to Sydney. It is unknown if more troops were going to be readied for travel to Port Moresby.

A report came from Cape Town that the freighters carrying US supplies should be leaving sometime today to head to Batavia. When they are a few days out we should receive reports.

He also reported that CAPT Stevens would be taking a force of one light cruiser and five destroyers to attack enemy shipping at Sambas. They are Task Force 5.

The briefing ended and we went to work. Toast and juice for breakfast.

SUBMARINE OPERATIONS

A report came in via the British Liaison Officer that the Dutch submarine HNLMS K XIV attacked a "large troop transport" and hit it with at least three torpedoes. The report indicated that the Japanese ship may have been the Huzi Maru (only ship of its class), a large and relatively fast transport. The submarine was then attacked by a small escort and had to dive deep. When the submarine surfaced later, there was no trace of enemy shipping. The submarine then resumed its patrol in the Celebes Sea. The intelligence section was notified.

There was also a report from the West Coast that a patrol plane had spotted a Japanese submarine on the surface 90 nautical miles southwest of Santa Barbara. They tried to attack but the submarine dove quickly and could not be struck.

HAWAII

There were no reports of enemy shipping and all outbound and inbound friendly shipping proceeded unharmed.

BROADER PACIFIC OCEAN

Wake Island was hit at sunrise, yet again, by some medium bombers coming up from the south. Some damage was scored on the eastern side of the island, but there were no casualties.

They attacked from higher altitude so that the light anti-aircraft guns were unable to effectively defend against them. They then turned slowly and headed back south.

A report from Canton Island indicated that they were still engaged in low level combat against landed Japanese ground troops.

PHILIPPINE ISLAND OPERATIONS

A heavily escorted raid hit Clark Field at noon local time today. There were roughly two dozen enemy bombers with "many" fighter escorts. The runway was heavily cratered and there were a few hits near the support area. Luckily, there were no friendly fighters left that were airworthy, so the damage was effectively negligible. This attack occurred as Japanese troops slightly to the north and northwest were setting up artillery locations to begin shelling friendly troops in the area. Philippine Army and US Army troops were busy digging in and bringing up artillery and ammunition for a protracted battle.

On the Island of Mindanao, the city of Oroquieta was being invaded by Japanese troops. It was unknown how many troops had landed. What was known was that the only major concentration of friendly troops was nearly a hundred miles away at Cagayan. There was nothing to stop the Japanese troops from taking the area.

CHINESE THEATER

Information came in regarding combat at Lang Son, Hwainan, Canton, Kweisui, Loyang, Kaifeng and Kweiteh. Some of the Japanese attacks were supported by dive bombers. The Chinese forces were holding but were unable to make any counter attacks. Supplies are low for Chinese forces and our ability to get them supplies will become more troublesome as the Japanese advance in Burma.

BRITISH AND ALLIED OPERATIONS

On the Malayan Peninsula, there were more reports of Japanese attacks. Retreating troops from Tavoy came under attack yet again from enemy medium bombers after first light. It was unknown how bad the casualties were; all that was received was a message indicating that they were under attack. They had no anti-aircraft weapons, so it was obvious that no damage was scored against any of the enemy bombers.

Kuantan was hit by another raid. A little over 20 medium bombers hit the area. The ground forces again refused to repair the damage caused. It was unknown when the Japanese ground forces would attack the area.

In the area of Celebes Island and Balikpapan, many Japanese strikes took place. It appears that the Japanese carriers are in the Gulf of Tomini in the northeastern area of Celebes Island. They launched airstrikes against Balikpapan and Manado. Balikpapan was hit particularly hard near the port. There was a small destroyer tender and an auxiliary ship that were both hit by bombs from Val dive bombers. In the two raids, almost 90 aircraft attacked. They did not, however, specifically target the defending Dutch troops which were still engaged in small unit combat against landed Japanese forces.

Manado has a small port that was hit by Kate torpedo bombers on level runs armed with a pair of 250 kg bombs each. There was some damage to the supply dump and some of the pier facilities were damaged as well.

We received many reports from CAPT Stevens' force that had headed to Sambas. The task force had left port on a high speed run and managed to get to Sambas just before sunrise. They ran into a freighter with a small escort both of which were quickly dispatched by gunfire. Both ships were seen to have sunk; the small escort actually blew up when hit by a 6" shell from HMS Mauritius. The class of the freighter was not listed in the report though it was still dark and difficult to see the ship type. The intelligence section was notified of this engagement.

Since the force finished their first engagement around 0515, they stayed a while in the area to look for more enemy shipping. Unfortunately, around an hour after sunrise (roughly 0835 local) they found more enemy ships. They were identified as a Kongo Class battleship, a Kuma Class light cruiser, an Asashio Class destroyer and a Fubuki Class destroyer. The seas were fair (3 ft. seas) and it was sunny and clear. Textbook surface battle weather.

Figure 36 - Japanese Kuma Class Light Cruiser

CAPT Stevens immediately ordered all ships to 30 knots and closed with the enemy force to engage between 8000 yards and 12000 yards making it difficult for the Kongo Class ship to engage with their main guns (again, the range between plunging fire and flat trajectory fire).

Over the next three hours, both forces wound up being in a line heading northwest trading shots. CAPT Stevens ordered course changes every 20 to 30 seconds as main batteries were reloading to fire; this negated the ability of the battleship to score any hits with their main armament. The enemy battleship was hit by a few 6" rounds from HMS Mauritius that could not have caused much damage (the shells were not big enough or fast enough velocity wise to penetrate the battleship's armor).

The Japanese light cruiser was hit by several 6" rounds from HMS Mauritius' aft main gun turret; the enemy cruiser was noted to be on fire. HMS Mauritius herself was hit by several rounds, none of which penetrated the deck armor. However, HMS Stronghold was hit by a 6" round from the Japanese light cruiser and also by a 5" round from one of the enemy destroyers; she was damaged fairly heavily and could only make 27 knots. At this point, CAPT Stevens ordered the rest of the force to keep to the speed HMS Stronghold could make. The battle continued.

The Asashio Class destroyer was hit repeatedly by main rounds from HMS Electra and HMS Encounter. The enemy destroyer was burning heavily and was falling out of formation. The Fubuki Class destroyer was hit by at least one round from HMS Express. The damage didn't look bad against the Fubuki Class destroyer.

By 1030 local, both forces were looking to disengage (probably because torpedo runs were ineffective and ammunition was running low). CAPT Stevens headed due west with aft main batteries firing on the Japanese ships; the Japanese commander headed to the northeast to break from the area with their aft batteries still firing on the British ships. Contact was reported lost when both forces were separated by roughly 15 nautical miles (30,000 yards).

CAPT Stevens then asked for reports (via lights and signal flags) as to the material condition of the ships. As earlier indicated, HMS Stronghold had suffered the most damage. While this information was being tabulated, Japanese torpedo bombers arrived from the northeast getting ready to attack. According to the report, a total of 14 Betty torpedo bombers came in to attack. Anti-aircraft fire from the British ships managed to damage at least six of the enemy bombers, but one of the bombers came in from the starboard side and managed to put a torpedo into HMS Mauritius. There were casualties onboard and some flooding, but CAPT Stevens reported that they will be able to make port.

The British Liaison Officer reported that the force was ordered to retire to Soerabaja in order to get the ships repaired and out of danger on the Malayan Peninsula. It should take them a couple of days to get to Soerabaja. There were no further attacks against the British ships for the rest of the day. The intelligence section was also notified of all of this message traffic.

In the Australian area, Lae came under assault from enemy seaborne troops on New Guinea. It was unknown how many enemy troops were landing and these reports were sent to Port Moresby to make sure that the troops there were on alert.

Intelligence

I missed the daily intelligence briefing because I was busy working on items related to Operation Singing Pumpkin. One of the other staff officers filled me in. There were no new confirmed kills (by confirmed, the intelligence section means confirming a named enemy ship with other methods of identification to confirm location and hopefully, method of sinking). The only piece of information that my coworker found interesting was that it was confirmed that a Japanese Naval Construction Battalion was located at Vigan on north Luzon in the Philippines.

OPERATION SINGING PUMPKIN PLANNING

COL Jeschke had a briefing at 1400 with two of his battalion commanders, MAJ Acosta (1st Battalion) and MAJ Shackelton (2nd Battalion). The 3rd Battalion commander (MAJ Thomas) was busy on a field exercise.

The current plan would be to have 1st and 2nd Battalion each do an assault from the seaward area near the seaplane landing and the airport on D-Day. Each battalion would land two of their companies in the first wave (keeping one company in reserve) and some machine guns and mortars. 3rd Battalion would land on D+1.

Also in the initial landing would be two batteries from the anti-aircraft battalion (all .50 caliber machine guns), one each to support each landing battalion. These machine guns would serve dual purpose; one to protect the ground troops should Japanese aircraft come in low and second to provide heavy machine gun support if the ground troops need it.

Discussion involved around whether or not some of the 75mm artillery batteries should land on the first day to provide support or if they should come ashore on D+1 or D+2 after some of the shore fire support ships head back to Pearl Harbor. Not that any of the Marines cared what I thought my personal opinion was that they should go ashore on D+2. One of the batteries should stay in the area of the airport while the rest are moved forward around the island. The 105mm batteries would provide the heavy support while the 75mm guns provide closer fire support.

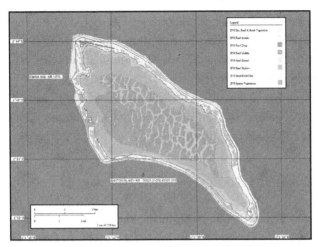

Figure 37 - Map of Canton Island

Support battalion troops will not be moving ashore until D+4 at the earliest. The engineers will be busy repairing the airport and working on the runway (in addition to building barracks and the like). What is currently unknown is how bad the coral is in the lagoon and how the reefs are. It would be an excellent facility and anchorage. I had to remember, that unlike in my time, a lagoon like this would be dredged and a port constructed without thought to environmental issues. National existence is at stake; other matters could be fixed in the future. This plan was going to be presented by COL Jeschke to ADM Nimitz tomorrow with our information and changes.

I smiled when I realized that MAJ Acosta and MAJ Shackleton were "friendly" rivals. Could be interesting; could be dangerous.

THEORIES AND INTENTIONS

Though Canton Island has not yet fallen, the plans for the invasion go forward. The first troops should be leaving in about three weeks. We're betting almost the entire Pacific Fleet on this operation. It makes me ill to think about what would happen if we were to fail.

The Japanese carriers are still near Celebes. It seems that Balikpapan and the rest of the area are actually the priority. More than likely for the oil supplies.

LATE DAY REPORTS

Pearl Harbor was busy during the day. A group of four tankers had refueled here during the day and were continuing their journey to Sydney, Australia to bring badly needed fuel supplies.

Another group of four tankers were unloading their fuel to the tank farm for further operations. This will take another day or so and then they will return to San Francisco to load up more. The great logistical tail back to the Continental United States was now in swing.

A group of three fleet cargo ships arrived late this afternoon. They are under the operational control of the Pacific Fleet now. They are awaiting orders.

The group of four converted fast liners left San Francisco to bring the 31st Pursuit Group to Sydney. They would come to Pearl Harbor first to refuel, then to Christmas Island to refuel and thence on to Sydney. When they drop off their troops and planes, they are to return to San Francisco by the same route. The fighters will then make their way up to Port Moresby.

The British reported that CAPT Stevens' group was able to make 23 knots and were heading to Soerabaja. Another report about the light cruiser HMS Danae was received indicating that they were still making for Soerabaja at 8 knots.

CAPT Rooks at Soerabaja reported that the Dutch destroyer HNLMS Van Ghent was fully repaired and was ready for orders.

It was almost 1900 and I missed dinner. I went to the Officer's Club for a quick sandwich and a beer. I went to my bungalow, took a shower and immediately went to bed.

Morning Brief

I didn't sleep well at all. The absurdity of my situation was beginning to make me wonder if I was in some sort of delusion. Is this real? It sure feels real. I'm stressed out more now than I was at the Naval Academy, more than when I was an Ensign on my first bridge watch, more than I was in the Persian Gulf thinking we entered a minefield. It's unreal.

In any case, duty calls.

I ate some toast with jam as we began the morning briefing. ADM Nimitz was meeting with the civilian authorities about some issue or another. The Operations Officer then began the briefing.

There was action on the West Coast. The destroyers USS Crosby, USS Kennison, USS Crane and USS Kilty were formed to execute offensive anti-submarine patrols on the coast. The force is known as "Chocolate 1" and is under the command of LCDR Collie. The remaining destroyers that were sent back to the coast (USS Allen, USS Talbot and USS Dent) were being held as convoy escorts for now.

Word also came from CAPT Rooks at Soerabaja. The submarine USS S-37 (CDR Easton) was putting to sea to head to the Gulf of Tomini to attack the carriers there.

All other US Forces were proceeding according to previously mentioned operational plans.

The British Liaison Officer reported that quite a few new developments were occurring in the Australian area.

First is that a squadron of transport aircraft were moved to Townsville. This will allow Australian forces to provide replacements and medical evacuation from Port Moresby. Also at Townsville arrived the Australian Cruiser Force. Since there were few large rounds used in their previous engagement it was decided to send them to Townsville as this would allow a quicker reaction against Japanese incursions on New Guinea.

Second, there was a report that the 14th Australian Brigade had arrived at Cooktown and that they needed supplies. A single light freighter was loading supplies at Townsville to bring them to Cooktown. A further five coastal/light freighters were loading up with supplies at Sydney to also make the run up to Cooktown. This should allow the forces on the ground at Cooktown to build up defenses.

The morning briefing ended and we went to work. I had some fresh fruit for breakfast; pineapple, excellent pineapple.

SUBMARINE OPERATIONS

There were no reports of friendly or enemy submarine attacks today. The only reports received were routine.

HAWAII

There were no major reports. All incoming and outgoing forces were proceeding according to plan.

BROADER PACIFIC OCEAN

Friendly forces were still unloading at Christmas Island and Palmyra. It would be a few more days at both locations before the shipping would be heading back to Pearl Harbor.

There was also a report of continuing low level combat at Canton Island. The Navy ground personnel were still trading pot shots with the Japanese; it is unknown when the Japanese will make their firm assault. The estimates of Japanese troop strengths change almost hourly.

PHILIPPINE ISLAND OPERATIONS

There were no major airstrikes at Luzon today. It was reported that the weather wasn't very good in the area; this probably had something to do with it. However, there was renewed ground combat north of Clark Field with the beginnings of an artillery duel. There were a few casualties to our side but none of the artillery pieces were put out of action. There is enough heavy artillery ammunition to last a few days.

At Manila, Japanese troops had pushed into the southern "suburbs" and were beginning an artillery attack against known friendly locations and against the main road junctions. There was no indication of enemy casualties. However, at least for now, friendly troops were holding.

CHINESE THEATER

There were reports of continued combat at Hwainan, Haichow, Lang Son, Kweisui, Loyang, Kaifeng, Canton and Kweiteh. There was a report of a defeat of Chinese forces near Sinyang. Chinese infantry was pushed back and the Japanese have taken control of the immediate area.

BRITISH AND ALLIED OPERATIONS

There were continued air attacks against remaining friendly troops that were pushed out of Victoria Point. It is dire for them there because there is no way to send a rescue team via ships to get them. They will try to make their way through Japanese lines heading north.

Further south on the Malayan Peninsula, there was a small airstrike against British troops at Malacca. There were a few casualties on the ground and no damage was scored against the enemy bombers.

In the west side of Borneo, there were a couple of attacks against Allied troops that were in the area of Singkawang. There were two confirmed strikes against facilities and troops there. Best reports showed a total of roughly 60 enemy bombers making the attacks. It was also reported that several of the Japanese bombers were damaged by anti-aircraft fire (apparently the second strike came it at only 5000'). They were seen leaving the area heading north, at least a half dozen of them trailing smoke of some kind.

On the east side of Borneo, the Japanese 8th Special Naval Landing Force was still engaged with the Dutch troops on the ground at Balikpapan. Neither side made any headway against the other.

Meanwhile, Celebes Island was attacked at two locations by Japanese carrier based planes. Makassar and Kendari were hit by Kate level bombers and Val dive bombers escorted by Zero fighters. There was light damage at both locations and there were no indications of enemy planes being shot down. It appeared that the carriers were moving south; they would then either head west to go back up the Makassar Straights or south and east to northern Australia.

The only major news from the Australian Theater was that more Japanese troops had landed at Lae. There was only a company of Australian troops present and they were engaged in combat against the invading Japanese troops.

Figure 38 - Japanese "Kate" Torpedo Bomber

INTELLIGENCE

The only major piece of information that came from the Intelligence Section today was confirmation of an enemy ship sunk at Kuching back on December 21st. The Meiu Maru (4875 tons) was confirmed sunk by radio intercepts and decryption. The ship was sunk by the British.

OPERATION SINGING PUMPKIN PLANNING

There was nothing new on this front. Our plans were presented to ADM Nimitz in the presence of COL Jeschke. No requests for information came out by the end of the day and no indications as to the viability of the operation were given to us. We were standing by to assist with any questions or to rework any specific portions of the plan. The stress on ADM Nimitz must be horrible.

THEORIES AND INTENTIONS

Oddly enough it was a relatively "slow." day. Nothing was really new except for tracking the Japanese carriers. All the operations were going on as planned, apparently for the Japanese as well.

LATE DAY REPORTS

There was a confirmed report showing the Japanese carriers around 60 nautical miles southeast of Kendari on the Island of Celebes. It was unknown which direction they were going to be turning to; they were heading due south when they were spotted.

There were no other major reports. I left for dinner and stopped by the Officer's Club for a quick beer.

Morning Brief

The weather was unusually odd today. Cloudy and kind of gloomy. The walk over to the headquarters building was nice because of the breeze. When I got the building we were just about ready to start the morning briefing.

The Operations Officer started by talking about Christmas Island. There was a lot of activity with the 2nd Marine Engineering Regiment; they were still busy building up the defensive positions with the 4th Marine Defense Battalion and were working on facilities. The runway was being worked on and there was equipment being unloaded that would help increase the capacity of the port. The patrol squadron VP-12 (equipped with Catalina flying boats) was running patrols to the west heading towards Canton Island. This would give warning if Japanese ships were heading towards Christmas Island.

Additionally, escorted fleet oilers had left Pearl Harbor today to bring fuel to the island for use as an intermediate fueling spot for ships transiting to Australia. They should reach Christmas Island in three or four days. It will take them a few days to completely unload as well.

The British Liaison Officer reported that elements of the 6th Australian Division were assembling at Aden after having been released from duty in North Africa. Shipping was being gathered to be sent to Aden to load up the troops to bring them either to Java or Australia.

Closer to Java, it was determined that HMS Danae will head to Batavia and dock there for a while to allow temporary repairs before heading down to Soerabaja. HMS Mauritius will still head to Soerabaja.

He also reported that the 77th Anti-Aircraft Regiment was packing up at Karachi to head by train to Chittagong. It turns out that Chittagong will be the linchpin to start a counter invasion heading south. This was a High Command strategic decision.

At New Guinea there were reports that the Japanese had "many ships" at Rabaul and at Lae. The Australians were sending their cruiser force to try to break up enemy shipping at Lae.

There were no questions from staff members and we were dismissed to head to our desks. Hot ham and cheese on toast for breakfast – I was hungry.

Submarine Operations

First, the submarines USS S-38 and USS S-39 both arrived early this morning at Soerabaja completing their patrols. The rollup reports from both LCDR Chapple and LCDR Coe (respectively) should be radioed to us sometime today. More than likely we will have the rollup by dinnertime.

USS Salmon (LCDR McKinney) made a report that they had found a Japanese freighter escorted by a destroyer. They fired two torpedoes at the freighter and then dove deep (they did not witness the strike). They confirmed that one torpedo hit; they heard the explosion on time. The destroyer was looking for them immediately but since they dove deep immediately the destroyer didn't even get close to them. They broke contact after around three hours submerged and surfaced to find the enemy ships away from the area. They then continued their patrol.

Figure 39 - USS S-36 (SS-141) shortly before commissioning

A couple of hours later, a report from USS S-36 (LCDR McKnight) found a Japanese unescorted freighter on the surface. The radio message indicated that the merchant code was "MFM" and an "Aden Maru" class freighter. The freighter was hit by three torpedoes in quick succession; the freighter sank in less than 15 minutes. The submarine then continued the patrol; the intelligence section was notified.

A report came from the British Liaison Officer that a Japanese submarine was seen near Cairns. The submarine was found because a light freighter that was bringing supplies up to Cooktown from Townsville was shelled by the deck gun from the submarine. The freighter put out a distress call but was eventually sunk. The lifeboats were heading west towards land (they were sunk around 35 nautical miles from the coastline). The freighter's name was the SS Pulganbar.

Hawaii

All inbound and outbound forces are proceeding according to plan. There were no reports of enemy submarines in the area today.

Broader Pacific Ocean

Wake Island was bombed yet again this morning. There were no casualties on the ground, but if these attacks continue it will be difficult for freighter SS Laida to offload the supplies (even if escorted by the destroyers). It is to be hoped that enough fuel is immediately offloaded so that the remaining Wildcat fighters can get into the air to provide air cover to continue unloading the badly needed supplies.

The anticipated Japanese assault on Canton Island began at sunrise. By 0930 local time, a final radio report was received from the island indicating that Japanese troops were just outside of their building. There were a little over 400 friendly troops stationed there; they are all either dead or prisoners of war. Operation Singing Pumpkin is still progressing on schedule.

Philippine Island Operations

The Philippines were very busy today. It started with an air raid on Clark Field by at least 20 Betty bombers escorted by fighters (Zero types). They damaged the runway and scored a direct hit on an O-47A aircraft with a large bomb; the aircraft was very obviously destroyed. One Betty bomber was damaged by ground fire.

Nichols Field near Manila was also attacked by a very large force of Sally medium bombers. The radio report indicated that at least 50 bombers were in the enemy force. They hit the runway pretty hard and caused some casualties on the ground as well. None of the enemy aircraft were damaged or shot down by ground fire.

Just off the coast, the minesweeper USS Bittern was attacked while patrolling off of Bataan maintaining the minefield. The ship was hit by a bomb and set on fire. The crew radioed that the ship will probably sink and that they were trying to get closer to Bataan so that they could abandon ship.

As these air attacks were going on there was a continued artillery duel going on in the southern areas of Manila. Casualties to the Japanese were unknown, but one of the 75mm field guns from the 1st Philippine Army Division was destroyed by a Japanese shell. It appears that the Japanese are trying to "soften up" the area prior to conducting an assault.

Meanwhile, a Japanese assault group began an attack against friendly troops northeast of Clark Field. They attacked with tanks in regimental strength along with infantry with heavy artillery support. The US 194th Tank Battalion and the US 192nd Tank Battalion laid in a decent ambush against the Japanese. They destroyed "many" enemy tanks for a loss of two friendly tanks. This was done to separate the infantry from the tanks to allow friendly artillery to cut apart the attacking wedges; this was done well by the 91st Philippine Army Division. None of our forces were pushed back from their defensive positions. Supplies however, are still a problem.

CHINESE THEATER

As usual, there was continued combat in China. The Japanese were tying more airpower into their attacks (dive bombers and medium tactical bombers). Combat was confirmed at Hwainan, Lang Son, Kaifeng, Kweisui, Loyang and Kweiteh.

Defeats were admitted at Sinyang, Canton and Chengting. At Sinyang, it was reported that some rear area Chinese troops were taken by surprise from Japanese infantry. They had to abandon the positions they had and fell back to the northwest.

At Canton, a Chinese Infantry Corps was attacked by a "significant" Japanese force. The remaining Chinese forces fell back to the southeast. Word from the Chinese leadership was that friendly casualties were "substantial". I'm not entirely sure what that means, but it can't be good.

The same story was repeated near Chengting. It was reported that at least 3000 friendly troops were killed or wounded (the majority were killed). The Chinese forces were under attack by at least three Japanese Infantry Brigades supported by artillery.

The Chinese High Command again asked for medical supplies, ammunition, weapons and food. They are having a very difficult time keeping their forces adequately supplied.

British and Allied Operations

On the Malayan Peninsula, radio contact was lost with the troops that had been retreating north from Victoria Point. It is unknown if the troops were captured or if their last radio set was destroyed or broken.

Kuantan was hit by an airstrike that was relatively small given the mass raids in the past. The airfield was hit by around 20 Betty bombers that damaged the runway further. No repairs were ordered.

Kuala Lumpur was assaulted by several regiments of Japanese troops during the day. They managed to push their way into the suburbs in the northeast area. The remnants of the Argylls Battalion are located there along with some anti-tank guns and some Burmese troops. They were conducting an active defense but they were heavily outnumbered.

Meanwhile, on the west side of Borneo, friendly troops at Singkawang were under attack from Japanese troops and aircraft. Two very large strikes against friendly ground troops occurred during the day that helped the Japanese ground troops. By mid-afternoon, friendly troops had been pushed out of the built up areas and were retreating south towards Pontianak. Friendly forces suffered at least 370 casualties.

On the east side of Borneo, Dutch troops were trading mortar rounds and rifle fire with invading Japanese forces. Neither side made any headway towards the other. The Japanese would have to bring in reinforcements or withdraw.

AUSTRALIA AND NEW GUINEA

Because this area will begin to have more significance, it will have its own section in my journal from day to day. North New Guinea is seeing many Japanese troops landing and the Australian cruiser force is still heading towards Lae to break up enemy shipping. I feel that this area will be getting more Japanese attention soon.

The freighter SS Steel Worker completed unloading supplies at Pago Pago and was beginning the return leg back to Sydney.

INTELLIGENCE

The first part of the 1600 report revolved around the area of Rabaul. It would seem that via radio intercepts that there were some Australian forces still falling back from Rabaul base. Since the reports were coming from Japanese sources it is difficult to determine how many friendly troops were still fighting. This information was sent to the British Liaison Officer.

There were also reports that lent credence to the thought that Tulagi had been occupied by the Japanese. This was done with decrypts and radio direction finding. There were no friendly troops on the island, so unless we send recon assets to find out for sure, we must assume that the Japanese are actually there.

Another interesting report came in concerning Malaya. The Japanese 36th Infantry Regiment was identified as being at Kota Bharu. They are probably a reinforcement unit that will start to march south to support attacks heading toward Singapore.

Operation Singing Pumpkin Planning

Word came that ADM Nimitz was pleased with the overall plan. What was occurring now was that the supply officers were working on the individual loads for each ship. Unless some other operational level problem comes up, the team I'm on will be informed of changes only.

Theories and Intentions

The Chinese Theater saw several setbacks with friendly troops being pushed back. The Philippines was holding for now, but that couldn't last long. Canton Island has officially fallen to the Japanese; Operation Singing Pumpkin is well planned and should take the island back.

Late Day Reports

The rollup report from USS S-38 was received. LCDR Chapple and his submarine are officially credited with 4875 tons sunk (Tyoko Maru on December 21st) by multiple verifications (intelligence, radio decrypts and reports). They are also credited with damaging another freighter on December 9th; this ship was not confirmed sunk. The rollup reports that they should be ready for another patrol in a few days.

The rollup report from USS S-39 was also received. LCDR Coe is officially credited with 830 tons sunk (Hakka Maru) confirmed by multiple other verification sources (mostly intelligence and radio decrypts). They have some equipment that needs to be fixed onboard their submarine and need a minimum of a week to complete the repairs.

A report via the British Liaison Officer stated that the sloop HMAS Warrego was leaving Melbourne and heading up to Townsville to begin anti-submarine patrols. Two other sloops that were escorting the 1st Australian Division to Port Moresby (HMAS Swan and HMAS Moresby) were ordered to break away from the Task Force and head to Townsville to meet HMAS Warrego also for anti-submarine patrols.

The Japanese carriers were placed as being near Makassar on the southwest peninsula of Celebes Island. It was surmised that they would head either north up the Makassar Straights or west through the Java Sea. It was unknown at this time.

I left for the day. The night breeze felt good and it smelled like fish for dinner at the Officer's Club. I went for a sandwich and a beer.

MORNING BRIEF

The Operations Officer began the morning meeting. I munched on some granola like substance as the briefing began.

The transport task force (Task Force 381) that unloaded Marines at Christmas Island should finish offloading the rest of the supplies and equipment today and then head back to Pearl Harbor.

Task Force 139 is heading towards Christmas Island. It has the fleet oilers USS Neosho and USS Platte along with four destroyers acting as escort. They are proceeding at 14 knots and have experienced no problems. They should arrive at their destination in around three days or so.

The fleet troop transport USS President Coolidge arrived late yesterday at Midway Island and began offloading supplies. It should only be a couple of days to fully offload the supplies and then the ship will head back to Pearl Harbor.

From the West Coast, word was received that the destroyer transport (APD type) USS Waters was released and would begin transit to Pearl Harbor from San Diego.

Also on the West Coast 2nd Fighter Command and some support troops were ordered to load up on some fast converted liners to begin the transit to Sydney. When they arrive there, they will then head up to Port Moresby to support fighter and medium bomber operations.

All other operations were proceeding as planned and no other major updates were needed.

The British Liaison Officer had nothing major to report this morning so we all went to work.

SUBMARINE OPERATIONS

A report came in from USS Porpoise (CDR Brewster) indicating that they had found an unescorted Japanese freighter around 150 nautical miles southwest of Formosa. They reported many problems with their Mark 14 Torpedoes. They had fired their last eight torpedoes, three circled around, two had been heard to hit the hull of the freighter and not explode and the remainder apparently ran too deep. The submarine surfaced and attacked the freighter with their deck gun. They fired off almost all of their gun ammunition over a four-hour running gun battle. The submarine also took a couple of small round hit that wounded two sailors on the submarine. The freighter was hit repeatedly (4" 50 caliber Mark 9 deck gun) and was burning brightly. Aircraft were seen and the submarine needed to dive to protect itself. After a few more hours, darkness had fallen and the submarine was heading to Soerabaja. They are completely out of torpedoes and have about a dozen gun rounds left. This will complete their patrol when they get back to port. The freighter was identified with code "MFM" as a Nanko Maru class freighter. It is unknown if the freighter sank. The Intelligence Section was notified.

HAWAII

Again, there were no major combat reports here. However, outbound tankers left port this morning and were heading back to the West Coast to reload fuel for delivery to Pearl Harbor. Also, USS Yorktown was only a day away from arriving. They were seen by PBY Catalina patrols heading in all directions looking for Japanese submarines.

BROADER PACIFIC OCEAN

The Japanese were not seen doing any major operations that were new today. We were not able to get any patrols over to Canton Island (the range was too great from Christmas Island). Our forces were working hard at Christmas Island building up the base and defenses there. It was beginning to look like all future operations in this general area would have Christmas Island as the major base.

PHILIPPINE ISLAND OPERATIONS

Reports of major combat in the vicinity of Clark Field filled up the airwaves today. The Japanese sent in medium bombers to support the major attack from the north and northeast areas around Clark Field. The attack was successfully defended with the Japanese being held to no gains. Reports from friendly forces put the Japanese force at a full division plus a reinforcing infantry brigade with tanks and lots of artillery support. It seemed like a lot of Japanese combat engineers were supporting the attack; they were trying to knock out key defensive positions leading into the area. Friendly casualties at the end of the day were just under 200 (mostly wounded, 31 killed). Japanese casualties were unknown but were thought to be "substantial".

At Manila, the artillery duel continued with small probing attacks being done by Japanese infantry groups. These attacks were supported by Japanese bombing runs and some aircraft loitering, possibly to feed information to the Japanese artillery. In any case, the front lines have not changed and it looks like the Japanese are content with continuing the artillery strikes.

CHINESE THEATER

There were new reports of combat at Pucheng. Reports were indicating that at least two Japanese divisions with support were attacking the area. The initial Japanese attack was repulsed by large Chinese units. There were also reports of airstrikes supporting the attack. This may become the crux of the next set of attacks.

There were also reports of combat at Kweiteh, Canton, Kaifeng, Hwainan, Loyang, Kweisui and Lang Son. At these locations the front lines didn't move much.

BRITISH AND ALLIED OPERATIONS

There was a Japanese invasion of Manado on the northeast end of Celebes Island. Initial reports showed at least a dozen enemy ships in the area providing support to the invasion forces. The shore batteries managed to damage one of the transports with a few rounds of 75mm ammunition. There was a Dutch garrison battalion of light infantry with some heavy weapons against what was estimated at 2000 or so Japanese troops. It did not look good for the Dutch troops.

On the west side of Borneo, friendly troops were still retreating towards Pontianak; it would take them a few days to get there on foot. On the east side of Borneo, the Dutch 6th Battalion is still trading shots with the landed Japanese troops. It is thought that once the Japanese run low on supplies and are whittled down a bit, the Dutch will aggressively attack the Japanese there.

On the Malayan Peninsula there were several major developments. The biggest setback occurred at Kuala Lumpur. It was reported that nearly 20,000 Japanese troops had attacked the area beginning at dawn. There was a heavy artillery bombardment that had walked forward based on the forward progress of the infantry. Combat engineers came forward with the attacking infantry to destroy hardpoints set up by the British and Burmese defenders. By the end of the day, all friendly forces had been pushed out of the city and were retreating towards Singapore. There were no reports as to friendly casualties but they were thought to be very heavy.

Kuantan was also subjected to another set of heavy air attacks. The only report received was that "more than 100 bombers" had attacked during the day. The entire area was hit, nearer the coast, the airfield, some of the spotted defensive positions that friendly troops had set up. As usual, friendly troops were not repairing any of the base facilities except for firing positions.

AUSTRALIA AND NEW GUINEA

There were some unconfirmed reports of Japanese airstrikes against Kavieng on the Bismarck Archipelago. Again, these were unconfirmed but it would make sense if the Japanese wanted to secure the Bismarck Sea. There are no patrol assets with the range to check out the area.

There were also reports of combat at Lae between a company of Australian Infantry and invading enemy forces. Casualties were unknown.

INTELLIGENCE

Figure 40 - IJN Kamikaze

The intelligence section gave a report that signals determined that the Japanese 146th Infantry Regiment was on transports heading to Davao in the Philippines. Right now there was nothing that could be done about this report.

Information leading to a confirmed kill was also reported today. The Japanese destroyer IJN Kamikaze was confirmed sunk by the British near Kota Bharu back on Christmas Day. The British Liaison Officer was notified.

OPERATION SINGING PUMPKIN PLANNING

There were no requests from our team today about Operation Singing Pumpkin. Of interesting note, the four chaplains assigned to the Operation were at the headquarters building meeting with ADM Nimitz. They drew straws to see which chaplain would be in the initial assault wave. As it turned out, one of the two Protestant chaplains would be making the initial run; the remaining three (another Protestant, a Catholic and a Jewish chaplain) would draw straws when the force arrives at Canton Island.

THEORIES AND INTENTIONS

With the Japanese moving swiftly on the Malayan Peninsula, it does not look good for the troops in Singapore. If memory serves, Singapore fell to the Japanese on February 15th,1942; if that was the case, then they are ahead on their timetable. Maybe it was a good thing to get the reinforcing troops to Java.

I am not sure about what the Japanese are doing in Celebes and on the east side of Borneo. Celebes doesn't have much in the way of raw resources needed, so I'm assuming that they are taking the island to make sure that they can adequately defend the area after they secure the oilfields and other raw materials in the region.

LATE DAY REPORTS

HMS Mauritius arrived at Soerabaja late today and assessments were begun determining the material condition of the ship. The escorting destroyers were also completing their assessments. The reports should be ready by the time we come back to work in the morning.

Also good news, HMS Danae arrived at Batavia. She immediately went pierside to begin some repairs before heading to either Soerabaja or to Columbo for drydock repairs. Material condition reports should be available in the morning.

The fleet cargo ship USS Castor completed unloading supplies at Christmas Island and was heading back to Pearl Harbor with the same three attending destroyers. Task Force Present that brought troops and supplies to Christmas Island also completed full unloading and was heading back to Pearl Harbor. This is good news.

There was a pork like substance for dinner tonight. It wasn't Spam. It wasn't bad. Sleep came quickly.

Morning Brief

After getting to the headquarters building I was told that a rotation would be put in place to start giving personnel a day off once in a while. The strain was beginning to show on everyone and some R&R was necessary. I thought back that I had a half a day off in the last 30 days. I must look terrible.

In any case, a busy morning brief began with a report by the British Liaison Officer. He began by discussing a report from CAPT Butler who was the commanding officer of HMS Danae. The ship was heavily damaged and it would take a little over two weeks to repair the ship enough to send her to a drydock somewhere. It was thought that it would be Columbo because of the limited space available at Soerabaja. HMS Tenedos (the escorting destroyer) reported that she would be ready for operations in 24 hours.

At Soerabaja, CAPT Stevens reported that the damage to HMS Mauritius wasn't as bad as originally thought, but that his ship wouldn't fit in the drydock. It would take a few days to shore up some of the damage and then the ship could head to Columbo for permanent repairs. The problem was that some of the forward compartments were damaged heavily and were flooded, but the damage was below the waterline and required drydock assistance (the divers didn't have the equipment to repair the damage pierside). The report also stated that CAPT Stevens was fairly confident that he could make 23 knots if he put to sea after temporary repairs.

HMS Stronghold took damage from enemy fire and would require a week in drydock to fix the hull damage; the damage to other parts of the ship could be repaired simultaneously.

HMS Electra would be joining her in the drydock as her damage was almost the same (she took a hit from an enemy 127mm shell that exploded damaging the hull, a couple of compartments and damaging a boiler). HMS Encounter had minor damage and would be ready in a couple of days and HMS Isis reported that she would be ready in 24 hours for operations.

The Liaison Officer then moved onto supply issues. The ships carrying US supplies were still advancing at 11 knots but would still take a couple of weeks to arrive at Java. A group of three more freighters were loading up with a mix of US and British supplies and would leave Cape Town either today or tomorrow. It was intended that groups would leave every few days to keep the lines open.

He also reported that the British 55th Infantry Brigade had taken up position to the east of Java at Banjoewangi in case the Japanese try an invasion there. He then yielded the floor to our Operations Officer.

Our portion of the morning briefing centered on a report from the West Coast that a further nine civilian freighters were loading up with supplies to begin shuttle runs to Pearl Harbor. Also, II Fighter Command and some base support troops were now well out to sea with a temporary destination of Sydney to support our forces in Port Moresby. The fighters had already left and it would be a while before the bombers were loaded up for shipment.

Here at Pearl Harbor, the battleships USS West Virginia and USS Maryland had sent reports indicating that they should be ready for operations in 12 days. This will allow them to support Operation Singing Pumpkin.

Japanese carriers were still near the area of Makassar. We were to notify ADM Nimitz if any major reports about this force were received; the carriers seem to have disappeared when they were last seen near Makassar. The Dutch were asked to send patrol planes there to see if the carriers were hanging around or if they had left the area.

We were then dismissed to our daily duties.

Submarine Operations

An interesting report was received from USS Perch (LCDR Hurt). They had seen an escorted convoy and made a dive to approach. They went deep and relatively fast (for a diesel submarine submerged on batteries) and when they popped up to take a look found themselves in the middle of the convoy. A freighter directly on the bow at about 1500 yards was "an MFM Daisin Maru class seen riding low forward, possibly previously damaged". This ship was allocated four torpedoes from the forward tubes. Aft of the submarine was "an MFM Aden Maru class freighter" that was allocated both aft torpedo tubes; the ship was only 1000 yards away. The ship forward of the submarine was hit by two of the four torpedoes; the ship aft was hit by both torpedoes fired at it. LCDR Hurt then dove deep and sent his submarine on a reciprocal course to the convoy to break quickly. Only one of the escorting destroyers came close and the depth charges were fairly far away. They stayed submerged for 6 hours before coming to periscope depth to take a look; no ships were seen so they surfaced and ran on their diesel engines to continue the patrol and recharge their batteries. The Intelligence Section was notified.

Hawaii

The only major items to report concerned the carrier USS Yorktown. She arrived around lunchtime today with her destroyer escort. All of the ships will be replenished and will await further orders. Some other ships should be coming in late today as well.

BROADER PACIFIC OCEAN

Wake Island was subjected to a fairly large raid. It was estimated that around 30 Betty bombers attacked the island today. There were no casualties on the ground. The freighter SS Laida should be arriving at Wake tomorrow with her destroyers. They moved to the north to come down so they could avoid being attacked by any bombers that regularly visit Wake. Again, priority is for fuel for the fighters (along with the spare parts), followed by all other supplies.

PHILIPPINE ISLAND OPERATIONS

There were reports of night air attacks against both Manila and Clark Field. At Clark Field the target appeared to be front line areas where friendly artillery was massed to attack the growing Japanese forces. At Manila it was localized to the south-central areas of the city where friendly troops had massed to provide defenses should the Japanese push into the city.

As it turned out, a Japanese attack materialized at dawn in southern Manila. Best information was that the assault was spearheaded by the Japanese 16th Division. They were engaged in combat with the remnants of four Philippine Army Divisions (the 1st, 71st, 41st and 51st along with a regiment of military police). The Japanese had pushed into the southern suburbs of the city but were taking heavy losses to infantry and machine gun teams in fortified positions that had to be destroyed one by one. The real problem was one of major firepower; the Japanese had brought up what was thought to be a full regiment of artillery to support the attack (good communications were seen between forward Japanese units and calls for fire). Casualties were unknown and combat was continuing as I am writing in this journal.

Back at Clark Field the Japanese continued to attack vigorously. Their tank regiments had run into some hastily laid minefields that disabled them whereupon they were shelled heavily by friendly artillery and attacked by platoon sized units with Molotov cocktails to destroy them. When this occurred, Japanese infantry would call in artillery on the attacking teams and then counterattack supported by combat engineers. The front line hadn't changed, but "a couple dozen" Japanese tanks were destroyed. Friendly casualty reports from the last 24 hours show that 71 friendly troops were wounded; Japanese casualties are unknown, but given their tactics they can't be good.

CHINESE THEATER

Combat continued at many locations as the Japanese continued their overall assault against Chinese forces. Combat at Hwainan, Lang Son, Kaifeng, Kweisui, Haichow, Loyang, Canton, Kweiteh and Pucheng. The defense was particularly effective at Pucheng and nowhere did the Japanese make significant gains.

BRITISH AND ALLIED OPERATIONS

Manado at the northeast corner of Celebes Island, saw Japanese troops landing during the entire course of the day.

The shore defense batteries that are made up of 75mm guns were firing almost the entire day as well (firing on landing craft, ships offshore and at the beaches where the Japanese were landing). It was reported that at least two of the troop transports were hit by the shore batteries, one of which was set afire. However, this did not deter the troops from landing. The final report of the day indicated that "thousands" of troops had landed and were engaged in continual combat with the single garrison battalion located there. The Dutch still owned the base at the end of the day, hanging on by a thread because they were so outnumbered.

Near Borneo, a Japanese surface group was found with at least one battleship in it, a "Kongo Class" and was attacked by Dutch level bombers with not hits being score on enemy shipping and no damage suffered by Dutch forces. Meanwhile, at Balikpapan, the situation had not changed with Japanese forces and Dutch infantry still locked in low level combat. The British Liaison Officer thought that the Dutch had intimated that available troops at Balikpapan may attack the Japanese before more troops land.

Kuantan, on the Malayan Peninsula, was hit by a mass raid again today. Nearly 100 bombers attacked in three separate waves and caused more destruction to the area. It is strange that they don't attack with amphibious troops or with troops from the north, but just keep bombing the place. Surely they must know that all the cruisers and destroyers have fallen back to Java. Strange.

Further to the north, approaching the area of Moulmein (itself, around 90 miles from Rangoon), a Japanese airstrike occurred. Fighters from the All-Volunteer Group flew the 90 miles to attack the aircraft. Two friendly fighters were shot down and a single enemy fighter was shot down (reports indicated that it was an "Oscar" type). Royal Air Force crews at Moulmein suffered some wounded.

AUSTRALIA AND NEW GUINEA

Shortland Island came under assault by Japanese amphibious forces today. There were a few civilians living there who radioed in the report. There are no troops there at all. In a related note, the British Liaison Officer reported that the Australian Cruiser Force was returning from Lae having found no enemy shipping. Their orders were changed and they are going to head to Shortland Island to attack the Japanese shipping there. They will head in from the southeast just in case the Japanese have aircraft available at Rabaul (this will require the ships to head further to the east before making the run in, but it will be safer for them). Also related, the company of troops at Lae were pushed back into the jungle; Lae now belongs to the Japanese.

INTELLIGENCE

Another enemy ship sunk was identified. The Japanese destroyer transport Shimakaze was confirmed sunk by signals traffic and decrypting. The ship was sunk by British forces at Kota Bharu on December 25th. Given the intensity of the combat that day it is not surprising that it is taking a while to determine exactly what happened there. The Intelligence Section also reported that they had received some information about the attack by USS Perch today based on the amount of traffic coming from that area and that they were working on decrypting it. They had no further information. They were also instructed to find information about the Japanese carriers; they had none.

OPERATION SINGING PUMPKIN PLANNING

We were ordered to do ship selection for Task Force Decamp; this is the Task Force for surface action in case a Japanese surface force tries to break up the invasion. The ships are:

- Battleships: USS Maryland and USS West Virginia
- Heavy Cruisers: USS New Orleans and USS Astoria
- Light Cruisers: USS Concord and USS Honolulu
- Destroyers: USS Craven, USS Gridley, USS Henley, USS Tucker, USS Cassin and USS Downes

Figure 41 - USS Honolulu (CL-48)

These selections were based on availability and capability. The force commander has not yet been selected.

THEORIES AND INTENTIONS

Now that the Japanese were actively attacking both Clark Field and Manila, it looks like they are trying to get to their "end game" with regards to operations on Luzon. Previous intelligence information tells us that Davao is next, but there is little that we can do about it; there are no forces available and the transit would be too dangerous. We will continue planning on Operation Singing Pumpkin and hit the Japanese there.

LATE DAY REPORTS

Some late day reports from the British Liaison Officer told us that there were "many" ships at Kuching. These ships were probably disgorging more troops to consolidate gains and look at what resources they could ship back to the Home Islands.

He also reported that the sloops HMAS Swan and HMAS Moresby had arrived at Townsville. They needed about a day to replenish then they would start anti-submarine patrols in the area while waiting for another sloop (HMAS Warrego coming up from Melbourne).

From the US side, Task Force 113 arrived at Sydney to meet with the heavy cruiser USS Pensacola for operations in the Australian Theater. The light cruisers USS Raleigh and USS Detroit arrived with the destroyers USS Cummings, USS Drayton and USS Lawton. Their orders have not yet been determined. Supplies and fuel are already on their way from the West Coast.

At Pearl Harbor, the fleet cargo ship USS Procyon arrived along with the aviation cargo ships USS Hammondsport and USS Kittyhawk. They were to replenish and await further orders.

I left at around 1800. I went to a poker game at the Officer's Club that lasted until 2300; I won about $6. They don't know what Texas Hold'em is here yet… I laughed inside at that; we played Stud and Draw. That one Commander (Larson I think his name was); he needs to learn how to bluff.

MORNING BRIEF

ADM Nimitz seemed well rested today. He had a devious little smile on his face as we got ready for the morning briefing. I wondered what that was all about.

The Operations Officer began with the West Coast. The freighters that were loading up yesterday have been designated as Charlie 9-2. They put to sea late yesterday and would make shuttle runs to Pearl Harbor. Another freighter force known as Charlie 10-5 was loading up today; they had 10 freighters in their force and would also run supplies. These supply runs had everything in them, food, ammunition, uniforms, spare parts; you name it. Just when I thought I figured out the naming convention, he told us that Charlie 4-9 was leaving the Panama Canal to head up to San Francisco; they had 12 civilian freighters. Oh well…

The four converted liners that brought troops to Pearl Harbor had arrived safely at San Francisco; they were standing by for further orders.

The freighter SS Laida should arrive at Wake Island today. We were to stand by on reports if they come under attack.

The submarine USS Sailfish (LCDR Voge) was departing Soerabaja to patrol the South China Sea between Palawan Island and Cam Ranh Bay and attack Japanese shipping. It was thought that replacement torpedoes, parts and other ammunition would be available for them at the end of the patrol so there was no reason to keep them in port.

The same went for the submarine USS Searaven (LCDR Aylward). They were to patrol the approaches west of North Borneo to attack Japanese shipping.

The British Liaison Officer reported that the three freighters mentioned yesterday had put to sea with a mixed bag of supplies for US and British forces at Java. They were to unload at Tjilatjap on the south central part of Java. Also, No. 232 Squadron made up of Hurricane fighters was loading up on the fast liner Empress Australia to head to Tjilatjap to offload the fighters and the pilots. The final destination of the squadron was not yet determined.

All other forces were proceeding as planned. The briefing ended and we went to our respective stations for the day's work.

Submarine Operations

The submarine USS Snapper (LCDR Stone) arrived at Soerabaja this morning completing their first war patrol. We expect the rollup report in around 24 hours. They are replenishing and repairing to get ready for another patrol. There were enough Mark 14 torpedoes available ashore for a full load for the submarine. There are only around 30 Mark 14 torpedoes left ashore before the supplies arrive from Cape Town.

A report from USS Tarpon (LCDR Wallace) found a freighter on the surface and attacked around sunrise this morning near Groot Natoena. They identified the ship as an MKFM code for a Husimi Maru class freighter. This might be a problem because a Husimi Maru is a troop transport. In any case, the ship was hit by two torpedoes and by the deck gun of the submarine. The ship was seen to have sunk in the presence of the submarine. The intelligence section was notified. The report also indicated that they were out of torpedoes and would fall back on Soerabaja to replenish.

USS Saury (LCDR Burnside) reported that they had found a large troop transport escorted by a couple of destroyers. They fired four torpedoes at the ship from 3000 yards. They hit with two of the torpedoes on the starboard side (both hits aft of the beam). They were immediately attacked by the destroyers and had to dive deep to break from the area. They were under attack for over two hours but managed to escape with no damage. The ship was identified as a code "MFM" for a Takatiho Maru transport. The submarine is continuing the patrol.

All during the afternoon, the destroyers USS Allen and USS Talbot were in a duel with a Japanese submarine off the West Coast near Coal Harbor, Vancouver Island. The submarine attacked them while they were escorting a freighter (the Ensley City). The submarine shadowed them and attacked the destroyers twice, not scoring any hits. The destroyers depth charged the submarine but it is unknown if the submarine was damaged.

HAWAII

There was no significant activity near Hawaii today. All expected friendly units were progressing in the vicinity without incident.

BROADER PACIFIC OCEAN

The freighter SS Laida arrived this morning but did not start unloading fuel, supplies and equipment until after 0900 due to a Japanese air raid. Just under 30 medium bombers attacked the island yet again. They were aiming for the locations where supplies would come to the island to make it difficult for resupply. No casualties were noted. More support forces will need to be sent to Wake Island in order to make the area more defensible.

Philippine Island Operations

Japanese troops were reported to be landing at Oroquieta on northwest Mindanao. Troop numbers were not known.

Combat continued at Clark Field and in southern Manila today. There were a few patrols from the Japanese that resulted in low level combat but no major assaults took place and friendly troops were still digging in. There was no change to the front lines.

Chinese Theater

There was little information except that there were reports of combat at Hwainan, Lang Son, Kweisui, Loyang, Kaifeng, Canton, Kweiteh and reports of a major assault at Pucheng that was repulsed (with losses). As usual, no reports of casualties were available.

British and Allied Operations

The invasion of Manado continued during the day today. More troops were unloaded and just like yesterday, were under fire from 75mm guns of shore batteries and mortar fire from the garrison there. Some fire was received from the escorting ships and an assault from Japanese infantry tried to take a couple of machine gun nests. These assaults were stopped cold, but the machine gun locations then came under mortar fire from Japanese troops. The machine gun crews fell back to other prepared positions and continued to fight the Japanese into the night.

There was an overnight air raid against Singapore by about a dozen Betty bombers. Searchlights coordinated with anti-aircraft units to have a confirmed kill (a Betty was shot down at 0120 local time). The bombers did manage to put a few bombs on the airfield. A Swordfish torpedo bomber was confirmed destroyed on the ground and several Blenheim bombers were damaged. The raid was over by 0140 local time).

Kuanatan was hit several times during the day. Total numbers of enemy bombers was not confirmed, but there were no losses to the Japanese. The facilities there are all but destroyed and yet the Japanese continue to attack.

Friendly troops were still falling back on Singapore and the engineers were working hard on firepoints, machine gun nests, artillery sites and creating obstacles. There would be quite a fight for the city.

Near Borneo, Japanese carriers were seen in the vicinity of Makassar. The carrier aircraft performed concentrated strikes at Makassar severely damaging the port facilities and the small runway near the port. It is possible that this will be the next target for an amphibious assault. There were rumors that a sortie of quick forces from Soerabaja may try to attack the carrier force.

At Balikpapan there was low level combat as usual and no major change to the front line between the Japanese 8th Special Naval Landing Force and the Dutch VI Battalion. Rumors persisted that the Dutch would counter-attack in the next day or so.

Australia and New Guinea

Port Moresby was attacked by enemy medium bombers at first light this morning. Around a dozen Betty medium bombers made a low level bombing run at about 5000 feet that took the base by surprise. They were targeting the port facilities. Only a single major hit on the facilities was noted and this damage was being repaired quickly.

Intelligence

The intelligence report concerned the Japanese carriers and probable responses by the Japanese to our assault of Canton Island. There was nothing revealed that we hadn't already known, but we were asked to prepare a response if the Japanese move their carriers into the area to break up our operation. Admittedly, I personally couldn't think of anything that could be done if more enemy ships showed up than we would expect. There wasn't much of a reserve to speak of and ADM Nimitz was firm that there would be a US carrier kept in reserve at Pearl Harbor.

Operation Singing Pumpkin Planning

There were no major requests from our team about the Invasion of Canton Island today.

Theories and Intentions

No new revelations today. I think that the operational tempo is starting to even out and we will become busier as Operation Singing Pumpkin gets closer to officially starting.

LATE DAY REPORTS

The rollup report from USS Snapper arrived at the end of the day. They are formally credited with sinking the Tazima Maru on December 22nd and damaging another ship on the 23rd (this ship was not confirmed sunk). Tonnage score for the patrol was 6475 tons. They should be ready to put to sea in a few days.

The troop transports USS U.S. Grant, USS Crescent City and USS Wharton arrived late today at Pearl Harbor. They will refuel and wait for further orders.

Figure 42 - USS Wharton (AP-7)

The converted liners carrying the 31st Pursuit Group to Australia arrived and quickly refueled. They then put immediately back out to sea to head to Christmas Island for another refueling and then would make the rest of the run to Sydney. They are moving at 22 knots.

I left at around 1830 for the night. Nothing special for dinner. Played a game of chess with an Ensign at the Officer's Club; he didn't know how to use his bishops on the attack. Sleep came quickly.

Morning Brief

It was raining today. It doesn't rain here that often. A good steady rain with winds coming in from the sea; I like the rain.

The Operations Officer began the briefing a little late. First on the list was a request from ADM Nimitz that ship selection be completed today for Task Force Loadstone pursuant to Operation Singing Pumpkin. Ships being selected for the forces are to remain in port until the operation begins.

Several submarines are leaving Pearl Harbor today for offensive operations in concert with Operation Singing Pumpkin to provide scouting and attacking forces in case the Japanese send a counter invasion force:

- USS Pollack (CDR Jameson) will patrol just west of Canton Island and engage any Japanese ships seen
- USS Trout (LCDR Fenno) will patrol northwest of Canton Island between Baker Island and the Gilbert Islands
- USS Cachalot (LCDR Christiansen) will patrol just east of the Gilbert Islands, just east of Tarawa
- USS Narwhal (LCDR Wilkins) will patrol in the Marshall Islands

Word was received from the West Coast that the 49th Pursuit Group (equipped with P-40E Warhawks) has been given orders to train up and get ready for deployment to the Pacific. They will be under II Fighter Command heading to Australia. They have been ordered to complete training by May 12th.

There were orders given for more support troops to form up and get ready to head to Wake Island. Hopefully the supplies being offloaded there will allow the remaining fighters to get off the ground to attack the bombers visiting the island daily.

All other US Forces are proceeding as planned and there are no major changes at this point.

The British Liaison Officer began his portion of the report. In Australia, the sloops HMAS Swan and HMAS Moresby, are to perform offensive anti-submarine patrols between Cairns and Cooktown. Smaller troop transports and freighters are redeploying to Townsville to better support Port Moresby. It will be a few days before the ships arrive.

Also reported was that the Australian Cruiser Force should reach Shortlands Island sometime in the next 24 hours to attack the enemy transports there. We are to stand by for those reports.

The morning briefing then ended. We had a quick breakfast of toast, oatmeal and some orange juice followed by a quick review of a newspaper. I then went to my desk to work on ship lists.

SUBMARINE OPERATIONS

A Japanese submarine attacked a group of freighters that had left San Diego with supplies for our forces in Australia around 150 nautical miles northeast of Christmas Island. The freighter SS Jacob Luckenbach was torpedoed and sunk. The crew managed to abandon ship with light casualties and were picked up by Catalina patrol planes.

The freighter Ensley City was heading up to Annette Island to drop off supplies escorted by the destroyers USS Allen and USS Talbot. USS Talbot's lookouts spotted a Japanese submarine and moved to attack it. The submarine was forced under and was depth charged several times. It is unknown if the submarine was damaged or sunk and the destroyer eventually lost contact with the submarine. The freighter kept on course and eventually made it to Annette Island late in the afternoon.

USS Seadragon (LCDR Ferrall) found a large Japanese surface group of combat ships (one reported at a battleship) and attempted to maneuver to attack in the Makassar Straights east of Balikpapan. The submarine was sighted by Japanese destroyers and had to dive deep and break from the area. It took them almost 5 hours to break contact. When they surfaced, the Japanese ships were long gone. The submarine suffered no damage.

Further north near Tawi Tawi the submarine USS Perch (LCDR Hurt) found an escorted Japanese freighter and attacked. Four torpedoes were fired at the ship (identified as a code MFM freighter "Taian Maru" class) and scored hits with three of the torpedoes; the ship was not seen to sink but it is unlikely that the ship is still on the surface. The submarine was then swarmed by a pair of escorts and a patrol plane. They dove deep and broke away slowly to the southeast. It took six hours to break contact. They then surfaced and resumed their patrol.

HAWAII

Figure 43 - USS Curtiss (AV-4)

The only major report here today is that the aviation support ship (seaplane tender) USS Curtiss had completed all repairs and was now ready for duty. All other forces were proceeding as planned.

BROADER PACIFIC OCEAN

The freighter SS Laida managed to unload about 30 tons of supplies at Wake Island. What wasn't known at the time is how bad the runway was damaged. The supplies offloaded are helping the engineers to get the runway operational again. There was another air raid that was concentrated against the defensive positions on the western side of the atoll. The Marines had suffered some wounded on the ground but went to repairing the fire points in case the Japanese try to make an assault. Fuel was also unloaded for the fighters (they should be able to get into the air after the runway is repaired).

PHILIPPINE ISLAND OPERATIONS

There were several air attacks during the day in the vicinity of Clark Field and Manila. Subic Bay also came under attack by air. These strikes were probably meant to support the artillery duels that were occurring at both locations. There were a few probing patrols by both our forces and the Japanese but there was no major assault made by the Japanese today. Casualties were relatively light.

CHINESE THEATER

Combat continued at the same locations today as yesterday. The only difference is that word was received from the Chinese command that they will attempt a counter attack tomorrow at Loyang to push the Japanese back into French Indochina.

BRITISH AND ALLIED OPERATIONS

There was much action at Manado today. The Japanese carriers had moved up near Manado to provide support for the amphibious assault. The carriers conducted strikes at Manado and Kendari. The strikes at Manado were specifically against troop locations and supply dumps. The strikes at Kendari were targeting the airfield.

At Manado, troops were unloading all day with the small boats making shuttle runs to the larger troop transports offshore. The 75mm shore batteries were causing casualties to the invading troops and damaging some of the transports but more and more troops were making it ashore and engaging the few Dutch troops available. The last report received indicated that over 14,000 troops had landed. The garrison and some support troops were overrun but some did manage to head south out of the area. The Japanese however did take the area and are now in control. A Dutch patrol plane did spot the battleship Yamashiro near Ternate; this report was sent to the intelligence section.

At Balikpapan, the Dutch VI Battalion attacked the Japanese trying to consolidate the landing area. Casualties were caused on both sides (38 Dutch soldiers were wounded), but the Dutch troops were unable to dislodge the Japanese. The situation remains the same.

Meanwhile, Rangoon and Kuantan were attacked by Japanese aircraft. As usual, Kuantan was damaged heavily by several raids and no enemy planes were shot down. However, at Rangoon, the situation wasn't exactly the same.

The All-Volunteer Group still had their aircraft from their 1st Squadron at Rangoon. They had two aircraft in the air when the alarm came in from a radar set located there. A further 14 aircraft got into the air and made it to altitude before the raid reached the airfield. Half of the fighters mixed it up with the Japanese fighters and the other half attacked the bombers. The bombers were Kate torpedo bombers making a level run at 12000 feet. All of the Kate bombers were shot down (there were a total of six) and one of the friendly fighters was shot down (no Japanese fighters were shot down). 1st Squadron may rotate out and send in another squadron in its place. Our pilots are getting better.

There were no reports of combat from Singapore.

AUSTRALIA AND NEW GUINEA

A radio operator on Guadalcanal in the vicinity of Tassafaronga reported that Japanese troops had landed and were moving inland. The operator reported that he was going to try to hide and continue to provide information. Reports were also received that the small town of Salamaua near Lae on New Guinea was bombed by Japanese aircraft this afternoon. The small airstrip in the area was heavily damaged.

Good news came from the Australian Cruiser Force. As it turns out, as we were having our morning briefing, they had arrived in the area of Shortlands. They found a Japanese force that was busy unloading troops; a force of five ships. There was a half-moon providing light for the force. The quick report indicated that a destroyer, a small escort, two freighters and a "large troop transport" were spotted by lookouts on HMAS Achilles (the van ship of the group).

HMAS Perth opened fire first with her 6 inch guns at a range of 8000 yards, attacking the Japanese destroyer (the report indicated that the destroyer was a Fubuki class). The Australian ships then turned so that all of their gun batteries would bear against the Japanese ships. HMAS Canberra fired an 8 inch round into the small escort; the escort blew up immediately and disappeared.

The Japanese destroyer did manage to hit HMAS Australia with a 5 inch round, but the shell did not have the power to penetrate the heavy cruiser's armor. After the HMAS Australia was hit by the shell, the captain ordered all batteries to fire on the Japanese destroyer. Multiple 8 inch rounds hit the destroyer and set it ablaze; after a few minutes, the destroyer's gun batteries fell silent and the ship began to slip under the waves.

The two freighters were receiving hits by gunfire from all the Australian ships; a few minutes later, a full torpedo barrage from the cruisers hit the freighters and the large troop transport. One of the freighters exploded (it might have been carrying munitions) and the other freighter was burning from stem to stern. At this point, due to the fires, it was noted that "many" troops were jumping into the sea from the freighters and from the large troop transport. This transport took many hits from Australian gun batteries and was hit by at least four torpedoes. This ship began to sink and more troops were seen jumping off to try to get away from the fires. At this point, the Australian commander (CAPT Getting) ordered a withdrawal to head to Sydney. All five of the Japanese ships were sunk and it is unknown how many troop casualties were caused. The intelligence section was notified of these reports.

Figure 44 - HMAS Perth (D29)

INTELLIGENCE

The intelligence officer giving the briefing indicated that they had a lot of traffic to go through concerning the Australian attack at Shortlands. They were attempting to sift through it and indicated some of the information was in the clear and not encrypted.

It was the opinion of the intelligence section that Celebes Island is the current main objective of the Japanese High Command. They have committed battleship groups, most of the carriers and a large portion of their transport fleet. With Manado in Japanese hands and further invasion expected, it will become the focus for the next several weeks.

They also reported that they have the names of a couple more ships confirmed sunk by multiple sources. The freighters Kashii Maru and Kano Maru were confirmed sunk on December 25th by the British near Kota Bharu.

There is also a confirmation on the patrol boat Toshi Maru #3, a 215 ton patrol boat that was sunk near Dadjangas which corroborates the report from the submarine USS Sturgeon on December 28th.

Sadly, there was no further information on regarding the intentions of the Japanese outside of Celebes Island. There exists the possibility that Borneo will be next, but the team was not sure.

OPERATION SINGING PUMPKIN PLANNING

The ships selected for Task Force Loadstone were completed before lunch and were sent up to ADM Nimitz for approval. The ships selected are:

- Heavy Cruisers:
    o USS Salt Lake City (flagship)
    o USS Louisville
    o USS Portland
    o USS Indianapolis
    o USS Northampton
    o USS Chester
- Destroyers:
    o USS Flusser
    o USS Aylwin

- o   USS Benham
- o   USS Ellet
- o   USS Farragut
- o   USS Dewey
- Troop Transports:
  - o   USS Wharton
  - o   USS U.S. Grant
  - o   USS Barnett
  - o   USS Henderson
  - o   USS Crescent City
  - o   USS William Ward Burrows

The heavy cruisers will provide the majority of the shore fire support. The destroyers will provide shore fire support and screen the force seaward from any enemy ships that might break through the main surface combat force. The troop transports are to be guarded at all costs and the Marines that are carried within.

Scheduled refits for USS Benham and USS Ellet will be postponed until after the completion of the operation.

THEORIES AND INTENTIONS

There is essentially nothing that can be done for the Philippines and for Celebes Island. I remain optimistic that Operation Singing Pumpkin will throw off the Japanese a bit and let them know that they are going to be attacked.

LATE DAY REPORTS

A late day report from more Dutch patrol planes gives further confirmation that Japanese battleships and carriers are in the vicinity of Celebes Island. The only confirmed battleship is the Yamashiro, with photographs being taken of the ship.

Just before dinner, the submarines USS Tambor, USS Grayling and USS Gar arrived at Pearl Harbor from bringing supplies to Wake Island. They are fixing minor damage and are readying for further orders.

Dinner was substandard "lasagna". I use quotes for a reason. I took a shower and decided to read some Hawthorne, "The House of the Seven Gables". The book reminded me of being back in college taking my literature class. Sleep came quickly.

MORNING BRIEF

The morning brief began as usual. USS President Coolidge is still unloading supplies at Midway Island; they are 40% unloaded and are continuing the operation.

The light cruiser USS Raleigh reported from Sydney that they need a couple of days to repair a problem with their engineering plant. They should be combat capable by January 14th at the latest.

All other US Forces were proceeding as planned and no major issues were reported since last night.

The British Liaison Officer reported that the 6th Australian Division has completed the withdrawal from North Africa and are standing by to be transported from Aden to Java. LTG Herring is the commanding officer and he is waiting for enough shipping to load up all of the troops and equipment. This should take a few more days.

No other major issues were in the briefing and the entire staff went to their desks after grabbing some food. I was hoping it would be a slow day.

SUBMARINE OPERATIONS

Just off the Australian coast near Bundaberg, the coastal freighter SS Yunnan was torpedoed and sunk by a Japanese submarine shortly after sunrise. There were casualties on the ship but the extent was not yet known. The freighter was on the run up to Cooktown to deliver supplies.

USS Swordfish (LCDR Smith) came across a small convoy at long range in the Celebes Sea. They manage to fire two torpedoes into the convoy from long range. They reported one torpedo hit a ship at which point the submarine dove deep (still at long range) and broke quickly from the area. It is unknown if the freighter sank.

USS Sargo (LCDR Jacobs) found a freighter escorted by a small patrol boat near Babeldaob. They fired two torpedoes at the freighter and were attacked by the patrol boat. They went deep and broke contact towards the freighter. Almost 45 minutes later, they went to periscope depth and saw the freighter at a range of about 2300 yards. The report identified the ship as a code MKKFKM for a Nagara Maru class freighter. The freighter was hit by two of the torpedoes forward of the beam on the starboard side. The submarine then dove deep to try to break away (again, breaking towards the freighter causing problems for the patrol boat). The submarine came up around an hour later to periscope depth and the previously struck freighter was behind the submarine and was down by the bow burning brightly. LCDR Jacobs then went deep again and snuck away from the area staying submerged for another two hours. When they came to the surface, the patrol boat was gone and burning oil was on the surface around 4 nautical miles behind the submarine. The submarine then resumed the patrol.

There were a couple of reports via CAPT Rooks from Java. The first report concerned the Dutch submarine HNLMS K XII; they found a small convoy south of Tawi Tawi and attacked. A Japanese freighter was hit by a torpedo and a small destroyer then tried to find the submarine. The submarine was not damaged in the encounter and the submarine was able to quickly continue the patrol. A few hours later the submarine saw another freighter and fired two torpedoes at the ship, hitting with both. The freighter went under the waves by the stern and was sunk.

Another report came in around lunchtime concerning the Dutch submarine HNLMS K XIV. They had found a Japanese convoy and attacked trying to torpedo a freighter. The torpedoes missed and the submarine was not detected; however the submarine could not make another immediate attack.

Hawaii

Task Force Present arrived back at Pearl Harbor around 0900 this morning. All of the ships were refueling and repairing any damage that they had. They were to stand by for further orders.

The fleet cargo ship USS Castor arrived around two hours later with her destroyer escorts and also replenished. Material condition of all ships that arrived back in port today were good.

Broader Pacific Ocean

Supplies were still being unloaded at Wake Island. The Japanese strikes were concentrated on troop concentrations to the west side of the atoll. All of the troops have immediate supplies and the supply dumps are slowly being filled. The runway is still not operational, but being worked on.

Philippine Island Operations

There were carrier air strikes against Davao today. The attacks were heavy and only a couple of carrier based bombers were damaged by anti-aircraft fire. It is possible that the Japanese may also order an amphibious assault directly at

Davao. There were reports of other air strikes on Mindanao, but they were unconfirmed by the end of the day.

On Luzon, there were air strikes against Subic Bay and Clark Field damaging more facilities. Ground combat kept up in terms of artillery duels at both Clark Field and Manila. There were some patrol actions on both sides, but nothing major occurred today. It did look like the Japanese were preparing for a major assault at Clark Field, but other than troop concentrations, there were no other indications.

Chinese Theater

There was a major attack at Wuchow that forced the Chinese to fall back with significant casualties. It doesn't seem like the Japanese have enough combat power to continue the pursuit.

There was also combat reported at Pucheng, Kweiteh, Canton, Kaifeng, Loyang, Kweisui, Hwainan and Lang Son. In these locations there were no major changes to the battle line.

British and Allied Operations

There was a major bombardment at Makassar by a couple of Japanese battleships and cruisers escorted by several destroyers. Defensive guns were unable to hit any of the Japanese ships and it may be a precursor to an invasion. There were 35 dead and 132 wounded Dutch soldiers in the vicinity. The carriers moved to the northeast to hit the Philippines.

On the Malayan Peninsula there were strikes yet again at Kuantan. No reports of numbers of bombers or damage on the ground; but at this point, the facilities have all been more or less destroyed.

At Balikpapan, it was quiet. No firing, no patrols, no nothing. The weather was bad and the Japanese performed no combat missions on the ground (neither did the Dutch).

AUSTRALIA AND NEW GUINEA

A report came in from Munda in the Solomon Islands that Japanese troops were landing. The Australian Cruiser Force would make a quick run in to see if anything could be done (much like at Shortlands). The cruisers had enough ammunition to attack shipping there but they were to basically perform a "reconnaissance in force". It would be safe to assume that Munda is occupied.

The only other major report indicated that an air strike had occurred at Wau on the northern side of New Guinea. No indications were received as to damage suffered or casualties.

INTELLIGENCE

The only interesting piece of information was confirmation of the sinking of the destroyer transport Aoi and the freighter Arizona Maru by the British at Kota Bharu on December 25th. There was little official intelligence and it appeared that there were a few problems with gaining information.

OPERATION SINGING PUMPKIN PLANNING

ADM Nimitz approved the force list for Task Force Loadstone. We were to stand by for any other requests.

THEORIES AND INTENTIONS

Considering the way things have been lately, this was a relatively calm day. I think that the Japanese will land at Makassar in Celebes and probably land at Davao in Mindanao. What I'm wondering is when they will attack and try to capture the oil wells on Sumatra and Java. Unlike World War II in my world, Java will be able to be held.

LATE DAY REPORTS

I had left for the day at 1600 to go for a swim before heading to dinner. I stopped by quickly after dinner to see if there were any major developments; there were none so I went to my bungalow to read for a while and then go to sleep.

JANUARY 11, 1942   DAY 36 OF THE WAR

<u>MORNING BRIEF</u>

I was well rested as I got to the headquarters building. It was nice to get out a little early yesterday and get a swim in. ADM Nimitz had some other Marine Officers with him this morning (none that I had seen from the 8th Marine Regiment). I think they were going over training schedules.

The Operations Officer began by letting us know that all other forces were proceeding as planned. The only major new piece of information was that the tanker MV Eidsvold would be making runs from Pearl Harbor to Christmas Island to deliver fuel.

As he was finishing up that piece of information ADM Nimitz came in from his office and asked that we provide information on ship selection for Task Force Recline and Task Force Stampede by noon today so that he could have the supply officers go over the requirements. The Operations Officer nodded and looked at all of us. We nodded in reply.

The British Liaison Officer reported that the only new information was that he confirmed that the Australian Cruiser Force would indeed go to Munda for a "reconnaissance in force". Essentially, they are a group of ships that are looking for trouble. He also reported that the Australian cruiser HMAS Adelaide would leave Port Moresby, run into Shortlands and then fall back to Townsville.

He also made a request that after USS Raleigh completes repairs that the US surface forces at Sydney redeploy to Townsville. The Operations Officer didn't have a problem with it but would get a confirmation from ADM Nimitz before the end of the day.

We then went to work after a quick bite to eat.

SUBMARINE OPERATIONS

A report arrived via the British Liaison Officer that the Dutch submarine HNLMS K XIV was attacked by a Japanese patrol near Jolo earlier today. There was no damage to the submarine and the patrol was continued after they broke contact.

A report came in from USS Sargo (LCDR Jacobs) near Peleliu that they had found and attacked a Japanese surface group. One of the ships was identified as "Kongo" class battleship with at least five destroyers acting as escort. The submarine fired two torpedoes at a destroyer and missed at which point three of the destroyers immediately began attacking the submarine. They had to stay submerged for four hours at which point the destroyers were breaking away at high speed towards Peleliu (more than likely to catch up with the battleship). The submarine then continued the patrol without damage.

HAWAII

There were no unusual incidents today.

BROADER PACIFIC OCEAN

Bad weather at Wake Island prevented the Japanese from attacking today and all other forces are proceeding according to plans. No major reports.

PHILIPPINE ISLAND OPERATIONS

On the Island of Mindanao, Japanese ships were seen off of Davao. They began shelling defensive positions ashore and small amounts of troops were seen landing in the area. This is must be a precursor to a major invasion.

On Luzon, there was a lot of combat at Clark Field. Several air raids attacked defensive positions and the airfield itself prior to a major Japanese assault; there was also a dive bomber attack against the facilities at Subic Bay. The Japanese infantry came out in a charge and were cut down by the concentrated machinegun fire and artillery. A mixed force of Japanese tanks and other vehicles also got into the fray and were attacked by the 192nd and 194th Tank Battalions. In all, the Japanese assault was stopped, but friendly troops were concerned about supplies and extra ammunition. They wouldn't be able to continuously repel assaults without resupply.

At Manila, low level patrol combat and artillery strikes kept that area deadly during the day. No major changes to the front line were experienced. The Manila area was experiencing many of the same supply problems that troops at Clark Field had. There were roughly 20,000 friendly troops located at Manila, not to mention the civilians that needed food as well. The situation is beginning to get desperate.

CHINESE THEATER

No reports were received from the Chinese Theater of Operations. The communications officer didn't know why because the frequency was not experiencing problems. This information was given to the Liaison from the State Department.

BRITISH AND ALLIED OPERATIONS

A troubling report was received that the forces at Balikpapan had been overrun by Japanese troops. It is possible that the Japanese 8th Special Naval Landing Force could have dislodged the Dutch battalion but that would have required local superiority (which was possible but not probable). All that was known is that over 400 casualties were sustained by the Dutch and that they had fallen back towards Samarinda. The oil wells and equipment were more or less intact.

Another unsettling report came from some radio operators on Morotai (northernmost island in the Moluccas chain). Japanese troops were seen to be landing. There was nothing that could be done about it.

On the Malayan Peninsula, friendly troops were continuing to fall back on Singapore and there were more bombing raids at Kuantan. There was talk of having the troops at Mersing also fall back to Singapore. A full decision has not been made yet. Right now the engineers at Singapore were busy making defensive positions and fortifying the island as quickly as possible. That battle is expected to be fierce.

AUSTRALIA AND NEW GUINEA

There were only two major reports here today. First was a report of an air raid that seemed to be focused on attacking Australian troops at Port Moresby. A total of 15 Sally bombers laid down an attack against one of the artillery units in the division. The bombs fell wide of the mark and one of the bombers was damaged by anti-aircraft fire (seen leaving to the north trailing smoke from their starboard engine). No casualties were suffered on the ground.

Second was word that Salamaua (a small town near Lae) was attacked by bombers. There was a small airfield there that was heavily damaged but there were no casualties on the ground (the airfield was not occupied at the time).

Intelligence

The intelligence report began with information about Rabaul. It seemed that there were at least 20,000 Japanese troops there working on facilities, airfields, fortifications and defensive positions. This location looks like it will be the entire lynchpin of the Japanese operations in the area.

There was also information to confirm that there are at least 30 or so ships located at Jolo. The reasoning for this is unknown; possibly the Japanese intend for the location to be a major resupply base or that they want it as a fortress.

Lastly, there was no information regarding the location of the Japanese carriers. No radio contact or confirmed reports (of note, there were no reports of carrier aircraft making attacks today).

There were no further confirmed kills.

Operation Singing Pumpkin Planning

\

We went to work almost immediately on these ship selection lists. As it turns out there were a few issues related to them that will be mentioned where appropriate.

Task Force Recline is the force that will bring the support troops to Canton Island after the 8th Marine Regiment secures the island:

Combat ships:
- Light Cruiser USS St. Louis (flagship)

Destroyers:
- USS Maury
- USS Mugford
- USS Blue
- USS Bagley

Troop Transports:
- USS Hugh L. Scott
- USS President Jackson
- USS President Monroe
- USS President Polk

Fleet Cargo Ships:
- USS Castor
- USS Procyon
- USS Arturus
- USS Bellatrix

The destroyers selected were originally scheduled for a minor refit this month but this refit will be postponed until the end of the operation. It is assumed that the fleet cargo ships will be combat loaded (less efficient but if a single ship is lost it won't cause the loss of a complete type of supply). The supply officers are working on the loading as I write this.

Task Force Stampede is the carrier group that will provide air support during the entire operation. This force contains the majority of the firepower and will protect the operation as a whole from enemy carriers should they arrive in addition to providing ground support to the Marines:

Figure 45 - USS Enterprise (CV-6)

Carriers:
-   USS Enterprise (flagship)
-   USS Yorktown
-   USS Lexington

Heavy Cruisers:
-   USS San Francisco
-   USS Minneapolis

Light Cruiser:
-   USS Phoenix

Destroyers:
-   USS Dunlap
-   USS Fanning
-   USS Mahan
-   USS Ralph Talbot
-   USS Patterson

- USS Jarvis
- USS McCall

We had the lists compiled and ready for ADM Nimitz by 1100 local. The Operations Officer would present it at noon today. No further requests came from ADM Nimitz to us for the rest of the day concerning Operation Singing Pumpkin.

THEORIES AND INTENTIONS

Jolo and Rabaul as major bases? I knew historically that Rabaul became a major base, but I did not think that Jolo did. More proof that I have altered history.

LATE DAY REPORTS

There was a report from the Australians that their redeployment of smaller troop transports was completed at Townsville when the ships arrived safely.

There was a frantic radio report from the USS Blackhawk (she is a destroyer tender) that she had managed to get out of Balikpapan as the Japanese took over the base. The ship is heading towards Soerabaja to support CAPT Rooks and the rest of the US Forces there.

I left after a strange day. Not terribly busy, but long. Most of the news that came in was bad news. I quietly returned to my bungalow after dinner and continued to read my book until I fell asleep.

MORNING BRIEF

First thing on the morning brief concerned the SS Florence D. and her escorting destroyers. They arrived back safely early this morning from their resupply mission. All of the ships are in good material condition and should be ready in about a day for further operations.

The remainder of the briefing concerned operations elsewhere. First, the US Forces in Sydney (USS Pensacola with two light cruisers and three destroyers) were redeploying at the request of the Australian High Command to Townsville to more adequately support operations in the Australian Theater. Supplies for US Forces are already on the way.

The British Liaison Officer reported that the Australian 4th Light Anti-Aircraft Regiment will begin loading up on smaller troop transports in Townsville for transport to Port Moresby. They should begin loading up tomorrow.

He also reported that HMS Danae would be leaving Merak on Java to head to Columbo for the drydock. The ship is still heavily damaged with some temporary repairs; hopefully enough to get them to Columbo.

The same was reported for HMS Mauritius. Though she isn't damaged as badly as HMS Danae, she still needs to get into a drydock and the facilities at Soerabaja can't fit a ship of that size.

The Australian cruiser HMAS Adelaide should be reaching Shortlands Island today (if not already there since it's still night there) to engage enemy shipping. After completing the mission they are to fall back on Sydney.

The Australian Cruiser Force should be reaching Munda as well. They are to engage enemy shipping and fall back on Sydney at the completion of their mission.

All other forces were proceeding as planned. There were no other major reports from the West Coast. We had breakfast (fruit and toast) and went to work.

Submarine Operations

There were no major reports from any of our submarines; nor any reports of attacks by enemy submarines.

Hawaii

The only major events today concerned the Harbor Master. His daily report included news that the light cruiser USS Helena and the aviation support ship USS Tangier completed repairs and had returned to service. All other forces were proceeding as planned.

Broader Pacific Ocean

Radio operators at Baker Island reported seeing Japanese ships and troops landing and then went off the air. The Staff now considers that island under Japanese control.

Philippine Island Operations

Clark Field and Subic Bay came under attack from air raids yet again today. Our forces in the Philippines were completely incapable of putting any fighters into the air to try to stop them. The enemy bombers proceeded to their targets unmolested.

While these air raids were executed, there was intense combat in the northern areas of Clark Field and in southern Manila. In both cases, the Japanese had only made minor gains while suffering heavy casualties (at least that is what the report had indicated). The reports also indicated that the main assault in southern Manila was being conducted by the Japanese 16th Division with some independent artillery support. At Clark Field, there were nearly 20,000 Japanese troops attacking supported by tanks and artillery (plus the air raids). The troops were holding for now but a couple of key defensive positions on the approach to Clark Field were captured by the Japanese. We were trying to find out more information.

Meanwhile, at Davao on Mindanao, a Japanese surface force was seen and troops were beginning an amphibious assault. There were no reports as to the number of enemy troops that had landed.

CHINESE THEATER

The problem from yesterday involved a loss of radio communications at the Chinese Headquarters. They had fixed the problem and have re-established contact. They reported ground combat at Hwainan, Lang Son, Kaifeng, Kweisui, Loyang, Canton, Kweiteh and Pucheng.

BRITISH AND ALLIED OPERATIONS

We received a report that there was a "good chance" that the Japanese had sent a surface force to Tarakan on the northeast coast of Borneo. There was a small Dutch combat ship there (something akin to a Coast Guard Cutter) and no further reports were received.

On the Malayan Peninsula there several air raids yet again at Kuantan. No word on casualties or even the number of enemy bombers that were involved in the attacks. All that was known was that fighters were escorting the bombers.

AUSTRALIA AND NEW GUINEA

Very troubling news came to us via the British Liaison Officer. He stated that a vexing and troubling report was received from HMAS Adelaide (the Australian light cruiser assigned to attack enemy shipping at Shortlands before falling back on Sydney). They reported seeing three enemy ships and that they were attacking; no further reports have been heard from them. The Australians and British are concerned; they are not answering calls and there have been no reports at all. If the ship does not answer in a week (enough time to make it back to Sydney), it is entirely possible that the ship was sunk.

The main Australian Cruiser Force had better luck attacking enemy shipping near Munda. They found a pair of enemy freighters attacked them and sank them both. The ships are now falling back on Sydney. It is hoped that the facilities at Townsville will be upgraded so that heavier ammunition can be moved properly to the ships from the port facilities. This will allow ships to be fully replenished without having to fall back on Sydney.

The only other major report from the Australian Theater concerned a Japanese air raid against Salamaua on New Guniea. Damage assessment has not yet been completed.

Intelligence

The intelligence report was mainly concerned with Operation Singing Pumpkin. There was an estimate of 2700 Japanese troops on the atoll and it was surmised that they would be concentrated near the airstrip and the approach to the interior to the atoll. There was no information about ship kills or the location of the *Kido Butai*.

Operation Singing Pumpkin Planning

There were no requests to me or my team today. Word on the staff floor was that ADM Nimitz was conferring with other flag officers to determine who would lead each force. ADM Nimitz would maintain overall operational control from here at Pearl Harbor.

Theories and Intentions

Nothing really new today. It appears, to me at least, that the Japanese are still rampaging but are strategically picking points that will be easy to defend. Hopefully we will be able to throw them off.

Late Day Reports

I was told that I was having tomorrow off and that my FBI handlers would take me into town for a day off. There was a new Operations Officer that would be coming in the same day I get back from my day off. As such, I left and did not attend any late day reports.

I spent a pleasant day off in Honolulu. I was always escorted by the FBI agents, who ate with me and had a few drinks with me. It was interesting to see how the city was very different from what I remembered. Very few high rise buildings and the beach seemed a bit rockier than I remember. It was still very easy to pick out Diamond Head and some of the other landmarks.

The conversation drifted between official and unofficial topics. I was told that a couple of scientists would be heading to Pearl Harbor to ask me about what I was working on when the "accident" occurred. I explained, yet again, that I was a computer scientist and not a physicist. These men didn't really care but I could see that when they thought I wasn't looking, they were taking notes.

After a pleasant dinner of what tasted like Thai food (at least the spices had a strong hint of lemongrass and crushed pepper) we headed back to Pearl Harbor. I went to the officers club and had quite a few beers and played some more poker. CDR Larson wasn't there tonight; I had quite a few heavy hands with a LCDR Gene Brown. He was a good player but I had beat him quite handily with a full boat of aces full of queens to have him pay for my bar tab. We agreed that we should play again; at least as long as his submarine doesn't ship out soon.

I listened to the radio with quite a heavy buzz and decided that it was probably in my best interest that I go to sleep. Sleep came quickly.

JANUARY 14, 1942   DAY 39 OF THE WAR

Morning Brief

I had a mild hangover as I went to the headquarters building. The new operations officer was waiting for me; CAPT Ringwood introduced himself in the presence of ADM Nimitz. Before the briefing, he took me aside to let me know that he didn't fully believe what I was about and that he would watch me closely. I told him that I fully understood because it didn't make any sense to me either. I had the feeling that he thought I was an undercover agent or something.

However, he did give me a quick rundown of what had happened the day before. The major catastrophe was that Davao on Mindanao had fallen to a Japanese amphibious assault; nearly 5000 troops had landed and the single company of Philippine infantry was overwhelmed. Baker Island was also under Japanese control.

The Japanese had also started an amphibious assault at Tarakan on the east coast of Borneo. The only good news there was that the base commander confirmed shooting up an enemy troop transport pretty good. Other than that, the Dutch troops were totally on the defensive.

In nearby Soerabaja, the submarine USS Tarpon had arrived, completing their patrol. The rollup report from LCDR Wallace should be available sometime today.

The British had ordered Australian troops on the Malayan Peninsula at Mersing to fall back on Singapore to bolster the defenses there. There was a full strength infantry brigade that would significantly help. The British also reported that HMS Mauritius had passed Merak heading back to Columbo. Also of note, they reported that repairs had been completed on the destroyer HMS Stronghold.

Nearer to home, the submarine USS Nautilus had completed her mission of bringing supplies to Wake Island and they were standing by for further orders. Also, the destroyer transport USS Waters arrived from the West Coast and was standing by for orders.

He then dismissed me to prepare for this morning's briefing. I saluted and joined the rest of the staff.

The regular morning briefing began with the British Liaison Officer in attendance, along with VADM Pye and ADM Nimitz. The briefing began with an emergency report from the submarine USS S-37 (CDR Easton). They were apparently moving into position to attack a Japanese convoy when they were seen by an escort. They dove immediately but were subjected to a particularly brutal depth charge attack (the report stated that they were in shallow waters so they couldn't get very deep). The submarine managed to break away but they were severely damaged and could only make 5 knots; they were heading back to Soerabaja with casualties on board.

A more happy report was received from the destroyer tender USS Black Foot; they had made good their escape from Balikpapan and had successfully made it to Soerabaja. They were under the operational command of CAPT Rooks and were providing support services to the US Forces at Soerabaja.

Nearer to Australia, the US force of cruisers and destroyers were still transiting to Townsville to support operations closer to Port Moresby. Along those lines, the fast transports with the 31st Pursuit Group onboard were approaching the Samoan Islands and were still making 22 knots on their journey to Sydney.

On the West Coast, an enemy submarine was seen around 120 nautical miles west-southwest of Santa Barbara and was attacked by a patrol plane. There was no word on damage to the enemy submarine but the patrol plane did make it back to base. There was also a report that more shipping was massing at San Francisco (mostly civilian freighters and tankers). Resupply and convoy operations were what was going to keep ADM Nimitz' command going.

The British Liaison Officer reported that it was now almost a certainty that the light cruiser HMAS Adelaide was sunk by enemy action. However, the Australian Cruiser Force was still making their way down to Sydney to re-provision before heading up to Townsville. The port facilities were being worked on and more equipment was being sent there from Sydney in order to transfer shells up to 8" size. The transfer boxes and cranes simply can't handle the weight yet. Supplies for US Forces are already on their way to Sydney from the West Coast and if necessary, supplies can be brought from the steady convoys going to Cape Town and transfer them to Perth on the west coast of Australia (from there, trains to the east coast).

ADM Nimitz had nothing for the staff today except to tell us to remain vigilant and be smarter, faster and better than our enemy. We were then dismissed for the day's work.

SUBMARINE OPERATIONS

A report from USS S-36 (LCDR McKnight) was received that gave good news of an attack against a Fubuki Class destroyer near Sandakan off the northeast coast of Borneo. The submarine fired two torpedoes at the destroyer and hit with one torpedo. Other escorts then began to hunt the submarine but they managed to slip away. It is unknown if the destroyer was sunk.

There were no reports of Japanese submarine attacks.

HAWAII

Welcome news was received that repairs to the destroyers USS Craven and USS Henley were completed. The destroyers were returned to the operational control of their destroyer squadrons.

BROADER PACIFIC OCEAN

Wake Island was subjected to a fairly large air raid in the early morning. The only good news is that the remaining Wildcat fighters managed to get into the air after repairs to the runway and unloading of fuel allowed some air operations. A total of 50 Betty medium bombers attacked and were met by the 7 remaining Wildcat fighters; 1 Betty was shot down and 2 others damaged. No losses were suffered by the Marines (VMF-211).

Figure 46 - USS Henley (DD-391)

PHILIPPINE ISLAND OPERATIONS

The Japanese were consolidating their gains in Davao on Mindanao and were content today to just continue an artillery duel at both Clark Field and in southern Manila. There were no major changes to the front lines.

There were apparently some ships that had escaped from Davao. Orders were being promulgated to send them to Soerabaja; it will take them at least a week to get there and they will have to run the gauntlet of enemy shipping to get there. It is still better than being sunk in place.

CHINESE THEATER

There were reports of continued combat at the usual locations, Hwainan, Lang Son, Kweisui, Loyang, Kaifeng, Canton, Kweiteh and Pucheng. There were no reports of major changes to the front lines in any of these locations.

BRITISH AND ALLIED OPERATIONS

The Dutch had a few bombers stationed at Samarinda on the east coast of Borneo and they were now bombing the Japanese troops located at Balikpapan. It was hoped that the bombing would cause casualties and slow any advance by land up to Samarinda giving the remnants of the VI KNIL Battalion time to dig defensive positions. Further to the north at Tarakan, Japanese troops continued to land and there was a battle beginning to develop between Japanese troops and the VII KNIL Battalion that is stationed there. Casualties were unknown at this time.

On the Malayan Peninsula, Kuantan was hit yet again by several raids that continued to add to the general carnage in that locale. There was nothing that the ground forces still located there could do. They were still under orders to not repair the runway or port facilities. It was noted that the bombers were escorted.

Meanwhile at Malacca, a determined assault by the Japanese 5th Division attacked the scratch force of infantry and support forces. Defenders at 0800 local included a total of 2845 troops; by 1600, only 1380 troops were combat effective (the rest being killed, wounded or captured). Casualties inflicted on the enemy were unknown and friendly forces were in full retreat heading towards Singapore.

A report was received from Dutch forces at Medan (on the Island of Sumatra) that they were under attack by Japanese bombers. The Japanese seemed to be attacking the troop concentrations and not the facilities. There were a few wounded on the ground.

Further to the north at Moulmein in Burma, a heavily escorted Japanese air strike was attacking Royal Air Force ground units. As it turns out, the All-Volunteer Group's 2nd Squadron was providing air cover. A furball of fighters were going at it while the bombers made their run (it was reported that the bombers were Kate types). A dozen fighters from 2nd Squadron mixed it up with almost 30 Zero fighters. When it was all over, a single Zero was shot down for the loss of four H81 fighters of the 2nd Squadron. Not a good showing but at least the Japanese know that they must fight in that area.

Australia and New Guinea

Port Moresby was hit by an air raid this morning conducted by around a dozen Betty medium bombers. They came in a little low (hoping to concentrate their bomb patterns) but were hit by anti-aircraft fire. One bomber was confirmed shot down. The runway had a couple of small craters that were quickly repaired. The problem should be partially alleviated when the 31st Pursuit Group arrives in around a week or so. The bombers did not appear to be escorted.

All other forces in this area were proceeding to plan and were not hindered by the Japanese in any way.

Intelligence

A major piece of intelligence showed that the Japanese had discussed via radio messages the loss of the fleet oiler Ken'yo Maru from the battle north of Lihue on December 19th. The kill is being credited to the destroyer USS Patterson based on analysis of the battle from the log reports. The ship was a 10,000 ton fleet oiler. It is possible that more of the ships from that battle were sunk and the intelligence section was working hard on further decrypts.

There was no information available on the location of the Japanese carriers. They were still looking for information.

Estimates of troop strength at Canton Island remained at 2500 troops; this information was shared with the Marines.

Operation Singing Pumpkin Planning

The only requests that came from ADM Nimitz concerned updating the ship lists with the return of USS Henley and

USS Craven. The Marines were still coordinating with the supply officers to make sure that the combat loads for the freighters and troop transports would meet the requirements of the operation.

THEORIES AND INTENTIONS

New attacks at Sumatra may indicate the next target for the Japanese if/when they consolidate gains on the Malayan Peninsula. It's obvious that they will push north into Burma as well.

LATE DAY REPORTS

The rollup report from the submarine USS Tarpon (LCDR Wallace) arrived this afternoon. They were officially credited with sinking the freighter Josho Maru on December 23rd and with torpedoing a freighter on January 8th that has not yet been confirmed. Total tonnage sunk and credited to the submarine as of now is 3675 tons. They should be ready in a few days to redeploy, but there are few torpedoes left at Soerabaja; the supplies have not yet arrived. USS Tarpon will receive a full loadout, but there are now only 8 Mark 14 torpedoes left in storage at Soerabaja along with 26 Mark 10 torpedoes.

The British Liaison Officer said that the first convoy with US supplies should reach Batavia in 11 days. It would then take another two days to offload and get the supplies on trains to head over to Soerabaja.

There was also a lengthy conversation between our staff and CAPT Ringwood concerning the battleships USS Nevada and USS Oklahoma. He wanted information about having the battleships escorted to the West Coast to complete repairs to free up space in Pearl Harbor; the battleships should be able to make at least 8 knots to head to San Francisco or Seattle for the dry docks there.

I then left for the day to have some dinner. I was given a glop of some kind of edible material; not very palatable. I went to my bungalow, listened to some music and went to sleep.

JANUARY 15, 1942   DAY 40 OF THE WAR

<u>MORNING BRIEF</u>

It was unnaturally cool today, felt like the temperature was in the high 40s or so. CAPT Ringwood began the briefing with ADM Nimitz in attendance.

First on the agenda concerned a report from CAPT Rooks at Soerabaja. He stated that the Dutch were sending a surface force of two light cruisers and three destroyers to perform a run in to Balikpapan. This is because aircraft had spotted a few Japanese tankers in the area and the Dutch commander thought that they were going to try to load up with oil to head back to the Home Islands. The force was under command of CAPT DeBoer. CAPT Rooks would receive a command from ADM Nimitz to not perform any sorties until further notice; supplies were too scarce and it made more sense to coordinate an attack should Japanese ships attempt to invade Bandjermasin on the south side of Borneo. For now they were to sit tight.

Next came Australia. Our forces had arrived safely at Townsville and were refueling. There were possibilities of conducting strikes at Munda or Shortlands. ADM Nimitz took it under advisement and would have an answer at the end of the day.

The Australians had notified us via the British Liaison Officer that they were loading up the 4th Light Anti-Aircraft Regiment at Townsville under escort of three sloops to bring them to Port Moresby. It would take a day or two to load up the troops, equipment and more supplies to put to sea. US Forces were requested to perform an operation to draw attention away from the transport force.

Lastly, reports from the West Coast indicated that convoy Charlie 15-1 would be loading up with needed supplies for Pearl Harbor. It should take them a day to load up and then put to sea. Also reported was that a further six freighters were transiting the Panama Canal to head to San Francisco for operations in the Pacific (convoy Charlie 15-B).

The British Liaison Officer had then reported that another convoy of three freighters was loading up at Cape Town with a mix of US and Allied supplies to head to Batavia. The logistics train was now working; albeit not in the quantities needed, but at least it's a start.

We were then dismissed and headed to our desks for work after a quick breakfast of oatmeal and fresh fruit. The pineapple was particularly sweet this morning.

SUBMARINE OPERATIONS

There were no reports of attacks by either our submarines or by Japanese submarines. Routine reports only where required.

HAWAII

The destroyer USS Gridley had all repairs completed and was returned to full duty today. The destroyer is ready for further operations. No other major reports were received here today.

BROADER PACIFIC OCEAN

Wake Island was hit by a small overnight raid that caused no damage and a larger raid just after dawn that seemed to be concentrated on the troop areas of the atoll. There were a few lightly wounded on the ground and no enemy planes were shot down. The previous day's raid had damaged the runway where the Wildcat fighters could barely land. Repairs were being made to the runway as quickly as possible.

PHILIPPINE ISLAND OPERATIONS

Reports from the Philippines were a bit confusing. First report was that the areas on north Mindanao around Cagayan were under attack by Japanese carrier based aircraft and that when the aircraft departed the area they headed south. This would put the carriers in the vicinity of the eastern edge of the Celebes Sea. This information was quickly put out to all commands.

The areas around Clark Field and Subic Bay were subjected to several air raids during the day. What was most interesting is that the 21st Philippine Army Division seemed to be taking the brunt of the attacks. It is probable that this is where the Japanese will try to push during their next major assault. We also received word that tanks from the 192nd Tank Battalion were heading to this area to bolster the defense.

All of this was occurring while a continued artillery duel was being conducted at both Clark Field and southern Manila. The Japanese seem content to continue these kinds of attacks; most likely while they marshal additional troops and supplies for a major push.

CHINESE THEATER

There was bad news near Wuchow. A Chinese force that was maintaining a base northwest of Wuchow was overrun by Japanese forces today causing "significant" casualties and forcing the remaining troops back. This was the only area where the Japanese had pushed the Chinese back today, with continued combat at Canton, Loyang, Kweisui, Hwainan, Kaifeng, Lang Son and Kweiteh. The State Department was trying to get the War Department to get more supplies to the Chinese, but right now there wasn't really a way to do it.

British and Allied Operations

Kendari on the southeast side of Celebes Island was subjected to an amphibious assault. Elements of the Japanese 52nd Division had gotten ashore taking the garrison by surprise. By noon time local, the troops were retreating towards Kolaka.

On Borneo, things weren't much better. Tarakan was under amphibious assault and Jesselton on the northern side of Borneo saw an amphibious invasion force arrive. Troop numbers were not known but there was little that could be done at either location. An uplifting report was received from the commander at Tarakan; the shore batteries managed to damage another troop transport ("heavily burning" the report read) and damage an enemy destroyer with hits by the 75mm and 120mm shore guns. That was the extent of the good news there.

Another Japanese air strike hit Medan on Sumatra today. There were a few wounded on the ground and the Dutch were asking if there was a way for us to help them. The only forces we have are at Soerabaja and they were to protect Java; the Dutch were on their own on Sumatra.

Quite a bit happened on the Malayan Peninsula. Overnight, there was an air raid to the north at Rangoon. The raid was ineffective but did wake up the pilots and ground crews.

There were several air raids against Kuantan. The Japanese Air Force must be using this location as a live fire training area; they visit it daily yet there is nothing to really be destroyed on the ground. Let them waste effort here.

The Royal Air Force sent some medium bombers to attack the Japanese forces at Malacca. A scratch force of Hudson and Blenheim bombers attacked forward marching elements of the 5th Japanese Division as they were forming up to head towards Singapore. The bombing seemed effective (the bombers came in at only 6000 feet). A recon plane later confirmed that no other forward movement of Japanese troops occurred by sunset. The raid was escorted by a dozen Buffalo fighters. These tactics may buy more time for Singapore to prepare fighting positions.

AUSTRALIA AND NEW GUINEA

The only major reports concerned an overnight air raid against Port Moresby that was ineffective and that enemy shipping was confirmed at Shortlands and Munda. This information was given immediately to ADM Nimitz.

INTELLIGENCE

Other than information on the Japanese carriers, the only piece of information provided was that the Japanese were probably going to attempt an amphibious assault at Buna in New Guinea. This was on the other side of the peninsula from Port Moresby. The intelligence section gave it from 7 to 11 days before the operation is attempted. This may alter plans regarding US Forces in the area and the Australian Cruiser Force.

OPERATION SINGING PUMPKIN PLANNING

The final supply and equipment loadouts for each ship were completed today and given to the Harbor Master and Chief Supply Officer. Loading of the equipment and supplies would begin today. Of interesting note, almost all of the available .30 caliber ammunition was being gathered to be loaded up. It was revealed that the large supply convoy heading from the West Coast was mostly loaded with small arms ammunition, grenades, extra machine guns, rifles and pistols. Only one of the freighters was loaded up with food. Factories back home were working three shifts to make ammunition; this was revealed to us today. Had we known, we might have modified the overall operational plan, but it is too late for that. ADM Nimitz was not pleased.

THEORIES AND INTENTIONS

New attacks and landings at Celebes Island with continued attacks at New Guinea indicate that they intend to completely isolate the Philippines from Australia. This makes sense. They are also consolidating oil resources on Borneo and will probably assault Sumatra before trying for Java. This makes defensive preparations on Java all the more important.

LATE DAY REPORTS

The rollup from USS Porpoise's first combat patrol was received. CDR Brewster's report stated that they had torpedoed a freighter on December 18th but the kill was not confirmed. They also torpedoed and gunned down a freighter on January 6th, but, yet again, the kill was not confirmed. For now, the submarine was credited with damaging two freighters. If the ships are later confirmed sunk, the submarine and her crew will be credited.

There were no other major late day reports and I left for dinner at 1830. I had a sandwich and a Coke. Some of the other officers were going to a movie tonight; I declined. I wanted sea air and some time to relax.

MORNING BRIEF

ADM Nimitz was not available this morning. He was conferring with the Governor of Hawaii on some matters. CAPT Ringwood began the morning briefing.

Orders were given to US Forces in Australia to sortie from Townsville and visit Shortlands followed by Munda to attack enemy shipping. They would then fall back to Sydney to load back up with 6" and 8" ammunition and then re-deploy back to Townsville. They would be Task Force 204 under command of CAPT Cummings.

The fast transports with the 31st Pursuit Group onboard were passing the Fiji Island and were a week from reaching Sydney. They were still making 22 knots.

Word came from the British Liaison Officer (who was absent this morning) that the Australian Cruiser Force had arrived safely at Sydney and were repairing damage and replenishing. They would stay in Sydney for two days and then redeploy to Townsville. The report also indicated that the freighter Steel Worker had returned from Pago Pago unscathed at Sydney.

CAPT Rooks reported from Java that the Dutch were sending another force of three destroyers to attack enemy shipping at Kendari where Japanese troops were consolidating gains. It was also noted that the force that left yesterday should reach Balikpapan today to attack enemy shipping.

From the West Coast, the submarine USS Silversides was released and would be heading to Pearl Harbor today. Also a further nine civilian freighters were released from Panama and were heading up to San Francisco; they were Charlie 15-C.

All other forces were proceeding as planned. We were then dismissed and went to breakfast before heading to our desks. Ham for breakfast; I made a sandwich with cheese and ate it with a glass of orange juice.

SUBMARINE OPERATIONS

A report was received from USS Salmon (LCDR McKinney) that they had spotted a damaged Fubuki Class destroyer and attacked near Balabac Island. They fired two torpedoes at the destroyer and hit with one. The destroyer was seen to have sunk by LCDR McKinney via the periscope (the destroyer went down by the stern). It is possible that this is the same destroyer damaged by USS S-36 a couple of days ago; if that is the case, then the kill would be shared. The information was sent to the intelligence section.

The tanker Eidsvold was attacked by a Japanese submarine around 75 nautical miles northeast of Christmas Island. The tanker was hit by three torpedoes and sank quickly. All that was received was the S.O.S. report, location and that they had been torpedoed. Catalina aircraft from Christmas Island were sent to look for survivors. Casualties were unknown and it is unknown if the submarine is patrolling that area or if they were transiting when the attack occurred.

HAWAII

There were no major reports at Hawaii today. All forces are proceeding as planned and no reports from the Harbor Master.

BROADER PACIFIC OCEAN

Wake Island was hit by a concentrated air strike of almost three dozen medium bombers. The bombers concentrated their attacks on the landings where the supplies were being landed. It is currently unknown why they don't actually attack the enemy shipping offloading the supplies.

PHILIPPINE ISLAND OPERATIONS

Artillery duels continued at Clark Field and southern Manila. No major ground was made by either side. Attacks at Clark Field were supported with aircraft but there were no concentrated attacks on any particular sector of the front.

CHINESE THEATER

There was a major Japanese assault at Pucheng that was repulsed with losses. This particular attack also had quite a few aircraft in support. The Chinese forces managed to hang on.

There was combat also at Kweiteh, Canton, Kaifeng, Loyang, Kweisui, Lang Son and Hwainan. Some of the attacks had air support but the majority were probing attacks.

BRITISH AND ALLIED OPERATIONS

There were continued amphibious assaults at Jesselton and Tarakan today. At Tarakan, the shore batteries managed to damage another troop transport and a freighter. This did not prevent the Japanese from continuing to land troops. It appeared that combat engineers had landed in addition to infantry units. The Dutch troops won't be able to hold out long without outside support.

At Jesselton, the landings were continuing with only sporadic resistance from the scratch infantry force there; there were no major shore batteries or defensive positions. By the end of the day, around 1100 Japanese troops had landed and were engaged with the small Royal Navy base contingent stationed there. It did not look good at all.

At Samarinda, Japanese troops had moved in from Balikpapan to the south. The remnants of the VI KNIL Battalion with some base support forces were engaged with the 8th Special Naval Landing Force. The Dutch troops inflicted more casualties on the Japanese but only at the expense of losing a key defensive position leading to the interior of the facilities. The Dutch had reported 31 troops wounded; no firm numbers on Japanese losses, but they are thought to be around 150 (this may be optimistic).

The Dutch ships under CAPT DeBoer managed to find a single Japanese freighter that was promptly shot up and sunk. It is probable that this ship was bringing in supplies for the Japanese troops on the ground. In any case, the ships then fell back towards Soerabaja.

On the western side of Borneo, Japanese troops had arrived from the march at Pontianak and attacked the troops at the base there. The defending friendly forces held off the attack; at least for now.

On the Malayan Peninsula, Kuantan was subjected to more attacks. No word on numbers or continued damage assessments. We were more or less in the dark.

On Sumatra, there was a confirmed Japanese air strike against Sabang on the very northern tip of the island. There were a few casualties on the ground and no damage was scored against the enemy aircraft. Types and numbers were not immediately available.

Word was also received from the Dutch via CAPT Rooks that they were now busy laying mines on the approaches to Palembang, a major oil producing area.

AUSTRALIA AND NEW GUINEA

Friendly forces were proceeding as planned and the troop transports with the 4th Light Anti-Aircraft Regiment had put to sea. The problem is that reports from Wau and Salamaua on the northern side of New Guinea indicated that they were under attack by carrier based aircraft.

A flash report was sent to CAPT Cummings to warn him and that it was up to him whether to continue with his current mission or to fall back on Townsville, but he was still to maintain radio silence.

No other major reports came from Australia during the day.

INTELLIGENCE

The intelligence section thought that the Japanese had split up the carriers; else there is no way that they could be attacking Mindanao and then be in the vicinity of Rabaul the following day. They maintained that they thought that Buna would be the next target on New Guinea.

Another report indicated that the patrol boat Toshi Maru #3 was sunk on December 28th near Dadjangas. This corroborates the report from the submarine USS Sturgeon.

OPERATION SINGING PUMPKIN PLANNING

Loading of ships continued and all ground troops involved with the operation were now in quarantine to make sure no word of the operation got out to civilians.

THEORIES AND INTENTIONS

There was nothing new today. Well, maybe carriers showing up at Rabaul. If the intelligence section was to be believed it makes sense. However, if the Japanese can have medium bombers at Rabaul, why bring in carriers?

LATE DAY REPORTS

There were no major late day reports. I left on time and grabbed a sandwich to eat at my bungalow. I was thinking a good poker game would be fun but I was too tired.

MORNING BRIEF

There are thunderstorms today. Visibility is crap and it was pouring. Not sure if that made me feel ominous or not.

ADM Nimitz was talking to CAPT Ringwood when I arrived at the headquarters building. They were discussing what they thought CAPT Cummings would do if they were in his situation. The briefing began shortly after I arrived.

There were only a few new developments. First, production was ramping up stateside and it was hoped that more aircraft would be produced. The Army Air Forces especially had a shortage.

Second, British forces were sending some supplies from Batavia to Singapore to help with the coming siege. Three faster freighters would make the run to bring the supplies.

Lastly, the submarine USS Finback was transiting the Panama Canal and would begin the trip to Pearl Harbor.

All other operations were proceeding as planned.

We were rather quickly dismissed and went to breakfast. Nothing special for breakfast. I then went to my desk.

SUBMARINE OPERATIONS

There were no reports of friendly or enemy submarine attacks today.

HAWAII

There were no major events at Hawaii today.

BROADER PACIFIC OCEAN

Bad weather prevented attacks against Wake Island today. The respite was very welcome as it will allow the engineers to repair facilities and get more supplies on the atoll. A major relief expedition should be attempted upon the completion of Operation Singing Pumpkin.

PHILIPPINE ISLAND OPERATIONS

Cotabato on the west side of Mindanao was under attack by an amphibious assault. It was unknown how many troops had landed, but it was irrelevant as no further help could be sent anyway.

On Luzon, Clark Field, Subic Bay and Manila were subjected to air strikes. Ground combat was limited to artillery fire and patrol actions. There were no major changes to the front line. Supplies are starting to run low for our forces there; they can't continue to expend ammunition at the current rate for much longer.

CHINESE THEATER

Combat continued at Hwainan, Lang Son, Kweisui, Loyang, Kaifeng, Canton and Kweiteh. No major changes to the front lines.

BRITISH AND ALLIED OPERATIONS

As usual, Kuantan was under heavy air attack. One of the guys on the staff thought it would be really neat if we could get a heavy fighter cover there for just one day to throw them off. Too bad it wouldn't work.

On Borneo, the Japanese attack at Jesselton continued without respite. Shore fire support was helping out the infantry that had landed. By the end of the day, the Royal Navy personnel were pushed to the northeast towards Kudat. Jesselton is now another Japanese base.

At Tarakan, the Dutch troops were having a slightly better time. They managed to fight off another attack led by Japanese combat engineers. The shore batteries helped out by putting more rounds into the same troop transport that was damaged yesterday. The situation is one of stalemate but it is one that the Dutch will eventually lose because there is no hope of reinforcement or resupply.

On the west side of Borneo, Japanese troops continued their attack at Pontianak. They managed to push through the defended area and force the defenders to retreat towards Ketapang. The route to Ketapang is through thick jungle and it will take the troops quite a while to get there. The good news is it will be just as difficult for the Japanese to pursue them. The only option the Japanese have is an amphibious assault against Ketapang before the Allied troops get there.

On the Malayan Peninsula, British bombers continued to attack forward elements of the Japanese 5th Division to slow their advance. It was known that they were causing casualties and it was helping friendly troops fall back on Singapore.

On Sumatra, Medan was again attacked by an air raid. This raid was reported as having around 30 twin engine bombers with escorts. The types were not immediately available but were thought to be Lily or Betty types.

AUSTRALIA AND NEW GUINEA

CAPT Cummings' force was discovered by Japanese patrol planes shortly after dawn. At that point it made no sense for the force to maintain radio silence. Just before noon they were attacked by a small force of Betty medium bombers on torpedo runs. None of the ships in the force were damaged and they were attacked near Vella Lavella. A message was received that indicated that the force would proceed with the original plan.

The only other reports concerned attacks against facilities near Salamaua and Nadzab; all in the general area of Lae. The Japanese must be considering pushing inland to these locations. The interesting piece is that the attacks were being done by carrier based aircraft.

INTELLIGENCE

There was no new information on ship kills or regarding new Japanese intentions. The code breakers were working as quickly as possible. The only item that the intelligence section was adamant on was that Buna would be invaded before the end of the month. I guess time would tell.

Some of the carriers were obviously noted in the areas around New Guinea. The intelligence section was split about mission of the carriers; either support the invasion or provide stop-gap firepower until Rabaul is fully up and operating.

OPERATION SINGING PUMPKIN PLANNING

Ships were still loading equipment and supplies. The troops wouldn't be loaded up until a day or so before the ships were due to leave port. There were no requests for information from our staff. I felt somehow useless in that aspect.

THEORIES AND INTENTIONS

Since carrier based aircraft are attacking the areas near Lae and only a few bombers were available to attack CAPT Cummings' force, it may indicate that they haven't fully consolidated the base at Rabaul. We should use this time to be slightly more aggressive before the base is fully ready.

LATE DAY REPORTS

There were no particularly interesting late day reports with the notable exception that USS S-36 had arrived at Soerabaja completing her patrol. My relief came in on time and I left on time. I had some pasta with marinara sauce and played some poker at the Officer's Club. I lost a buck and a half; LCDR Brown took me with an ace high straight. Classical music on the radio. I drifted off to sleep to lilting violins.

JANUARY 18, 1942   DAY 43 OF THE WAR

<u>MORNING BRIEF</u>

The storms were subsiding a bit and one could see the sun poking out through the clouds. CAPT Ringwood passed me a cup of coffee; I explained that I prefer tea. He laughed and shook his head as he walked away.

The morning briefing began. The Dutch force under CAPT DeBoer arrived safely at Soerabaja overnight. There were no casualties to the force and the report from CAPT Rooks indicated that the Dutch ships were in good material condition.

The Dutch destroyer force did not find any ships at Kendari but were going to head back and look again. They wanted to hit back at the Japanese forces bad; ADM Nimitz thought it was a bit too aggressive.

In the Australian area, Task Force 204 under CAPT Cummings should be hitting Shortlands today; he may be able to hit Munda today as well. We were to stand by for any reports.

Task Force 108 of fast transports carrying the 31st Pursuit Group was passing Norfolk Island and was only a few days away from Sydney. The force is still making 22 knots.

Nearer to home, the submarine USS Plunger (CDR Perry) was leaving Pearl Harbor today to patrol around Truk Island.

All other forces were proceeding as planned. There was no report from the British Liaison Officer (he was present but it looked like there was nothing to report).

As we were dismissed to the day's duties, the radio operators came in to notify us that something major was happening. Breakfast did not look appealing; runny eggs and cold toast. I took some toast and jam and went to my desk and began listening in on the reports.

SUBMARINE OPERATIONS

USS Permit (LCDR Hurst) found and attacked a freighter with torpedoes south of Swatow, China. The ship was listed as code "MFM" for an Ehime Class freighter. Four torpedoes were fired with three hits. The ship was sunk and the submarine continued the patrol.

USS Seawolf (LCDR Warder) was spotted by a Japanese escort near Batan Island and had to dive to escape. The escort attempted to make contact with the submarine and dropped some depth charges, but they were nowhere near the submarine. They eventually broke contact and continued their patrol.

A Japanese submarine attacked a US flagged freighter just west of Victoria, British Columbia. The torpedoes missed and the escorting destroyer USS Dent attempted to attack the submarine. After a two hour sub hunt where some depth charges were dropped, USS Dent broke contact and resumed escort of the freighter. It was unknown if there was damage to the enemy submarine.

HAWAII

There were no major reports and all forces were proceeding as planned.

BROADER PACIFIC OCEAN

Strangely quiet. No raids at Wake, nothing at Canton Island, Christmas Island or any other areas. I'll have to take a look to see what the weather is like at Wake Island. Any delays by the Japanese would be simply unforgiveable with the troops on the ropes like they are.

PHILIPPINE ISLAND OPERATIONS

A report was received from Cotabato on Mindanao about Japanese troop strengths. It appeared that just under 4000 troops had landed and they were engaged with a scratch infantry force of Philippine Army reservists. The area was secured by the Japanese by the end of the day and there were reports of heavy casualties to the reservists. Not good news.

Meanwhile, on Luzon, the Japanese made a determined attack in the southern areas of Manila. They managed to push into the city a few hundred yards but were taking heavy casualties from Philippine Army troops (the remnants of the 1st, 41st, 51st and 71st Infantry Divisions were in the city along with some US Forces). All that was known is that 300 friendly troops were wounded and killed. No information on the Japanese casualties.

The areas around Clark Field continued patrol and artillery actions with no major assault. There were bombing raids against front line areas and friendly casualties were not known.

CHINESE THEATER

There was combat again today in the usual locations; Hwainan, Lang Son, Kweisui, Loyang, Kaifeng, Canton, Kweiteh and Pucheng. There was significant combat at Pucheng, but Chinese forces held. As usual, there was not a single report of casualty numbers to either side.

BRITISH AND ALLIED OPERATIONS

Not surprisingly, there were several air strikes against Kuantan. There were no indications as to numbers, but there were reports of Japanese troops being seen. These troops were not landed via amphibious assault but had come from the interior. A request was sent to see what the estimate of enemy troop strengths are.

On Sumatra, the garrison at Medan was attacked again by an air raid. It was confirmed that there were at least 40 wounded on the ground. There was very little that could be done.

Tarakan saw more ground combat today. The Japanese combat engineers are pushing against the hard defensive positions set up by the Dutch infantry. All that was known was that the Dutch suffered 26 casualties (all wounded). The Japanese attack was stopped cold. The problem is that the attacks will continue while the Dutch don't really have hope of reinforcement or relief.

AUSTRALIA AND NEW GUINEA

When the radio operator came into the morning briefing to let us know that messages were flying it was because CAPT Cummings and his battle force had found Japanese shipping at Shortlands. The intelligence section also sent a runner because the Japanese were sending frantic messages, some of them in the clear, to call for help. It appeared that the freighters and troop transports were in the process of either loading or unloading troops and there were many casualties.

As best as we could make it out, the ships entered the area at around 0400 local time and came across a small force at a range of only 2000 yards. This happened because one of the navigators on staff figured that there was almost no moon at that location making spotting difficult. When the ships opened fire on the first two ships encountered, the message indicated "a very small escort and an MFM freighter of the Aden Class". CAPT Dawley on USS Detroit fired on the small escort with his main guns (6 inch guns) and when hit, the small escort simply blew up. The freighter was fired on by LCDR Fitzgerald on USS Lamson; they fired torpedoes and when the torpedo hit, he ordered 5" gunfire on the freighter. The freighter was sunk in a matter of minutes; one of the shell hits caused the freighter to explode (probably carrying ammunition for ground forces). This part of the battle took less than 15 minutes.

Around an hour later, more radio messages came in reporting that they found another enemy surface force. The report said that they found the ships at 4000 yards indicating a little bit of nautical twilight, and the ships were identified as:

- A small escort, possibly a patrol boat
- An "Uyo Maru" large fleet auxiliary (used for troops and cargo)
- A code "MKFKM" for a Bangkok Maru armed merchant cruiser
- A code "MFFMK" for a Shanghi Maru class troop transport

Figure 47 - USS Drayton (DD-366)

411

It is important to note that the codes are from the ship recognition manuals and should help the intelligence section confirm kills later. In any case, signal lights between the US ships ordered each of the ships to take targets. Fire was concentrated on the armed merchant cruiser first (they were the most heavily armed) and the patrol boat. An 8" round from USS Pensacola blew up the patrol boat and a concentrated torpedo spread from the destroyer USS Drayton under the command of LCDR Cooper destroyed the armed merchant cruiser. The Uyo Maru class ship then drew the ire of the entire force (the ship was fairly large at around 7000 tons). Several shell hits from the US force and a torpedo hit caused the ship to capsize and sink. During this, the troop transport made a run for a rain squall to hide; they had escaped for now.

As dawn broke over the area, CAPT Cummings ordered the force to the east at 12 knots. They then spotted another small force around 0715 with the report stating "a very small escort, possibly a sub chaser and ship with code MKFKM for a Kyushu Maru class freighter". The force was spotted at 7000 yards. USS Pensacola's main guns made short work of the escort and then the heavy cruiser shifted fire to the freighter. The other ships in the force were saving their ammunition for now and USS Pensacola sank the ship unassisted with the final salvo of rounds hitting the freighter at only 2000 yards. The freighter sank by the stern.

At 0840 local, CAPT Cummings then ordered the force back to the west to take advantage of some clouds and rain. When they doubled back, they came across the troop transport that had gotten away during the earlier engagements. The ship was spotted at 13000 yards; CAPT Cummings ordered the light cruisers USS Detroit and USS Raleigh to open fire with their main 6" gun batteries. When the range closed to 6000 yards, he ordered the destroyers to also fire with their 5" main batteries. The troop transport was raked with fire from stem to stern and was seen to sink at around 0955 local.

It was at this point that aircraft were spotted by lookouts. Around two dozen medium bombers appeared and made bombing runs against the force. The ships were able to avoid the falling bombs (the report estimated an altitude of 11000 feet for the attackers). The report indicated that they were Sally medium bombers with escorts (the escort fighter types were not identified). CAPT Cummings then ordered his force into a rain squall that was moving up from the south.

The force stayed in the rain squall until around 1400 local, at which time it was decided that the force would start heading towards Munda. Lookouts spotted a freighter hull down on the horizon. CAPT Cummings had his force intercept the freighter. It was identified as a code MFM for an Aden Class freighter. USS Pensacola opened fire at 24000 yards. After around an hour of firing, the freighter was sunk by combined gunfire of the force at a range of 8000 yards. At this point, another air raid was spotted, medium bombers at an estimated altitude of 12000 feet. Again, the bombs were fairly easily avoided, but one bomb did land only 200 yards from the destroyer USS Cummings. This attack had ended around 1615 local and CAPT Cummings ordered the force to head towards Munda after the aircraft were seen to leave the area.

Very long day for that task force. It is expected that they should reach Munda overnight tonight. One final report from the float planes of USS Pensacola reported some ships to the south, heading south, possibly to Australia or to New Caledonia. This information was sent to the British Liaison Officer.

The only other information from the Australian area is that there was an overnight air raid at Port Moresby that caused some damage to the airfield facilities and that there were troops landing at Kavieng; nothing could be done about the new invasion.

INTELLIGENCE

The intelligence briefing began with them stating that no new confirmed kills were determined and then they quickly went to information about what was happening at Shortlands. Most of the information came from messages sent in the clear, but some quick items have been decrypted. As it turns out, there is more shipping in the area but the ships that were attacked were almost fully loaded up with troops. As best as they could make out, there were 22000 troops in transit in the area and the ships that were attacked were carrying almost 17000 troops between them. It is almost with certainty that heavy casualties were caused to the troops that were being carried and they were trying to find out which units were in the area.

They also stated that if the ships were sunk it would mean that almost 30000 tons of merchant and fleet shipping were destroyed. The best news possible is going to depend on enemy troops losses; even if the killed to wounded ratio is low, the equivalent of an entire Japanese division has been shattered (it will take the wounded and rescued time to reorganize and most of their equipment would be on the transports). If that were the case then it would take even longer for the division to be combat effective.

OPERATION SINGING PUMPKIN PLANNING

No reports or requests. The ships are still loading up with equipment and supplies.

THEORIES AND INTENTIONS

I am reminded of a lesson from the Naval Academy in my timeline where we studied Soviet Admiral Gorshkov. He stated that the best way to defend against an amphibious assault is to destroy it on the ships during transit to the battlezone. This attack by CAPT Cummings is the next best thing. The troops are packed and unable to defend themselves against a naval assault. I wonder if the Japanese will try the same with us.

LATE DAY REPORTS

The rollup report from USS S-36 was received. LCDR McKnight and his crew were credited with sinking the Brisbane Maru on December 19th (5935 tons), damaging another freighter on December 24th, damaging a destroyer on January 14th and they claimed another freighter sunk on January 5th that has not yet been confirmed. If the kill is later confirmed it will be added to the tally. The submarine is performing minor repairs and has fully loaded out with Mark 10 torpedoes. They are standing by for further orders.

Other than the report of other shipping heading south towards the areas of Australia and New Caledonia, there were no major late reports. I went to dinner, had decent fried chicken with a baked potato and carrots. I took a walk after dinner with the cooler air in my hair; then I realized I should probably get a haircut. I got to my bungalow, took a shower and went to bed.

MORNING BRIEF

I didn't sleep well last night. Don't know why. I'm just tired and a little cranky.

CAPT Ringwood began the morning briefing. The fleet cargo ship USS Almaack arrived very early this morning and was reprovisioning. They should be ready for more operations in a day or two.

All other US Forces were proceeding as planned; CAPT Cummings' force should reach Munda if they're not already there. We were to stand by for any reports.

The British Liaison Officer reported that the transports carrying the Australian 4th Light Anti-Aircraft Regiment should be reaching Port Moresby today. They are also carrying more building supplies, food, ammunition and some aviation fuel.

Figure 48 - HMAS Voyager (D31)

The Australian Cruiser Force is leaving Sydney to redeploy to Townsville. They also picked up a couple of destroyers to add to the force (HMAS Stuart and HMAS Voyager). They are to stand by for further orders during transit in light of the shipping discovered by CAPT Cummings' force yesterday.

The destroyer HMS Tenedos will make a quick run in to Djambi on Sumatra; a lone Japanese ship was seen heading to the area and it might be a small invasion force.

All other Allied forces were proceeding as planned.

Breakfast was toast with some tea. I also grabbed some extra bread to munch on while working at my desk. We left to go to our stations for the day's work.

SUBMARINE OPERATIONS

USS Sturgeon (LCDR Wright) found a small convoy near Dadjangas and attacked. They fired two torpedoes at a freighter/transport (unidentified) and hit with one. The escort immediately began looking for the submarine so LCDR Wright dove deep and broke away on a reciprocal heading. They escaped after three hours and when they surfaced, the convoy was gone. They then resumed their patrol.

HAWAII

Nothing significant to report here today.

BROADER PACIFIC OCEAN

A Japanese force was seen heading towards Midway Island; the only ship identified was a light cruiser. Orders were immediately sent to USS President Coolidge to cease unloading supplies and immediately come back to Pearl Harbor. The ship complied.

The fleet cargo ship USS Alchiba with her escorting destroyers have completed their resupply mission and are heading back to Pearl Harbor.

PHILIPPINE ISLAND OPERATIONS

There were several air raids against the Subic Bay area and Clark Field. Ground combat was still low level patrol actions and artillery duels; there has not been a major change to the front line. The same holds true for Manila. The gains from yesterday are being consolidated at loss to the Japanese; Philippine snipers and sharpshooters are making life difficult for advancing troops. Troop movements on Mindanao are currently unknown.

CHINESE THEATER

There was a major push by the Japanese at Pucheng with a multi-division attack that was successfully defended by Chinese forces. Casualties, as usual, were not known. There was also combat at Kweiteh, Canton, Loyang, Kweisui, Kaifeng, Lang Son and Hwainan.

BRITISH AND ALLIED OPERATIONS

Japanese troops finally made their presence felt at Kuantan. A mixed infantry/tank regiment began attacking the troop concentrations in the area after a concentrated air strike. The troops initially were doing ok, but some forward positions were overrun. The problem is that the troops are cut off from Singapore, so they have to fight in place. Casualties were not immediately known.

The Royal Air Force was now bombing the Japanese lead units only 70 miles from Singapore. The lead elements are just outside of Johore Bahru. This is not a good thing. Australian troops were pulled back intact to contribute to the defense of Singapore and supplies are being dispatched.

On Borneo, there was continued combat at Samarinda and Tarakan. The lines had not changed and casualties for Dutch troops were light. The problem was one of supply, particularly for Tarakan, but not quite as bad at Samarinda.

Australia and New Guinea

CAPT Cummings' force got to the vicinity of Munda in a thick fog. It was too dangerous to attempt to head in the reefs without good navigation. They waited until sunrise and the fog refused to lift, so they began a slow withdrawal towards Sydney. When the fog did finally lift, they were shadowed by a Japanese patrol aircraft. At that point, CAPT Cummings ordered all ships up to formation speed (20 knots) and dutifully left the area. They did run into a single freighter, USS Pensacola put an 8" round into the ship from 24000 yards but CAPT Cummings thought it imprudent to press the attack while still being shadowed by the patrol plane. The force continued on to Sydney for the rest of the day without incident. They should reach Sydney in a few days.

Troops and equipment of the Australian 4th Light Anti-Aircraft Regiment began unloading this morning as the transports arrived at Port Moresby. Priority was given to the troops and anti-aircraft guns followed by all other supplies and munitions.

There was an attack near Lae by land based medium bombers; damage assessment was unknown as were casualties. Curious as to what the Japanese hope to attain with those air strikes. There was also a late afternoon strike against rear positions of the 1st Australian Division. The raid was fairly ineffective.

Meanwhile, Kavieng was overrun by Japanese troops during the day. The single radio operator there (there were no troops) stated that hundreds of troops had landed and that he was surrendering.

INTELLIGENCE

A kill was confirmed on December 30th, the freighter Kashi Maru (1650 tons) was confirmed sunk by the Dutch near Balikpapan. There was no other major intelligence.

OPERATION SINGING PUMPKIN PLANNING

I was pulled to a quick meeting to discuss the overall plan with other officers. I had been worried that the Japanese might mine the area and voiced my opinion. It was decided that a force of six destroyer minesweepers would be going with the invasion force to reduce the mine threat. No force name was yet decided. We should have a list of ships ready for tomorrow. The initial list has the following ships:

- USS Elliot
- USS Chandler
- USS Zane
- USS Hovey
- USS Boggs
- USS Trevor

The force will probably be called "Task Force Broom"; a clever play on words. In any case the minesweeping force will be directly attached to the initial assault forces (Task Force Loadstone). They can also provide shore fire support in a pinch as well.

Theories and Intentions

We simply can't figure out what the Japanese are doing by bombing the areas around Lae; do they not know that our forces have evacuated? That might make sense, but it would stand to reason that the Japanese troops that have landed would send out patrols to learn this information.

Late Day Reports

Word was received from the West Coast that the battleship USS Colorado was fully repaired, refitted and ready for operations. We were waiting for word that she would be assigned to the Pacific Fleet (obvious, but the ship can't move until the orders are signed). Not sure what's left as far as escorts to get the ship safely to Pearl Harbor. The battleship will probably begin movement after the completion of Singing Pumpkin.

There were no major reports coming in late, so I left as soon as my relief arrived. Dinner wasn't bad, ham steak with cheese potatoes (or something that looked like it; it wasn't bad). I went for a haircut and then to my bungalow. Classical music on the radio as I fell asleep.

<u>MORNING BRIEF</u>

ADM Nimitz was conferring with the Marines as I entered the building. They were making sure that all was coordinated between the Navy and themselves for the upcoming operation. All was proceeding to plan.

CAPT Ringwood started the briefing by telling us that the submarines USS Tambor, USS Triton, USS Gar and USS Grayling were redeploying to Sydney to form the nucleus of Submarine Forces Southwest Pacific. They were leaving Pearl Harbor today.

The transports carrying the 31st Pursuit Group should be arriving at Sydney today. The aircraft are to be reassembled and flown up to Townsville or Cairns by their pilots and then begin rotations at Port Moresby. The transports are also carrying spare parts, extra ammunition and other supplies for US Forces.

On Java, CAPT Rooks sent a report that the Dutch were sending a force of two light cruisers and three destroyers (the same ships from the previous operation) to Pontianak to attack Japanese shipping. The destroyers that had gone to Kendari should be reaching their objective today.

The British Liaison Officer notified us that three freighters were loaded up with supplies and heading up to Singapore from Batavia. These supplies should help with the siege and prevent the city from falling to Japanese assault. He also let us know that the freighters loaded with supplies for our forces were only a few days away from Batavia. A more in depth report would be made once a report was received from the freighters.

We were asked if there were any questions. There were none. We were then dismissed for the day for our duties.

SUBMARINE OPERATIONS

USS Sargo (LCDR Jacobs) was damaged by enemy air attack while performing a crash dive to escape. The submarine is damaged (though not severely) and is making 18 knots to Soerabaja for repairs.

USS Seawolf (LCDR Warder) found themselves under attack most of the day. They had found a Japanese convoy and had positioned themselves for attack but were sighted by some enemy patrol boats. There were two separate actions during the day where the submarine was depth charged; there was no damage to the submarine, but the submarine was also unable to successfully complete an attack against the freighters in the convoy. The submarine then resumed their patrol.

HAWAII

There was nothing significant to report at Hawaii today.

BROADER PACIFIC OCEAN

Wake Island was subject to two separate air raids during the morning. The runway was heavily damaged and the fighters could not get off the ground. The engineers were working as quickly as possible to get the airfield working but every time they managed to make some headway on the repairs, Betty bombers would come in and cause more damage. The island is in desperate need of more anti-aircraft defenses. When ADM Nimitz heard this report he ordered us to think about a force to be delivered to help with both the repairs on the island and more anti-aircraft guns. We started looking at available equipment and troops to be sent there. More than likely they would not be able to be sent until after the completion of Operation Singing Pumpkin.

PHILIPPINE ISLAND OPERATIONS

The areas around Clark Field were subjected to several air raids during the day. Reports were sketchy as to the number of enemy bombers and their targets. The Japanese did attempt a major offensive in the areas around Clark Field but the 91st Philippine Army Division with support from the 194th Tank Battalion managed to hold against a concentrated infantry assault supported by artillery and a few tanks. The Japanese troops were caught in the open and were under severe fire from the field guns and machineguns of friendly troops. There were few friendly casualties, but the Japanese had "hundreds of casualties".

Around Manila, there were no airstrikes and the ground combat was limited to patrol actions and artillery strikes. The local weather was worse south of Manila than it was in the more northern areas around Clark Field. The remaining Philippine Army units around Manila have been reorganized under the II Philippine Corps. This will allow (theoretically) for a more coordinated defense.

There were no reports from friendly units on Mindanao. This is concerning to the staff; the headquarters units have not answered calls and the main headquarters at the Bataan Peninsula have no information as to what is happening on Mindanao.

Chinese Theater

A troubling report was received that a Chinese infantry corps was defeated and pushed back with heavy casualties near Kaifeng. We were trying to find out more information but the Liaison with the Chinese said that there was "nothing to worry about", but anytime the front lines are sundered, it is cause for alarm. We are monitoring the situation.

There were also reports of combat at Pucheng, Kweiteh, Canton, Loyang, Kweisui and Lan Son.

British and Allied Operations

On the Malayan Peninsula there was good news and bad news. The good news is that all of the Australian troops managed to make it to Singapore. The bad news is that Johore Bahru was overrun by a combined tank and light infantry assault. There were no friendly troops there; they had all fallen back on Singapore.

A little to the north at Kuantan, friendly troops were engaged by a Japanese infantry regiment supported by tanks. They were losing the battle and only hanging on by a thread. By the end of the day, friendly troops were pushed completely out of the original base area (that was still more or less destroyed by the constant air strikes). It was unknown how many troops had survived.

On Borneo, reports were received that combat was continuing at Tarakan and Samarinda. Dutch troops were holding and the shore batteries at Tarakan had shot up another troop transport (the ship was reported as heavily damaged and on fire from repeated hits by 120mm and 75mm gun emplacements).

Meanwhile, at Kendari on Celebes Island, the Dutch destroyers managed to find a small escorted troop convoy loading up the troops that had invaded Kendari. The destroyers worked up to full speed and attacked the Japanese ships. The battle began roughly an hour before dawn and the ships had spotted each other at 11000 yards. LCDR Schotel (the force commander) opened fire on the larger escort (reported as a destroyer) with the main guns from HNLMS Bankert. The smaller escort (reported as a patrol boat) drew the fire from HNLMS Van Nes and HNLMS Witte de With. After around a half an hour of exchanging fire, HNLMS Witte de With was hit several times by main gun rounds from the Japanese destroyer that caused significant damage and started some fairly large fires.

HNLMS Van Nes was signaled to concentrate fire on the enemy destroyer. The Japanese destroyer was eventually sunk after repeated hits by 120mm gunfire from the two Dutch destroyers. The troop transport and the patrol boat were then attacked as LCDR Schotel ordered a withdrawal due to the damage to HNLMS Witte de With. The patrol boat was heavily damaged and the troop transport was hit by at least 30 main gun rounds (120mm in both armor piercing and high explosive shells). The troop transport was on fire and the other freighter in the enemy force was hit by a few rounds. LCDR Shotel reported that he was retiring to Soerabaja at best possible speed for repairs and replenishment. The report indicated that they could make 22 knots (mostly due to the damage to HNLMS Witte de With). A full report on the material condition of the ships will be available when they reach port.

AUSTRALIA AND NEW GUINEA

The troop transports that were in the process of unloading the 4th Light Anti-Aircraft Regiment came under air attack by Betty bombers; probably from Rabaul. The troop transport USS Chaumont and the converted liner SS Ormiston were both sunk by torpedo hits from the bombers (USS Chaumont took a torpedo hit midships that quickly flooded the main spaces; SS Ormiston was hit by two torpedoes forward of the beam and sank by the bow). The troops had offloaded, but the remaining supplies and equipment were sunk in the harbor. There was no damage suffered by the attacking bombers. The sloops that were escorting the transports tried to provide fire support but they were unable to deter the attackers. This punctuates the need for fighters at Port Moresby. Casualties to the ships crews were unknown at this time.

As it turns out, at the end of the day the fast converted liners carrying the 31st Pursuit Group arrived at Sydney and they are beginning to unload the aircraft and pilots. It will be a day or two before the aircraft are ready to fly. The plan is to have the pilots fly the planes up to Cairns for their garrison location before rotating squadrons to Port Moresby.

INTELLIGENCE

There were a couple more confirmed ship kills from the intelligence section. The freighters Brazil Maru and Huso Maru were confirmed sunk near Balikpapan by Dutch destroyers on December 30th.

There was no word on additional shipping or troops at Canton Island and we were to stand by for any other reports.

There was a separate squad of intelligence analysts to support Singing Pumpkin.

Figure 49 - USS Chaumont (AP-5)

OPERATION SINGING PUMPKIN PLANNING

The destroyer minesweeper selection was approved, as well as the task force name. The ship captains were given their orders this afternoon and then left to prepare their ships and crews; the crews were not told where they were going except for the navigators.

No other requests were made of our staff on this today.

THEORIES AND INTENTIONS

I didn't think there was anything really new here. Attacks against Port Moresby are increasing as expected and the Japanese are trying to secure Borneo and Celebes. What I think will be interesting is what will happen at Singapore. We were told that the defenses were strong and there will be a fierce battle, unless the British surrender; which I don't think will happen again in my current timeline.

LATE DAY REPORTS

The only interesting late day reports came via the British Liaison Officer. He reported that the destroyer HMS Tenedos had arrived safely at Soerabaja and that the convoy with supplies for US Forces at Soerabaja are only a day out of Batavia. This made ADM Nimitz happy because he was concerned about the ability of our forces to make a contribution to the overall effort; something that couldn't be done without the ships and submarines being adequately supplied.

I then left for the day. Dinner was substandard (don't even know what it was; meat or fish). I then had a lengthy conversation with one of the FBI guys who was assigned to watch over me. I told him that we had completely changed the timeline and that I thought I might cause more damage than help. He laughed; he didn't really seem to believe I was who I said I was. I then laughed a bit; I remembered a few things about J. Edgar Hoover. I kept them to myself... don't need a broken nose.

MORNING BRIEF

Just like in my timeline, sometimes a Tuesday feels like a Wednesday; or maybe you just want it to. It was sunny and just a bit warm. I am hoping it'll be a good day.

CAPT Ringwood began the briefing; ADM Nimitz was not present and no reason was given. I guess at my paygrade they won't always tell me anyway. Before starting the morning briefing, CAPT Ringwood informed us that Operation Singing Pumpkin was no longer in the planning stage, it was now in execution. Ships were loading up, troops were briefed and there was little more planning to be done.

The first items were regarding a report sent from CAPT Rooks at Soerabaja. The Dutch were fairly certain that the surface force under CAPT DeBoer should be making contact with the Japanese at Pontianak sometime today. They also reported that the destroyer HNLMS Witte de With has fallen back from the rest of the destroyer formation; the other destroyers were ordered to do so. It was expected that the HNLMS Banckert and HNLMS Van Nes should reach Soerabaja sometime today; HNLMS Witte de With will take another full day to reach port.

CAPT Rooks also reported that on his authority, the submarines USS Snapper, USS Sculpin and USS Sealion were loading up with as much food as possible and were under orders to offload the food at Bataan. This was not a violation of any orders; his orders not to sortie related to the surface force only; he had discretion on the submarines. It is thought that 150 tons of food should be able to be delivered. The submarines were putting to sea today. The force is under the command of LCDR Stone.

The British Liaison Officer then began his report. At Java, the converted liner Empress Australia carrying No. 232 Squadron comprised of Hurricane fighters should reach Tjilatjap in the next two days. It was not known where the squadron would base themselves; more than likely Batavia.

He then continued by reminding us that the British freighters carrying US supplies should reach Batavia today and immediately begin unloading the cargo. The Dutch had provided rolling stock and locomotives to bring the cargo over to Soerabaja. He would keep the staff up to date on any developments.

He then reported that the light cruiser HMS Mauritius had arrived safely at Columbo. Initial reports from the harbor master there indicated that a minimum of three weeks in drydock would fully repair the ship. The ship could not go to the drydock until HMS Prince of Wales completes the hull repairs (repairs to internal systems, the superstructure and other weapons could be completed pierside). Once the battleship is out of the drydock, HMS Mauritius should be able to go in (probably with HMS Danae, she was only a few days from Columbo; there was enough drydock space to hold both cruisers).

There was a report from Singapore about defensive preparedness. There were roughly 7200 infantry and 31000 other troops for the defense of the city. Supplies were making their way there from Java and it was thought that there was enough artillery to stop the Japanese assault. The troops were still digging in but had created dozens of hard, fixed fire spots and would make any advance into the city very costly for the Japanese. The few medium bombers available would shift targets to hit the supply dumps the Japanese are creating at

Johore Bharu. There was no further information at the start of the day.

He also reported that at Aden, the Australian 6th Infantry Division was beginning to load up on transports with destroyer escorts to transit to Batavia. They would make a refueling spot at Columbo and then offload the division before returning to Aden. The transit would take a couple of weeks at least.

CAPT Ringwood then took back the floor and reported some items from the West Coast. The battleship USS Colorado would be leaving Seattle with five attending destroyers. The destroyers were older and were reserve ships. They have been released to the Pacific Fleet. They would be leaving port in the next 24 hours. The force is under the command of CAPT D'Alessio.

He then moved on to another force of fast converted liners that are carrying the troops of II Fighter Command and some support troops for the buildup of forces at Australia. They had passed Fiji Island on their way to Sydney and were making 19 knots.

The final item for the morning dealt with the 8th Pursuit Group equipped with P-39 Airacobras. They were at full establishment and were training; they would be released to the Pacific Fleet for employment on April 1st of this year. More forces were training.

There were no questions from the staff so we were dismissed for the day's work. Breakfast was actually not bad. I made a breakfast sandwich with ham, scrambled eggs and cheese. Also had more pineapple; it's just too good here.

SUBMARINE OPERATIONS

A report from USS Salmon (LCDR McKinney) was received that they had found a large Japanese convoy near Balabac Island. They had fired two torpedoes at a large freighter (identified as code MFM for a Biyo Maru class freighter). The torpedoes had missed and they were then attacked by a pair of escorts. The submarine was forced deep and they were bracketed in by the escorts so the only option was to break away from the convoy. It took nearly 4 hours for them to break contact. They then surfaced to recharge their batteries and continue their patrol. There was no damage to the submarine.

The submarine USS Permit (LCDR Hurst) came across a Japanese destroyer that was moving quickly (report stated "around 20 knots") to the north near Calayan Island. LCDR Hurst fired four torpedoes for no hits. It might be that the torpedoes had run too deep or they were too wide of the destroyer. The destroyer did not even know it was under attack because they never turned around or tried to find the submarine. Approximately 30 minutes later, the submarine surfaced and continued their patrol.

HAWAII

The fleet cargo ship USS Alchiba arrived with her escorting destroyers around lunchtime today. All ships from the force are performing minor repairs and replenishing in anticipation of further orders.

The Harbor Master arrived around 1300 this afternoon to report that the battleships USS Maryland and USS West Virginia had completed minor overhaul and refits and were ready for duty. The ship captains were reporting to ADM Nimitz and VADM Pye at the same time.

Broader Pacific Ocean

There was bad news from Wake Island. The Japanese changed their tactics and attacked the ships that were delivering the supplies to the atoll. The freighter SS Laida was torpedoed by a large force of Betty bombers (over 40 were in the attack). The fighters at Wake could not get off the ground because the runway was still too heavily damaged. The freighter was more or less stationary because they were offloading the supplies but the destroyers could still make 20 knots (they kept at least some of their boilers hot) and managed to work up some speed before the bombers arrived. There was a total of 6 minutes from sighting by lookouts and radar until they arrived. The destroyers were also attacked but not damaged; Laida was hit and sunk (there was a large explosion and fire, only six of the crew were rescued). One bomber was confirmed shot down by USS Balch and five more were damaged (confirmed trailing smoke) by the entire force. ADM Nimitz was notified immediately and ordered us to have orders sent to get the destroyers out of there.

ADM Nimitz wanted us to start finding a way to get anti-aircraft guns and more fighters to the Island. We were to start formal planning tomorrow and it would be called Operation Spinning Whistle. Again, I wondered idly where these names come from.

Philippine Island Operations

There were a couple of air raids at Subic Bay and at Clark Field. These raids didn't do much damage. Ground combat at

Clark Field was limited to patrol actions and some low level fire fights.

At Manila, there was a major push by the Japanese. The Japanese had reinforced the 16th Division and were making wedges in the defense of the city. They had suffered dearly for the advances, but had pushed back elements of the 41st Philippine Army Division. The center of the city and the vital areas north were still firmly in friendly hands, but the troops were beginning to run low on supplies and none were forthcoming. There were 20000 friendly troops in the city and they could hold temporarily, but overall, the situation did not look good. There was nothing that could bring in copious amounts of supplies, only what we could bring in by submarine and that would not be enough.

CHINESE THEATER

The Japanese had mounted a significant offensive around the areas at Pucheng. According to our Liaison with the Chinese, there were 18000 Chinese troops in that area and were engaged with the Japanese. The troops there were "holding" and had inflicted "significant" casualties on the enemy. Our staff still wasn't sure what that really meant.

There were also reports of lower level combat at Kweiteh, Canton, Loyang, Kweisui, Lang Son and Hwainan. There was not a lot of information on these locations but if there were major problems we'd be able to figure it out (at least that's what I think).

BRITISH AND ALLIED OPERATIONS

On Borneo at Tarakan there was a major defeat. As the Japanese combat engineers had kept the attention of Dutch troops focused on them, almost an entire division had landed over the last few days to a smaller beach further north (by about 6 miles) that was undefended due to lack of troops. These Japanese troops were fully assembled and performed a pincer move against the Dutch troops coming from inland and from the sea; this also coincided with an air raid by medium bombers probably launched from Saigon. The Dutch troops were heavily outnumbered and were being overrun. A final report stated that the remaining survivors were falling back on Tandjoengselor to the south. Casualties were unknown.

Samarinda was still holding against the Japanese and there were no major reports from the troops there.

The good news from the Dutch command came from CAPT DeBoer's force that managed to reach Pontianak without incident. They found a lone Japanese freighter that was shot up and sunk. This report was sent to the intelligence section. The Dutch ships were falling back on Soerabaja after the action.

On the Malayan Peninsula, there were reports from recon aircraft that Japanese troops were landing from the sea at Mersing; our troops had evacuated to Singapore several days ago. Since there were no friendly troops to resist the invasion, it is assumed that the Japanese have successfully gotten inland and now control the facilities located there.

When these reports were received, we were also informed via the British Liaison Officer that the freighters with supplies for Singapore had arrived and were unloading. He also took the liberty to let us know that the freighters with US supplies had arrived at Batavia on Java and were unloading their cargo (priority was given to torpedoes for the submarines and spare parts for the surface ships).

There was also a confirmed report of a large air strike against the facilities at Medan on Sumatra. The airfield was heavily damaged (there were no aircraft stationed there, so not really a major problem) but the supply dumps were damaged and on fire, so this might be the bigger problem. There is a coastal gun battalion stationed there and they are on 24 hour watch looking for the possibility of invasion.

Australia and New Guinea

Bad weather kept more enemy bombers from attacking the transports unloading supplies at Port Moresby. The troops had completed offloading first, so the loss of the ships from yesterday, while bad, did not cripple the 4th Light Anti-Aircraft Regiment. We were waiting for reports about how quickly the P-39 fighters could be sent up to Cairns. It seems that all other forces were proceeding as planned.

There was also an unconfirmed report of a Japanese air strike against Salamaua, but there was no damage report and no information regarding types of bombers or numbers.

Intelligence

There was a lot of data presented here today. ADM Nimitz made it a point to attend.

The action involving US ships at Shortlands Island (some are referring to it as the Battle of Shortlands Island; not much of a battle, more like we destroyed a lot of freighters, but I digress) took most of the report. As it turns out the intelligence section managed to decode some information about the units that were on the transports there.

If the reports from the Japanese were accurate, 3259 Japanese troops were killed, 11854 were wounded or "unable to contribute". Also listed were over 100 artillery pieces and mortars and "countless" small arms and other equipment that were lost. This would make the unit that was attacked almost a full Japanese division with supporting elements. The intelligence analysts were not 100% sure which division was in the area but were trying to figure it out.

They also reported that they have pinpointed a lot of enemy radio chatter at Guadalcanal (not surprising) and even more at Shortlands. The attack by CAPT Cummings' force may have seriously set back plans for the Japanese in the Solomon Islands.

There were also a lot of Japanese radio communications coming from Watampone on Celebes Island. This information was passed to the Dutch via CAPT Rooks; the Dutch probably didn't have any troops there, or else we would've heard something by now.

There were no other confirmation of confirmed kills.

ADM Nimitz told all of us to think of ways that we might be able to use this information to further upend Japanese plans in the area and wanted ideas via CAPT Ringwood tomorrow morning.

Operation Singing Pumpkin Execution

The transports and fleet cargo ships were still being loaded. There were no requests from our staff today.

Theories and Intentions

We had to take a look to see what was left in order to get done what ADM Nimitz was asking. This was aggressive without major carrier support to run interference for Wake Island until the runway was operating with sufficient fighter support. Not an easy task. I was tasked with being the lead for the planning. It feels like I'm back at the Academy – here, quick, do all of this with almost nothing. Time to see if that training helped.

Late Day Reports

USS President Coolidge arrived safely at Pearl Harbor in the early evening hours. There were no casualties on the ship, the ship was in good material condition and they were standing by for further orders.

It was confirmed that orders were acknowledged from the destroyers that were escorting the now destroyed freighter SS Laida. They were leaving Wake Island immediately to head back to Pearl Harbor.

Word was received from the West Coast that the overhaul for the battleship USS New Mexico had been completed and the ship was ready at San Francisco. The ship had not yet been released to the Pacific Fleet and escorts would have to be assembled to get the battleship to Pearl Harbor.

A report was received from CAPT Rooks at Soerabaja that the Dutch destroyers HNLMS Banckert and HNLMS Van Nes had arrived safely and were performing repairs and replenishment. HNLMS Witte de With was still a full day out.

The British Liaison Officer reported that two British submarines were heading towards Columbo to begin offensive patrols. It would be a while before the submarines (HMS Trusty and HMS Truant) were available.

Figure 50 - P-39 Fighter

A rollup report from the 31st Pursuit Group was received that showed the number of fighters ready to go. The 39th Pursuit Squadron had 11 fighters ready, the 40th had 6 fighters ready and the 41st had only 3 fighters ready. The headquarters squadron had none. The ground crews were getting them ready as quickly as possible. More support troops were on the way, but it was imperative to get the fighters ready immediately.

I left for the night. Had some pork with a decent sauce, rice and veggies for dinner. I stopped by the Officer's Club to see if anyone was there to play some poker. The club was pretty sparse with people. I left dejected, went to my bungalow, took a shower and continued to read my book until I fell asleep.

JANUARY 22, 1942   DAY 47 OF THE WAR

<u>MORNING BRIEF</u>

I was very tired today and yet there seemed to be a bit of energy in the headquarters building. I had a meeting over at Hickham Field at 0500 this morning to discuss items with COL Hobbs, US Army about his anti-aircraft regiment. I had been given permission by CAPT Ringwood to discuss an upcoming operation with him about the readiness of his unit and the material condition of his equipment. As it turns out, COL Hobbs' unit would be useful for Operation Spinning Whistle.

ADM Nimitz was in fine spirits when we entered the briefing room. He began the briefing by reminding us that we were doing good work and that despite some setbacks, we were putting our nation into the position for victory. As I stood there, I remembered reading Thucydides; "but to the brave, few words are as good as many".

CAPT Ringwood began on Java. What we didn't know is that on the original convoy to Cape Town there were 115 shipyard personnel on the freighters. They were also on the convoy that arrived at Batavia. They were heading over to Soerabaja to take up shop and provide repair, upgrade, overhaul and other services to our ships and submarines there. CAPT Rooks was very happy about this; most of the destroyers were older "Clemson" Class ships from the First World War. Any upgrades or maintenance activities are going to be most welcome.

The manifest of supplies in the cargo was quite interesting. Ammunition (8 inch, 6 inch, 5 inch, 4 inch, 3 inch, .50 caliber machine gun ammo, Mark 15 torpedoes for the surface ships,

Mark 10 and Mark 14 torpedoes for the submarines and depth charges), food, uniforms, spare parts, some machine tools for the shipyard workers, everything. This first shipment will keep our ships supplied and supported for several engagements.

There was also a report from CAPT Rooks about the destroyers HNLMS Van Nes and HNLMS Banckert. Both of the destroyers had received some light damage and would require three days of maintenance and repair to be fully combat capable. HNLMS Witte de With should arrive at Soerabaja sometime in the next 24 hours.

The British Liaison Officer requested to be heard at this point since we were talking about Java. They were sending out a sortie of five destroyers under the command of CDR Powers to make a run into Mersing to try to attack Japanese shipping there. The destroyers would make the run at 36 knots (these were their faster destroyers; lighter gun armament, but quite a few torpedoes).

CAPT Ringwood then moved the briefing to the West Coast. The battleship USS Colorado with escorting destroyers were well out to sea making 21 knots and performing drills on the way to Pearl Harbor. Reinforcements are always welcome. Word was also received that more shipping and ground unit formations would become available for use in the Pacific as they pass readiness tests.

Here locally, CAPT Ringwood announced that starting tomorrow there would be formal planning for Operation Spinning Whistle. Since this was a smaller operation, I was named as its lead. I then informed the floor that I had talked to COL Hobbs of the 251st Coastal Anti-Aircraft Regiment and his unit could pack up and deploy when ordered. They were fully equipped with .50 caliber machine guns, 37mm anti-aircraft guns and a dozen 3 inch, M3 anti-aircraft guns that had a ceiling of 29800 feet. These heavy guns would ensure that any Japanese aircraft that tried to attack Wake would come under fire at any altitude. I was going to find troops and equipment to form a scratch base force of engineers and aircraft maintenance personnel for transport to Wake as well. CAPT Ringwood then took back the floor and gave it to the British Liaison Officer.

The British Liaison Officer reported that five smaller freighters assigned to resupply Cooktown had returned to Townsville without incident. He also reported that ground crews were helping to get the P-39 fighters ready at Sydney and that trains had been dedicated to getting the personnel, spare parts and ammunition up to Cairns from Sydney. The same would happen when the next converted fast liners arrive with support troops and II Fighter Command.

There were no questions from the staff, so we were dismissed for breakfast and our work for the day. I had some juice, fruit and toast. I went to the canteen and grabbed a bottle of Coke for some caffeine to wake me up and then went to my desk.

SUBMARINE OPERATIONS

There was a lot going on in the world of submarines today and the majority of it was not good.

First bad news came from USS S-37 (CDR Easton). They had been slowly heading back to Soerabaja after having been severely damaged in an engagement on January 14th. Apparently, the damage was exceptionally severe as the submarine could only make 5 knots on the surface. The hull was severely damaged and out of the crew of 42, only 6 were uninjured. On the journey to Soerabaja, 5 of the crew had died, being buried at sea. When the submarine was around

60 nautical miles from Soerabaja, they issued an SOS. The pumps were failing and the submarine was taking on more water and slowly sinking by the stern. A couple of tugboats were immediately dispatched but took 4 hours to get to the submarine's location. The crew took to the lifeboats as the submarine sank. Six more men had died during the sinking and it was confirmed by the crew that CDR Easton was the last one off the submarine (he was also injured with a broken arm, broken ribs and some severe lacerations to his head and face). The survivors were picked up by the tugboats and were in Soerabaja by sunset. CAPT Rooks sent a message that he had sent some medical supplies to the shore hospital to help the survivors and that he would debrief CDR Easton personally. The logbook of the submarine was saved as well.

A report was received from USS Permit (LCDR Hurst) that they had been in a five hour running battle with a couple of enemy escorts that had spotted them while on patrol near Calayan. One of the ships was a destroyer and the other was a smaller escort. An attack was launched against the destroyer to no avail (a spread of four torpedoes fired, no hits). The submarine was depth charged but managed to evade the escorts and eventually resume their patrol.

USS Perch (LCDR Hurt) performed a successful attack against an unescorted Japanese freighter near Tawi Tawi. The report stated that the freighter was a code MFKMK for a Hoeisan Maru class freighter. USS Perch attacked on the surface and the freighter was torpedoed and then hit with the deck gun of the submarine to finish the job. The freighter sank in full view of the crew. This report was sent to the intelligence section.

Off the coast of Coal Harbor on the Canadian Pacific areas, the freighter SS Steel Navigator was torpedoed and sunk by a Japanese submarine. Float planes are heading to the area to try to find survivors.

Very bad news off the West Coast near San Clemente Island. A small convoy of four freighters on their way to Pearl Harbor with supplies and equipment were attacked by a Japanese submarine. The freighters SS Santa Teresa and SS Minnesotan were both torpedoed and sunk. The surviving crew was making for San Clemente Island in the lifeboats and patrol planes were monitoring their progress.

The bad news didn't stop there. HNLMS Witte de With was attacked by a Japanese submarine only 150 nautical miles from Soerabaja. The destroyer was sunk with heavy loss of life. CAPT Rooks was monitoring the situation.

When all these reports were reviewed by ADM Nimitz, he sank in his chair. More escort ships were needed to protect the West Coast convoys. This would limit offensive capability. He asked for a message to be sent to the Commander on the West Coast to rework the convoy system to utilize the limited number of escorts. A report was received that more destroyers would be sent to both the West Coast Command and to Pacific Command. They would be transiting the Panama Canal tomorrow.

HAWAII

There were no major reports near the headquarters today. All forces were proceeding as planned.

BROADER PACIFIC OCEAN

Wake Island was not attacked today; that is a rarity. All other areas were relatively quiet; no major reports.

PHILIPPINE ISLAND OPERATIONS

There was a major Japanese push in the areas around Clark Field today. Forward elements of a Japanese division managed to push back troops of the 21st Philippine Army Division in a planned elastic defense which allowed the 192nd and 194th Tank Battalions to counterattack the Japanese infantry in the open. This caused the Japanese to fall back in disarray causing many casualties. The front lines ended the day in more or less the same position they were in at the start of the day.

At Manila there were continued patrol actions and small artillery and mortar strikes in support of the patrols. There were a couple of air strikes against suspected friendly locations, but the commander had his troops move positions overnight. No changes to the front lines.

CHINESE THEATER

The Japanese must think that the areas around Pucheng are valuable because they kept up the pressure on Chinese units in that area with another attack. The Chinese were holding but casualties were beginning to mount and the problem, as always, was one of keeping the Chinese troops supplied.

There were also reports of combat at Kweiteh, Canton, Loyang, Hwainan, Kweisui and Lang Son.

BRITISH AND ALLIED OPERATIONS

The British Liaison Officer reported that the Japanese had attempted to do a quick attack to seize Singapore. The British, Australian, Indian and Burmese troops were waiting for them.

The attack was performed by an infantry regiment that was heavily supported by tanks.

The tanks attempted to move forward quickly in shallow fording areas and near bridges. They ran into a carefully prepared minefield that took out many of the tanks. When the infantry moved forward to support the tanks stuck in the minefield (possibly combat engineers), artillery and machineguns hit the infantry trying to move forward. The ending result was massive carnage. When the forward units were making their reports up the chain of command, it was confirmed that there were 57 burning and abandoned tanks near the front lines and there were "hundreds" of Japanese bodies. Artillery units were firing on likely Japanese assembly areas and the limited number of bombers available were hitting supply dumps in the rear areas. The Japanese did not attempt any daylight raids at Singapore but did manage to attack during the previous night; one of the bombers was confirmed shot down by anti-aircraft fire and there were a few aircraft lightly damaged on the ground.

It wasn't all good news on Borneo. Japanese troops had captured Kudat on the northern coast pushing further inland. At Tandjoengselor, Japanese troops were pursuing the remnants of the troops that survived the taking of Tarakan. There was continued combat at Samarinda with no major change to the front lines and there was little to be done with regards to relief or resupply.

And the most troubling report is that an amphibious force had appeared at Makassar on Celebes and was landing troops. When this report was received, CAPT Rooks added an addendum where he had requested permission to sortie to attack the amphibious force (now that he was being supplied). ADM Nimitz sent a reply back saying to coordinate with the

Dutch, but that he had permission to perform the mission if the Dutch allowed him to.

On Sumatra, Medan was again subjected to air strikes. They were small in comparison to earlier strikes, but still managed to cause casualties on the ground to the coastal gun battalion stationed there.

Figure 51 - USS Republic (AP-33)

AUSTRALIA AND NEW GUINEA

The Australian Cruiser Force successfully arrived at Townsville and was refueling. They would probably be sent on a sortie soon; the Solomon Islands became "target rich". The problem would be dealing with the air threat.

At Port Moresby, more bombers attacked the transports unloading supplies; the transport USS Republic was hit by a torpedo. This ship is a large transport and it was thought that the force would retire to Townsville without fully completing unloading of supplies. The air threat would cost too many ships until the fighters at Sydney began making their way to Port Moresby. We were expecting a late day report on the number of fighters ready from the 31st Pursuit Group.

INTELLIGENCE

The first item concerned the attacks on the West Coast by enemy submarines. The intelligence section had no information to suggest that there was another refueling spot in the North Pacific. While it was unlikely, it wasn't a complete impossibility. Sounded like a cop-out to me.

They did manage to confirm another kill. The Tatuno Maru was confirmed sunk on December 31st by radio decrypts and operational analysis. This kill is credited to the submarine USS Seal from their radio report. They were working on other data concerning the British attacks at Kota Bharu and Sambas on December 31st, as well but had no firm data to suggest any particular kills.

OPERATION SINGING PUMPKIN EXECUTION

RADM Francis Rockwell arrived at the headquarters for a conference with ADM Nimitz. It seems that RADM Rockwell is the commander of Task Force Loadstone. After a one hour meeting, he left to go to his flagship, USS Salt Lake City.

We were told that the remaining flag officers would be arriving tomorrow for final orders and briefings. The spring is being compressed; it will soon fire off at Canton Island.

THEORIES AND INTENTIONS

The Japanese managed major submarine attacks today on the West Coast. Three freighters sunk for no damage is unacceptable. Something has to be done to alleviate this. It is possible that there is another refueling area in the North Pacific; we might want to send recon elements out there, perhaps a single carrier to scout the area.

LATE DAY REPORTS

The 31st Pursuit Group reported that they now had 31 fighters ready, the 39th Squadron had 17, the 40th Squadron had 9 and the 41st Squadron had 5 ready. This is up from a total of 20 yesterday. Once the 39th Squadron is ready, they will ferry-flight up to Cairns. These fighters are badly needed.

A report arrived from CAPT Cummings that his force arrived safely at Sydney. As soon as they have replenished ammunition and fuel they will redeploy to Townsville for further operations.

Convoy Charlie 4-9 arrived safely at San Francisco. They are to wait for escorts before convoying up to bring more supplies to Pearl Harbor. We can't afford to lose more freighters; logistics will become more and more important as the war progresses.

A report was received from the Canadians that they are sending three more corvettes to perform offensive anti-submarine patrols off of Coal Harbor.

I left for the day at 1830 and got leftovers at the dining facility. Basically, they gave me a sandwich and some vegetables. The veggies actually weren't bad; peas and carrots. I then stopped by the Officer's Club for a beer and then went to sleep at 2200 after a quick shower. I was very tired. The breeze through the trees was very soothing.

JANUARY 23, 1942   DAY 48 OF THE WAR

<u>MORNING BRIEF</u>

Present at this morning's brief were RADM Withers, RADM Shafroth, LCDR Agnew and VADM William "Bull" Halsey. This was to introduce them as the force commanders for Task Force Recline, Task Force Decamp, Task Force Broom and Task Force Stampede, respectively. It was made plain to the staff that VADM Halsey would be the overall force commander with his flag on the carrier USS Enterprise. He would answer to ADM Nimitz and all other forces would fall under him for Operation Singing Pumpkin. The chain of command was firm and the entire staff nodded in acknowledgement.

CAPT Ringwood then began the briefing. Overnight, ADM Nimitz received word from CAPT Rooks that the Dutch were more than happy to allow our forces to attack Japanese shipping at Makassar and Watampone on Celebes Island. CAPT Rooks would lead the first force consisting of the heavy cruiser USS Houston, the light cruiser USS Marblehead and five attending destroyers (USS Barker, USS John D. Edwards, USS Paul Jones, USS Peary and USS Whipple). They would attack shipping at Makassar. CAPT Farrell with the light cruiser USS Boise and four destroyers (USS Alden, USS Bulmer, USS Parrott and USS Pillsbury) would attack Watampone.

The report also stated that the submarine USS S-40 (LCDR Lucker) would patrol the areas between the Java Sea and Banda Sea south of Makassar. Also performing a sortie would be the submarine USS S-41 (LCDR Holley) that would patrol further to the east in the Bandas Sea, east of Kendari.

The British Liaison Officer then reported that the five British destroyers that were going to attack shipping at Mersing had their objective changed to Kuantan when patrol aircraft discovered that the Japanese ships had withdrawn. The ships were in good material condition and proceeding at 20 knots; they would make their attack runs at a full speed of 36 knots.

He also reported that the light cruiser HMS Danae had reached Columbo safely. Initial reports indicated that the ship will be in drydock for at least two months to repair all the damage. HMS Prince of Wales is still taking up the drydock for at least another week and then HMS Danae and HMS Mauritius will then enter the drydock for repairs.

Troops at Singapore are in a strong position and are being resupplied by ships from Java. More supplies will be dispatched to Java from Cape Town.

He also reported that the transports bringing troops and supplies to Port Moresby were ordered to cease operations and immediately return to Townsville because of the threat of air attack.

CAPT Ringwood then continued the briefing with information coming from the West Coast. A force of one light cruiser and three destroyers were released to head to Pearl Harbor from the Panama Canal; the light cruiser is USS Trenton and the destroyers are USS Sims, USS Hughes and USS Anderson. A further six destroyers are released and are heading up to San Francisco. They are USS Hammann, USS Mustin, USS Russell, USS O'Brien, USS Walke and USS Morris. They will form the nucleus of convoy operations until more suitable escorts are found.

Two more submarines have completed transit of the Panama Canal and are heading to Pearl Harbor: USS Gato and USS Grampus. They are now in transit and are making 15 knots.

SUBMARINE OPERATIONS

USS Seawolf (LCDR Warder) reported that they had found a Japanese convoy near Batan Island and were maneuvering on the surface to a more advantageous position when they were spotted by one of the escorts and were forced to dive. The escorts did not make firm contact with the submarine and they were able to sneak away and surface. When they did, the convoy was gone and the submarine resumed the patrol.

The Dutch reported that the submarine HNLMS O19 found a large enemy convoy and attacked. They managed to put a torpedo into a freighter and then were pounced on by a couple of destroyers. The submarine managed to break contact after several hours and resume their patrol. It is unknown if the freighter sank. This report was sent to the intelligence section.

Another friendly freighter was attacked today near Alliford Bay. The small freighter SS Nebraskan was torpedoed and sunk. They radioed an SOS and then went off the air. ADM Nimitz looked very upset at this report.

HAWAII

Aside from marshalling of forces for Operation Singing Pumpkin, there was nothing to report at Hawaii.

BROADER PACIFIC OCEAN

There was a large air raid against Wake Island. One Wildcat fighter managed to get into the air and attacked the bombers (Betty types). The pilot managed to damage one of the bombers before being forced away by defensive fire from the bombers. The runway was hit pretty hard and the maintenance sheds were busted open again by direct hits. They desperately need more support at Wake.

PHILIPPINE ISLAND OPERATIONS

Combat on Luzon at Manila and Clark Field were restricted to patrol actions. There was not a major push at either location. The biggest problem is that supplies of all kinds were running out; food, medical supplies, ammunition. Unless we can figure out a way to get major supplies there, friendly troops will eventually be defeated.

On Mindanao, scratch Philippine Army troops were engaged by Japanese troops that came into the western areas of Butuan. The Japanese did not yet get into the vital areas around Butuan, but the troops will not be able to do much to stop them before they do get there.

CHINESE THEATER

High intensity combat had apparently wound down at Pucheng. The reports from our Liaison indicated that combat in that area had been one of patrol actions today. The same could not be said for Canton; the Chinese troops there had held on after a determined assault by Japanese infantry. Casualties were not known.

There was also combat at Kweiteh, Loyang, Kweisui, Lang Son and Hwainan.

BRITISH AND ALLIED OPERATIONS

Figure 52 - USS Boise (CL-47)

CAPT Rooks' force could not penetrate the exceptionally thick fog with any certainty of finding enemy ships prudent with navigational safety. Therefore, he ordered a withdrawal and will try again tomorrow.

CAPT Farrell did not have the same problem near Watampone and found a small Japanese force at sunrise. They found a freighter identified as code MKFKM for a Tamon Maru class freighter, a small escort and a destroyer of the Nokaze class. CAPT Farrell ordered his ships to open fire at 16,000 yards. Over the next two hours, the enemy destroyer was hit several times, but managed to cause some damage to friendly forces.

USS Bulmer took a hit from the 120mm guns of the enemy destroyer that plunged down two decks and exploded. Four sailors were killed and nine wounded while a fire started from the hit. Damage control parties immediately went to work as USS Bulmer continued to fight. USS Pillsbury took a hit that exploded on one of the forward main gun turrets that put the turret out of action. The remaining turrets were still in the fight. USS Alden took a hit to the superstructure from the freighter that caused some superficial damage and wounded five sailors. USS Boise was hit by a main gun round from the enemy destroyer but the armor of the light cruiser was too tough for the enemy round to cause damage.

The enemy destroyer drew the majority of the fire during the battle and was hit multiple times by 4" fire from US destroyers and a few 3" rounds. The destroyer was burning and slowing down when it was hit by several 6" rounds from USS Boise. At that point, the guns from the enemy destroyer stopped firing and the rest of the US force swarmed in with main guns and secondary guns on the destroyers while USS Boise engaged the other escort.

The other escort, which was some kind of converted patrol boat was hit repeatedly by 6" gunfire from USS Boise which eventually sank it. There wasn't a lot of information to identify the type of hull the enemy ship was converted from, but it was confirmed as sunk.

When the enemy destroyer and patrol boat were sunk, the large freighter was hit repeatedly by main guns from all the ships. The coup de grace was delivered by a torpedo from USS Pillsbury which hit the cargo space that had something volatile; the ship then blew up.

Because of the damage to the destroyers in his force, CAPT Farrell ordered a retirement back to Soerabaja. There were no other reports from his force for the rest of the day.

Makassar saw some low level combat from the troops that had landed and it appeared, at least for now that they can hold. When the fog lifts, CAPT Rooks' force will attack the transports. There were also reports that the troops that had fallen back from Manado to Sidate were under attack by advance elements of Japanese infantry.

On Borneo, there was continued combat at Samarinda and Tandjoengselor. There was scant information and there was no way to know for sure what was happening.

On Sumatra, the Japanese continued their air bombardment of facilities and troops at Medan. Reports from the Dutch indicated that there were almost 100 wounded troops from the attacks. However, heavy equipment and major artillery were untouched.

Singapore was again subjected to a major Japanese assault. Reports indicated that just under 30000 enemy troops were attacking. The troops tried to push into Singapore from all areas that had a modest connection to the rest of the peninsula. Infantry moved forward with artillery support and in some places, tanks. The great majority of the advances were stopped by Allied infantry and machineguns, but there was a small foothold on the northeast side of Singapore. It was planned that the 27th Australian Brigade would counter-attack that area tomorrow. The Japanese were suffering horrendous losses, because the attack was actually halted. The intelligence section was notified to see if they could find information from radio decrypts. This is very different from my timeline where GEN Percival had surrendered before even trying to defend against an invasion. I can say with certainty that the timeline is completely shot now; it is unknown what the history will now read.

AUSTRALIA AND NEW GUINEA

Port Moresby was attacked overnight by some bombers that did no damage to facilities or troops. The same could not be said for the ships trying to get back to Townsville. The ships in the force were attacked continuously by Betty bombers on torpedo runs for almost a full hour. The transport SS Idomeneus took four torpedo hits in quick succession and sank in less than 5 minutes. There were few survivors.

The escorts were not faring any better. The sloop HMAS Swan was hit by two torpedoes and sank along with the sloop HMAS Moresby. The transport SS Lycaon was torpedoed and set on fire. It is unknown if the ship will make it back to Townsville. The Japanese suffered damage to three of their bombers; they were seen leaving the area trailing smoke. The day was a disaster for the force.

INTELLIGENCE

Oddly, there wasn't much from the intelligence section today. Their biggest concern (that echoed ours) is that there is no information on battleships or carriers from the Japanese fleet. Where are they?

OPERATION SINGING PUMPKIN EXECUTION

All combat troops and support troops were loaded upon their respective ships. The fleet cargo ships were combat loaded with equipment and supplies and ready to execute the plan. VADM Halsey reported that the forces would proceed according to plan. He looked like he was looking for blood; his look actually made me shudder.

OPERATION SPINNING WHISTLE PLANNING

I had requested information on the material condition of the ships left after all forces for Singing Pumpkin are taken into account. All that was left was one carrier (USS Saratoga), one heavy cruiser, three light cruisers, four destroyers, three troop transports, three fleet cargo ships and two aircraft cargo ships (these ships carry aircraft fully assembled). In my estimation, it was not enough. I wrote up the report and sent it up the chain via CAPT Ringwood to ADM Nimitz. I expected an interesting conversation tomorrow.

THEORIES AND INTENTIONS

We simply don't have enough combat power to push through to Wake Island without some serious losses. The problem is one of air cover. Carriers would have to provide fighter cover while the runway is repaired and fighters can get off the ground. Anti-aircraft guns would help but would not completely fix the problem. It might be possible to do a quick invasion using the light cruisers and destroyers to screen the transports but it will be risky. If the bombers keep attacking the atoll while the troops land it might work, but even with the light cruisers and destroyers running interference, there would be losses.

LATE DAY REPORTS

The transports that had delivered the 31st Pursuit Group have offloaded all of their aircraft, parts, supplies and sundries. They put to sea late today to head back to San Francisco.

COL Wirth sent a report (he is the commander of the 31st Pursuit Group) that the 39th Squadron (LTC Iverson) had 18 aircraft ready and needed two days to complete the rest of the aircraft. The 40th Squadron (COL Ward) had 16 aircraft ready and needed five days to complete the rest of the aircraft (two aircraft suffered damage during unloading). The 41st Squadron (LTC Wilder) had 8 aircraft ready and needed three days to complete the rest of the aircraft. The Headquarters Squadron still had no aircraft ready and needed four days to get their aircraft ready. It was determined that they would only move in full squadron strength.

The transports carrying II Fighter Command and support troops should reach Sydney by tomorrow.

At Java, CAPT DeBoer's ships arrived safely and were performing maintenance and repairs. They would need a few days to be fully combat capable but were able to complete missions if absolutely necessary.

On the other side of Java, the converted liner Empress Australia arrived at Tjilatjap and was unloading pilots and aircraft of No. 232 Squadron equipped with Hurricane fighters. After the aircraft are put together they would probably go to Soerabaja to provide top cover.

Some Dutch ships had escaped Tarakan and were making their way to Soerabaja. It would be a few more days before they got there and they were keeping radio silence to not attract attention from the Japanese.

I was very tired. I grabbed a quick sandwich and went to my bungalow. I listened to some soothing classical music as I rubbed my temples. How can I help the troops at Wake without putting too many ships in danger… how can I… how can I…

MORNING BRIEF

I was told that I would have a meeting with ADM Nimitz, VADM Pye and CAPT Ringwood at 1100 today to discuss my report concerning Operation Spinning Whistle. In the meantime I was to keep working on the planning and to support the rest of the Operations Section as usual.

The briefing began with the British Liaison Officer. He reported that three more freighters were loading up at Cape Town with a mixed bag of US and Allied supplies and munitions to be delivered to Tjilatjap. The freighters were putting to sea either late today or early tomorrow.

Next on his agenda was about the Australian 6th Division. The troops and equipment were loaded up on two separate convoys and were going to Batavia. This arrangement was to minimize risk; the larger convoy would stop off at Columbo to refuel (mostly for the destroyers). The smaller convoy would not need to stop. The first convoy is a 15 knot convoy, the second is a 13 knot convoy. It is imperative to get the entire division safely to Java (the savagery of the fighting at Singapore must have sobered up the British Command a bit).

He then discussed the force of five destroyers that were going to Kuantan; if the weather is good, they should make their objective in the next 24 hours, otherwise it will take two days. Recon planes indicated that there are a lot of freighters there, probably offloading equipment and supplies.

Last on his agenda concerned the ships at Columbo. The battleship HMS Prince of Wales would be able to finish fitting out pierside; this will get the ship out of the drydock and allow the light cruisers in to start repairs. The Harbor Master there thinks this could be done in 24 hours.

The only new information on our side is that the submarine USS S-36 (CDR Allison) would be performing a combat patrol in the areas between Celebes Island and Taliaboe Island. This should allow them to hit ships going to Kendari from the north.

Operation Singing Pumpkin would commence in 24 hours. All troops were loaded, all equipment and supplies loaded, ship captains briefed and on lock down.

There were no questions so we went to our desks for the day's work.

Submarine Operations

Of interesting note, the logs from USS S-37 under the command of CDR Easton were reviewed and it was the opinion of the other officers doing the review that while the submarine was lost, there appeared to be no overt acts by CDR Easton in the performance of his duties. He will not appear before a review board and his service was considered above that required by a submarine captain. The wounded were being cared for and the dead were treated with the respect demanded of the Naval Service. The families would be notified.

USS Swordfish (LCDR Smith) found a large, heavily escorted convoy passing the straights near Donggala. Apparently hoping to narrow the odds a bit, they fired two torpedoes at a destroyer. Both missed and the submarine had to dive deep, but was bracketed by depth charges that exploded close but did not cause damage. It took the submarine almost 3 ½ hours to sneak away. When the submarine surfaced, the convoy was long gone so they resumed their patrol.

Hawaii

Aside from waiting to launch Operation Singing Pumpkin, the submarine USS Silversides arrived safely from transit across the Pacific. The submarine is replenishing and standing by for further orders.

Broader Pacific Ocean

There were no major reports on our outposts. Even Wake Island did not see enemy aircraft today.

Philippine Island Operations

There were multiple air strikes against facilities in and around Subic Bay and Clark Field. One of the raids seemed to be concentrated on the 21st Philippine Army Division's front area. There were a few casualties on the ground and no major attack materialized. Patrol actions and artillery strikes were the order of the day. While there weren't any air strikes against the troops at Manila there was what could be termed a "recon in force" by Japanese troops that was successfully defended in the southern regions of the city. Supplies are running low.

On Mindanao, the areas west of Butuan were under attack again. This time, the troops managed to hold quite well when reinforcing cavalry troops arrived to cut off a company of Japanese infantry that was then assaulted. Many of the enemy troops were killed and wounded but they managed to break out of the tactical encirclement to rejoin their lines. This action stalled the Japanese assault.

CHINESE THEATER

There were reports of combat at Hwainan, Kweisui, Loyang, Canton, Kweiteh and Pucheng. It is thought that the Japanese will attempt another major attack near Pucheng in the next day or two.

There were also reports of a major Japanese push in the areas around Lang Son. The Japanese were held for now, but the problem for the Chinese troops is one of supply.

BRITISH AND ALLIED OPERATIONS

Again there was heavy fog at Makassar and CAPT Rooks had to turn the force around. The radio report received stated that he was going to try to get in one more time before fully retiring to Soerabaja. Meanwhile, CAPT Farrell's force returned to Soerabaja. A full report on the material condition of his ships should be available by the end of the day. Ground forces at Makassar were engaged with Japanese troops but there was no hard data to determine the severity of the situation.

There were reports of a night strike at Batavia. There was a single small bomb hit on the runway and one of the bombers was seen to be on fire as the planes left the area. They might have come from Pontianak.

On Borneo, the areas around Sandakan saw Japanese troops landing. Some radio operators reported seeing Japanese troops and then the radios went off the air. There were also reports of patrol level combat at Samarinda with no major changes to the front lines there.

At Singapore, more enemy troops were moving into the immediate area. It was estimated that 37000 Japanese troops were in position to attack the city. Patrol actions and a small counter-attack by Australian troops restored the original lines but the situation is getting dire and major assault by the Japanese will result in large casualties to both sides.

Some friendly bombers made attacks against supply dumps at Johore Bharu and attacked a troop concentration just across the water on the Peninsula. The raids were reported as "successful", but we're not quite sure what that means.

Friendly artillery is firing on suspected and confirmed Japanese positions around the city. More supplies and ammunition will be sent to Singapore from Java. GEN Percival reported that he has just under 31000 troops available. The day's patrol actions and minor counter attack resulted in 13 dead and 78 wounded. Enemy casualties are unknown at this time.

On Sumatra, there were several air raids against Medan that caused significant casualties on the ground (reports indicated that over 200 troops were injured in some way). There was also an attack against the facilities at Langsa; no reports of casualties or damage.

Further to the north, there was a night air raid against Rangoon; a couple of fighters were damaged on the ground but there is no other significant damage. One of the enemy bombers was hit by ground fire and could be seen with an engine on fire as it left the area.

AUSTRALIA AND NEW GUINEA

There was bad news from Luganville on Espiritu Santo Island as some Japanese troops had landed and were taking over the area. There were no friendly troops and this area is too close to New Caledonia and the Fiji Islands. ADM Nimitz seemed a bit unhinged by this report. I suspect something may have to be done here. If I remembered correctly, in my timeline, this became a major base for Allied forces and the Japanese had never landed there. The timeline I've created has taken another strange turn.

There were reports of an attack on facilities at Wau near Lae, but other than that, there really were no other strikes. The retreating ships from Port Moresby were making their way to Townsville and all other forces were proceeding as planned. The fighters landed at Sydney were still shaking out and our surface force under CAPT Cummings is still proceeding to Townsville. I would expect that the Australians will try another hit and run with their cruiser force; we'll see tomorrow, I guess.

INTELLIGENCE

The intelligence section was pre-occupied with the capture of Luganville and with Operation Singing Pumpkin. They had no new information on kills and were still extremely nervous.

OPERATION SINGING PUMPKIN EXECUTION

We were just waiting for the execution signal to begin. We were expecting the signal to be sent by ADM Nimitz at 1700 tomorrow.

OPERATION SPINNING WHISTLE PLANNING

I went to our meeting at 1100 as ordered. ADM Nimitz asked me if I thought that this operation was too aggressive. I stood quietly for a moment before saying yes. He asked why. I stated that I could not determine if there was acceptable risk or excessive risk. A single carrier would not be able to provide enough fighter coverage and it would put the carrier at risk. The light cruisers and destroyers would provide some protection but it would not be enough, unless the Japanese bombers turned their complete attention to the atoll instead of the ships.

ADM Nimitz then sat silent. After a few moments he told me to continue planning and that it might have to happen anyway. I came to attention, saluted and stated I'd figure something out that would minimize risk.

As I later worked on the plan it came to me that the operation *could* happen. If the ships picked were fast, the troops and equipment were unloaded in record time and the anti-aircraft guns emplaced, it could work. I went back to the overall plan and chewed on it in the back of my head as I worked on other projects.

Theories and Intentions

My mind was almost too preoccupied with Spinning Whistle to give serious consideration to the capture of Luganville. If the Japanese have the ability to significantly build up that area then they'd be able to just about cut off Australia from the West Coast of the United States and Hawaii. This would make resupply difficult at best.

Late Day Reports

A late day report was received from CAPT Farrell concerning the ships in his force. USS Bulmar was pretty heavily damaged and would require four days in the drydock. As it turned out, when the shell exploded inside the destroyer the hull was damaged in several places and would need to be repaired. The damage to USS Alden would take three days to repair pierside; some of the main support structures in the superstructure were damaged by the enemy hit and would need to be re-welded. Lastly, USS Pillsbury would need just one day to repair some damage to the forward 4 inch gun turret. USS Boise was in good material condition.

There were no other major reports so I left at 1800 to get some dinner. I sat idly chewing my food staring off in the distance thinking about how I could get the 251st Coastal Anti-Aircraft Regiment to Wake with supporting troops without getting ships sunk or people killed. What constitutes acceptable risk? How many men could be lost to consider the operation a "success"?

After dinner I went for a walk and continued to think. By the time I got near my bungalow it was almost midnight. I took a quick shower and laid down. Sleep came quickly considering my thoughts...

MORNING BRIEF

The air was warm and it was sunny. I felt revived like somehow I had figured something out. I felt like I needed to doodle or to get near a chalkboard – whiteboards haven't been invented yet.

ADM Nimitz looked concerned as we started the briefing. He began the briefing today. He stood in front of all of us and told us that the first major offensive operation of our war was about to begin. At 1600, unless some major information changed things, he would send VADM Halsey code word "trumpeter". This would indicate the start of Operation Singing Pumpkin. We were to discuss it with nobody outside the room. We all nodded in affirmation of the order. He then turned over the floor to CAPT Ringwood.

CAPT Ringwood started the briefing by reading an early morning report from CAPT Rooks. He was bringing his force to try to hit Makassar yet again and was hoping for better weather. There were still reports of over a dozen transports and freighters assisting with the invasion and CAPT Rooks desperately wanted to smash the force.

The next item concerned the West Coast. A couple more Yard Patrol Craft (YP in Navy parlance) were being sent to Los Angeles to form another coastal anti-submarine squadron to work around San Clemente Island. They were leaving San Diego this morning and should be at Los Angeles by late afternoon.

He then turned the floor over to the British Liaison Officer.

The British destroyers will hit Kuantan today as their last report indicated that they were only 60 nautical miles from their objective. They were waiting for night to attack.

HMS Mauritius and HMS Danae did in fact get into the drydock late yesterday and the battleship HMS Prince of Wales was finishing repairs pierside. The battleship should be ready in a couple of weeks, but HMS Danae will be in drydock for at least two months.

A report from the Australians indicated that they were sending their cruiser force on a sortie to attack Japanese shipping at Shortlands again. They would come in from the southeast to minimize detection chances by Japanese patrol aircraft. US surface forces should arrive at Townsville sometime today.

The freighters that were carrying US supplies to Batavia have completely offloaded their cargo and were returning to Cape Town for another load. Word was also received that the shipyard workers were unloading their equipment at Soerabaja.

He had nothing further to report.

CAPT Ringwood then dismissed us to the day's work. Before I left the room for breakfast he ordered me to a conference at 1100 about Spinning Whistle. I acknowledged the order.

I ate a bacon sandwich for breakfast with some fresh orange juice – at least it tasted fresh.

SUBMARINE OPERATIONS

USS S-40 (LCDR Lucker) sent a report that they had found an escorted freighter near Salajar. The ship was identified as code MFM for a Biyo Maru class freighter. They fired two torpedoes at the freighter for no hits. Neither the escort nor the freighter realized they were under attack and the submarine was not in a position to re-attack. They broke contact on a reciprocal heading, surfaced and resumed their patrol.

USS Salmon (LCDR McKinney) reported that they had found a small convoy and attacked north of Borneo. They fired four torpedoes at a large ship identified as code MKFKM for an Aikoku Maru class troop transport. They hit with one of the torpedoes and had to break from the area due to the escorts. The escorts were not able to make contact with the submarine and after a couple of hours the submarine surfaced and resumed their patrol.

USS Pike (LCDR New) found and attacked an escorted freighter near Brunei. Four torpedoes were fired at the freighter identified as code MFMK for a Bengal Maru class freighter. One of the torpedoes hit the freighter on the port beam. The escort (more than likely a submarine chaser) tried to make contact with the submarine to perform a depth charge attack. The escort was unable to do so and the submarine broke contact a little over an hour later. After the submarine surfaced and recharged their batteries, they resumed their patrol. It is unknown at this time if the freighter sank and the convoy was no longer in the area.

HAWAII

Aside from the start of Operation Singing Pumpkin, there were no major events at Hawaii today.

BROADER PACIFIC OCEAN

Talk about bad timing. A report was received at around 1500 that said that Wake Island was under an amphibious assault. Several troop transports were seen on the horizon. The 5 inch gun batteries began firing on the approaching ships and then began firing on the landing boats that were approaching the shore. MAJ Deveraux had his reaction force of infantry meet the attack at the point of entry while trying to hold them. His report stated that this would allow him to counter-attack when appropriate. As the infantry and machinegun teams met the attack, the few mortars that he had were firing on the Japanese troops landing at the water's edge. He had ordered that at 1700, all 5 inch guns would train on the Japanese landing site and fire a barrage; this to coincide with a counter-attack supported by mortar fire. The artillery was too much for the Japanese; some of the troops began boarding boats to head back to the landing ships, others tried to valiantly attack the Marines. Those that attacked the Marines were cut down by machinegun fire; those that headed back were under 5 inch gunfire. By nightfall, the situation appeared to be well in hand. The problem is nobody knew if more troops would try to land.

Radio operators on the Island of Funafuti reported that Japanese troops were landing. Funafuti is the southernmost island in the Ellice Islands chain. This report was immediately brought to the attention of ADM Nimitz.

PHILIPPINE ISLAND OPERATIONS

Much like yesterday, the air strikes were directed mostly at the sector where the 21st Philippine Army Division is defending. There were some other strikes against Subic Bay and a small one at Clark Field, but the majority of the firepower was directed against the forward positions of the Division. At around noon, a concentrated assault against this sector took place. It was reported that the Japanese took severe losses but it was also admitted that the forward positions were taken by the Japanese. This is causing a small bulge in the line and could be used tactically by the Japanese. There was also a problem that it was getting more difficult to find fuel for the tanks of the 192nd and 194th Battalions. This will make it more difficult for the troops to continue to defend the area. Without more supplies, the defenses will eventually crumble and there is nothing we can do to get them more except by submarine.

Combat at Manila was at the platoon level and mostly directed at patrol actions and probing actions. An acute shortage of supplies was also beginning to be felt here as well.

The western areas of Butuan came under determined assault yet again today. Philippine troops were pushed back around four miles closer to Butuan. The Japanese were bringing up tanks and there were not many anti-tank guns with the defending troops.

Basilan Island also fell to an amphibious assault today. There were no friendly troops on that island so it was not that difficult for the Japanese to take it.

CHINESE THEATER

There were reports of combat at Kweiteh, Canton, Loyang, Kweisui, Lang Son and Hwainan. There were no reports about casualties to either side, as usual.

BRITISH AND ALLIED OPERATIONS

CAPT Rooks' force had paused roughly 55 nautical miles west of Makassar waiting for the next bout of darkness before heading into try to shoot up the Japanese ships. The force was guessing that it was not the right conditions for fog; if it is, the ships will turn back to Soerabaja. Meanwhile, more Japanese troops were landed at Makassar and the Dutch troops were engaging them. The problem is that they were outnumbered and a little after noon, it was reported that the Dutch positions had been overrun. Casualties were unknown and there were no other messages received from Makassar. Once Makassar fell silent, CAPT Rooks made the decision to head back to Soerabaja at full speed.

In the areas around Singapore it was very busy, deadly and crazy. The British destroyer force did indeed find Japanese shipping at Kuantan; they found literally dozens of freighters with light escort. From midnight until first light, a total of 36 larger freighters, 8 small freighters and 3 escort ships were found. CDR Powers ordered the ships to concentrate initial gunfire on the escorts, holding fire until the range had closed. The escorts were identified as a larger escort, possibly a small destroyer, a patrol boat and a submarine chaser. Gunfire was to be used on the escorts while torpedoes could be fired at the freighters.

HMS Thanet fired torpedoes at a freighter from 8000 yards on a broad set of bearings; there were so many ships that the torpedoes were bound to hit something. One of the freighters was hit in quick succession by three torpedoes around the time it was expected that the torpedoes would hit. The freighter blew up and sank almost immediately. Torpedoes from the other destroyers (HMS Scout, HMS Stronghold, HMS Tenedos and HMS Thracian) hit three other freighters that were burning brightly.

At this point, the smaller escort estimated to be a submarine chaser was taking a large number of hits from the main guns of the destroyers. The ship was slowly sinking and on fire; none of the guns from the enemy ship were firing. At that point, the larger escort came from behind one of the freighters and opened fire on the destroyers. This action immediately drew the ire of HMS Thracian and HMS Thanet. The escort ship was hit repeatedly by main guns and even anti-aircraft guns from the destroyers (they were separated by only 2000 yards).

As the large escort was being shot up, the patrol boat came down from the north from behind another freighter and got into a gunnery duel with HMS Stronghold. The patrol boat was hit by several shells from the forward main guns from HMS Stronghold and that made it difficult to return fire. The patrol boat was burning brightly and not firing so HMS Stronghold then began firing on the freighters. All of the destroyers began firing on the freighters; CDR Powers issued a fire at will command. The destroyers kept firing until they were at 30% ammunition at which point CDR Powers ordered a general withdrawal to head back to Soerabaja. The destroyers were pouring fire into the freighters for over four hours at this point and it was beginning to get light.

This is where the fight turned even more savage. As the destroyers were making their withdrawal they were attacked by aircraft. The Japanese must have been pissed off something awful because seven separate air raids occurred during the daylight hours. Luckily for the destroyers, they were close enough that they could call for support from the fighters of the Royal Air Force at Singapore.

The fighters (Buffalo types) of No. 21, 243, 453 and 488 Squadrons scrambled to protect the destroyers. They were itching for a fight anyway. During the course of the day, a total of 55 bombers of different types (Betty, Sally and even a few Kates) attacked the destroyers escorted by a total of 34 fighters (Zero and Oscar types) mixed it up with 27 fighters from Singapore.

By sunset, 4 of the Buffalo fighters were shot down. The Japanese suffered losses of two Betty bombers shot down by the fighters, a further one shot down by anti-aircraft fire from HMS Scout, two Kate bombers shot down, one Zero fighter shot down, one Oscar fighter shot down and three Sally bombers damaged. No damage was scored against the destroyers by enemy air action – a feat in itself. The destroyers are working up more speed to head back to Singapore.

While all of this crazy action was going on, the Japanese were attacking the areas around Singapore with tanks and infantry. Allied troops were using artillery to separate the infantry from the tanks and then ambush the tanks. The tanks were hit by larger anti-aircraft guns that were not being used for air defense. Dozens of Japanese tanks were burning by the end of the day and the combat engineers that were coming up to support them were being cut down by machinegun and artillery fire. GEN Percival reported that he had 25 dead and 115 wounded in the day's fighting; he did admit that it is easier to defend which is why they had worked so hard making reinforced firepoints. These firepoints were needed because GEN Percival estimated the enemy force at being a reinforced infantry corps.

There were also counterattacks made by air units, but these didn't work out so well. The port facilities at Mersing were attacked by some Hudson medium bombers escorted by Buffalo fighters at first light. This raid went well enough and the bombers reported seeing at least a couple of bombs hit vital areas of the port. Only a single Claude type fighter rose to meet the attackers and the Buffalo fighters were effective in protecting the bombers from a single fighter.

An hour later, nine Vildebeest torpedo bombers went looking for enemy ships near Mersing. They were escorted by 15 Buffalo fighters. No enemy fighters came to meet the Royal Air Force and the torpedo bombers (armed with a pair of 500 lb. bombs because of a torpedo shortage) did not cause any damage to the ships located there.

At around noon, disaster struck. Another flight of nine Vildebeest torpedo bombers revisited the area looking to attack the ships there. They were escorted by 13 Buffalo fighters. The problem is that they were bounced by 21 Oscar fighters. During the ensuing fight, 4 of the Buffalo fighters and 5 of the Vildebeest bombers were shot down for no loss to the Japanese. Not good at all. That was the last offensive mission for the Royal Air Force today. Both sides ended the day licking their wounds.

Needless to say, we sent all of this information to the intelligence section to see if they could decrypt messages to help out with the overall situation.

As the vicious combat was occurring in the areas around Singapore, an air strike was occurring at Batavia. Nine Betty bombers were attacking the freighters that had just completed their mission of resupplying Singapore. Half a dozen B-339 fighters met the attackers from the Dutch Air Force. Three Betty bombers were shot down, and a fourth damaged but they still managed to attack the freighters putting a torpedo into the SS Langkoeas. The freighter later sank but most of the crew was rescued.

On Borneo, combat continued at Samarinda with the Japanese making a determined assault that gained some ground but eventually petered out before pushing the Dutch troops completely out of their defense area. Around Sidate, combat was confined to patrol and squad level action. No major changes to the front line.

AUSTRALIA AND NEW GUINEA

There was bad weather over most of New Guinea today and there were no strikes performed by the Japanese. The

Australian Cruiser Force was proceeding according to plan and should be able to attack Japanese shipping at Shortlands in a few days. The remaining transports from resupplying Port Moresby were still making their way towards Townsville.

INTELLIGENCE

The intelligence section had notified us that they knew something major was happening around Kuantan because of the level of radio traffic coming from that area. They were working on those messages as well as the backlog of messages from the previous weeks. They had no new data for us today and were very concerned that nothing has been seen or heard about the Japanese carriers for some time.

They shared ADM Nimitz' concern that the taking of Espiritu Santo Island could have far reaching effects on our ability to continue to support Australia.

With regards to Operation Singing Pumpkin, they had not changed their estimate of enemy troops at Canton Island; it is still at 2500.

OPERATION SINGING PUMPKIN EXECUTION

At 1550 local time just an hour after it was learned that Wake Island was under amphibious assault, ADM Nimitz ordered "trumpeter" be sent to VADM Halsey on the carrier USS Enterprise. The order would then be sent to RADM Rockwell on the heavy cruiser USS Salt Lake City. The 8th Marine Regiment was just ordered to be the pointy end of the spear. The operation is a go.

OPERATION SPINNING WHISTLE PLANNING

When summoned at 1100 by CAPT Ringwood, I was asked to sit at a large table with himself and ADM Nimitz. They asked what I had considered about the operation. I explained that I thought I had found a solution.

When the destroyers arrive from escorting the freighter Laida that was sunk by Japanese attack at Wake, I could use those ships to bolster the overall air defense of the force. I could use two of the light cruisers (USS Honolulu and USS Helena) and eight destroyers to escort three troop transports, two fleet cargo ships and an aircraft cargo ship carrying additional fighters. My plan called for the ships to come down from the northeast; this would make it difficult for the Japanese to spot the force and to have a quick offload of the forces, like an amphibious assault. This would negate the need for using conventional offload which takes forever due to the lack of facilities at Wake.

The risks were:

1. Possibility of Japanese air attack.
2. Possibility of losing some of the heavy equipment when trying to move it like an amphibious assault (i.e. the heavy anti-aircraft guns).
3. Possibility of elements of the Japanese fleet arriving that would overwhelm the cruisers and destroyers.

I then went over the information gained from the 251st Coastal Artillery Regiment and my conversation with LTC Rutins about putting together a base force (the Army command would label it the 119th Base Force). In all, I felt confident that the troops and equipment could be offloaded in 48 to 72 hours and the force would keep the destroyers and light cruisers mobile as a perimeter around the fleet cargo ships and troop transports to maximize the anti-aircraft coverage.

ADM Nimitz asked how quickly it could be pulled off – I replied that it would take a minimum of 5 days to marshal the forces and get them loaded up with enough supplies. This also took into consideration that four of the destroyers were returning from Wake and would give them two days to do repairs and replenishment before leaving again.

CAPT Ringwood congratulated me on a job well done and ADM Nimitz told us both that he would consider it and have an answer for me tomorrow. In light of the new invasion of Wake Island, I'm not too sure if this operation will be attempted.

THEORIES AND INTENTIONS

The Japanese are doing things that never happened in my timeline and this timeline is quickly spiraling out of control. Other than understanding the Japanese ships and tactics, I feel that I am becoming a liability. However, I have no choice but to continue to support the Pacific Fleet staff.

LATE DAY REPORTS

CAPT Cummings' force arrived at Townsville late today. They were to stand by for further orders and would probably sortie if the Japanese tried a landing at Buna or if they came around and tried to openly assault Port Moresby.

A report was received that II Fighter Command had arrived at Sydney with other support troops. They were unloading and getting ready to board trains to get to Townsville. From there they will either go to Cairns or to Port Moresby.

A couple of straggler ships that had escaped from Tarakan had made it to Soerabaja. A small British tanker and a small Dutch oiler had arrived and were reporting to their respective Naval Representatives. Other ships were expected to follow.

At this point, I left for the day. It was almost 1730 and I could see some of the ships from Task Force Loadstone beginning to leave port. I went down to the waterfront to watch them leave. The destroyers left first, followed by the cruisers and then finally the troop transports.

As I watched them leave I thought about their transit and the combat that awaits them. I thought about the new invasion of Wake Island. I thought about how I had completely changed the timeline. I thought about how World War II will be different in my timeline.

My choices have had a bigger impact than I ever thought possible.

Is it possible that I killed more people by saving some on December 7th?

Tomorrow may hold the answer. In the meantime, I need dinner.

PICTURES, MAPS AND FIGURES

PHOTO ATTRIBUTIONS

Figure 1: "USS Maryland (BB-46) underway in 1935" by U.S. Navy (photo 80-G-463249) - This media is available in the holdings of the National Archives and Records Administration, cataloged under the ARC Identifier (National Archives Identifier) 520812. Licensed under Public domain via Wikimedia Commons - http://commons.wikimedia.org/wiki/File:USS_Maryland_(BB-46)_underway_in_1935.jpg#mediaviewer/File:USS_Maryland_(BB-46)_underway_in_1935.jpg.

Figure 2: Map hand drawn by the Author.

Figure 3: Map of Java (1920) from http://home.ia.nl, Public Domain

Figure 4: "HMS Repulse leaving Singapore" by Adams W L G (Captain), Commanding Officer, HMS CORINTHIANPost-Work: User:W.wolny - This is photograph A 29069 from the collections of the Imperial War Museums (collection no. 4700-01). Licensed under Public domain via Wikimedia Commons - http://commons.wikimedia.org/wiki/File:HMS_Repulse_leaving_Singapore.jpg#mediaviewer/File:HMS_Repulse_leaving_Singapore.jpg

Figure 5: "USS Seal (SS-183)" by U.S.Navy - http://www.history.navy.mil/photos/images/h91000/h91833c.htm http://www.history.navy.mil/photos/images/h91000/h91833.jpg. Licensed under Public domain via Wikimedia Commons - http://commons.wikimedia.org/wiki/File:USS_Seal_(SS-183).jpg#mediaviewer/File:USS_Seal_(SS-183).jpg

Figure 6: "USS Louisville SLV Green" by Allan C. Green 1878 - 1954 - State Library of Victoria [1]. Licensed under Public domain via Wikimedia Commons - http://commons.wikimedia.

org/wiki/File:USS_Louisville_SLV_Green.jpg#mediaviewer/
File:USS_Louisville_SLV_Green

Figure 7: "G4M-50s". Licensed under Public domain via Wikimedia Commons - http://commons.wikimedia.org/wiki/File:G4M-50s.jpg#mediaviewer/File:G4M-50s.jpg

Figure 8: "Curtiss P-40 Warhawk USAF". Licensed under Public domain via Wikimedia Commons - http://commons.wikimedia.org/wiki/File:Curtiss_P-40_Warhawk_USAF.JPG#mediaviewer/File:Curtiss_P-40_Warhawk_USAF.JPG

Figure 9: "Mark 14 torpedo side view and interior mechanisms, Torpedoes Mark 14 and 23 Types, OP 635, March 24 1945" by United States Navy - http://www.hnsa.org/doc/torpedo/index.htm#pg7. Licensed under Public domain via Wikimedia Commons - http://commons.wikimedia.org/wiki/File:Mark_14_torpedo_side_view_and_interior_mechanisms,_Torpedoes_Mark_14_and_23_Types,_OP_635,_March_24_1945.jpg#mediaviewer/File:Mark_14_torpedo_side_view_and_interior_mechanisms,_Torpedoes_Mark_14_and_23_Types,_OP_635,_March_24_1945.jpg

Figure 10: "Japanese Battleship Nagato 1944" by 不明 (Unknown) - 呉市海事歴史科学館 Kure Maritime City Historical Museum. Licensed under Public domain via Wikimedia Commons - http://commons.wikimedia.org/wiki/File:Japanese_Battleship_Nagato_1944.jpg#mediaviewer/File:Japanese_Battleship_Nagato_1944.jpg

Figure 11: "Zero Akagi Dec1941" by Japanese military personnel - Official U.S. Navy photograph 80-G-182252, now in the collections of the U.S. National Archives.. Licensed under Public domain via Wikimedia Commons - http://commons.wikimedia.org/wiki/File:Zero_Akagi_Dec1941.jpg#mediaviewer/File:Zero_Akagi_Dec1941.jpg

Figure 12: "USS Pope (DD-225)" by USN - Official U.S. Navy photograph NH 90123.. Licensed under Public domain via Wikimedia Commons - http://commons.wikimedia.org/wiki/File:USS_Pope_(DD-225).jpg#mediaviewer/File:USS_Pope_(DD-225).jpg

Figure 13: Map hand drawn by the Author

Figure 14: "HMS Mauritius moored" by Royal Navy official photographer - This is photograph FL 15132 from the collections of the Imperial War Museums (collection no. 8308-29). Licensed under Public domain via Wikimedia Commons - http://commons.wikimedia.org/wiki/File:HMS_Mauritius_moored.jpg#mediaviewer/File:HMS_Mauritius_moored.jpg

Figure 15: "USS Marblehead (CL-12)-San Diego" by USN - Official U.S. Navy photograph NH 64611.. Licensed under Public domain via Wikimedia Commons - http://commons.wikimedia.org/wiki/File:USS_Marblehead_(CL-12)-San_Diego.jpg#mediaviewer/File:USS_Marblehead_(CL-12)-San_Diego.jpg

Figure 16: "USS Tulsa (PG-22)" by Original uploader was Bellhalla at en.wikipedia - US Navy Photo http://www.history.navy.mil/danfs/t9/tulsa.htm. Licensed under Public domain via Wikimedia Commons - http://commons.wikimedia.org/wiki/File:USS_Tulsa_(PG-22).png#mediaviewer/File:USS_Tulsa_(PG-22).png

Figure 17: By U.S. Marine Corps History and Museums Division [Public domain], via Wikimedia Commons http://upload.wikimedia.org/wikipedia/commons/9/9b/Wake_Island_map_Dec_1941.PNG

Figure 18: "Rabaul - map". Licensed under Public domain via Wikimedia Commons - http://commons.wikimedia.org/wiki/File:Rabaul_-_map.jpg#mediaviewer/File:Rabaul_-_map.jpg

Figure 19: "USS Houston". Licensed under Public domain via Wikimedia Commons - http://commons.wikimedia.org/wiki/File:USS_Houston.jpg#mediaviewer/File:USS_Houston.jpg

Figure 20: "Akebono II" by Shizuo Fukui - Kure Maritime Museum, Japanese Naval Warship Photo Album: Destroyers, edited by Kazushige Todaka, p. 67. Licensed under Public domain via Wikimedia Commons - http://commons.wikimedia.org/wiki/File:Akebono_II.jpg#mediaviewer/File:Akebono_II.jpg

Figure 21: "FEAF Philippines Map - 7 December 1941" by United States Air Force - Edmonds, Walter D. 1951, They Fought With What They Had: The Story of the Army Air Forces in the Southwest Pacific, 1941-1942, Office of Air Force History (Zenger Pub June 1982 reprint), ISBN-10: 0892010681. Licensed under Public domain via Wikimedia Commons http://commons.wikimedia.org/wiki/File%3AFEAF_Philippines_Map_-_7_December_1941.jpg

Figure 22: "HMS Electra" by Royal Navy official photographer Post-Work: User:W.wolny - This is photograph FL 24524 from the collections of the Imperial War Museums (collection no. 8308-29). Licensed under Public domain via Wikimedia Commons http://commons.wikimedia.org/wiki/File%3AHMS_Electra.jpg

Figure 23: "USSGridleyDD380" by Original uploader was RasputinAXP at en.wikipedia - Originally from en.wikipedia; Licensed under Public domain via Wikimedia Commons - http://commons.wikimedia.org/wiki/File:USSGridleyDD380.jpg#mediaviewer/File:USSGridleyDD380.jpg

Figure 24: "Ki-21 97juubaku b" by "Akemi shashinkan" at Chitose-cho Hamamatsu, Shizuoka, Japan. 浜松市千歳町のアケミ写真館撮影。 - http://blog.goo.ne.jp/summer-ochibo/e/24fba1a5ce67541945b839573f95a376 after trimming.. Licensed under Public domain via Wikimedia Commons - http://commons.wikimedia.

org/wiki/File:Ki-21_97juubaku_b.jpg#mediaviewer/File:Ki-21_97juubaku_b.jpg

Figure 25: "HMS Danae (D44)" by Royal Navy official photographer - This is photograph FL 791 from the collections of the Imperial War Museums (collection no. 8308-29). Licensed under Public domain via Wikimedia Commons - http://commons.wikimedia.org/wiki/File:HMS_Danae_(D44).jpg#mediaviewer/File:HMS_Danae_(D44).jpg

Figure 26: "HMS Tenedos (H04) IWM FL 019818" by Royal Navy official photographer - This is photograph FL 19818 from the collections of the Imperial War Museums (collection no. 8308-29). Licensed under Public domain via Wikimedia Commons - http://commons.wikimedia.org/wiki/File:HMS_Tenedos_(H04)_IWM_FL_019818.jpg#mediaviewer/File:HMS_Tenedos_(H04)_IWM_FL_019818.jpg

Figure 27: "HMS Tenedos (H04) IWM FL 019818" by Royal Navy official photographer - This is photograph FL 19818 from the collections of the Imperial War Museums (collection no. 8308-29). Licensed under Public domain via Wikimedia Commons - http://commons.wikimedia.org/wiki/File:HMS_Tenedos_(H04)_IWM_FL_019818.jpg#mediaviewer/File:HMS_Tenedos_(H04)_IWM_FL_019818.jpg

Figure 28: "BrewsterBuffalosMkIRAAFSingaporeOctober1941" by British Government - This is photograph [http://www.iwm.org.uk/collections/item/object/205207914 K630] from the collections of the Imperial War Museums. Originally uploaded to EN Wikipedia as en:Image:Bbf.JPG by Wolcott 5 March 2007.Latest version of image uploaded by Grant65 30 May 2007.. Licensed under Public domain via Wikimedia Commons

Figure 29: "StateLibQld 1 90148 Macdhui (ship)" by This file is lacking author information. - Item is held by John Oxley Library,

State Library of Queensland.. Licensed under Public domain via Wikimedia Commons - http://commons.wikimedia.org/wiki/ File:StateLibQld 1 90148 Macdhui (ship).jpg#mediaviewer/ File:StateLibQld 1 90148 Macdhui (ship).jpg

Figure 30: "HNLMS Evertsen SLV Green" by Allan C. Green 1878 - 1954 - State Library of Victoria [1]. Licensed under Public domain via Wikimedia Commons - http://commons.wikimedia. org/wiki/File:HNLMS Evertsen SLV Green.jpg#mediaviewer/ File:HNLMS Evertsen SLV Green.jpg

Figure 31: Map hand drawn by Author

Figure 32: "USS Yorktown (CV-5) Jul1937" by U.S. Navy photo 19-N-17424 - This media is available in the holdings of the National Archives and Records Administration, cataloged under the ARC Identifier (National Archives Identifier) 513026. Licensed under Public domain via Wikimedia Commons - http://commons. wikimedia.org/wiki/File:USS Yorktown (CV-5) Jul1937. jpg#mediaviewer/File:USS Yorktown (CV-5) Jul1937.jpg

Figure 33: "HNLMS Piet Hein (full speed)" by Dutch Navy personnel - Schepen van de Koninklijke Marine in W.O.II. Licensed under Public domain via Wikimedia Commons - http://commons. wikimedia.org/wiki/File:HNLMS Piet Hein (full speed). jpg#mediaviewer/File:HNLMS Piet Hein (full speed).jpg

Figure 34: "Myōkō trials 1941" by Japanese navy - http://articleimage. nicoblomaga.jp/image/160/2013/1/8/18db6783700a90c9dd531bf 8ec9ea6262aea2a541384421877.jpg. Licensed under Public domain via Wikimedia Commons - http://commons.wikimedia.org/wiki/ File:My%C5%8Dk%C5%8D trials 1941.jpg#mediaviewer/ File:My%C5%8Dk%C5%8D trials 1941.jpg

Figure 35: "USSArcturus" by Original uploader was Lou Sander at en.wikipedia - Transferred from en.wikipedia; transferred to

Commons by User:Benchill using CommonsHelper.. Licensed under Public domain via Wikimedia Commons - http://commons.wikimedia.org/wiki/File:USSArcturus.jpg#mediaviewer/File:USSArcturus.jpg

Figure 36: "Japanese cruiser Kitakami in 1935" by Unknown - Mikasa Memorial Museum. Licensed under Public domain via Wikimedia Commons - http://commons.wikimedia.org/wiki/File:Japanese_cruiser_Kitakami_in_1935.jpg#mediaviewer/File:Japanese_cruiser_Kitakami_in_1935.jpg

Figure 37: "Canton Atoll Map" by EVS-Islands - Flickr. Licensed under Creative Commons Attribution 2.0 via Wikimedia Commons - http://commons.wikimedia.org/wiki/File:Canton_Atoll_Map.jpg#mediaviewer/File:Canton_Atoll_Map.jpg

Figure 38: "Kate B5N1 Akagi dummy torpedo". Licensed under Public domain via Wikimedia Commons - http://commons.wikimedia.org/wiki/File:Kate_B5N1_Akagi_dummy_torpedo.jpg#mediaviewer/File:Kate_B5N1_Akagi_dummy_torpedo.jpg

Figure 39: ""USS S-36;H51827" by U.S. Naval Historical Center Photograph. - http://www.history.navy.mil/photos/images/h51000/h51827c.htm http://www.history.navy.mil/photos/images/h51000/h51827.jpg. Licensed under Public domain via Wikimedia Commons - http://commons.wikimedia.org/wiki/File:USS_S-36;H51827.jpg#mediaviewer/File:USS_S-36;H51827.jpg

Figure 40: "Kamikaze II" by Shizuo Fukui - Kure Maritime Museum, Japanese Naval Warship Photo Album: Destroyers, edited by Kazushige Todaka, p. 26. Licensed under Public domain via Wikimedia Commons - http://commons.wikimedia.org/wiki/File:Kamikaze_II.jpg#mediaviewer/File:Kamikaze_II.jpg

Figure 41: "USS Honolulu 1941". Licensed under Public domain via Wikimedia Commons - http://commons.wikimedia. org/wiki/File:USS_Honolulu_1941.jpg#mediaviewer/ File:USS_Honolulu_1941.jpg

Figure 42: "USS Wharton 1941". Via Wikipedia - Licensed under Public domain via Wikimedia Commons http:// en.wikipedia.org/wiki/File:USS_Wharton_1941.jpg#mediaviewer/ File:USS_Wharton_1941.jpg

Figure 43: "USS Curtiss (AV-4) in 1940" by USN; Original uploader was David Newton at en.wikipedia 28 March 2005 (original upload date) - U.S. Naval Historical Center photograph NH 55535; Transferred from en.wikipedia. Licensed under Public domain via Wikimedia Commons - http://commons.wikimedia. org/wiki/File:USS_Curtiss_(AV-4)_in_1940.jpg#mediaviewer/ File:USS_Curtiss_(AV-4)_in_1940.jpg

Figure 44: "HMAS Perth (AWM 301166)" by Not stated (Credit: Naval Historical Collection) - This image is available from the Collection Database of the Australian War Memorial. Licensed under Public domain via Wikimedia Commons - http://commons. wikimedia.org/wiki/File:HMAS_Perth_(AWM_301166). jpg#mediaviewer/File:HMAS_Perth_(AWM_301166).jpg

Figure 45: "USS Enterprise (April 1939)" by USN (official U.S. Navy photo 80-G-463246) - This media is available in the holdings of the National Archives and Records Administration, cataloged under the ARC Identifier (National Archives Identifier) 520587. Licensed under Public domain via Wikimedia Commons - http://commons.wikimedia.org/ wiki/File:USS_Enterprise_(April_1939).jpg#mediaviewer/ File:USS_Enterprise_(April_1939).jpg

Figure 46: "USS Henley (DD-391)" by Original uploader was ScottyBoy900Q at en.wikipedia - Originally from en.wikipedia;

description page is/was here.. Licensed under Public domain via Wikimedia Commons - http://commons.wikimedia.org/wiki/File:USS_Henley_(DD-391).jpg#mediaviewer/File:USS_Henley_(DD-391).jpg

Figure 47: "UssDraytonDD366" by This file is lacking author information. - Licensed under Public domain via Wikimedia Commons - http://commons.wikimedia.org/wiki/File:USSDraytonDD366.jpg#mediaviewer/File:USSDraytonDD366.jpg

Figure 48: "HMAS Voyager (AWM 301643)". Licensed under Public domain via Wikimedia Commons - http://commons.wikimedia.org/wiki/File:HMAS_Voyager_(AWM_301643).jpg#mediaviewer/File:HMAS_Voyager_(AWM_301643).jpg

Figure 49: "USS Chaumont AP-5 off Shanghai 1937" by Unknown - Navsource Online - Photo courtesy of Vice Admiral M. L. Deyo, USN (Ret.), 1973. US Navy Photo # NH 77810 from the collections of the US Naval Historical Center. Licensed under Public domain via Wikimedia Commons - http://commons.wikimedia.org/wiki/File:USS_Chaumont_AP-5_off_Shanghai_1937.jpg#mediaviewer/File:USS_Chaumont_AP-5_off_Shanghai_1937.jpg

Figure 50: "P-39 1". Licensed under Public domain via Wikimedia Commons - http://commons.wikimedia.org/wiki/File:P-39_1.jpg#mediaviewer/File:P-39_1.jpg

Figure 51: "StateLibQld 1 101348" by This file is lacking author information. - Item is held by John Oxley Library, State Library of Queensland. Licensed under Public domain via Wikimedia Commons - http://commons.wikimedia.org/wiki/File:StateLibQld_1_101348.jpg#mediaviewer/File:StateLibQld_1_101348.jpg

Figure 52: "USS Boise (CL-47) underway 1938" by U.S. Navy Bureau of Ships photo 19-N-19153 - This media is available in the holdings of